PRAISE FOR
GREY SISTER

"Vivid worldbuilding and fast-paced action enhance this powerful coming-of-age story. Readers who loved *Red Sister* will find this second series outing even more compelling."
— *Library Journal* (starred review)

"Great worldbuilding and dynamic characters. . . . A brilliant fantasy book that is highly recommended for all adult and YA fantasy collections." — *Booklist* (starred review)

"Lawrence's suspenseful account of Nona's efforts to complete her training and gain control over her powers balances action and introspection, and will keep readers hooked."
— *Publishers Weekly*

PRAISE FOR
RED SISTER

"Dark, passionate, tense, with a female hero anyone could relate to—I was utterly fascinated! This is no pretty, flowery tale, but one of vastly different people struggling to survive when a hostile government comes to power."
— Tamora Pierce, #1 *New York Times* bestselling author of *Tempests and Slaughter*

"Fabulous, in-depth worldbuilding, great characters, and, as always with Lawrence, plotting that is fresh and unpredictable. . . . If you like fresh, take-no-prisoners fantasy, this is for you."
— Rick Riordan, #1 *New York Times* bestselling author of *The Burning Maze*

"The lyrical excellence of previous books is present in full force here, and it's fair to say that Mark Lawrence has evolved into a master of his craft. In *Red Sister* he has produced a novel that is as thought-provoking as it is entertaining, and as poignant as it is ferocious. Highly recommended."
— Anthony Ryan, *New York Times* bestselling author of *The Empire of Ashes*

Ace Books by Mark Lawrence

The Broken Empire

PRINCE OF THORNS
KING OF THORNS
EMPEROR OF THORNS

The Red Queen's War

PRINCE OF FOOLS
THE LIAR'S KEY
THE WHEEL OF OSHEIM

The Book of the Ancestor

RED SISTER
GREY SISTER

GREY SISTER

Second Book of the Ancestor

MARK LAWRENCE

ACE
New York

ACE
Published by Berkley
An imprint of Penguin Random House LLC
1745 Broadway, New York, NY 10019

ISBN: 9781101988909

Ace hardcover edition / April 2018
Ace mass-market edition / February 2019

Printed in the United States of America
1 3 5 7 9 10 8 6 4 2

Cover art by Bastien Lecouffe Deharme
Cover design by Judith Lagerman

For my grandmother,
Beatrice "BG" Georgina,
who knew with absolute certainty
that I would be a ship's captain

ACKNOWLEDGEMENTS

I'm enormously grateful to Agnes Meszaros, without whose beta reading Nona's story would have been very different and far less fun to write. She worked tirelessly and refused to let me get away with anything but my best effort.

I should also thank, as always, Jessica Wade at Ace for steering this ship, and all her team including Alexis Nixon and Miranda Hill for efforts on my behalf. And of course my agent, Ian Drury, and the team at Sheil Land.

THE STORY SO FAR

———— ✦ ————

FOR THOSE OF you who have had to wait a while for this
book I provide brief catch-up notes to Book One, so that
your memories may be refreshed and I can avoid the awk-
wardness of having to have characters tell each other things
they already know for your benefit.

Here I carry forward only what is of importance to the tale
that follows.

You may find yourself wondering about Keot when he is mentioned. You're supposed to wonder. You will find out. He's not
mentioned in Book One.

Abeth is a planet orbiting a dying red sun. It is sheathed in ice
and the vast majority of its people live in a fifty-mile-wide
ice-walled corridor around the equator.

An artificial moon, a great orbiting mirror, keeps the Corridor
free of ice by focusing the sun's rays into it each night.

When, thousands of years ago, the four original tribes of men
came to Abeth from the stars they found the ruins of a vanished people they call the Missing.

The empire is bounded by the lands of the Scithrowl to the
east and by the Sea of Marn to the west. Across the sea the
Durns rule. At the end of Book One Durnish invaders were
raiding inland from the coast.

As the sun weakens, the ice continues a slow advance despite the warmth of the moon's nightly focus. As the Corridor is squeezed nations look to their neighbours for new territory.

The empire's nobility are the Sis. The suffix is attached to the name of ennobled families e.g. Tacsis, Jotsis etc.

The four original tribes that came to Abeth were the gerant, hunska, marjal, and quantal. Their blood sometimes shows in the current population, conferring unique powers. The gerant grow very large, the hunska are fantastically swift, the marjal can manifest all manner of minor to medium magics, including shadow weaving, sigil writing, and mastery of elements. The quantal can access the raw power of the Path and manipulate the threads that are woven to create reality.

The ships that brought the tribes from the stars were said to have been powered by shiphearts. A small number of these orbs exist within the empire and are highly valued, as they enhance the magical abilities of quantals and marjals.

The Missing left behind structures called Arks. Three exist within the Corridor. The emperor's palace is built around one. There are no reliable records of anyone being able to open the Ark, but a faked prophecy predicts the coming of a Chosen One who will be able to.

Nona Grey is a peasant child from a nameless village. She was given to the child-taker Giljohn who sold her to the Caltess, where ring-fighters are trained and pitted against each other.

Nona ended up at the Convent of Sweet Mercy, where novices are trained in service to the Ancestor. Novices take orders as one of four classes of nun. Holy Sister (entirely religious duties), Grey Sister/Sister of Discretion (trained in assassination and stealth), Red Sister/Martial Sister (trained in combat), Holy Witch/Mystic Sister (trained to walk the Path).

Nona has proven to be a triple-blood. An incredibly rare occurrence. She has hunska, marjal, and quantal skills. Nona has wholly black eyes, a side-effect from taking a dangerous antidote. She has no shadow, having cut it free whilst fighting Yisht.

Yisht is a woman of the ice-tribes and is in the employ of the emperor's sister Sherzal. Yisht stole the Sweet Mercy shipheart and killed Nona's friend Hessa.

Nona is hated by Lord Thuran Tacsis as she first wounded and later killed his son Raymel, a gerant ring-fighter. She is also hated by Thuran's surviving son, Lano. The Tacsis sent assassins, known as Noi-Guin, after Nona. Once hired, the Noi-Guin rarely cease their efforts until the target is dead, even if it requires years of patience.

During the theft of the shipheart Nona was betrayed by her friend and fellow novice Clera Ghomal. Among Nona's remaining friends are novices Ara, Darla, Ruli, and Jula. Arabella Jotsis is from a powerful family and a rare two-blood, having both hunska and quantal skills. Darla is the daughter of an important officer in the emperor's armies and has gerant blood. Ruli has minor marjal skills. Jula is very studious and hopes to become a Holy Sister.

Zole is a significant novice. She is from the ice-tribes and came to the convent at Sherzal's insistence, used as an unwitting distraction to help in the theft of the shipheart. She is the only known four-blood with access to all the skills of the original tribes. Many consider her to be the Chosen One from prophecy. Under the prophecy Zole is the Argatha, and Nona is her Shield.

The Convent of Sweet Mercy is led by Abbess Glass, a woman whose connections in the Church and beyond reach further than expected.

Most senior among the nuns are the sister superiors, Wheel and Rose. Sister Wheel teaches Spirit classes. Sister Rose runs the sanatorium. Other important figures are Sister Tallow, who teaches Blade; Sister Pan, who teaches Path; and Sister Apple, who teaches Shade. Sister Kettle is a Grey Sister based at the convent. She and Apple are lovers.

There are four classes/stages that novices move through as they train to take holy orders as nuns. Red Class, Grey Class, Mystic Class, and Holy Class. Book One ended with Nona in Grey Class, aged around eleven or twelve.

Novices take new names when they become nuns. Nona will become Sister Cage. Ara will be Sister Thorn.

Book One ended with Nona having just killed Raymel Tacsis in the wilds. Sisters Kettle and Apple were secretly watching over the novices but Kettle was poisoned by a Noi-Guin assassin tracking Nona, and Apple has gone to her aid.

PROLOGUE

———————◆———————

The dissolution of any monastery or convent is not
something to be lightly undertaken. Even the might of
House Tacsis, whose line was born of emperors, may not
suffice.

Lano Tacsis came to the Rock of Faith garbed for war, his
armour Ark-steel made bloody by the light of a thousand
crimson stars. Before him the serried ranks of his personal
guard, the iron core of the Tacsis army, forged by his father.
Soldiers tempered in battles upon the empire's eastern borders
and in the west upon the beaches of the Marn.

But Lano's confidence rested on more than the spears of his
army. Noi-Guin walked with him, brought from the shadowed
halls of the Tetragode.

When a child is given to the Noi-Guin it is sacrificed to the
dark. Some few may survive the training but the adult who
then descends the fortress walls on a moonless stretch of night
a decade and more later will be a different person. They will
have been cut free of any allegiance to parent or sibling,
pruned from the Ancestor's tree. They will be Noi-Guin—
instruments of death, beyond morality, beneath religion, dedicated only to the task they have been given. The richest among
the Sis may purchase their services but few missions require
more than one child of the Tetragode. None living remember
more than three acting together. Even the oldest stories never
speak of more than five. Eight walked with Lano Tacsis the day
he came to the convent that stood upon the Rock of Faith.

"Nona Grey? You're sure?" Lano raised his visor to squint
at the dark figure standing alone in the path of his army, tiny

before the great band of pillars. "Sister Cage . . . returned to Sweet Mercy." Fist smacked palm, gauntlets clashing. "Oh this is perfect! I feared she had gone despite my instructions." A glance to his left. "It's her, you're sure?"

Clera Ghomal lifted her dark eyes to him. "Of course. Which other would let me go?"

SISTER CAGE WAITED, shadowless among the shadows of the pillars. The old nuns and young novices watched from within the stone forest behind her. When the Tacsis came and the blood began to flow Sister Rose would still be fighting her own battle somewhere back there, striving to save Sister Thorn from her injuries. Clera had left Thorn bleeding. She could have killed her in a moment. But she didn't. At least there was that.

The sword Cage held offered its sharpness to the world, and the Corridor wind, divided by its edge, hissed in pain. Cage's sister had waited for her battle, hunting her centre, seeking silence and stillness while the Pelarthi advanced. Few Red Sisters had ever left the Convent of Sweet Mercy better able than Sister Thorn to practise what the mistresses of Blade and Path had taught them.

Sister Cage walked to a different beat.

The holy disdain anger, for what faith is not, at its core, about acceptance of things you cannot change? The wise call wrath unwise for few truths are to be found there. Those who rule us stamp upon rage for they see it clearly, knowing it for the fire that it is, and who invites such hungry flames among that which they possess?

To Sister Cage though, fury was a weapon. She opened herself to the anger she had held at bay. Her friend lay dying. *Her friend.* There is a purity in rage. It will burn out sorrow. For a time. It will burn out fear. Even cruelty and hatred will seek shelter, rage wants none of them, only to destroy. Rage is the gift our nature gives to us, shaped by untold years. Why discard it?

Every law of church or state seeks to separate you from your anger. Every rule is there to tame you—to take from your hands that which you should own. Every stricture aims to place the vengeance that is yours in the grasp of courts, juries, justice and judges. Books of law look to replace what you know to be right with lines of ink. Prisons and executioners stand only to keep your hands from the blood of those who have wronged you. Every part of it exists to put time and distance between deed and consequence. To lift us from our animal nature, to cage and tame the beast.

Sister Cage watched her enemy, bright in steel upon the Rock.

Hers the anger of an ocean wave rolling over deep waters to spend its white fury against the shore, one and then the next, relentless, tearing down high cliffs, pounding rocks to pebbles, grinding pebbles to sand, and thus are mountains laid low. Hers the storm's wrath, thunder-shaken, sharp with lightning, blown on a wind that rips the oldest trees from the hardness of the ground. Hers the defiance of stone, raised in outrage against cold skies. Hers the anger that sits like broken glass within a chest, the anger that will allow no sleep, no retreat, no compromise.

NONA GREY RAISES her head and regards her foe through midnight eyes. Perhaps it is just the reflection of the torchlight but somewhere in their darkness a red flame seems to burn.

"I am my own cage." She lifts her sword. "And I have opened the door."

1

———————◆———————

THERE ARE MANY poisons that will induce madness but none perhaps quite so effective as love. Sister Apple carried a hundred antidotes but she had drunk that particular draught of her own free will, knowing there was no cure.

Thorn and briar tore at her, the ice-wind howled, even the land opposed her with its steepness, with the long miles, the ground iron-hard. The Poisoner pressed on, worn, feeling each of her thirty years, her range-coat shredded in places, the tatters dancing to please the wind.

When the deer-track broke from cover to cross a broad and rutted track Apple followed without hesitation, eyes on the ranks of trees resuming their march on the far side.

"Stop!" A harsh cry close at hand.

Apple ignored it. Kettle had summoned her. She knew the direction, the distance, and the pain. Kettle had called her. Kettle would never call her from her watch, not even if her life were in danger. But she *had* called.

"Stop!" More voices raised, the dialect sharp-angled and hard to attach meaning to.

The treeline stood ten yards away across a ditch. Once she reached the shadows beneath the branches she would be safe. An arrow zipped past her. Apple glanced along the road.

Five Durnishmen spanned the width, their quilted armour salt-stained and mud-spattered, the iron plates sewn on shoulders and forearms brown with rust. Apple could reach the trees before the men caught her—but not before the next arrow or spear did.

Cursing, she reached both hands into her coat pockets.

Some of the obscenities she uttered had probably never been spoken by a nun before. Even the Durnishmen seemed surprised.

"Don't kill me. I'm worth more to you alive." Apple tried not to sound as if she were lecturing a class. She drew her hands out, a wax capsule of boneless in one, a wrap of grey mustard in the other, and a small white pill between finger and thumb. She popped the pill into her mouth, hoping it was bitterwill. She had all the antidotes ordered inside the many inner pockets of her habit, but reaching in to recover one would be asking to get shot, so she chanced to memory, feel, and luck, fishing in the outer pocket of her range-coat.

"You . . . are nun?" The tallest of them took a pace forward, spear levelled. He was older than the other four. Weathered.

"Yes. A Holy Sister." She swallowed the pill, grimacing. It tasted like bitterwill. The four younger raiders, all with the same dark and shaggy hair, tightened their grip on their weapons, muttering to pagan gods. Perhaps one nun in a hundred was anything other than a Holy Sister but with the stories told in Durn they couldn't be blamed for thinking every woman in a habit was a Red Sister, or a Holy Witch just itching to blast them to smoking ruin. "A nun. From the convent."

"Convent." The leader rolled the word around his mouth. "Convent." He spat it past frost-cracked lips.

Apple nodded. She bit back on her desire to say, "With the big golden statue." The men had to walk into the trap themselves. If they sensed her leading them she would be dead in moments.

The leader glanced back at his men, gabbling out words that so nearly made sense. Durnish was like empire tongue put through a mincer and sprinkled with spice. She had the feeling that if they would just speak a little more slowly and change the emphasis it would all become comprehensible. Apple caught the two words that might keep her alive though. "Convent" and "gold." She broke the capsule of boneless in her fist and rubbed her fingers over her palm to spread the syrupy contents before wiping the hand over the back of her other and her wrist.

"You. Take us to convent." The man advanced another two paces gesturing with his spear for her to move.

"I won't!" Apple tried to sound scared rather than impatient. She thought of Kettle in danger, injured maybe, and fear entered her voice. "I can't. It's forbidden." She had to get them close. She couldn't do much if they prodded her ahead of them at the point of a spear. She let her gaze flit between the faces of the men, offering a wavering defiance. A defiance that they might enjoy breaking.

The leader motioned and two of his men advanced to grab Apple's arms. A third kept his bow ready, half-drawn, arrow pointing her way, daring her to run. The last leaned on his spear, grinning vacantly.

Apple feigned panic, raising her hands to intercept those that reached for her, but offering too little resistance to invite blows. One of the pair seemed to need no excuse and slapped her anyway, a hard, callused hand across the face. She spat blood and cried out for mercy. Both men were smeared with the clear boneless syrup now, sticky on their fingers.

The slapper twisted one arm behind her while the other made to open her coat, perhaps forgetting that the Ancestor's brides take a vow of poverty. Knowing he would find her array of poisons and cures rather than any gold or silver Apple wailed piteously, raising her clenched fist to remind them she had something more obviously hidden.

Slapper grunted incomprehensible syllables to Robber and the man abandoned the coat-ties to pry Apple's hand open. In taking hold of it he got a second dose of boneless wiped across the palm of his hand. With the bitterwill to counter the poison Apple felt only a numbness where the syrup coated her, the strength in her arms untouched.

Apple began crying out, keeping her fist clenched against Robber's weakening efforts. Slapper tried to twist her into submission and it hurt like fire but she managed enough resistance to stop him breaking the arm behind her. At the same time Apple threw herself left then right, her progress always towards the leader and the archer though she never once glanced their way. The Durns' hobnails slid on the mud. The remaining subordinates laughed uproariously at their comrades' efforts, making no move to help. The leader, snorting in disgust, motioned the archer forward then jammed his spear-butt into the mud and followed to intercept the group as they made a weaving approach.

Neither Slapper nor Robber yet seemed to understand that they had been poisoned, presumably believing instead that Apple was an abnormally strong woman, perhaps drawing some animal strength from the depths of her terror. Apple wrenched her fist to her face as the officer reached them. She blew through her closed hand, a short sharp puff, and a cloud of powder from the crushed wrap bloomed around the man's head. The edge of the cloud caught the archer just behind him.

True terror loaned Apple the strength to throw herself backwards, falling from the Durns' clutches to the rutted mud. She had seen what grey mustard could do and nothing in her array of antidotes would reduce the pain and disfigurement of it to an acceptable level.

The officer's screams shattered the air, the breath for his second cry sucking mustard spores into his lungs. The archer fell back, scratching at his eyes. Slapper and Robber staggered away, tripping and stumbling. Which left Apple empty-handed, on the ground, with one able-bodied foe just yards away, spear in hand.

Another person's distress exerts a certain fascination; the man stood in slack-jawed horror watching the officer claw his face to ruin. Apple glanced at the shadows between the trees. So close: a quick scramble could see her safe in their embrace. The need to be speeding towards Kettle drew at her even more strongly than the desire to escape. But Sisters of Discretion swear more than just vows of piety and poverty. Suppressing an impatient snarl, Apple drew her knife. She rose slowly from the mud amid the officer's bubbling screams, the archer's curses, and the struggles of the other two Durnishmen trying and failing to get to their feet. Her headdress had come loose and red hair spilled around her shoulders. The last of her coat-ties gave and her range-coat opened about her like the dark wings of a raptor. She held her knife ready to throw, a pouch of ground deadruff in the other hand in case she got the chance to take the spearman alive.

The raider saw her at the last moment, dragging his gaze from the frothing officer, now fallen into the ditch. As he low-ered his spear Apple's hand rose in an underarm throw and an instant later the hilt of her knife jutted beneath his chin. He sat down, clutching his throat in confusion.

The archer stumbled close by, blinded with tears and blood. Apple took up a dropped spear and ran it through the man's chest. Next she went to offer mercy to the officer, now a twisting thing of mud and grass in the icy ditch water. She left him in a crimson bath and considered the two fallen Durns, Slapper and Robber. One had his face towards her and tracked the bloody tip of her spear with his eyes. Apple frowned, her gaze wandering to the treeline again, eager to be off. She had no stomach for killing helpless foes. In truth she had no stomach for killing. She had always been a better teacher than a doer.

Apple crouched. "Sisters of Discretion are supposed to pass unseen and be impossible to take unawares." She took two purple pills from her habit, brilliant groundwort. She had cured and prepared the roots herself, pressed the pills and sealed them in wax. "It's all very embarrassing. I won't tell if you don't." She peeled the pills quickly and popped one into the mouth of each man then rolled them so they wouldn't choke. "If nobody finds and kills you before you can move again—and believe me you deserve to be found and killed—then my advice is to run all the way back to your boat."

She wiped her hand on Slapper's cloak. The groundwort would make them sick for a week. A month if they swallowed too much. She considered leaving her dagger in the spearman's neck, but went to retrieve it, pulling the blade free with a shudder of revulsion. In the next moment she was moving, running for the trees, red blade in hand.

APPLE HAD ALWAYS been a teacher first, lacking the iron for the darkest shades of grey-work. Kettle though, she would never fail to do what was required, without relish or complaint. A perfect weapon. When duty called her she had the capacity to put her sweet nature in a box, ready for collection when the mission was complete. The thought of what it would take to get her to call for help made Apple shudder. Kettle would never willingly make Apple abandon the abbess's orders. Arabella Jotsis stood alone in the wild now, unwatched.

Apple pressed on, using all her resolve to pace herself rather than to sprint. Miles lay ahead. She dodged around trees, following a deer track for a while then leaving it to pursue a stream, rotten with ice.

Kettle had been watching Nona. Had something happened to the child? She was fearless, fierce, and quicker than thinking, but there were more dangerous things out in the Corridor than Nona Grey. Perhaps it was Nona that needed help . . . Apple shook the thought away: the pain had been Kettle's, and the fear.

A swirling fog came in, lifted somewhere by the moon's focus and carried perhaps for days in the ice-wind. The forest clutched at her, sought to trip her at every step, tried to lure her from her path with easier tracks. In the blind whiteness Apple found her way, following the faint echo of Kettle's cry through the shadow.

Many miles became few miles and, as the fog cleared, became a singular remaining mile. The land had opened up into heath where the soil stood too thin and too sour for crops. Farmsteads lay scattered, raising sheep and goats; few houses stood close enough to see one from the next. Apple picked up speed, running now as she crossed rough ground, divided here and there by grassed-over lanes and collapsed walls of dry stone. Ahead the land dipped. In the broad valley a stream threaded its path between stands of trees before losing itself in a thicker extent of woodland. Kettle waited among those woods, Apple could feel it; her nearness tugged at the scar her shadow-cry had left.

Apple slowed as she approached the first trees. She had been careless before: her haste had delivered her into the hands of men she could have stepped around unnoticed if she had kept her focus. She moved between two elms and the shadows flowed around her, raised with both hands. Shade-work had always come easy to her. Darkness pooled in her palms. When the shadows answered her will it felt as if she had remembered some name that had long escaped her, or recognized the solution to a puzzle, a sort of mental relief, joy almost. Other shadow-magic had been worked within the woods. The empty spaces shivered with the echoes of it. Kettle's cry lay there, sharp and deep, but other traces too, the sour workings of Noi-Guin. Apple had tasted their like before, back at Sweet Mercy on the night Thuran Tacsis had sent two of them to kill Nona. Quite how they had failed in that task was beyond her.

Apple wrapped herself in darkness and sought the pa-

tience of the Grey Sister. Mistress Path had taught her the
mantras twenty years ago and Apple had made them part of
her own foundation, woven through her core. Today though,
with Kettle's distress throbbing through the shadow, patience
came hard.

The undergrowth scratched and tore and rustled with each
step Apple took. She felt as raw as any novice, her woodcraft
rusty with disuse, certain that her advance would be heard by
any foe within a thousand yards. Bait the trap. A tactic as old
as killing. Leave a comrade, a friend, a lover wounded, then
wait and watch. A Noi-Guin could be resting among the
branches of any tree, crossbow ready, bolt envenomed.

Kettle wouldn't have called me if that were true. Apple advanced, leaving patience behind her but bringing the shadows.

All that drew her eyes to Kettle was the bond between
them. The nun lay at the base of a great frost-oak, the length
of her body fitting around the rise and fall of roots. Leaves
covered her range-coat, leaves and mud, her headdress gone,
the spread of raven hair showing the paleness of her face only
in thin slices. She lay sprawled like a dead thing, a part of the
forest floor, a work of camouflage of which any Grey Sister
would be proud.

"Kettle!" Apple came to her side, the fear of an assassin's
bow crushed beneath the certainty that Kettle lay dead and
that no purpose remained to her in the world. She took Kettle's
muddy fingers in her own, shocked by the coldness of them.
"Kettle . . . it's me." She choked on the words, overwhelmed,
while her other hand, still calm, sought the nun's pulse with
practised ease. Nothing. No . . . not nothing, a whisper.

Apple reached to pull Kettle to her, to lift her from the cold
ground, but saw the hilt of the knife, jutting from her side just
above the hip. She touched a finger to the pommel, an iron
ball. Leather binding wound the grip. She recognized the dagger. Kettle had shown one like it to her after it was confiscated
from Nona. Noi-Guin for certain then. The one that got away.
Apple eased her lover onto her lap and sat for a moment, hugging her, eyes squeezed tight against the tears. Seconds later
she drew a deep shuddering breath and strove for calm.

Think.

Apple set Kettle back upon the ground and stripped her

own range-coat to lie her on. With Kettle arranged on the coat she examined her for other injuries, checking the colour of her skin, lifting an eyelid, listening to her breath, watching the speed with which circulation returned to her extremities when pinched. She took a thin leather tube from the collection within her habit and broke the seal. Already the cold was making her shiver. She tipped the liquid into Kettle's mouth, sat back, and watched. The knife was the only wound. It must have been coated with blade-venom but there were no strong indications to narrow down the type.

For the longest minute in Apple's life nothing happened. All about her the trees groaned against the wind, their leaves seething. Then Kettle twitched, spluttered and started to choke. Apple seized her head. "Easy! Just breathe."

"W-where?" Any further question became lost in coughing and choking. One hand clutched at the range-coat just above the knife. "Hurts."

"I told you to breathe, idiot."

"A-Appy?" Kettle rolled her head to see, eyes squinting as if the light were too bright. Her skin was bone-white, lips almost blue. "Sister." The faintest smile.

"I've given you adrene, it won't last long. Tell me what you've taken. Quick!"

"Nona. She made me call." Kettle slurred the words, staring past Apple at the leaves, black against a white sky. "Gone now."

Apple shook her. "What did you take? It's important!"

"B—" Kettle blinked, trying to focus. "Black cure." Her breath came shallow and fast. "And . . . kalewort."

"Kalewort?"

"I—was cold. Thought it . . . might be nightweed on—"

"Who puts nightweed in blade-venom?" Apple shook her head. "Where's the assassin?"

"Gone." Kettle's eyes closed and her head flopped back.

Apple bit her lip. The black cure should have had more effect whatever the Noi-Guin had used. She tasted blood and frowned. Her mind lay blank. Nothing in her great store of lore suggested a cause or cure.

Despair closed about Apple. Her lips moved, reciting venoms, none of which fitted the symptoms. Tendrils of shadow caught around Kettle, moving across her in wisps. Apple stared, her brow furrowed, mind racing. On the white inch of wrist exposed before Kettle's range-coat swallowed her arm, a line of shadow followed the path of the largest vein.

"No?" Apple motioned the shadows around her forward and like a dark sea they washed over Kettle. As they drew back traces of shadow remained, held by her veins as a lodestone will hold powdered iron, revealing the invisible lines of its influence. "Yes!"

She grabbed Kettle's face in both hands. "Wake up! Kettle, wake up!" Kettle lay, as boneless as the Durns in the road. Apple slapped her. "Wake up! It was dark-venom."

"I'm dead then." Kettle rolled her eyes open. "I'm so sorry." A glistening tear pooled in the corner of her eye. She lifted a hand, as if it were the heaviest thing in the world, to Apple's cheek. "You're bleeding."

Apple took the fingers and kissed them. "You are my blood."

The darkness began to thicken around them, shadows streaming towards Apple, clotting about her.

"What are . . . you doing?" The smoothness of Kettle's brow furrowed and her hand dropped back to her side.

"Saving you," Apple said. The effort of drawing so much shadow so fast tightened her voice. She felt a coldness in her bones, an ache behind her eyes.

"H-how?" Kettle sought her eyes. "There's no way."

"There is a way." Apple saw Kettle only because the darkness ran so deep in her. Night enfolded them both now, a fist of darkness within the depths of a forest grown lighter as its shadows were stolen. "I have to push you into shadow."

"No." Kettle managed to shake her head. "The Ancestor—"

"I have to. It's the only way." Apple gathered the darkness around her hands until even to her night-born sight they were holes cut in the shape of her body, without depth or contrast. The Noi-Guin pushed the best of their killers into the shadow, as far as their minds could bear it. It broke some of them. Others were lost in the dark places behind the world. But the price Kettle feared to pay was her soul. The Church taught that those who walked too far into the shadow would never join the Ancestor in unity.

"Don't." Kettle lacked the strength to raise her hands again. "Sister Wheel . . . says the Ancestor—"

"Fuck Wheel, and fuck the Ancestor." Apple set one hand to Kettle's chest, kneeling above her, ready to push. She took the hilt of the knife in her other hand. "You're mine and I won't lose you." She bent her head and tears fell. "Let me do it." Her mouth twitched and the words came out broken. "Please."

"Poisoner." Kettle found the strength to raise a hand, running white fingers into the flame of Apple's hair. She held her a moment. "Poison me."

And with a cry Apple pressed down with one black palm, all her strength behind it, and with the other drew the assassin's knife from the wound, pulling with the steel and blood an inky venom born of the darkness that dwells between stars.

2

---◆---

Two Years Later

"HAVE YOU COME for the laundry?" The tall girl, a willowy blonde with a narrow beauty to her, stood away from her bed and bent to pull the linens from it. A titter ran among the other novices getting undressed around the room. Mystic Class had the whole of the dormitory's second floor and the beds were well spaced around the walls, with desks between them.

Nona had been warned about Joeli Namsis. Her family held lands to the west and kept a close alliance with Thuran Tacsis. "Yes," she said, and stepped forward quickly, taking the bundled sheets with hunska swiftness. She returned to the doorway and threw the bedding down the stairs. Across the skin of her back Keot trembled with laughter.

"Now, which bed is mine? Or must I take one?" Nona looked around at their faces, a dozen of them, variously astonished or horrified, a couple even amused. Of all the novices from Nona's time in Red Class she was the first to join Mystic. Three of the girls from her time in Grey Class had reached Mystic ahead of her: Mally, a hunska prime who had been head-girl, had a bed close to the door; Alata watched her, dark-eyed, from the far side of the room, the ritual patterning of her scars a black web across arms and cheeks; and Darla who had joined the week before, grinning beneath the brown mop of her hair, the hugeness of her contriving to make the larger Mystic beds look small.

"Well that was a mistake, peasant." Joeli came to stand before Nona.

"Mistakes are how we learn." Nona looked expectantly past Joeli's shoulder towards an empty bed.

"Perhaps I should teach you another lesson." Joeli raised a hand, fingers spread. A white haze of lines filled Nona's Pathsight. Some said Joeli was the best thread-worker in the convent, and since Hessa's death Nona supposed it could be true. Using any kind of Path-power outside a lesson however was a surefire way to get your back shredded with a wire-willow cane, no matter which family name you bore.

Nona looked up, meeting the green slits of Joeli's stare, and spoke with all the sincerity she could muster. "I love you as a sister, and when we die we will be together in the Ancestor, our bloods mixed." A warmth spread across her back as Keot sank into her flesh. A moment later he had wrapped himself around her tongue. "But I must warn you, sister, that a sickness runs in me, and if you fashion yourself my enemy I will make a ruin of your life, for I am born of war."

Joeli stared at Nona, eyes widening as if recognizing a promise rather than a threat. Then laughter burst from her in a clean, controlled peal, confidence pushing aside sensible fear. "What dramatics! 'I am born of war.'" Joeli mimicked Keot's words accented heavily towards the peasants' dialect. "You were born of a mud hut in the wilds." She glanced at her friends. "What a strange creature this novice is. I can see why Sister Hearth was keen to get her out of her class." She turned away.

Nona resisted the urge as Keot tried to make her arm rise to seize the girl's neck. Instead she turned towards an empty bed with a snarl, angry at the lapse of concentration that had let Keot speak for her.

"I will make a ruin of your life," Keot?

You should let me. That bitch means trouble for you.

Nona sat on the bed she had chosen, one of a pair too neat to belong to anyone. She pushed her small bag of possessions under the desk, spare clothes mainly. Joeli was already in animated conversation with three novices across the room, laughter and glances in her direction punctuating their conversation. A fourth girl returned from the stairwell with the sheets Nona had thrown.

If you kill one of them the others will respect you.
Shut up.

The door opened again and Zole walked in, arms folded across the bag she had brought from the Grey dormitory. When Nona had left the classroom where Sister Hearth had examined her merit certificates Zole had been waiting outside the door. They had both nodded acknowledgement but it wasn't in the ice-triber's nature to volunteer information.

"Another one?" Joeli raised her voice in complaint.

Zole's face registered no expression as she scanned the room, eyes dark above broad cheekbones. She wore her face like a mask. Nona could count on one hand the times she had seen her smile or scowl.

"I—" Joeli seemed about to expand upon her displeasure but for once her supposedly forgotten aristocracy fell short, eclipsed by Zole's celebrity. Novices rose on all sides along with an excited babble of voices as they moved to welcome the Argatha. Nona decided against shielding her, though she was sure Zole would rather see the novices knocked down than endure their attentions.

Zole made slow but sure progress towards the bed beside Nona, answering questions and flattery with curt nods. On the few occasions she did reply she offered only single words. Most of them "no." Outside the convent it was far worse. Her secret had been uncovered just months after they had returned from the ranging. Some said Sherzal herself had spread the news, but whatever the truth all of Verity soon whispered that Zole was the four-blood spoken of in the Argatha prophecy, the Chosen One come to drive back the ice and bring salvation! And the rest of the empire knew within another month. Pilgrims came to sit in vigil beyond the pillars even on days when the abbess stationed a sister at the base of the Vinery Stair to tell them there was no chance of an audience with Novice Zole.

Zole reached the bed and drove the last couple of novices away with a glower. The Argatha prophecy had been a constant in Sister Wheel's Spirit classes for almost three years now, and she had managed to infect a fair proportion of the convent with her zeal, including most of the novices. At least the ones who didn't know Zole.

"You're making friends almost as quickly as I am." Nona stood and stripped off her habit.

Zole shrugged. "None of them are bleeding."

Nona knelt to dig in her bag for her nightdress. Keot could sink from view for a few moments and knew enough not to be seen. Nona had explained to him that the nuns would seek to burn him out before throwing her from the convent—over a cliff if she were unlucky. Nobody tainted by a devil could stay in service to the Ancestor, even after the taint had been driven from them with hot irons. Sister Wheel's lessons had left no room for doubt on that account.

"Welcome to Mystic, shrimp." Darla came to the foot of Nona's bed, somewhat comical in her tent of a nightdress, her arms, thick with muscle, straining out of short frilly sleeves. "Nice entrance."

"I do my best." Nona stepped out of her underskirts and pulled her own nightdress over her head as fast as possible. In Grey dorm they mocked her for being shy, but it was Keot who prompted the haste. Also she was shy.

"She threatened to kill Joeli before she'd even reached her bed," Darla said to Zole. "And she didn't even have a crowd trying to get in her way."

Zole looked up from her bag, one hand wrapped around the carved tooth of some sea-monster. "Good. I do not like that Joeli."

"You don't like anyone," Nona said.

Zole shrugged.

"And besides, I didn't threaten to kill her."

"'I will make a ruin of your life,'" Darla quoted through a broad grin.

"That's maiming at best," Nona said. "And I seem to remember my welcome to Grey wasn't too warm either."

Darla kept her grin. "That was just a kicking. Joeli's a whole lot more dangerous. A thread-worker can mess you up. And she doesn't even need to do that. She has lots of friends. Too many novices in this class are thinking they might not take their vows, just go back to their families. And when you start to think like that you also start to think how helpful it is to have friends like the Namsis."

"A devil got my tongue," Nona said. "I should have held it more tightly."

I spoke truth. The fortress of you is built of such moments, they are stones dropped into the well of your tomorrow.

Shut up.

Nona checked the bed for spiders and other welcome gifts then slipped under the blanket, yawning. Darla laughed. "Get your beauty sleep, Shield." She slapped the bed. "Long day tomorrow. You're with the big girls now."

All around the room novices were climbing beneath thick blankets, Alata sleeping alone until Leeni got her merit certificate in Spirit. Something Sister Wheel seemed to be taking particular pleasure in denying her. Joeli Namsis wore only her tawny skin to her bed, perhaps proud of her woman's body. Nona looked away. She would miss Ara's presence in the bed beside hers, close enough to reach out and touch. She yawned again and stared at the shadow-dance across the beams above her. At heart she was still a child of the Grey and no matter how warm a room might be she would never be at ease with nakedness, even in the bathhouse. Ruli had taught Nona the steam-weaving trick that she had first shown them at the sink-hole in the focus moon, and when possible Nona wore a robe of steam around the bath-pool. Keot hid across the sole of her left foot at such times.

Shadows are nothing. Talk to me instead.

Shut up.

You should thank me. Your enemies make you what you are. Your foes shape your life more than friends ever could. This Joeli is good practice.

Nona ignored Keot and watched the shadows. Most novices with marjal blood could make them dance to their own tune, but such tricks were put beyond her reach the day she cut her own shadow loose. The day she launched it at Yisht to try to save Hessa. She had failed. She had lost both her friend and her shadow, and Yisht had escaped with the shipheart. Sleep came slowly as it always did, fighting to overcome the anger. She finally fell asleep wondering where her shadow might be now, and dreamed of being lost in dark places.

3

———— ✦ ————

"In Mystic we use edged steel." Sister Tallow spoke to Zole and Nona above the clash of swordplay as the other novices sparred in widely spaced pairs across the sand of Blade Hall. She held two naked blades, forge-iron rather than the Ark-steel of a Red Sister's weapon, but visibly sharp. Each had the same curve as a sister-blade and each was the same length, about as long as a man's arm from shoulder to fingertips. "There are some lessons that must be written in scars."

Sister Tallow offered the hilts. Nona took hers, clumsy in her new gauntlets. Like her new blade-habit the gloves were reinforced with strips of iron sewn into the padding. They wouldn't stop every hit but they would lessen the chances of blood being spilled.

"It's a good sword." Zole swung hers then circled the point in front of her.

Nona lifted her own, finding it heavier than the blunted Grey Class blades. She felt awkward in her blade-habit, as if she were wading in the bath-pool. Red Sisters wore black-skin but that had been scavenged from the hulls of the ships that carried the four tribes to Abeth and was worth more than its weight in gold. Far more. An experienced Red Sister had to die or become a Holy before a new one could get her armour.

"You two spar. I'll watch." Sister Tallow pointed to a clear patch of sand. "No showing off. We have serious and dangerous work ahead of us, and I would rather send you on to Holy Class with the same number of fingers and eyes you had when you arrived in Mystic."

Nona squared up to Zole. The ice-triber stood as tall as

Sister Tallow now, her gerant blood perhaps starting to show. Nona remained a head shorter. She supposed she was around fifteen but when she came from the village she had scarcely realized there were dates and certainly hadn't known on which one she had been born.

"What are the rules?" Nona asked. Behind her thoughts Keot yammered for blood and made his opinions on rules quite clear.

"No killing thrusts." Sister Tallow stepped back.

"That's it?" Nona had no more time for inquiry. Zole pulled the mesh-mask over her face and moved to attack. Nona pulled her own down and lifted her sword.

Zole came in fast as she always did, offering no quarter. Sister Tallow never had to lecture the girl on controlling her temper. Nona wasn't sure Zole had one. Ara said if they cut the Chosen One open they'd find ice at her core.

Nona's world narrowed to the flickering of blades and the clash of iron. With her speed matched Nona had to rely on training, on the memory that Sister Tallow had imprinted on her muscles. Deeper than that even—on her bones. She mounted a desperate defence against the stronger girl, acutely aware that the edge she met with her own could open ruinous wounds, even slice a limb off, gone in the blink of an eye, beyond repair. Zole would hardly care if she took all four fingers from Nona's sword hand at the knuckle.

"Stop!" Sister Tallow raised an arm.

Nona put up her blade, relieved.

"Your fear is beating you." Sister Tallow pinned Nona with narrow eyes. "Zole doesn't even have to try."

"I'm not afraid!" A snarl. And a lie. Blade-work held a fear for Nona that was absent when she fought empty-handed. Perhaps it had started with Raymel Tacsis swinging his sword at her as exhaustion robbed her speed. Perhaps before. Against most novices blade-work was just a game, but facing hunska primes and full-bloods her control slipped away and slaughterhouse images crept in.

"Find your centre, novice. Wear your serenity like a second skin." Tallow motioned for them to continue.

Nona scowled and raised her blade. Serenity had never helped her find the Path. It had been passion that led her there.

Rage. On the blade-path, suspended high above the ground in the chamber behind the changing room, it had been the discovery that she needed to slide rather than stick that made her stop falling. Where the other novices stepped with ever greater caution Nona had raced in.

Zole came at her again, efficient, relentless, cold. Their blades clashed and clashed again. Serenity would wrap up the fear that hampered her, but it would also keep away the anger that she needed. Nona had to have her heart in the battle or it wasn't a battle at all, just some game. What she required was the right balance.

Nona swung at Zole's side. The ice-triber stepped inside the blow, trapping Nona's wrist against her ribs and laying her own blade along the thick collar around Nona's neck.

"Break!" Tallow raised her hand. "Work through the standard thrust and parry routines. And think on my instruction, novice. They don't call me Mistress Blade for nothing . . ."

AFTER THE LESSON there was time for half an hour at blade-path before hitting the bathhouse. Nona changed into the lightest of her combat habits and joined the other Mystic novices who had chosen to practise.

She found that most of the class were there, half on the platform high above the net, half below staring up at the show. Even Darla, who Nona almost never saw in the chamber, had turned up. Joeli too, at the doorway down below, watching with her three closest cronies. The blonde girl, Mesha, stood at her side, and before them the hunska half-bloods Elani and Crocey, solid and sly, so similar they might be twins. A novice from Holy Class joined them. One Nona often saw walking with Joeli.

Nona found a spot on the platform's edge beside Zole and sat, dangling her legs over the drop. "Now you're in Mystic you'll get to go on the ice-ranging."

Zole grunted.

"You notice how they put us up a class on the same day?" Nona watched Alata on the blade-path. She moved well and had covered half the distance.

"That's Wheel's doing. She wants Argatha and Shield together. She has been sitting on my merit certificate until they were ready to let you up," Zole said.

Nona narrowed her gaze and, as if her stare had become a weapon, Alata faltered, slipped, and fell with an oath.

"It is your temper that held you where you were," Zole continued, gazing into space.

"I—" Nona bit off a sharp reply. It was true. Mostly true. Keot had returned with her from the Corridor ranging. She had lost a shadow, lost two friends, and gained a devil. Nona supposed she had never been the mildest of novices but with a devil beneath her skin she had turned wild. It had taken the best part of two years to get the upper hand, to slowly regain control and concentration, and even more slowly to regain the trust and respect of the sisters who taught her. "I wasn't holding *you* back, if that's what you think."

Zole shrugged. Everyone knew she'd been ready for Mystic Class for an age, but the abbess didn't want her ice-ranging. Abbess Glass didn't think Zole would come back. More importantly Sherzal didn't want her to go. Her opinion counted in the matter. Despite very obviously being behind the theft of the convent's shipheart the emperor's sister remained free, unpunished, and a power in the land. If anything she had tightened her grip on the Inquisition since the theft.

Another novice fell from the blade-path. Nona didn't register which. "So why *did* they let you move up?"

"I do not know." Zole hardly seemed to care. If Nona hadn't met Tarkax she would have imagined everyone from the tribes to be carved from ice.

Zole stood to take her turn on the blade-path. Several of the novices raised a cheer as if they were pilgrims crowding on the Rock, hoping to see a miracle. They at least looked embarrassed when Zole turned to stare at them.

Nona watched Zole's progress without truly seeing. Zole was right that her temper had held her down. Keot might fan the flames but the fire had been there before the devil came to warm himself in its midst. Four devils had found Raymel Tacsis while he waited to cross the Path and enter death. They had made their home within his flesh. The focused will of Academics in Thuran Tacsis's pay had kept Raymel from joining the Ancestor, and in time they had returned him to health, alive but changed. But not even the power of the Academy could drive a devil from a man's flesh if it found enough sin to anchor it.

Before the Tacsis giant died Nona had thrust her knife into his back a score of times. Perhaps more: it had been a frenzy. Three of the four devils had returned to the hollow places from where devils watch eternity, but the fourth, spilling out with Raymel's blood, had slipped through some crack into Nona. At first he had seemed only a scarlet stain on Nona's knife-hand, one that refused to be washed away with the gore that had reached up past her elbows. But later, in the depths of the night, he had spoken to her. He called himself Keot and claimed it had been neither the blood nor the rage that had let him get under her skin. Rather it had been the pleasure Nona had taken in driving the knife home into her enemy. That had been the crack into which he had squeezed.

"You're up." A novice tapped Nona's shoulder.

"What?" Nona shook away her thoughts and went to stand at the start of the blade-path. Another girl reset the pendulum.

"Let's see you do your trick then." Joeli's voice from below, sounding for all the world as if she were in her father's halls and Nona was the entertainment, an acrobat hired to amuse.

Nona ran onto the cold, swaying pipe. She never slid along it except late at night when she came to clear her mind. Greasing her feet left the blade-path slippery and brought howls of protest from everyone but the handful of novices who had taken up her approach. Even so, whenever she took the path she went quickly. On the twisting narrowness of the blade-path pipe she ran faster than a non-hunska could sprint. The quickness of it gave the path beneath her feet too little time to sway or shift. In eight counts she had run up the first twist of the spiral. When sliding Nona took the inner path, letting her speed hold her to the metal as she turned momentarily upside-down inside the spiral. Running, she took the outer path and jumped from the top of the first turn to the second, then to the third, breaking the rules. The leap from the last turn of the spiral to the next flattish section was a dangerous one, several yards, risking injury if she missed and struck the pipe in passing.

"Cheat!" Joeli's cry as Nona took off.

Keot twisted beneath her skin, scalding hot. Both feet hit the bar, but neither met it perfectly and on the blade-path one tiny error is multiplied with every step. Over-correction built on over-correction and five paces later Nona fell. No sound escaped her. The bounce of the net brought her to her feet and a moment later she landed cat-footed among the watchers.

"So, you cheated and then you fell." Joeli put herself between Nona and the doorway.

Kill her!

Nona ignored Keot, slipping between Joeli and the tall girl from Holy.

At least cut an ear off . . .

Nona had her hand on the door before Joeli spoke again. "Did you cheat when you murdered Raymel Tacsis?"

Nona turned around.

"I can see it doesn't take thread-work to pull your strings." Joeli's smile was an ugly thing.

Better. Make sure you scar her face.

"Raymel Tacsis sought to kill me out in the wilds. I killed him first."

"There were half a dozen of you, including Tarkax Ice-Spear. Raymel came alone." Joeli managed to sound disgusted at the injustice of it.

"I heard she had some gerant helping her." The girl from Holy Class wrinkled her nose at the thought of it, somehow ignoring the fact that Raymel stood close on nine foot tall and had sent his soldiers in first. "That girl . . ." She snapped her fingers, trying to recall a name. "You know the one . . . The fat—"

"Sorry." Darla rubbed her elbow where it had struck the Holy Class novice in the face. She peered down at her, sprawled on the floor, moaning. "Didn't see you there."

Nona didn't try to hide her grin. "I killed Raymel Tacsis. He was a murderer and I doubt many worse men have drawn breath. If that damaged your family connections at court or inconvenienced the Namsis in any way . . . I don't care." She turned to go. "You'll have to work harder than that to provoke me, Joeli."

"Of course the person who really pulled your strings was back here while you were murdering your betters out in the Corridor."

Nona found herself facing Joeli again without remembering turning around.

"A pity she was killed in the cave-in while her conspirator escaped with the shipheart," Joeli said. "I would have liked to have seen the peasant bitch drowned for her crimes against this convent. What did they call her? Hop-along! That was—"

"Hessa." Nona found herself pinning Joeli to the floor. Her hand scarlet around the girl's throat where Keot burned across her skin. "Her name was Hessa."

Finish her! Tear her neck open! Keot fought Nona as she struggled to draw her hand back. Shouts of alarm rang out all around her, novices seized her shoulders, and still she couldn't withdraw her hand though the trembling fingers, caught in a war between her and Keot, exerted no pressure.

As Darla lifted her clear Nona managed to force Keot into the shadows of her habit sleeve. Joeli's throat slipped undamaged from her grip, just the faint white impression of fingers left to record the event. The girl's eyes narrowed and she started to choke, clutching at her neck. Darla carried Nona out through the door, and the wave of Joeli's concerned friends closed in around her. Their voices followed Nona, raised in such outrage that you might think Joeli lay disembowelled in a pool of her own gore. The last thing Nona saw through the ring of backs were Joeli's eyes seeking hers, a small but triumphant smile on her lips.

4

———— ✦ ————

"I HEAR YOU'VE been making friends in your new class."
Ara sat herself down beside Nona, golden hair frothing
around her shoulders.

"How—"

"Ruli told me. You know there's nothing happens at Sweet
Mercy without Ruli knowing minutes later. I think it's her
secret marjal talent. You have your claws, Ruli has gossip-
magic." Ara nodded at Ruli, crossing the novice cloister to join
them.

"I heard you put Joeli in the sanatorium!" Ruli sat heavily
on Nona's other side, habit billowing around her, cheeks red
with excitement.

"I hardly touched her." Nona frowned. Joeli had come to
the Academia Tower with a shawl around her neck. In the
corridor outside the lesson she came up to Nona and held her
gaze for a long moment, pale green eyes fixed upon Nona's
black orbs without a flicker of fear. "Hessa's name is so important to you? And yet you've never even visited the spot where
she died. If you really thought Yisht killed Hessa . . . wouldn't
you want to find her murderer?" She turned away then with
just a hint of a smile, her words echoing in Nona's head.

A minute later Sister Rail had called the novices into the
classroom. Inevitably she spotted Joeli's neck scarf and asked
about this departure from the novice uniform. Joeli had, in a
croaking whisper wholly absent in the corridor, related a lurid
tale of being throttled. Sister Rail had sent her to the sanatorium to be checked over and had fixed Nona with a steely eye.
Sister Rule had been huge, straining every seam of her habit.

Her replacement, Rail, was a short, painfully thin woman whose habit flapped around her. Both nuns controlled their class with a very firm hand, but Rule's had at least been fair and she had welcomed questions, valuing cleverness of any kind. Although she'd endured just a handful of lessons so far it seemed clear to Nona that Sister Rail most valued the ability to recite what the mistress said. She appeared to consider questions to be a form of stupidity and contrary ideas tantamount to mutiny.

Nona looked around at her friends on the cloister bench. "Really. I had a hand on Joeli's neck but I held back. I didn't choke her."

The pause, just a beat of silence, reminded Nona that even friends needed a moment to swallow unlikely statements, true or not.

"Rosie won't be taken in by a pretend croak," Ruli said. "She'll send Joeli on her way soon enough."

But Joeli hadn't returned to class. She wasn't in the cloister either, and Joeli loved to hold court beneath the centre oak during breaks. Nona glanced at her friends. They had seen her rages, back before she started to master Keot, and those hadn't been pretty scenes. Fortunately Zole had suffered the worst of them, mostly out on the sands of Blade Hall, and had never complained . . . probably because she usually won the fight. And even when Keot had his hooks set deep into the meat of her emotions Nona had never used her flaw-blades or raised her hand against a novice not training for the Red.

"So, senior novice!" Jula hailed. She bent over Nona's shoulder, lowering her voice. "Are you too grand to come 'below' with us now?" She cropped her mousey hair short these days. It tickled Nona's ear.

"Try to stop me." Nona grinned. Jula had always been the most bookish and law-abiding of novices but since her discovery, close by the Seren Way, of a hidden entrance into the caves there had been no end to her enthusiasm for clandestine exploration.

Darla came to join them, shouldering her way through the building crowd. "Oh Ancestor, that Sister Rail will kill me with those lessons. I don't care which emperor annexed what territory."

"You should!" Ruli said. "Your father's promotion is any day now, and generals are always annexing something."

Darla scowled, sitting heavily on the bench. "And I don't care which tax caused what revolt. The only good thing to happen in that lesson was Joeli leaving."

"Seriously, though." Ruli pushed aside the long pale fall of her hair and turned back to Nona. "Keep a lid on that temper. Sister Wheel would happily push you off the cliff and have Ara as Shield. And what would you do out there in the world if the abbess had to throw you out?"

Ara nodded. "Joeli's trouble. She's got half the mistresses on her side and a lot more friends inside the convent than you do. Then you have to think about how many friends she has outside. Just because they like her family's money rather than her doesn't stop them being dangerous. The Namsis are as well placed as my family, plus if you're discharged from the order they'd happily murder you just to earn favour with the Tacsis."

"Sometimes I think I'd like to go out there and let them try."

"Nona!" Ruli looked shocked.

"What? It's the only way I'm ever going to find Yisht. She's not going to come back here and let me kill her." Nona scowled up at the grey sky, which was darkening by the moment. The cloister roofs opposite lay white, plastered by the ice-wind. The centre oak's branches tossed randomly as the wind sought its direction, the Corridor wind trying to reassert itself. The tree's leaves were wrapped so tightly against the cold that the branches seemed bare. "Joeli said bad things about Hessa. That's what got to me."

"That's how she is. Pulling strings, even if it's not thread-work," Ara said. "She's even got on the Poisoner's good side because she's so good at brewing up nastiness in a pot. So watch what you touch around her! And she poisons minds just as easily. The girl's got a tongue on her. It wasn't bad luck you fell foul of her straight off. She made it happen. Perhaps she even had it hot for Raymel Tacsis. She wouldn't be the first Namsis matched to a Tacsis."

Nona stared at the novices out on the gravelled yard, jaw clenched. Ara was right and the truth of it burned her. She'd been manipulated, moulded to the Namsis girl's desire. Her eyes found Zole, alone as usual, sitting with her back to the centre oak, knees drawn up. Joeli could never sway Zole. The ice-triber gave out nothing for anyone to take a hold of. Since the bloodshed at the Devil's Spine all those years ago Zole had perhaps spoken a hundred words to Nona. Most of them singular and days apart.

"So, are we cave hunting tonight?" Ruli asked.

"Don't you ever sleep?" Darla was distinctly less keen than the rest of them when it came to exploring the tunnels riddling the Rock of Faith.

Ruli stuck her tongue out. "So, are we?"

"It's dangerous." Ara closed her fingers, signing that Ruli should lower her voice.

Ara didn't just mean the chance of getting lost or injured. After the theft of the shipheart Abbess Glass had made clear that any novices exploring the convent's undercaves would find themselves stripped of the habit, too untrustworthy to marry the Ancestor. And it seemed that all the rules were being more strictly enforced these days, Sister Wheel's determination to root out wrongdoing more zealous from one day to the next.

"It's the only exciting thing we do outside Blade class." Ruli pouted. Jula had discovered the fissure hidden just past one of the many turns of the Seren Way, but it had been Ruli who convinced the novices that the caves it led to were just caves, not directly under the convent and so not the convent's undercaves. On that basis they had begun their explorations. Discovery would undoubtedly bring punishment, but wouldn't see them turned out into the world. Besides . . . they weren't going to be discovered!

"I . . ." An uneasiness ran through Nona—having no world outside Sweet Mercy to return to she had always been the one of them with most to lose. "Perhaps we shouldn't . . ." Across the cloister she saw a face at a window, above the galleried walkway. Joeli? Watching her? Smiling with the mouth that had sullied Hessa's name. Nona knew she wouldn't find any clues to Yisht's whereabouts on top of the Rock. And Joeli had been right. Nona had failed her friend. For three long years Nona's struggles with mastering Keot and the enormity of the challenge in finding justice for Hessa had kept her from action.

Perhaps there really was something in the caves that might help. Maybe they could find a passage to the convent under-caves. She owed it to her friend to visit the place where she had died. Maybe Hessa had left some clue for Nona that might lead to her killer. Even at twelve Hessa had had few equals when it came to thread-work and bathed in the power of the shipheart she might have accomplished miracles. "Oh hells, let's do it!"

A raindrop hit the back of Nona's hand. A fat raindrop, close to freezing. A heartbeat later a salvo scattered down around them. As one the novices joined the rush for the shelter of the galleries, and behind them the black sky opened, hurling down the rain as if each drop were intended to be fatal. By the time Nona looked again for the window where Joeli had been the rain had drawn a curtain across it.

Sister Pail found Nona with her friends as they huddled together watching the downpour. "You're to appear before the convent table tonight at eighth bell, that's Ferra, not Bray." She stood regarding Nona with mild distaste, her habit beaded with water.

"Why? What's she done?" Ghenna, small and dark, working her way out of a clump of Red Class novices.

Sister Pail kept her gaze on Nona. "The abbess doesn't approve of novices trying to murder other novices."

5

---✦---

ABBESS GLASS

"ANY OTHER BUSINESS before we invite the judge to make his petition?" Abbess Glass looked up from her notes. Along both sides of the long table nuns returned her gaze. All except Sister Kettle, still recording the minutes of the last item in the ledger of record. A chamber beneath the scriptorium held piles of such ledgers, filled with minutes, stacked to the ceiling in columns that marched off into the mildewed gloom. Enough minutes to constitute hours, weeks, decades. Never to be read. But authority must leave a trail or how else will it be held to account, and without checks, or at least the potential for them, authority, like any power, corrupts. "Other business?"

"Nona Grey." Sister Rail laid a hand upon the table. It was, like the rest of her, little more than skin and bones, the long nails jagged at the ends.

"Again?" Abbess Glass sighed and flexed her own hand. The burn scar across her palm had remained stiff despite all of Sister Rose's oils and unguents, allowing only limited movement. At times like these she let the echo of that old pain remind her that it had been Nona who saved her from the fire.

"Again." Sister Rail inclined her head. On the table her nails dug at the wood.

"Really?" Abbess Glass had disliked Sister Rail within moments of her arrival from the Convent of Silent Devotion, but by that point Sister Rule had already departed on her sabbatical and nobody else could teach Academia to all four classes. Besides, Rail had other qualifications Glass required, and one did not have to like one's pieces in order to play them. "Tell me."

"She attacked and very nearly maimed Novice Joeli within hours of joining Mystic Class." The bony hand on the table became a bony fist. The candle flames jumped as if Sister Rail had struck the wood and set the candlesticks shuddering.

"I wonder that Sister Spire hasn't brought this to my attention." Abbess Glass looked to the nun in question. Nona's new class mistress was another recent addition to the convent, a young Holy Sister returned from three years' ministering to the sick on the far borders of Archon Anasta's see.

"Sister Spire didn't know anything about it." Sister Spire raised an eyebrow and turned her gaze on Sister Rail.

"The girl came to me in confidence." Sister Rail made a sour pucker of her mouth. Rail's family were a very minor branch of the Namsis tree and she had petitioned the abbess before on Novice Joeli's behalf.

The abbess frowned, wondering what "almost maiming" the novice had entailed. "And what do you propose we do?" She could see her breath before her. White hands pulled her robes tighter. The cold never left the hall; the heating pipes lay freezing since the shipheart had been taken. "Do you have a punishment in mind, sister?"

"Reduce the girl to convent helper," Sister Rail replied without hesitation. "That's what she deserves. At the very least she must be returned to Grey Class and whipped before the Ancestor's dome."

"I vote she be whipped and then reduced to helper." Sister Wheel leaned forward, elbows on the table. "Or banished."

"Perhaps we could hear some evidence first, sister? Before moving to sentencing." The abbess raised her hand to forestall Wheel's reply. "Did someone think to summon the girls?" She drank from the cup beside her, wishing the water were wine.

"I saw them waiting in the corridor." Sister Apple had arrived late and sat at the far end of the table.

Abbess Glass gestured towards the door. The ice had been surging for three years straight, all the nations of the Corridor squeezed tight against their borders, bursting for war, and here she sat arbitrating the disputes of children.

Sister Apple's footsteps echoed in the bare hall. She spoke a word to the junior nun outside and moments later Joeli Namsis limped in, one hand at her throat, blonde hair in disarray. Nona Grey stalked in behind her. She looked twice the size of the painfully thin stray the abbess had brought from Verity more than five years earlier. Her unnerving all-black eyes seemed to challenge each nun in turn. She stood as tall as several at the table now, still slim, but Abbess Glass knew the body beneath that habit was corded with muscle. The abbess frowned at the state of Nona's hair, a short and spiky shock as consumingly black as her eyes. Efforts to tame it over the years had singularly failed.

Abbess Glass nodded to Sister Spire.

"If you could outline your grievance, Novice Joeli?"

Joeli looked as if nothing but determination kept her upright, sagging around her unspecified injuries. She dragged her bad leg a step closer to the table and spoke in a cracked whisper, holding her neck. "I was watching the class at bladepath. The new girl fell and seemed to think it was my fault. She beat me to the ground and tried to kill me."

"Novice Nona?" Sister Spire gave her an inquiring look.

"I did knock her down. If I had tried to kill her she would be dead."

Sister Spire frowned. She had blunt features, not unkindly arranged, marred by a burn that ran across her forehead and down the side of her face. "Novice Joeli, how did Novice Nona try to kill you?"

"She . . ." Joeli stifled a sob. "She strangled me. She said she would kill me. She said it before she even chose her bed! And . . . and then she wrapped her hands around my throat and . . ." Another sob. "They had to pull her off me."

"Is this true, Novice Nona?" Sister Spire asked.

"It was one hand. And for a few seconds. But yes." Nona furrowed her brow, looking furiously at the ground.

"And how long would you say you were throttled for, Novice Joeli?"

"I . . . it could be minutes. I blacked out after a while."

Sister Wheel banged her fist to the table and the shadows danced. "Any period of time one novice spends strangling another is too long. What are we even discussing? Take her habit.

She'll never be fit for her vows. Novice Arabella can take the Ordeal of the Shield and serve the Argatha in her place."

High above them the shutters rattled as the ice-wind picked up strength. It always seemed to be an ice-wind these days.

Abbess Glass stared at the two novices. She knew Joeli to be manipulative and spiteful, unable to forget her family's privilege. On the other hand she was a quantal prime with rare skill at thread-work and was an accomplished poisoner to boot. Nona of course was too precious to be lost to the Church, a three-blood, fast as a devil and with a temper to match. The abbess would not lose sight of the girl—but Nona might just have made keeping her in the order impossible. If she had deliberately injured another novice Nona had done about the only thing that could get Sister Rose to agree with Sister Wheel on something. Sister Rose spent too much time repairing bodies to forgive deliberate and unwarranted harm caused in anger. She wouldn't let a training blade be put in any hand that might seek the life of another novice. Together both sister superiors could overrule the abbess.

Sister Spire frowned. "Have you anything to say in your defence, Novice Nona?"

"I didn't try to kill her. I barely squeezed her neck."

Joeli straightened, lowering the hand from beneath her chin and pulling down the collar of her habit. Along both sides of her throat livid bruises told the story of fingers pressed deep, the black imprints surrounded by a halo of yellowing flesh. Sister Wheel drew in a sharp breath. Sister Rail thumped the table in outrage. "This! This is the work of someone who has no place within our order."

Abbess Glass felt the tide turn. She presided over a convent where a score of novices could do the miraculous, some moving faster than thought, some weaving shadows, or fire, and some few walking the Ancestor's Path, returning from it echoing with the power of the divine. And yet given a choice she would never once consider exchanging for any of that the gift the Ancestor had given to her. People were a magic and a mystery, no matter whether they were low-born or high, no matter whether it was soil or spells they turned their hands to, whether they were geniuses or fools. There were few who saw past faces, past status, past what people said to what they meant. Abbess Glass knew she didn't see far into the puzzle, but she saw further than most, and it gave her an edge. An edge so sharp that most of those she cut didn't even know it until it was far too late. Right now though, all her gift told her was that the room had shifted and Nona stood on the brink.

Across the table from Sister Wheel, Sister Rose lowered her head, lips pressed tight, brow furrowed.

"Are there no witnesses?" Sister Kettle asked, looking up from her recording. Surprise registered on several faces. Sister Kettle never spoke up at convent table—it wasn't her place to—less than ten years into her vows. She came to record, not to speak, but so soon returned from a long and arduous mission she might be forgiven her lapse.

"There are many witnesses!" Sister Rail brightened, showing narrow teeth in a narrow smile. "Let me—"

"Joeli is a very popular novice." Abbess Glass spoke over Mistress Academic. "Many of the girls may be swayed by personal loyalties, turning suspicion into fact."

"Would you summon the accused's friends instead?" Sister Rail demanded.

"We need a witness who would satisfy all of us as impartial and true." The abbess studied the grain of the table between her spread hands as if such a hope were impossible.

Sister Wheel took the bait. "The Chosen One was there!" She looked up in triumph.

Sisters Tallow and Apple suppressed long-suffering sighs.

"Let it be Novice Zole then." The abbess nodded to Kettle who hurried to the door. "At least nobody can accuse her of being friends with either party. Or anyone else. Nona and Joeli can wait outside."

Kettle led the pair to the door and returned to the table having sent for Zole. The shadows clung to the nun as she walked, like cobwebs. They mottled her face as if they were stains running across her skin. When Apple had brought Kettle back, injured and changed, there hadn't been one person at the table who had thought the convent still held a place for her, not now she walked in darkness as the Noi-Guin do. That had been a long debate. A long night and a longer morning. But at length Glass had steered the sisters to the decision she wanted.

"You know there is no safe place for Nona if she were to

leave this convent." Sister Apple spoke to the table in general, her gaze avoiding Sister Wheel and Sister Spire. "We've waited more than a generation for a three-blood novice and now you want to send her out to our enemies because of a fight with a girl who's never forgotten she was born Sis. Joeli's two parts spite, one part privilege."

"She is a member of our sisterhood!" Wheel glared across the table. "And she was nearly killed whilst under the protection of the Ancestor."

"Attempted murder is punishable by the oven. She would be of no danger to us then." Sister Rail spoke lightly as if the matter were of little consequence. "She would fall into nobody else's hands."

"In Sweet Mercy we drown rather than cook," said the abbess, without humour. "And we have managed to avoid capital punishment for several decades. I do not intend to start again today."

Raised voices in the corridor drew their eyes to the doorway. Abbess Glass prayed the novices weren't fighting again. The argument drew closer and she relaxed, hearing a man's complaint. A brief knocking and the heated debate outside continued.

"Come!"

Sister Pail burst in. "He won't listen! I told him to stay!" She still looked like a child to Abbess Glass, just two years in the habit. It took an effort not to call her Novice Suleri. Behind her came Zole, ice-spattered and glowering at the world with impartial dislike. Behind Zole a tall white-haired man encompassed by the thickest of velvet robes.

"Irvone!" Abbess Glass rose to greet the judge. The other nuns followed suit, Sister Rose struggling to rise having sat too long and weighing three times what was healthy.

A young man, burdened under books of law, hastened around the judge to introduce him.

"Judge Irvone Galamsis offers the abbess of Sweet Mercy convent his greetings and felicitations on this the ninety-seventh anniversary of Emperor Royan Anstsis's victory over the Pelarthi insurrection."

"Ah, that. How could we forget?" Abbess Glass broadened her smile into the most genuine imitation at her disposal. "Irvone!

How nice to have the pleasure of your company again. It's been what . . . three years?"

"Forgive the intrusion, dear abbess." Irvone inclined his head towards a bow. "But on seeing the arrival of the young lady about whom I've come all this way to petition you I felt I must be heard."

Abbess Glass considered having the judge escorted from the hall, perhaps even from the convent, but it would be an expensive pleasure. Better to hand over the small victory of a seat at the convent table in order to compensate the loss awaiting him. She gestured to a vacant chair and the judge's assistant pulled it out for him.

"Stand at the end of the table, Novice Zole." Abbess Glass indicated the spot before glancing towards Sister Pail. "Bring Nona and Joeli back, sister."

Accused and accuser re-entered the hall a moment after the junior nun exited. Sister Apple craned her neck to watch Joeli with particular attention, her eyes narrow. Further along the table Sister Pan coughed and muttered about the cold.

"Novice Zole, what can you tell us about this morning's incident at blade-path?" Abbess Glass favoured the girl with a warm smile, knowing that it would not be returned.

"Novice Joeli accused Novice Hessa of helping Yisht to steal the shipheart," Zole said. "Nona knocked her down."

"I would have wanted to knock her down myself," Abbess Glass said.

"I would have." Sister Tallow kept a flinty gaze on Joeli. "No 'wanted' about it."

"And then Nona strangled her!" Sister Rail said.

Zole shook her head. "She held Joeli's neck. There was no strangling."

Sister Wheel harrumphed in irritation but couldn't bring herself to contradict the Chosen One. Beside her Sister Rail looked daggers at Nona then raised a hand towards Joeli. "Of course she was strangled! You can see it!"

"No." Zole shook her head again. "It did not happen."

"But the bruises!" Sister Rail banged the table. "You think we're blind?"

"The evidence does seem compelling." Irvone nodded, candlelight glinting on the gold circlet around his hair.

Zole shrugged.

"This is nonsense." Rail looked around the table. "We should vote and then the abbess will decide."

Abbess Glass puffed out her cheeks. There were only two votes that mattered, the rest she could overrule, but if the convent's two sister superiors united against her the matter would have to go to the archons or the high priest. Such public dissent would weaken her position and Nona would likely be found guilty in any case. "Let us vote then."

"Guilty." Sister Rail folded her arms.

"Innocent." Sister Apple frowned, still watching the novices.

"I abstain." Sister Pan huddled within the range-coat she never removed these days.

"Innocent," Sister Tallow said. "If Nona wanted the girl dead she would have cut her head off."

As Mistress Spirit, Sister Wheel could vote first with the other mistresses, but as a sister superior she could also vote last. She waved for the class nuns to vote.

"Guilty." Sister Oak, Red Class mistress, looked down.

"Guilty." Sister Hearth had replaced Sister Flint as Grey Class mistress and had witnessed the worst of Nona's rages while she struggled to control Keot.

Sister Spire seemed unwilling to speak but at last spoke in a small voice. "Guilty."

"Innocent." Sister Fork of Holy Class smiled encouragingly at Nona.

"Sister Wheel?" Abbess Glass inquired.

"I . . ." The older nun goggled at her, jaw clenching and unclenching. "I am sure the Chosen One had told us what she saw . . . but . . ." The words seemed to hurt her. "She may not have seen everything. And this novice is guilty of many crimes. So I say, guilty."

"Sister Rose?"

Sister Rose shifted her bulk unhappily in her chair. "I wish you had come to me, Joeli. I have salves that would have helped your poor throat." She looked at the abbess, brown eyes glistening. "I'm sorry . . . but I can't sanction this level of violence against fellow novices, especially in one so talented in battle. What will come next? I—"

"Joeli didn't come to you?" Abbess Glass asked. That didn't sound like Joeli Namsis at all. The girl would go to the sanatorium with a splinter and try to stay for a week. Especially if she could lay the blame for the splinter at someone else's feet.

"No." Sister Rose shot the novice a sympathetic look. "That was unreasonable of me. She couldn't be expected to brave an ice-wind in her condition. But if she had sent word I would have come. Sister Rail really should have told me."

"Why would you not seek Sister Rose's attention?" Sister Apple stood from her chair and advanced on Joeli.

"I didn't want to bother—"

"You're bothering all of us now, Joeli. You bothered Mistress Academia before lunch. And yet you didn't present yourself to our own sweet Rosie to ease your suffering?" She stalked around the novice, peering at her neck. "Show me your hands."

Joeli instinctively hid them in the pockets of her habit. Apple reached out and took the closest one, pulling it towards her face, palm up. "Come." She led the novice to the table, holding the hand towards the candles. "See?"

"I see four fingers and a thumb." Judge Irvone covered a yawn.

Sister Apple ignored him. "This yellow staining here. Do you see it?"

Abbess Glass leaned forward. The girl's fingers were faintly yellow here and there, the colour of an old bruise almost faded from sight.

"Wodewort and burn-cotton. Careful preparation with an alkali base gives you Ulhen's ointment." Sister Apple released Joeli's hand.

Sister Rose scraped her chair back and came to see. "It has a role in the treatment of some chronic skin conditions but you have to be pretty desperate to use it. The main side-effect is severe bruising." She stepped back and looked Joeli in the face. The novice bowed her head. "Oh, Joeli! You didn't?"

"She choked me." Joeli spoke softly and without conviction, staring down at her hands.

"I've a pill that will get the truth out of you soon enough!" Sister Apple turned to make for the door.

"Stay." The abbess raised her hand. "Potions and pills have no role at convent table. We have no evidence of their accuracy nor Church sanction to rely on such." She ignored Apple's raised eyebrows. Sometimes the nun's enthusiasm for her own works overrode common sense. Such cards were not to be revealed or played over novices and before an audience like Irvone Galamsis. "I will say, however, that it seems impossible that we condemn Novice Nona to any harsh punishment on the basis of what we have seen and heard. Both of you girls are confined to convent this seven-day and neither of you will eat lunch until the seven-day after that. If there is any more fighting between you I shall be asking Sister Tallow to break out the wire-willow. Now go. And count yourselves lucky! Run!"

The novices hastened to the door. "Not you, Zole."

Zole turned as the other two vanished through the doorway. For a moment she seemed to be considering whether to obey. Then with a shrug she closed the door and returned to the table.

"So, to your business, Irvone," Abbess Glass said. "You came with a petition concerning Novice Zole."

"Indeed. Once more I come seeking the return of a novice." He inclined his head, full of gravitas, consulting the notes his assistant had set before him. It had always amused Glass quite how closely the judge resembled the statues and images the heretic Scithrowl made of the Ancestor, the mane of his white hair and blade of his nose making him seem wisdom incarnate rather than the most corruptible of Verity's three high court judges. Irvone cleared his throat. "Fortunately on this occasion the novice is to be returned to the bosom of her loving family rather than to her appointment with the gallows."

"And the loving family in question would be . . ."

"Our own esteemed royal family!" Irvone smiled. "Young Zole is to be returned to House Lansis itself, and the arms of her mother, the honourable Sherzal."

A low mutter ran the length of the table. Sister Wheel struggled to contain her outrage, and failed. "The Argatha belongs to the Church! She's not some royal toy!"

The judge kept his eyes on Abbess Glass, ignoring Wheel's outburst.

"The emperor's sisters have standing invitations to visit the convent any time they like," Abbess Glass said. "I would be delighted to discuss this matter in person with Sherzal."

Irvone forced a smile and spread his hands. "I fear the honourable Sherzal is uncertain about the nature of her welcome after the wild slanders spread at court at the time of the convent's . . . unfortunate loss."

"Certainly she would be still more welcome if she came visiting with the shipheart that was stolen from us. But we're hardly likely to take the emperor's sister prisoner or raise our hands against her are we, Irvone? We are brides of the Ancestor, pledged to peace." She gestured at the stern faces around the table. Sister Tallow in particular looked no more than a blink from killing someone.

Irvone glanced around the seated nuns with a nervous frown. "That's as may be, abbess. However, Sherzal is within her rights to demand the return of her child."

"Her ward," Abbess Glass corrected.

"Adopted child."

"Adopted in absentia? She was her ward when she arrived."

"A recent development," the judge acknowledged. "But entirely legal. Zole is Sherzal's heir. Trained in her palace for some years before being entrusted into your care until such time—"

"Until such time as I see fit to discharge her from her pledge of service."

"Until such time as Sherzal, Zole's parent and guardian, calls for her return." Irvone turned to his assistant who already had the uppermost of his books open at a ribbon-marked page.

"Yes. Yes." Abbess Glass waved the matter aside. "Again, Irvone, you come to us with a matter properly covered by Church law. Sherzal should take any concerns she may have to High Priest Nevis and they will be dealt with through the correct ecclesiastical channels."

"It's a bad time to be imposing Church law over secular law, abbess." The judge shrugged within his robe.

"One is not imposed over the other, judge." Abbess Glass reached for her water again, mouth dry. Irvone Galamsis might be greedy and lacking morals, but he wasn't stupid. After three years of narrowing, the Corridor ran with rumours of fresh wars. When the ice advanced something else had to give.

Such times were poor ones to remind an emperor that some of the empire's most deadly resources were not his to control but must be lent to his purpose through the goodwill of the Church. "Each law has its own domain where it applies without challenge from the other."

"Reaching for Church law can get your fingers burned . . ." The judge let his eyes linger on Abbess Glass's right hand. "In any event, I had the idea that under Church law the issue of family rights versus convent authority over novices was somewhat vexed. Is that territory you really wish to wander into?"

"Was there anything else, judge?"

Judge Irvone sat back in his chair, impassive save for a hard gleam in his eyes. "The honourable Sherzal was most insistent that Zole not go on the ice in any of the exercises your novices may undertake. I'm sure we can all agree on that. After all, none of us wish to lose the child."

The abbess glanced at Zole who had stood so impassive and immobile that it took an effort to remember she was there at all. "Sherzal told us that Zole was the only survivor from the town of Ytis on the empire's border with Scithrowl. Why would she be in any particular danger on the ice?"

The judge narrowed his eyes. "She spent her early years on the ice and unfortunately spent considerable time in the company of the criminal, Yisht, who stole the Sweet Mercy shipheart. It is possible she might wish to return to her parents' tribe on the ice or to seek Yisht's tribe out of some misplaced affection for the fugitive." He turned in his chair to face Zole. "I'm sure you'd like to swap your habit for something a bit more fashionable and join Sherzal at her palace, wouldn't you? There's a grand party coming up. She has exciting plans and wants you to be part of them!"

Zole regarded the judge without expression. "There are many things here I have yet to learn."

"But Sherzal has teachers for you, child! Safira is waiting to resume your weapons training, and Sherzal can call upon instructors from the Academy itself!"

"I will ask the abbess for guidance," Zole said.

"And I will give it." Glass hid her surprise and placed both hands flat upon the table. "Now, have you any more business to discuss, Irvone?"

The judge shook his head in resignation. "This is a poor decision, abbess."

"Even so."

And with that push Abbess Glass set a new game in play, one domino falling into the next. So many pieces to fall, so many chances to fail. No one but her understood the game yet, but that didn't mean she would win it. A thrill of fear ran through her. But the ice pressed in on both sides and somewhere high above them the moon continued its fall. It was time to move.

6

NONA LAY AWAKE her second night in the Mystic dormitory thinking she would never sleep. Joeli had retired to her cluster of friends and then to bed with nothing but hard looks thrown in Nona's direction. Even so when the lamps were extinguished Nona curled beneath her blankets wondering if there and then in the darkness the girl was picking at the jumble of her thoughts, seeking loose threads on which to pull.

However long Nona tossed and turned before her dreams took her it was not long enough to see Zole return. In the morning the ice-triber rose early and was leaving the room as Nona threw back her covers.

Nona finally trapped her at breakfast, taking her seat next to Zole who sat, head lowered, eating with her usual dedication as if it were a chore to be accomplished as swiftly as possible. Nona picked up her fork, glancing at the heaped and steaming bowls lined along the middle of the table. "You didn't see me." She kept her voice low, leaning towards Zole. "In blade-path you didn't see what happened."

"No."

"But you told the convent table that you did . . ."

"No."

"But you said—"

"I told them you didn't strangle the girl."

"But you didn't see . . ."

"Are you given to lying?" Zole looked up from her porridge.

"No . . ."

"The abbess says words are steps along a path—the important thing is to get where you're going." Zole shrugged and returned to her porridge.

Nona hesitated then spoke. "Is this because I saved your life when Raymel . . ."

Zole swallowed. "My life was only in danger because of your actions."

"What? I saved—"

"If you had killed Raymel Tacsis at your first attempt I would not have been lying poisoned in a cave. You should have cut his head off."

Nona sat back. Zole hadn't spoken so many words in a row to her for years, perhaps ever. Over on the Grey table Ara and Ruli were laughing at Jula who seemed to be demonstrating knife moves with a spoon. Nona grinned. It would be good when they joined her in Mystic. She'd feel safer sleeping in the same room as Joeli Namsis with Ara in the next bed.

"You should hide him better." Zole pushed her bowl back.

"Sorry?" Nona turned from watching her friends.

"You are careless. You lack control. I have seen him at your wrists when we fight, and at your neck when you are screeching."

"I don't screech!"

"Like a haunt-owl."

"I—" Nona suddenly realized that whether she screeched or not wasn't the important thing here. She lowered her voice, staring at Zole's dark eyes. "You don't know what you're talking about! You've seen nothing!"

Zole shrugged. "On the ice we know the *klaulathu*. We do not run from them screaming 'devils' like you people huddling in the Corridor."

Nona restrained herself from pointing out that Zole had been huddling with them for at least the past five years. "*Klaulathu?* Do you know how to get rid of them?"

Keot rose along her spine. *I can only leave when you die.*

Zole stood. "It is possible but hard. Better to live with him. They are of the Missing, you understand this? Pieces of the Missing that they abandoned before they crossed the Path." She walked off, leaving Nona openmouthed.

"Looked as though you got more than three words out of

the Argatha!" Darla sat down heavily beside Nona and started to heap her plate.

"Well, I *am* her Shield!" Nona reached for the food too. She made it a point of honour to always eat more than Darla managed, and Darla had an appetite most bears would envy.

"Path first today," Darla grumbled. She took three smoked kippers.

"Not too bad." Nona took four.

"For you maybe. For me it's a choice between meditation until my brain runs out of my ears, or begging off to see if I can get past four steps on blade-path."

Nona shovelled eggs and kept a diplomatic silence. Darla had the worst sense of balance of any novice at the convent. Path lessons for those with quantal blood at least consisted of more than hunting for serenity, clarity, and patience. Nona had a much more interesting time under Sister Pan's close guidance, but every attempt to reach the Path was a reminder of the day Hessa died. With the shipheart gone, reaching the Path, which had always been a trial, became a feat of near-impossible difficulty. On the day Nona had fought Raymel somehow the depth of her anger, or being thread-bound to Hessa who was so close to the shipheart, had let her run the Path. In the years since, Nona had touched the Path on just a dozen occasions. Only in recent months had Nona regained the same level of competence without the shipheart's presence as she had when it was kept at the convent.

"Practise the patience trance," Nona advised. "It'll make the lesson more bearable." She crammed an overfull fork into her mouth.

Darla grimaced. "I don't have the patience to learn the patience trance. It's a vicious circle." She filled her mouth too and they chomped at each other a while. Despite the gerant girl welcoming Nona to their first class together with a beating, they'd become firm friends, not that an outside observer would know it from the number of insults Darla threw Nona's way.

ZOLE, JOELI AND Nona entered Path Tower by three different doors. Nona had found the east held a sense of rightness about it that the others lacked. Joeli came through the west in opposition. Zole came through the north, perhaps remembering her origins out on the ice.

In the classroom at the top of the tower they found themselves seats amid the play of light from the stained glass windows. The classroom was freezing as usual and the novices' breath misted before them. The tower had been built without fireplaces, relying on the shipheart warming the oil pipes that ran the length of the structure. Sigils on the pipes closest to the shipheart had converted its power into heat. Many of the convent's buildings had been adapted since the loss and the wind now stripped the smoke from a score of chimneys, but Sister Pan had resisted change.

"Welcome Mystic Class girls, welcome." The ancient woman sat on her treasure chest, wrapped in a fox-fur robe for which the abbess had sought special dispensation from the high priest on account of Sister Pan being close on a hundred with nobody left alive who could say whether each year was now taking her closer to that century mark or further past it. "Zole and Nona have joined us! It's a rare class that boasts three quantals."

Two days earlier Joeli had been the only quantal in the class and the sole recipient of Sister Pan's attentions. Joeli scowled and wrapped the illegal shawl tighter around the faked bruising on her neck. She didn't look well pleased at having to share.

"Clarity today, girls." Sister Pan rubbed her hand over her stump and huddled deeper into her furs. "I've put the etching of the Holothian labyrinth against the wall." She nodded for Darla to uncover it. "There is a second path from door to tomb. First find your clarity, then find that route. Eyes only." She glanced at Darla as she sat down: the gerant had been known to leave her chair and try tracing paths with her finger. "Zole, Nona, and Joeli will accompany me."

The three novices fell in behind Mistress Path. At least the practice rooms were warmer, lacking windows. And if they were lucky Sister Pan would let them use any Path-energy they managed to channel to heat the room first before trying anything more complex.

Nona allowed her vision to defocus and summoned the Path's image out of the blurred confusion. She let the flickers of light from Pan's lantern fuse into a single burning line and followed it, her feet somehow losing contact with the reality of stone steps.

"Follow close." Sister Pan's voice, disembodied in a space both vast beyond measure and small beyond imagining. "A different room today."

Nona stumbled out of the void into a narrow curving chamber very similar to the one in which she had practised her Path-work for the years since her gift showed. It stood between the spiral of the central stair and the circle of the tower's outer wall, occupying another third of the space. The only difference lay in the nature of the sigils inlaid in silver upon the ceiling, floor, and every wall. These ones were smaller, more complex, less tightly bound. In places loops and trails from one overwrote the next, and no two looked the same.

"The thread-room." She hadn't meant to speak. Hessa had told her about the chamber.

"It's time you and Zole got to grips with thread-work," Sister Pan said. "Walking the Path arms a Mystic Sister with forces that are very hard to use for anything but destruction. Here we focus on the more subtle Path-arts, but although they are gentle one must never underestimate them. I believe our own dear abbess has some hint of quantal blood and a rare unconscious talent for the most ephemeral thread-work. Done right, a gentle pull here, a touch there, a breath just sufficient to set a thread vibrating . . . and kings may be toppled, wars turned, the weak raised up." She gave the lantern to Joeli who moved to light three others. "Thread-work is a delicate art, which is why you two have never been any good at it. It rewards patience, observation, and empathy. There is no violence to it, though that does not preclude its use for malice. Hate can be a cold thing." She pushed Nona aside and stood between her and Zole. Nona heard the creak of Pan's bones as she moved. When the nun stood hunched at her side Nona realized with sudden surprise that she was taller than the old woman, and more solid. A single blow would shatter Sister Pan. A sense of unease came over Nona. It felt wrong somehow that so much knowledge and experience could be so fragile.

"I will show you." Sister Pan raised her hand and stared into the space beyond it.

Nona waited, watching. When Nona had arrived at the convent Sister Pan had loomed over her as all the other nuns did. There were still more secrets locked in her head than Nona could ever learn, the keys to powers untold . . . and yet she looked so small, so frail, waiting to cross the Path, so close that the devils must be licking their lips.

She is old, but I would not dare her.

Nona looked again. Keot was never one to miss a chance to boast. It gave her comfort to know he feared Mistress Path.

"Watch!" The air before Sister Pan filled with the bright complexity of the Path, a moving, living thing, twisting through more dimensions than the eye could fathom. "When wool is spun on the wheel a single length of yarn is wound around the spindle. But all around that strand of yarn there is a halo of loose pieces, fibres of wool not quite twisted in, wandering out from the main body."

As Sister Pan spoke the Path dimmed and in the air all around it threads appeared, like stars when the sun has fled the sky. "The threads are not the Path but they are of the Path. And because the Path goes everywhere and runs through all things, so do the threads."

Nona wondered if Sister Pan had chosen to speak of yarn to explain the matter because she knew Nona was a peasant and might not understand a different analogy so well. She was still wondering about it when she became aware that her mouth was open. She closed her jaw with a snap and wiped her lips. The image Sister Pan had made was mesmerizing. With an effort she tore her gaze from it.

"It's fascinating is it not?" Sister Pan's smile was a narrow white crescent in the darkness of her face. "I could watch it forever."

The slow motion of the threads reflected in Zole's and Joeli's eyes.

"There's a danger there," Sister Pan said. "The Path will throw you, sooner or later, but the threads will hold you. If you lack the will to free yourself they will keep you until your years have run from you and all that remains is to cross the

Path into darkness." She waved at the pattern and it faded, releasing the others.

Joeli blinked and focused on Nona. "Mistress Path, you said that these two novices have no talent for thread-work because they're so predisposed to violence. But do you think they might just be violent because they know they lack the talent for deeper work?" A small smile played on her lips, as if the humiliation at the convent table had never happened.

Sister Pan waggled her hand. "We shall see. Path-work is closer to the brute force approach of the Red Sister, and thread-work more subtle, like the arts of the Grey Sister, all stealth and guile. Mystic Sisters shade either towards the Red or Grey."

"I would rather be open. Straightforward. Honest." Nona wrinkled her nose. "Manipulating people, using them, feels wrong. It feels like . . . lies. People should be allowed free will . . ."

Sister Pan barked a laugh. "We're all puppets. Other people pull our strings every moment of every day. The only difference between us and Sayan-Ra dancing in the street show is that we can also pull our own strings and those of others. Threads aren't something external to the world that only a privileged few can touch. Every time you speak to someone threads are pulled. Every glance exchanged. Every punch thrown. Every kindness shown. In thread-work we are just more direct about it. More focused." She turned and fixed Nona with her dark eyes. "You need to know how to draw a thread or how will you prevent your own from being drawn?" She reached forward, plucking at the air with finger and thumb. "At first it will help you to visualize the task, see it before you, use your hands. It's nonsense of course. Not needed. But the mind loves the familiar. There!" She pinched and pulled. "How do you feel, Nona?"

"Hungry!" Nona clapped both hands across her stomach. "Starved!"

"Basic needs, simple emotions, are the easiest to influence." Sister Pan opened her fingers as if releasing what she held. "And now?"

"Full of breakfast." Nona laughed despite herself, then frowned. "But you couldn't do that with just words."

"I couldn't?" Sister Pan tilted her head. "If I described a roast chicken in exquisite detail, steaming on a plate of buttered potatoes, its skin golden and crisp, seasoned with salt and pepper . . . your mouth wouldn't begin to water? Your stomach rumble?"

Nona's mouth had already filled with saliva. When it came to food her strings were remarkably easy to pull. "Hessa worked with threads when she tried to stop Yisht stealing the shipheart." She shot an angry glance at Joeli then frowned at Zole, who still, years later, felt tainted by that association. "And I saw it because we were thread-bound."

"Young Hessa was a remarkable talent. I've not seen another so gifted at such an age in all the years I've taught. She was a great loss." Sister Pan settled her hand on Nona's shoulder. "And perhaps you will have an aptitude for thread-binding, novice. It's a rare skill and difficult to achieve but always greatly aided by strong and honest friendship between both parties. It only ever works between quantals though. You need to share the same blood."

Sister Pan stepped back and addressed them all. "Two things you should always remember. Firstly: you can never pull the same thread twice. Every action you take changes the thing you act upon and changes its connections to the world. Secondly: you can never pull just a single thread. Every thread is bound to every other, sometimes through many links, though always fewer than you might imagine. Pull one thread and others are pulled: the effect spreads like a ripple on a pond. You can play at thread-work and think that you are alone, but if you pull on a strand of a web hard enough and often enough . . . a spider will come. It is the same with the threads that bind the universe. Sooner or later you will be noticed. The "spiders" will, like as not, be humans, older, more powerful quantal thread-workers, marjal sorcerers with particular talents, intuitives such as Abbess Glass. But there are bigger spiders out there too. This world is not ours: it is older than us, the Missing were gone before our ships beached here. When the Corridor was a thousand miles wide and there was no moon in the sky they were gone. Echoes of them live among the threads, vibrations that will not fade. And there are others; their servants and things more ancient still. So tread softly, work sparingly, and hope." She waved her stump at the walls. "In here, however, there is no need for hope. The sigils seal us from the world, and the few threads that penetrate even these walls are beyond your reach."

The morning's exercises began with Nona and Zole paired, each seeking to visualize the threads that bound the other to the world.

"See the Path first," Sister Pan instructed. "Each of you must see it as it runs through the other. You know it from your dreams. You hunt it in the serenity trance. You follow it every moment of your life. And when the Ancestor grants you grace, you walk it."

Nona stared at Zole, at the black hair laid flat against her blunt skull, the stone-dark eyes, the broad cheekbones, the reddish hue of her skin as if the burn of the ice-wind had never left it, and the short, hard line of her mouth. She tried to see through the ice-triber to the Path, past her wide shoulders, past the height and strength of her. Time seemed both to race and to crawl in exercises like this. It always felt as if she had been at it an age, and when she stopped, Nona often discovered that the hours between one bell and the next had been devoured and yet with hindsight her efforts felt like just the work of minutes.

At first the Path showed as a single line, half-imagined, dividing Zole's imperfect symmetry. In the next instant Nona saw it as Sister Pan had shown it, flexing at right angles to the world. A single, bright Path. The only difference being that where Sister Pan's had been haloed by the diffuse white infinity of threads straying from the Path, each following its own convolutions before ending or returning to join the whole, Nona saw just the Path and nothing else.

"I see her threads," Zole said.

"Good work, novice. Try to follow one back to where it left the Path," Sister Pan called from across the room where she was working with Joeli on some more advanced matter. "Keep at it, Nona: there is still a little while before it's time to return."

Nona felt the familiar sense of surprise, a nearly whole

class spent and nothing to show for it. She gritted her teeth and stared harder. The Path twisted across her vision, threadless. A bead of sweat rolled down her neck, the muscles of her jaw twitched and bunched. Her vision blurred. Nothing.

Help me! Nona never called on Keot but she needed this.

Helping is not in my nature.

Nona stared at Zole, willing her threads to appear. Abbess Glass had had Sister Pan try thread-work to hunt down Yisht and the shipheart of course, and without success, but Nona had been there, in Hessa's head, watched her as the shipheart's power filled her and sharpened her talents into something keen enough to dissect reality. They had been thread-bound. There had been an unbreakable connection. Something of it could have survived. Must have survived. For more than two years Nona had waited to be taught these arts. Years spent waiting for a chance to use them to avenge Hessa. And now . . . nothing. She hadn't the skill!

"Well, novice?" Sister Pan touched Nona's shoulder. "Have you been successful?"

Nona tore her stare away from Zole, her eyes hot and dry, too wide open yet unwilling to close. She found herself sweat-soaked and aching in every limb. "She doesn't have any!" Behind Sister Pan Joeli's laughter tinkled like silver coins.

Sister Pan shook her head. "Of course she does. Every living thing, every dead thing, and every thing that has never lived is bound by threads. Stone, bone, tree, and thee." She pushed Nona aside and took her place. "Allow me to . . ." She paused, frowned, and squinted. Then blinked. "That is quite remarkable. More remarkable, to me, than the fact that four bloods run in your veins, Zole."

Zole glowered at the old nun.

"She really doesn't have any threads?" Nona asked, feeling vindicated.

"Of course she has threads!" Sister Pan snapped. "Were you not listening to me?" She frowned again. "But only the deepest and most fundamental, those hardest to find. Where there should be a myriad blazing around her, there are just a few, and buried deep in the stuff of the world. I have never seen the like."

As if it had been holding its tongue and waiting for Sister

Pan to pause Bray tolled, the sound of the bell reaching them faintly through the stones.

"Come." Sister Pan waved for them to follow. "I will consider this later." And she began to walk the path that would take a nun through walls.

7

———— ◆ ————

"**H**URRY UP!" JULA beckoned at them from down the rock passage, a black shape behind her lantern.

"Breathe out. I'll pull." Nona grabbed Darla's wrist and heaved as the girl exhaled. Behind Darla the outside world intruded as a line of brightness, glimpsed through the cliff-face.

Darla lurched forward, gasping for air, free of the crevice. Further down the passage Ruli gave a brief round of sarcastic applause. "I still have that grease if we need it!"

"I'll give her grease," Darla growled, and followed as Nona hurried to catch the others. The Seren Way was not as well travelled as the Vinery Stair and the chances of discovery were small, but the longer it took Darla to squeeze through into the caverns the greater that chance grew.

Nobody had ever told the novices that they weren't to explore the caves and passages that riddled the plateau but Nona always had the strong impression that this was because they hadn't asked, and also because all the entrances known to the nuns were barred and gated, the locks inscribed with sigils to defeat any form of picking. When Jula had first discovered the caves a year earlier Nona had moved their weekly meeting underground where the chances of detection shrank to zero. Nominally the objective of the group was to recover the shipheart but for Nona it had always been about killing Yisht.

"Hold up!" Nona and Darla closed the last few yards on the others. Jula and Ara carried the only two lanterns and the footing was treacherous. "If we break our ankles back here it's you lot who'll have to carry us out!"

"We'll just leave you here and say you ran away with city boys." Ketti, the last of their number, grinned and made kiss-mouths. The hunska girl was just a few inches shorter than Darla now, though thin as a rail. She talked about city boys a lot and it was a wonder to Nona that she preferred to spend her seven-day exploring the darkness beneath the Rock of Faith rather than going into Verity to giggle at the opposite sex across Thaybur Square.

"Come on!" Ara led off, eager to reach new ground.

At the first fork where a smaller passage led steeply down Ketti took her block of chalk and reinforced the letter on the wall that indicated the path to take. The moisture tended to blur the marks. They moved on in single file, Darla at the rear, demonstrating her impressive range of oaths as she repeatedly grazed her head on the rock above.

Nona called a halt at Round Cave a hundred yards from the entrance. Darla had come up with the name, and whilst un-imaginative it was at least accurate.

"Who's got something to report?" Nona looked to Ruli first. Ruli was on gossip duty, gathering any snippet of infor-mation that leaked into the convent through its connections with the outside world. Ruli had a talent for both creating and gathering gossip.

"I do! I really do!" Jula stepped forward, half-raising her hand before remembering that she wasn't in class. "I was read-ing the appendices in Levinin's older works. Everyone always quotes from the *Seven Histories of Marn* but—"

"What did you find?" Darla had even less patience for Jula's booklore than the others.

"More about shiphearts in one page than I've discovered in all the books I've searched through since we started looking!" Jula grinned. "According to Levinin there were four shiphearts within the empire's boundaries: the one at Sweet Mercy which is most closely tuned to quantals; another we knew about in the Noi-Guin's keeping at the Tetragode, which is attuned to marjals; one he says is rumoured in the city of Tru; and one from a gerant ship in the keeping of the mage Atoan."

Ara frowned. "I've never heard of a city called Tru or a mage called Atoan. And if a shipheart were in a city someone would own it or it would get taken."

Jula nodded. "Levinin was writing two hundred years ago. Tru is under the ice now. The black ice! And it was ruins before the ice took it. Tru's a city the Missing left. And Atoan died years ago but he had a son Jaltone who was also a mage and somehow is still alive!"

"Him I've heard of," Darla said. "He lives on the coast and helped General Hillan when the Durnish tried to land at Port Treen two years ago. My father was the general's second-in-command."

"It's interesting and everything . . ." Ruli said. "But I don't see how it helps us. We're not going to walk up to the Tetragode and—"

"It helps us because we know where Sherzal will have to look next," said Ara.

"And we *are* going to the ice . . ." Everyone went on the ice-ranging in Mystic Class. Over the ice though, not under it. Nona remembered her father's tales about hunting in the ice tunnels. The worst of them, the scariest stories, were from the time he ventured into the grey ice. The trip he never came back from was the one to the black.

"The ice is a big place. And Tallow is never going to take us up to the black ice. Even if it wasn't on the Scithrowl side of the mountains." Darla shivered. "Let's go explore some caves!"

Nona looked around the circle of lantern-lit faces. "Any more contributions? No?"

Jula bit her lip. "Well I thought it was interesting." She shrugged and led off.

IT TOOK LESS than half an hour's walk to reach the furthest limit of their explorations, but to expand their territory initially had taken the best part of a year, following dead ends or routes that grew too narrow or too dangerous. In several places they had fixed knotted ropes to aid in difficult climbs. It was Nona's private hope that they would find an alternative route into the convent undercaves but there were no guarantees that the two systems connected.

"I love it down here." Jula fell in beside Nona as they trekked the Gullet, a long water-smoothed passage wide enough to walk shoulder to shoulder. "It's so quiet. Just the drip of water. And footsteps. And Darla swearing."

They passed a stand of stalagmites, blunt and glistening in the lantern light. Ketti said nothing. Even she had grown tired of her innuendo after the tenth or twelfth time. A little further along a veil of dripping water crossed the passage. Nona hunched and pressed on through the icy deluge. Five tight winding twists rising steeply took them past the niche where two skeletons lay, limed over with rock-scale. One grown and one a child, locked together. A rusty stain between them may once have been a knife. They always made Nona sad, huddled there in the dark, watching with empty sockets as the centuries scurried by.

After the rising turns came a scramble up a rockfall, with the cavern roof slanting just three feet above. Finally a cliff some twenty yards high, perhaps once a waterfall, the wet stone offering few handholds. Fortunately the old watercourse had allowed room to swing and throw a grapple. The locating and pilfering of both rope and hook had taken a week but the hours spent trying to catch some edge far above them had seemed much longer. On perhaps the seventieth throw Darla had snagged the hook and Ruli, the lightest of them, had scrambled up. The rope was now secure and knotted at intervals. Climbing it brought them to the limits of their exploration, a roundish chamber, mud-floored, from which three new passages led.

Nona stood with Ara, Jula, and Ruli, catching their breath, staring at the exits, Ketti and Darla still climbing behind them.

"I want to get under the convent," Nona said. She blinked. She hadn't been intending to speak, but now the words had left her mouth she realized it was better that the truth was out. For three years she had seen the only route to revenge on Yisht to be training. To make herself into a weapon suited to the task of finding then destroying the woman. Neither would be easy. The empire was large, and Yisht expert at hiding, deadly when found. Nona had been very lucky in their first encounter and had still only just survived. But Joeli's taunting had put into Nona's mind the idea that there might be some clue at the spot where Hessa died. Something the nuns had overlooked. Something her friend had left for her alone. It was a very faint hope. Too faint perhaps to justify exposing her companions to such dangers . . . but Joeli's words were an itch that refused to be scratched. *"Hessa's name is so important to you? And yet you've never even visited the spot where she died."* The accusation repeated in her mind, an echo that grew rather than died away.

"I need to visit the shipheart vault." Nona spoke the words into the silence that had followed her first statement.

"Because we won't be in enough trouble just for being in the tunnels," Ruli said. "We should go where we're more likely to be caught and will have broken more rules."

Jula frowned. Despite her cleverness sarcasm always seemed to go over her head. "But—"

"I'm banned from leaving the convent until next seven-day in any case," Nona said. "So if I'm right under it I'll be breaking fewer rules."

"Go back to the vault?" Ara asked, raising her lantern to inspect Nona's face. "That's madness. Abbess Glass will throw us out. You know what she said about the undercaves!"

"I have to." Nona had to see it for herself. She had to set her hands to the spot where Hessa had died. Perhaps some clue remained that would help her find Yisht. "I have to. For Hessa. I felt her die. The rocks. Yisht's knife. I felt all of it. If there's justice to be had, or revenge, it starts there, where it happened."

"I don't want to go near the convent. The sinkhole's too close." Ketti got to her feet behind them after finishing the climb. "There could be tunnel-floods." She shuddered.

"I still say they'll have the undercaves blocked off." Darla followed Ketti into the chamber, brushing grit from her habit.

"Maybe. But it's as good a direction to explore as any other," Ara said. Nona thanked her silently.

"I don't know . . ." Darla shook her head. "The abbess wasn't joking when she put the undercaves off-limits. She wrote it in the book and everything . . ."

"That was over two years ago." Ara came to Nona's defence. "Plus, if they didn't know Yisht was there for all those weeks and she was going to and fro from her room, they won't know we're there if we come from underneath for a quick look. Right, Nona?"

Nona nodded. She owed it to Hessa. She had let years slide by and done nothing to avenge her. Her friend had died and Nona had hidden in the convent, well fed, cared for, whilst Yisht walked the world with Hessa's blood on her hands. But though the Corridor might be a narrow girdle to the globe it was still too wide for a lone child to find a woman like that who didn't want to be found. And Yisht was an ice-triber. She might be anywhere in the vastness of the ice. "I can't do this alone." The gate to Shade class had a sigil-scribed lock now: the thing would have to be blown off its hinges to gain access without the key. Coming at the Dome of the Ancestor and the shipheart chamber from below was the best option.

"I'll help." Jula spoke up, her voice thin in the cavern's void.

Nona offered her a smile. Jula put an arm around her shoulders for the briefest hug.

"So . . ." Nona, even less at ease with physical affection than Jula, waved a hand at the tunnel mouths.

"That one." Jula pointed to the leftmost tunnel, boulder-choked and leading down. She had an instinct for direction below ground that had proved uncanny. "Though it doesn't look very safe."

Ara led on and they followed, stepping over fallen rock, some of it still jagged. After a hundred yards or so the passage broadened and became a cavern so wide it swallowed their light and gave nothing back. For a moment Ara halted and they all held quiet listening to the silence and to the drip . . . drip . . . drip of water that was somehow part of the vastness of the silence. Nona glanced about at the novices around her, all illuminated on one side and dark on the other, and for an instant found herself outside her body, suddenly aware of herself as a tiny mote of life, warmth, and light in the black and endless convolutions of the cave system. Now more than ever she felt the irony that the Rock of Faith, named for the foundations of their religion, lay rotten with voids and secret ways, permeable and ever-changing.

"We should go across," Jula said, her voice small in all that empty space. She didn't sound as if she wanted to.

Ketti marked the wall with her chalk and drew an arrow on the floor.

"We should follow the wall. We're less likely to get lost," Darla said.

Ara took them to the left, staying close to the wall. Stalagmites rose in small delicate forests, stalactites descended in curtains where the cave curved down, glistening with an iridescent sheen like the carapace of a beetle.

"Stop." Ruli turned and stared into the darkness beyond the lanterns' reach. Nona stopped, the others too.

"What?" Jula raised her light.

"Didn't you hear it?"

"No." Darla loomed beside her, her shadow swinging.

"Something's out there, coming for us," Ruli said, wide-eyed.

"There's nothing living in these caves," Darla said. "We would have seen bones or dung. What did it sound like?"

"Dry." Ruli shivered.

"Dry?"

"I want to go back," Ruli said.

Ara advanced a few yards, lantern high. "There's something here."

Nona crowded forward with the others, leaving Ruli in deepening shadow.

"What is it?" Ketti frowned.

To Nona's eye it seemed that a shadowy forest of misshapen stalagmites covered the cavern floor, some curving over in ways that such growths are not supposed to.

"Bones." Jula saw it first.

From one instant to the next the scene switched from one of confusion to one of horror. Skeletons, calcified like those back in the niche, but more thickly: dozens of them.

"Some of these have been here for an age." Ara pointed to a stony ribcage from which straw-thin stalactites dripped, and to a skull distorted by the weight of stalagmite growing upon it, like a candle from which half the wax had run.

Jula bent over to inspect something by the wall.

"We *really* need to go!" Ruli called at them, not having moved from where she stood. "Can't you feel it?"

"I don't . . ." But then Nona felt it and held her tongue. Something scraping at the edges of her senses, a dry touch from which her mind recoiled.

Holothour.

What?

Nona felt Keot moving beneath the skin of her back. Normally he was silent in the caves.

You should run.

You always tell me to fight.

Now I'm telling you to run.

"We should go back. Now!" Nona turned to follow Ruli who had already started to run back the way they came, into the blind darkness.

"What're you scared of?" Darla called after them. "There's nothing here." She laughed. "And neither of you have a lantern."

Nona stopped at the margins of the lighted area, infected by a disembodied fear.

What's out there, Keot?

Something Missing-bred. Something hungry. Run!

"We need to go. Trust me." Nona's voice sounded thin in the emptiness of the cavern. Behind her the sounds of Ruli's stumbling panic.

Ara frowned then followed. "I don't understand you, but I trust you." Jula fell in behind her. Darla, with the light now retreating from her, snarled in frustration and hurried after them.

The six novices picked up the pace, shadows swinging all around them. Nona could make out Ruli ahead, feeling her way. With each passing moment it seemed that something gathered itself behind them, as if the space now echoing with their footfalls was drawing in its breath. Nona felt the horror of it crawl along her spine. The darkness held something awful. Something ancient and waiting. The need to be gone made her heart pound and tightened her breathing into gasps.

"Oh blood!" Even Darla felt it now, her face white.

Nona knew with cold certainty that beyond the margins of

their illumination the calcified bones stretched out yard upon yard, innumerable victims lying in meticulous order. How many centuries had they watched the darkness? And she knew that among them paced a horror. She felt it now, individual, condensing out of the night, taking form. Perhaps it wore a man's shape. Perhaps even her own. And if it ever raised its face to her she would drown in nightmare.

By the time they reached the chamber where they had chosen between the three unexplored passages all of them were running. Ruli was already on the rope. Jula didn't wait for her to get off. Ara stood with her back to the cliff, lantern high, staring at the tunnel mouth. Ketti and Darla crouched by the edge urging the others down. It was all Nona could do not to push between them and make her own grab for the rope.

"Ancestor! Hurry it up!" The cry broke from her.

Ruli and Jula reached the bottom together and went sprawling in a clatter of loose stones. Ketti began to climb. The darkness in the tunnel seemed to thicken, rejecting the light from Ara's lantern.

"It's coming!" Darla was sliding over the edge, hands white on the rope, her feet just a yard above Ketti's head.

"We can't stay!" It was all Nona could do not to scream. Fear filled her, trembling in every limb, fluttering the breath in her lungs. "Ara, come on!"

They descended the rope on top of one another, lanterns hooked to belts, burning their palms as they slipped from knot to knot.

A confusion of swinging lanterns, sharp rocks, and snatching shadows followed. Screaming, panting, glimpses of chalk symbols, running, scrambling, and finally a desperate squeeze and they lay in the improbable brightness of day, sprawled on the Seren Way, gasping for breath.

There in the light, with a cold wind blowing and the plains stretching out below them towards the distant smokes of Verity their flight seemed suddenly foolish.

"I'm never going in there again. Ever." Darla rolled over onto her back, her habit torn and smeared with mud.

"What were we running from?" Ketti asked.

"The first time when serenity would have really helped us . . ." Ara sat up shaking her head.

"And we ran!" Nona couldn't believe she hadn't reached for her serenity. Some novices still took a while to sink into the trance but many could summon the mindset in a few moments. The fear had got into her before she thought to wall it away.

"Ancestor! Look at us!" Jula stretched out her habit. Grey underskirt showed through a tear as long as her hand. Nona glanced down at herself. Smears of mud streaked her in horizontal lines where she had collided with walls on the mad dash out.

"Sister Wheel will kill us!" Ruli examined herself in horror.

"Sister Mop you mean," Ara said.

"Both of them will!" Ketti jumped to her feet. "Let's get back!"

"You're worried about Wheel and Mop?" Nona pointed at the dark slot hidden back along the cliff side. "What about that. Just now?"

Jula frowned and brushed a grimy hand back over her hair. "I'm not going in there again." She looked down again at the rip. "Oh we're in so much trouble."

Darla followed Ketti, muttering to herself. Jula and Ruli set off up the track behind them. "Ara?" Nona stood amazed. "What happened in there? Why are they just leaving?"

Ara looked puzzled. The smudge of dirt just below her right cheekbone only seemed to make her more beautiful. She narrowed her eyes as if trying to capture some memory, then shook her head. "I don't think we should come back." She glanced once towards the fissure, shuddered, and turned to go.

"What's that?" Nona pointed to something gleaming among the rocks at Ara's feet.

"Oh." Ara didn't look down. "It's just a knife. Jula picked it up in the . . ." She shrugged and turned to walk away.

"Stay." Nona caught Ara's hand in hers. "That thing in there . . . that monster. You remember it? Yes?" Their fingers laced. Ara's blue eyes met the darkness of Nona's and for a moment there was a recognition of . . . something. Each took a step towards the other.

"No." Ara shook her head. "I'm sorry." The fragile moment broke. She pulled free and hurried after the others. And Nona felt as if some chance that might never come again had escaped her.

Nona stood watching the five of them wind their way up the track zigzagging its way towards the plateau.

What just happened?

You shouldn't go back to the caves.

Don't you try and pretend something didn't just chase us out of there.

It did. A holothour. I told you.

So why are Ara and the others walking away?

They don't want to die.

I mean why are they more concerned about having to wash their habits and stitch a few tears . . . There's something more to this. Don't lie to me, demon. I'll force you into my fingers and hold them to the flame again.

I'll chew your bones and make you spit blood!

But you know I'll win. So tell me.

The fear untied them.

Untied?

The threads that bound them to that place, to these caves—the fear untied them. It set those memories loose. By the time they reach the top this will all have been a dream for them. The holothour made them forget.

And me? Why do I still care?

I protected you.

I don't believe you. You're made of lies.

Nona bent to pick up the knife. "I know this weapon." A straight blade, dark iron, just a faint tracery of rust, the pommel an iron ball, a narrow strip of leather wound around the hilt. A throwing knife. She had found one of the same design in her bed once, and seen another jutting from Sister Kettle's side.

Keot reached above the collar of her habit, a hot flush rising. *I know it too.*

You liar. How would you?

The woman who held it came to see a dead man.

Why?

To understand the person who killed him, so that she might in turn kill them.

Nona asked the question though she knew the answer. *Who did she come to see?*

Raymel Tacsis. He was dead but the mages wouldn't let him die. And I was the first to find my way beneath his skin.

And the woman?

Was a Noi-Guin. Tasked to kill you.

8

---◆---

IN THE WEEK that followed Nona tried each day to broach the subject but none of her friends would do much more than admit, under pressure, that there *might* be caves beneath the Rock. It reached the point at which Nona saw Jula pretend not to notice her and turn a corner in order to avoid the chance of further questioning. She decided to drop the matter for a few days and see if the holothour's mark would wear off and return her companions to her.

Mystic Class lessons continued to challenge. Nona improved with the sword, practising a handful of basic cut-and-thrust combinations until they started to feel natural. In Spirit Sister Wheel set them the task of writing an essay about a saint of their choice. Nona took herself to the convent library—the smaller one attached to the scriptorium rather than the larger store of holy texts held within the Dome of the Ancestor—to research. By the week's end she had found three possible candidates from antiquity, all of whom had something in their story that would offend Mistress Spirit.

Sister Pan continued to immerse Nona, Zole and Joeli in thread-work, showing them new tricks. Sometimes she would demonstrate thread effects most easily achieved whilst in the serenity trance, at other times fine-work requiring the clarity trance. Changing a person's mood was something that might be achieved in a serenity trance; changing a particular decision required clarity. Neither were quick or easy to achieve, and Sister Pan warned that some people were much harder to manipulate than others.

Nona applied these lessons to the problem of the mark the

holothour had set upon her friends. She could see the damage in the halo of threads around each girl but the solution lay beyond her skill. In the serenity trance she could see connections that must be undone or loosened. And in the clarity trance she could see entanglements on the smallest scale that would need to be unravelled. But working on either problem would make the other worse. They needed to be worked on together. Which required two people. And the only thread-worker she trusted to help, Ara, whose skills were pretty basic, was also one of those who needed fixing.

Sister Pan might be able to solve the problem but she clearly didn't bother herself with thread-work on novices or she would have noticed Zole's peculiar lack long ago. Nona could draw Sister Pan's attention to the area of damage but the old woman would ask questions, and as she said, "Everything's connected." Give Sister Pan one corner and she would soon pull out the whole story, and that would be the end of their adventuring.

SHADE LESSONS FOCUSED on disguise. A whole week passed without mention of poisons, save to note some that were useful in small doses for altering the hue of a person's skin or the colour of their eyes. Sister Apple likened the business of disguise to an extended lie told with the body, with the tone of one's voice, and with the clothes that wrapped you. In Mystic Class every novice took the first of the Grey Trials, which involved crossing Thaybur Square undetected by other class members. Good disguise skills were a must!

In Academia Sister Rail made a spirited attempt to bore the class to death with mathematics. Nona felt she had achieved under Sister Rule, at great personal cost, a tenuous grip on arithmetic. A triumph, considering there were few people in her village who could count past twelve with confidence. Sister Rail introduced her to algebra, and not gently. The only moment of interest came when Darla, despairing of letters that were numbers but not any particular number, demanded to know what use such things were.

"Our forebears used algebra to build the moon, novice!" Sister Rail drew herself to her full height, which wasn't much more than Darla's when seated. "The curve of its mirror is governed by equations like these." A gesture to the chalk scrawls behind her. "It's how they tightened the focus as the world grew colder. Other equations allow it to be steered as it was in the past, tilted to deal with the uneven advance of the ice."

Nona frowned. Jula had mentioned something about changing the focus of the moon. Something she'd read about the Ark years ago: whoever owned the Ark could speak to the moon. "It could be a weapon."

"What's that, Nona? Your expertise extends past assaulting classmates and reaches the moon now?" Sister Rail tilted her head in enquiry.

Tittered laughter around Joeli.

"It could be a weapon. If the focus was narrowed further it could burn cities."

"Nonsense. The moon is not a weapon of war. There's no reason to believe the focus can be narrowed to that degree even if someone wanted to do it." Sister Rail waved the suggestion away with a bony hand.

"If it can be tilted it could be steered from the Corridor entirely then returned," Nona said, staring at the glistening white of the globe on Rail's desk. "Whole nations could be denied the focus and the ice would swallow them. It could melt vast lakes on the ice then connect them to the Corridor, washing away armies and cities . . ."

"We were discussing the formula for a circle." Sister Rail banged a heel to the floorboards and the lesson sank back into a confusion of letters and symbols.

Nona had let the nun's words slide past her and sat gazing at the distorted sky offered through puddle-glass windows. Memory filled her vision. Yisht stumbling away chased by shadow, the shipheart in her hand. Four shiphearts to open the Ark? One Ark to control the moon. One moon to own the world?

BY THE SEVEN-DAY nothing had changed in the others' reaction to talk of returning to the caves. Not ready to explore alone, Nona agreed to accompany Ara on a visit to Terra Mensis, a distant cousin of hers.

"It'll be great to get you off the Rock for once!" Ara grinned, hugging her range-coat around her.

"I don't think the abbess plans to let me out on my own even when I've got the Red." Nona peered around the pillar, squinting against the ice-wind. The Mensis escort was late. They were sending a dozen of their house guard, enough to satisfy Abbess Glass that neither Ara nor Nona would be at risk from kidnap or assassination.

"There is no point to strength if it is never tested." Zole stood in the open before the pillar forest, scowling at the world. Nona had been surprised when Ara extended the invitation to the ice-triber, more surprised when she accepted, and astounded when Abbess Glass permitted it. Nona supposed that Zole felt as trapped as she did on the Rock. Perhaps the abbess worried that if Zole felt too trapped she would simply run away.

Sister Kettle leaned against the pillar beside Nona and rolled her eyes, grinning. When Nona had heard the abbess was demanding an escort of her own in addition to the house troops she had worried they might get stuck with Sister Scar, Sister Rock or someone equally joyless. Perhaps even Sister Tallow. Nona respected Tallow but didn't imagine she would be a particularly lenient chaperone in Verity. The arrival of Sister Kettle to watch over them had been a pleasant surprise. She still looked too young to be a nun. In the bathhouse with the black shock of her hair shaved to her scalp she could easily pass as a novice.

"They're coming." Kettle kept her back to the pillar.

Nona leaned out again. "Don't see them." She spat an ice-flake. "Zole?"

Zole stood silent, leaning into the wind. Then, just as Nona was about to repeat herself, "I see something."

A few minutes later the twelve guards swaddled in black furs that now hung with ice gathered around the nun and three novices. Sister Kettle cast an eye over each of them in turn then nodded and allowed them to lead the way, back towards the Vinery Stair.

"Your cousin won't be pleased to see me and Zole with you." Nona knew that any Sis would spot her peasant roots no matter how many years of convent education she might be carrying on top of them. "Well, she might be pleased to see Zole." The Argatha was a novelty. The rich could overlook low breeding in a novelty.

"The Chosen One can hardly travel without her Shield."
Ara grinned, face red from the wind. "And besides, Terra will
like what I tell her to like. The Mensis have been scions to the
Jotsis for generations." At Nona's frown she elaborated. "We
get to boss them about."

The Vinery Stair led down from the Rock of Faith along a
gradient gentle enough for cart and horse, though Nona would
not want to be that horse. Below them the vineyards huddled
against the base of the Rock, sheltered from the worst of the
wind. The vines had their leaves folded tight. They wouldn't
open until the ice-wind relented, although Sister Hoe—who
had charge of the wine-making—had told Nona that a heavy
dose of fertilizer would coax most plants to open their leaves
whatever the weather.

"They can't abide to lose the chance," the old woman had
said. "Worried some other plant will thieve it first. They're not
so different from people really. There's not much most wouldn't
risk to stop a rival having the benefit of something they want."

AT THE BOTTOM of the Vinery Stair a turnpike gate offered
token resistance to any without proper business up at the convent and it was here that a crowd of perhaps two dozen pilgrims waited.

"That must be her!" A shout from the crowd.

Zole lowered her head, pulling the hood of her range-coat
down across her face. The opposite of what Sister Apple had
been teaching them all week. And rather than inconspicuous
she just looked guilty.

"It must be!"

"All those guards!"

"She's here!"

"Be watchful." Sister Kettle stepped to the front, tapping the
lead guardsman's shoulder. "Clear a path. Don't hurt anyone."

As the guardsmen approached to pull the pike aside the
crowd parted, letting a man emerge with his burden. Hulking
in his sheepskins he must have had a touch or more of gerant,
and in his arms he carried a child, limp and pale.

"He's sick. The Argatha can heal him." The boy he offered
up showed no signs of life. He looked to have no more than six

years, seven at most. "Please." Somehow the plea from so big a man in so deep a voice tore at Nona, making her eyes prickle.

A few of the guardsmen turned to stare at Zole. Nobody had named her to them but perhaps the red of her ice-tribe skin was enough.

"It's her!" Figures around the man with the child pointed Zole out, following the guardsmen's looks.

"Bless me, Argatha!"

"I just need to touch her."

The mass of people began to surge forward. With an oath Zole turned and ran back along the Vinery Stair.

"Zole! You don't have to—" Kettle turned, hand raised, but Zole had quick feet and was gone. The pilgrims sighed with a single voice, disappointment rising.

"It wasn't her."

"The Argatha wouldn't run."

Ara caught Nona's gaze, biting her lip, a small shake of her head. "You're lucky to have her. I'm lucky to have you. Neither of us would want this."

Kettle went to examine the child in the man's arms. He stepped back at her approach, as if sensing the shadow in her, but the crowd held him.

"I'm sorry." Kettle lifted her fingers from the boy's neck. "The Ancestor has your son. He is a link in a chain without end, still joined to you, still joined to everyone who has ever cared for him. We will all be one in the Ancestor. Nothing passes from this world that is not remembered."

They left then, walking towards the distant city.

Ara moved to walk beside Kettle. "Well spoken, sister."

Kettle shook her head. "A parent's grief runs deeper than words can reach, novice. We speak them to help ourselves."

THE MENSIS ESCORT forged a passage through the tight-packed streets of Verity with practised ease. They seemed more confident within the city walls, and in their midst Nona thought she had a taste of what it must be like to be born of money and name.

She watched the colour and variety of the crowd, the density and energy of it. With no shadow, wholly black eyes, and no apparent talent for disguise, Nona had begun to despair of passing the Shade Trial. But reminded of the city's chaos the prospect of crossing Thaybur Square unchallenged seemed to inch from totally impossible towards merely very unlikely.

"The Shade wardrobe doesn't match this . . ." Nona watched a woman pass by in a cloak of dark green velvet trimmed with fox fur. To stand a chance in the Shade Trial and cross the square unchallenged by her classmates her disguise would have to be perfect.

"No?" Ara hadn't yet been introduced to the wardrobe. "I should think the older novices can recognize most of what the Poisoner has in there anyway. A lot of the girls get clothes from outside for the trial . . ." Ara trailed off, presumably remembering Nona's poverty and complete lack of family in Verity.

Nona had thought the variety and quality packed into the Shade wardrobe was astounding, but seeing Verity's streets again she reassessed her opinion.

"I'll work something out." She kept on walking.

THE HOUSE THE guardsmen led them to was set back among trees behind a high wall on a street lined with grand homes. Nona had seen buildings to dwarf it: the Dome of the Ancestor, the Academy, and the palace itself, but never a private home. Windows marched for a hundred yards to either side of a great portal of polished redwood. Enormous sandstone blocks had been fitted together to build the walls, each block meeting the next with such precision that even without mortar the smallest insect would find no space to crawl between them.

A doorman opened the doors as Ara climbed the stairs.

"I'll explore the gardens," Kettle said.

"You don't have to, sister." Ara gestured to the doorway. "Join us. Please."

Kettle shook her head, faint shadows flowing like the memory of past bruises. "I'll be close when you're ready to leave."

A FOOTMAN LED Ara and Nona through the Mensis foyer. Having spent so much time in the Dome of the Ancestor meant that Nona was able not to gape at the mosaicked floor and towering marble columns. The corridor that led from the foyer was punctuated by niches though and the statuettes and vases within held Nona's gaze, filling her hands with a longing to touch. She found it hard to imagine that anyone lived here, day by day, striding through these corridors and knowing that they owned it all.

Nona suddenly felt very drab and dull in her habit and wondered what this high lady would make of her. It felt like little more than a sack compared to the finery she'd seen in Verity's streets. At the same time she had to admit that Ara somehow managed to look beautiful in hers, the simplicity of it contrasting the gold of her hair, the hard lines of her body evident as she moved.

The footman knocked on an imposing set of double doors, then entered. "The Lady Arabella Jotsis to see you ma'am, and her companion."

Ara strode into the room, a sumptuously appointed chamber strewn with stuffed couches and deep chairs that looked so comfortable they might swallow a person whole. High above them the ceiling had been painted sky-blue and clouds scattered the plaster heavens.

"Terra! You're looking wonderful! This is my friend Nona. She's Shield to the Argatha and she'll make the best Red Sister the empire's seen!" Ara spoke with an animation Nona had never witnessed in her before and in the accent she'd brought with her to the convent more than five years earlier, each word clipped short and stressed in strange places.

There's something wrong with your friend. Keot ran up her neck, spreading across her scalp beneath the black thicket of her hair.

She's fitting in. Shut up and stay hidden.

"Arabella!" Terra stood from her chair, a tall girl in a sparkling green dress, her hair long and sandy, confined by a gold band, her face pleasant enough, though dominated by an unfortunate nose. "Nona, do sit down." She glanced around. "I thought we were expecting"—she raised her hands palms forward and shook them in mock adulation—"the Chosen One! No?"

Ara fell dramatically onto the nearest couch. "No. We discovered her hidden weakness. She's allergic to being adored."

"No matter. In any case, I have a guest of my own to share!"

Terra's pout gave way to a mischievous smile, any disappointment forgotten. Nona found herself liking the young woman. "You brought your warrior—behold mine!" She leaned across to ring a silver bell on a small stand beside her chair and looked towards the main doors.

"Do they have to do battle?" Ara grinned, following Terra's gaze.

Nona shifted in the comfort of her chair, wondering that Terra considered her a warrior. She didn't seem to realize that Ara could probably defeat any man in her house guard without breaking a sweat.

It's hard to see old friends with new eyes.

What would you know? You don't have any friends. Nona tried to force Keot down onto her back but abandoned the effort as the doors began to open.

A tall, darkly handsome man walked in. The black sweep of his hair reached past a starched white collar. His jacket, deepest purple and embroidered with silver wire in the bold designs favoured by Verity's gentry, must have cost a year's salary for the average city worker.

"I know him!" Ara sat up, suddenly interested.

"You should, he's one of the empire's finest ring-fighters!" Terra clapped her hands, excited.

Nona stared at Ara and her friend. They were discussing the man as if he wasn't there. She looked back, apologetic, seeing his face properly for the first time. "Regol?"

"Indeed." Regol sketched a bow. "At your service, Nona the Nun." She recognized the sardonic smile and the dark humour in his eyes even if she didn't recognize the finery he wore now.

"You've met?" Terra clapped again. "Where? You must tell me!"

"The last time I saw little Nona she was on her back, surrendering to me," Regol said.

Terra frowned. "Surely novices aren't allowed to do that sort of thing?" She grinned again, all curiosity. "What *have* you been up to, Nona?"

"He'd kicked me in the chest then elbowed me in the head." Nona remembered that it had hurt, a lot. "I reckoned I should let him win and save my strength for someone I really didn't like."

"A big ginger gerant." Regol nodded. "And technically you *did* win that fight against Denam."

"Denam?" Terra looked shocked. "That man's a monster. Nona couldn't have . . ."

"You were what? Twelve at the time?" Regol shook his head. "Denam never quite lived that down . . ."

"I don't believe—" Terra started towards her feet.

Ara set a hand to her cousin's leg. "It's true. But Denam lost by disqualification. He tried to attack Nona outside the ring."

Regol came and took the chair beside Nona, uninvited. "From what I hear you could have killed both of us that day if you'd wanted to."

Terra stared at him. Regol nodded. "Magic." He mouthed the word silently and nodded again.

Terra began to tell Ara about Regol's victories in the Caltess. Nona leaned back, letting it wash over her. She found herself watching Regol, who in turn kept his gaze on Terra, smiling that smile of his. Nona shook her head. It seemed she and Ara weren't the only ones with magic at their disposal: Regol appeared able to fascinate the other two just by sitting there, and she'd found herself being drawn into it too, letting her gaze wander the length of him. Perhaps he had a touch of the marjal empathy that Markus had once spoken of.

In time lunch was served and the four of them went through to a dining room that was even longer, wider, and taller than the Sweet Mercy refectory where fifty novices ate their meals. In the centre stood a long, polished table down which Nona had a sudden urge to slide, sending a dozen candlesticks flying. She suppressed the urge and took a seat opposite Regol at one end. Terra and Ara sat to either side of him. Watching them, Nona realized that Terra must be a good few years older than Ara and herself, perhaps eighteen or nineteen, of an age with Regol. A spike of jealousy drove its way into her: Terra, living her grand life beneath her father's golden roof, producing Regol as a novelty for the entertainment of her friend.

If you killed her you could take her house and claim the male.

Shut up, Keot.

Nona turned her attention to the bowl of soup that had been set before her. A delicious aroma rose from the orangey liquid.

She had no idea what the ingredients might be. Several silver spoons were arranged around the place setting. She took the nearest, a fluted affair, and applied it gingerly to the liquid. The bowl itself was finest porcelain, eggshell-thin and delicately painted with lilacs. Nona took each spoonful in mortal fear that she might somehow damage the bowl.

"Nona? What do you think?"

"What?" Nona looked up, suddenly worried she had been slurping. "Yes?"

Regol, who had asked the question, gave her a puzzled look. *If you want to breed with him you should just tell him so.*

"I don't—" *I don't want to breed with him and if you don't shut up I will force you into my little finger and CUT IT OFF!* "Sorry . . ."

"Is the soup disagreeing with you?" Terra looked concerned.

"Something was," Nona said. Then, seeing Terra's distress, "No, not the soup, it's lovely. What's in it?"

Terra brightened. "Do you know, I've never thought to ask. I can summon the cook. It's persimmon and something, I expect. Everyone is eating persimmons these days. I had one with codfish at Dora Reesis's the other day! I'll have Edris get the cook—"

"No need! It's lovely." Nona bent her head and took another spoon, consuming it as silently as a Sister of Discretion.

What's a persimmon?

I have no idea. And shut up.

Keot slid down the back of her neck, curling towards her stomach, presumably to investigate in person.

The meal moved from soup to fish, four servants required so that the plates could be simultaneously swept away and replaced. Ara and Terra chattered about this or that lady of the Sis, though Terra's knowledge of who wore what dress and which colour was in favour at court seemed to wear down even Ara's tolerance for such detail. At last Ara swept the blonde sheath of her hair over one shoulder and turned those blue eyes of hers on Regol. "Have you beaten any other novices senseless lately?"

"No." Regol shook his head sorrowfully. "That's a treat reserved for apprentices. I get to dance with Gretcha now, and she punches *hard*!"

"Yours is a dangerous profession, sir." Ara pushed her plate back.

"It has its advantages." Regol mopped his plate with a hunk of bread, his manners those of the Caltess. "Free lunches, for example."

"Where else have you dined?" Ara arched an eyebrow. She looked much older than her fifteen years, Nona thought.

"It's where I *will* dine that interests me most." A degree of genuine excitement broke through Regol's habitual mask. "Sherzal herself has requested the pleasure of my company at her palace!"

Nona sat up at that, almost toppling the exquisite glass they'd brought her water in. "Sherzal!"

Ara half-raised her hand, a placatory gesture. "Ring-fighters are popular guests at many high tables. Raymel Tacsis made the whole business fashionable and it's a trend that seems to have outlived him."

Terra's smile had a touch of nerves about it. "I hear Sherzal takes all manner of pleasure in the company of ring-fighters. Keep your guard up, Regol."

"Always, lady." He nodded. "Around Gretcha especially, but hardly less so in the homes of the rich and powerful. Present company excepted of course."

They all laughed at that, though probably for four different reasons.

"And when, pray tell, is Sherzal to have the pleasure of your company, Regol?" Ara asked, every bit the Sis.

"Just over a month." Regol dipped his spoon into the soup, clearing it with an admirable lack of slurping. "The feast of . . . Stevvan?"

"Oh!" Terra clapped. "The feast of Stevvan? You won't be alone then, Regol dear. Everyone who is anyone is going. Sherzal has sent out invitations by the cartload. I doubt there'll be a Sis mansion with anyone under fifty left in it that day. I wouldn't be surprised if she hasn't invited Durnish princes and Scithrowl warlords! She's promised something *spectacular*!"

"I can hardly wait." Regol seemed disappointed to learn his meals at the palace would likely prove less intimate than he had expected.

The main courses arrived: individual peafowls, deliciously

roasted and garnished with mushrooms, then redketch, fished from the meltwater rivers off the southern ice. Nona ate with dedication, amazed at the idea that food could be so much better than what was served in the Sweet Mercy refectory, which she had considered to be a paradise.

Hard on the heels of the servants removing the second set of plates came a maid bearing a tray of porcelain cups each brimming with a fragrant, steaming liquid. Nona peered at hers uncertainly.

"It's chai, Nona." Ara picked up hers. "An infusion of leaves from Gerula. Drunk in all the best houses."

Gerula rang a bell, a land far to the east. Nona picked up her cup and sniffed.

"It's an acquired taste." Regol grinned at her across the table. "You have to work at enjoying many of the most expensive things in life!"

Something hit the door with such violence that the lock burst open. Surprise set Nona's cup slipping from her fingers. Instinct kicked in and Nona dug into the moment. Even with whatever threat might be exposed as the door continued its swing Nona's first act was to catch the cup again, intercepting its lazy fall and setting it on the table.

By the time the door stood wide enough to reveal Sister Kettle, Nona, Ara, and Regol were all on their feet, chairs tumbling behind them. The swinging door banged against the wall.

"Don't drink it!" The chairs crashed to the floor as Kettle walked into the room. Her gaze seemingly fixed on Regol.

"Wh—" Terra, still seated with her cup halfway to her lips, blinked and looked around her, astonished to see everyone else standing.

"Don't drink it," Kettle repeated, leaning over the table to take the steaming cup from Terra's hand.

Nona followed Kettle's gaze. Not Regol—the serving maid behind him. Regol, understanding, spun around, but the woman caught him by the wrist and neck, pressing on a nerve cluster to force him to his knees.

"The chai isn't poisoned, Kettle." The woman stood straight, looking less like a serving maid with each passing second.

She lied to you. With her body. Like your poisoned apple has been trying to teach you.

"I came to speak with Zole. If I'd wanted your novices dead you would be collecting their warm corpses now." The woman let Regol go with a shove that sent him sprawling. She was younger than Nona had thought, perhaps as young as Kettle, her hair hunska-black, tied into a tight plait. Dark eyes watched from above high cheekbones. There was a hard beauty to her. And a threat.

"I know you." Regol from the floor, rubbing his neck. "You come to the Caltess forging every year and watch the novices." His pursed lips took on a rueful smile. "My charms failed me last year. And the year before."

"Zole's not here, Safira," Kettle said, moving to put herself between the woman and the table. "What made you think she might be?"

"I didn't tell anyone." Terra found her feet at last. "I swear it!"

"I can see she's not here." Safira stepped towards the door. "I'll leave you to your dessert. Your maid's unconscious in a cupboard in the cold pantry."

Kettle moved to block Safira's exit. Regol gained his feet, wincing,

Who is this female? You know her too. Keot edged towards Nona's neck, a red flush rising.

Safira. She trained Zole for the emperor's sister. She was banished from the convent years ago when she stabbed Kettle.

At last! Keot pushed Nona's flaw-blades into being. *Someone you can kill.*

No. But Nona made no effort to dispel her blades.

"Get out of my way, Mai." Safira advanced on the door.

Mai?

Must be Kettle's real name. Shut up.

"You're coming to the convent. There are questions to be answered." Kettle settled into a blade-fist stance, soft-form, arms raised.

"I'm not." Safira echoed the stance.

"She knows about Yisht and the shipheart!" Nona leapt onto the table, her concern for the crockery forgotten. *Jump on her! Shred her flesh. Open her body!* Keot spread, shading crimson along her limbs.

"And she stabbed Kettle!" Ara hissed.

Safira shook her head, a narrow smile on her lips. "It wasn't like that. You don't know anything. You're children."

"It was a bit like that." Kettle kept her eyes on Safira's.

"Apple poisoned her against me, Nona."

Nona blinked, surprised to find herself addressed.

Safira continued. "Apple does that. You'll find out but it will be too late by then. Sherzal is our only hope. Crucical lacks the imagination. Velera is a blunt weapon. We can sink together with the emperor or some of us can swim."

"Sherzal—"

"Sherzal didn't order your friend's death, Nona. Yisht is dangerous but you use the tools you have." Safira glanced towards her. "I'm not your enemy. The Noi-Guin haven't forgotten you. That's a warning from a friend."

Nona shook her head. "If you're a friend you can come and tell your stories to the abbess. She'll know what to make of them." She moved to the table's edge, feet careful, avoiding the plates. Ara and Regol advanced too.

"No! Just me." Kettle's command was iron. Surprise at such authority from the nun held Nona in her place. Kettle was always smiles and fun. Nona didn't recognize this Kettle.

In the next moment the two women closed to fight, Safira sweeping her leg to topple Kettle. Both employed the strain of blade-fist favoured by Sisters of Discretion, their combat fluid. Where Sister Tallow concentrated on blocking and on blows aimed to inflict as much damage in as short a time as possible the grey-fist centred on evasion and on unbalancing the opponent, often seeming more of a dance. The two moved in a flowing contest of position and stability, flurries of blows finding nothing but air. It might be a dance, and a beautiful one at that, but Nona knew the form held scores of moves for disabling or killing a less skilled opponent in a quiet and efficient manner, any of which could be used in a heartbeat if either woman gained sufficient advantage.

A quick clash, hands finding purchase, a rapid adjustment of feet, grips broken. Kettle and Safira spun apart, both unbalanced. A moment later they closed again, punches ducked, kicks evaded with the minimum twist necessary, Kettle a blur of swirling habit. Without warning Kettle managed to seize Safira's trailing plait and, yanking her head back, drove an elbow into her face.

Safira stepped back, panting, wiping the blood from her nose. "As much as I love to play with you, Mai, I don't have time for this." She opened her hand to reveal a small leather tube, pitch-sealed. "Grey mustard. Not really the ideal condiment for social gatherings. Perhaps I should just go?"

Kettle stepped back from the door, eyes hard.

Throw yourself on her! You could cut her hand off before she—

No. Nona didn't know much about grey mustard but she knew it was a poison that Sister Apple didn't let any novice work with until they reached Holy Class, and then only if they were marked for the Grey.

Safira opened the door and turned in the doorway, finding Nona again. "Tell Zole what I said. Sherzal is bound for greatness and there is a place for both of you at her side."

A moment later she was gone.

9

---◆---

O N SEVEN-DAY THEY heated the pool water. With the shipheart gone it now required that coal be burned in a chamber beneath the laundry where the pipes lay exposed. Black smoke belched from the new chimney and the Corridor wind stripped it away. Come evening, after four hours, the water steamed. On some six-days during the freeze Nona had to break a film of ice in the bathhouse, so the seven-day was a blessing. After four hours burning coal the pool was as hot as it would get and almost as hot as in the year she had joined Sweet Mercy.

Nona and Ara had returned from lunch with Terra Mensis in Verity in good time to bathe but Nona left the dormitories late, deep in her considerations. She hadn't spoken to Zole and remained undecided about what to do with Safira's message. Probably she should let the abbess decide.

Kettle had been quiet on the journey back, locked in her thoughts. The best thing to come out of the visit had been when, as they were leaving, Ara had asked Terra to let Nona borrow some clothes the next time she was in town.

"It's a convent thing," she had said. "A sort of fancy dress. I don't know what she'll want."

"Of course . . ." Terra had seemed uncertain, perhaps imagining her finest dress walking out the door along with borrowed jewellery.

"Servant's uniform perhaps. Or a wig if you still have some?" Ara had said.

Terra brightened considerably at that. "Arabella! I have so many wigs! Velera wore that silver one three years ago and . . .

well, you know . . . but now? Nobody wears them. You can have six if you want, Nona!"

THE OTHER NOVICES had rushed off to enjoy the heat, Ara with them, as soon as the message went out that Sister Mop had opened the bathhouse doors. Nona had lain on her bed staring at the ceiling, ignoring Keot's urgings. He loved the pool.

The holothour filled her thoughts. The memory of that consuming fear. The anger she felt at the shame of it. The creature's mark on her friends. Of all the novices who came with Nona from the caves that day only Ara would even acknowledge they existed. The others grew irritated if she talked about them and would try to change the subject, and failing that just walk away. Even Ara, though she agreed there *were* caves, and that a hidden entrance existed, was vague and evasive when it came to talking about what might be down there and whether they had ever explored together.

Take me to the bathhouse!

You just want to see the novices naked.

I am older than your civilization and find your bodies no more attractive than those of spiders.

It's no big thing to be centuries old if you can't remember anything further back than a few years ago.

Keot seemed to know very little. He didn't even know what he was or where he came from. Or if he did he wasn't telling. He claimed to enjoy the heat of the water, but every time Nona's attention wandered she would find him trying to creep into one of her eyes to see better.

At last Nona rolled off her bed and left the dormitory. She needed to be free of the day's grime, not least the sweat of that remembered fear. She also wanted an end to Keot's moaning. The dorms lay silent. Her feet echoed on the stairs. Nobody stayed long when the pool was steaming.

"I thought you were never coming." Joeli Namsis stepped into her path in the entrance hall, emerging from the Red dorm. Nona had been too deep in thought to see her until the last moment. Apart from her air of cruelty her appearance— tall, with golden hair cascading around her shoulders—was very similar to Ara's. "I suppose it must be true. Peasants do like being dirty."

Two girls, so alike they might be true sisters, came out behind her: Elani and Crocey, Joeli's constant companions, both hunska half-bloods. Two more exited from Grey dorm. These two, on her right, were from Holy Class, both of them marked for Red Sisters. Elani and Crocey stepped past Joeli, both holding quarterstaffs. Not from the Blade Hall stores but rough pieces of timber that looked to have been looted from the cooper's yard.

Joeli smiled. "I don't think you'll report us however badly we beat you. But I'm quite eager to get into the world and put my skills to use, so being thrown out would be a price I'm willing to pay to see you crawl, Nona."

"My price is higher." Keot got into Nona's tongue. "But holding your guts in my hands will cover it."

Nona bit down on further threats and the air around her fingers shimmered as flaw-blades sprang into being. She wouldn't cut a novice except to save her life—but the quarter-staffs would get no mercy and dicing them would put fear into Joeli's friends. The convent knew her secret now, but knowing and seeing were different things. Nona let the planet spin to a near halt and stepped forward, offering no defence. She snapped out an arm at the nearest staff. The half-bloods were fast by normal standards but her speed made them seem slow. Her hand swung past the staff close to where the girl gripped it. The wood, that should have been sliced into sections, remained untouched.

Nona glanced down at her fingers. The flaw-shimmer had gone from them. Just the tingling in her bones remained as it so often did when she withdrew their sharpness from the world.

Nona stepped away quickly. A look up revealed both the older hunska novices coming at her around the sides of the other two. Joeli was falling back behind the staff-bearers, her hands still raised in a plucking motion.

She pulled your claws back in.

Why didn't you stop her? You stopped the holothour drawing my threads!

Then she would know I exist. But if you want to kill her . . .

Nona snarled and twisted into the first of the empty-handed novices, a lean girl named Meera, a prime with several years' advantage. Nona's anger pushed her speed towards its limits. She hammered her forearm into Meera's throat and caught the girl's shoulder to vault over her reaching arm, bringing both feet into the middle of the staff held by Elani behind her. The half-blood stood mired in the moment, her face contorted in a roar. The staff splintered and Nona's momentum carried her through Meera's grasp, both heels thudding into Elani's stomach, bringing her down.

Nona came out of her roll beside Joeli. Kicking the girl's knee resulted in a satisfying crunch but she should have focused on Hellan, the other hunska, a full-blood, taller and more heavily built than Meera. Hellan thundered into Nona, barrelling her to the ground even as Joeli began to scream.

They fought as they fell, battling for holds. Hellan had the weight and strength advantage, Nona an edge on speed. Nona's struggle to free her arms from where Hellan had pinned them to her sides only succeeded in moving the girl further up her body so they fell face to face. Unable to break free, Nona settled for bending her leg and turning her heel to the ground so the impact with the floor would power her knee into Hellan's thigh. In addition, to prevent the back of her head crashing against the flagstones Nona drove forward at the last instant, hammering her forehead into Hellan's nose.

The ground knocked the wind from Nona's lungs and she lay for a moment, her vision full of strange lights, and Hellan's blood. A large, fast something drove through the confusion of flashes. The heel of a quarterstaff hammering down towards her face. Nona turned her head and the wood grazed her ear before cracking against the stone beside her.

With a roar Nona forced Hellan off her and rolled clear, a slow and ungainly move with Hellan still clutching at her. The swing of the quarterstaff couldn't be avoided. Nona took the blow on the triceps of her left arm. Better a bruise than a fracture. She swept Crocey's legs from beneath her as she rose. Elani came at her now, swinging half her broken staff in each hand. Behind her Meera staggered towards the fray, clutching her throat, blood on her chin.

Nona caught one of the shortened staffs in her hand, using it as a lever to twist Elani's arm while she blocked the other on her forearm. Without hesitation, and still holding the trapped staff, she threw her body weight down on Elani's twisted elbow. It snapped beneath her.

On the ground Hellan caught at Nona's ankle. Meera brought her to the floor with a grappling lunge and tried to pin her, and at the same time Crocey rose to her feet, swinging her quarterstaff with renewed fury at the parts of Nona still exposed.

Nona's rage grew. She felt the blows of the staff as distant thuds against her legs and sides. Blinded with blood, she saw the Path coiling bright before her mind's eye. With one hand Nona sought Hellan's eyes, stiff-fingered. With the other she shielded her head while seeking to fasten her teeth in the flesh and standing tendons of Meera's neck. She might go down but any she left standing would be insufficient to carry the dead away.

"No!"

Before her jaws could snap shut, before she touched the awful power of the Path, Meera was hauled away from her, her body sailing through the doorway into Grey dorm. Something big loomed over Nona and Hellan. Nona blinked the blood away. A hulking figure. A quarterstaff hammered into the figure's shoulder, wood splintering.

"Really?" Darla's voice.

Darla turned and flattened the surprised Crocey with a punch. She kicked Hellan away and scooped Nona up with one arm. "Come on, you." She strode through the main door into the rain-laced wind, Nona over her shoulder. Behind them someone was screaming in pain. Joeli probably. Or Elani. Or both.

After two corners and a hundred yards Darla set Nona down against the back wall of the scriptorium. "Let's have a look."

"I'm all right." Nona didn't feel all right. Her arm wouldn't talk to her and her mind was red with Keot howling for murder.

"You don't look all right. You're covered in blood." Darla poked at Nona's face, blunt-fingered. "I should take you to Rosie."

"No." Once in the sanatorium it took forever to get out. "It's not my blood."

"This stuff is." Darla pulled splinters from Nona's calf. "They jumped you, huh?"

Nona let her head flop to her chest. Her ribs hurt at each breath. "Don't think any of them will be jumping anyone again in a hurry."

"What should we do?" Darla glanced to the corners for approaching trouble.

"Nothing." Nona tried to rise and failed. "Get me to the bathhouse. I'll see what will wash off."

"But . . . Joeli and the others? You made a mess in there."

Nona laid her head back against the wall, smelling only blood rather than the usual sharpness of hides from the scriptorium's back room where they cured them for book binding.

Darla tried again. "If I hadn't—"

"If you hadn't come back I'd have killed at least one of them." Nona spoke the words slowly. "And they probably would have killed me to stop me getting a second." She drew another painful breath and stood with the help of the wall. "They'll go to the sanatorium with tales of falling down steps. Joeli doesn't want to go up before the convent table again. She thought her lot would give me a beating—not so bad as this one—and escape without a scratch. She's too used to people rolling over for her."

With an arm over Darla's shoulder Nona limped to the bathhouse.

Tonight we will slice their throats as they sleep.

We won't.

You said you were born of war!

You said that with my tongue. And war is a longer game than battle. For now we wait.

Nona realized she was using "we" and shuddered. Keot might be under her skin but she wanted him no deeper than that.

Two novices were leaving as they arrived, their hair steaming. Both offered wondering looks but said nothing. In the hot moistness of the changing room the warmth enfolded them, shot through with the shouts, splashes, and laughter of girls crowding the pool. Darla sat Nona on a bench and stripped her own habit with a few quick motions. Every inch of her lay thick with muscle, as if it wanted to burst free.

"Don't drown." And Darla walked off towards the water.

Nona sighed and began the slow process of disrobing. The fingers of her left hand were too clumsy for her ties, and she winced at every stretch or lift. At last she stepped from her smallclothes and limped after Darla into the mist, too tired to weave it around her.

10

———— ✦ ————

ABBESS GLASS

"COME IN, SISTER." Abbess Glass motioned Sister Kettle from the doorway and pointed to the chair before her desk.

The nun flashed a nervous smile and hurried across. Glass had never truly fathomed the girl. Even if she hadn't summoned her she would have known it was Kettle at the door by the tentative knock, the hesitation. Was this the disguise she wore at convent, or the real girl? It was the Kettle she remembered from classes, a lithe girl, sharp-featured, with an impish smile, Novice Mai Tanner, middle daughter of a cobbler who plied his trade on the steps of Leather Street in Verity. Given over to the convent when her mother was taken. Mai had told the other novices it was the weeping sickness, but in truth a sailor had taken her mother: new love and new horizons. Abandonment of one's sons and daughters was perhaps a sadder tale than the random cruelty of disease. Little wonder the child tied herself so tightly to the Ancestor in whom all bonds of blood are bound and drawn tight.

"Sit."

Sister Kettle took her seat, hands folded in her lap, shoulders hunched although a fire burned in the hearth. Outside the convent Kettle's deeds had earned her a reputation for deadly efficiency that few Sisters of Discretion could surpass. Inside she appeared the same friendly, awkward girl Glass had watched grow. Was one an act and the other truth, or were both masks she chose to wear? Glass's instincts rarely failed her but here they gave her nothing.

"I'm sorry that this is the first chance for us to speak properly since your return from the ice," Glass said. "The last few weeks have been busy. You've seen some of it yourself at the convent table, and in Verity . . ." She wondered how deeply Kettle had been affected by meeting Safira at the Mensis house. To Glass's mind a knife was a very effective way to cut off any relationship but the bonds of affection Kettle formed were resilient ones and she had been very close to Safira for years. In that respect she shared much with Nona. Whilst the novice condemned the actions of her friend Clera Ghomal, actions that included personal treachery, she would still not condemn the girl herself. Loyalty of that degree seemed like a way to get yourself killed . . . but then what was the Ancestor's creed if not about bonds? The importance of them and the strength that outlasted years and deeds.

"Before we get to your mission report . . . this business with Safira."

Kettle flinched. The abbess doubted she would have reacted at all if she were outside the convent, if she had her Grey-face on, but here in her home, here she let her guard down, allowed herself both to be vulnerable and to be loved.

Glass started again. "You said Safira knew Zole was coming. Who took the message to Lord Mensis?"

"Sister Pail."

"Hmmm." As Novice Suleri, Sister Pail had been somewhat impetuous and hot-tempered but never someone Glass would have considered easily corrupted. The abbess wasn't naïve enough to think that anyone was incorruptible, but Sister Pail wouldn't be her choice as the weakest link in the convent's chain. "Someone let the news slip, and not many of us knew. Look into it when you've time."

Kettle nodded. "If Sherzal has an ear in Sweet Mercy I'll cut it off."

Glass shook her head. "If Sherzal has an ear in Sweet Mercy I want to decide what it hears. Now, to the matter in hand." She picked up the report before her. "You've been out in the world, Kettle. Getting your hands dirty once again. Doing the things that let others sleep at night. Necessary things, but cruel. Such acts can taint us, if we let them."

"I am already tainted, Mother." Kettle raised her dark eyes and Glass for a moment felt her own weakness, her own taint.

"They call me abbess now."

Kettle returned her gaze to her hands.

Glass's given title had been Reverend Mother and the novices called her Mother. She had not long buried Able and while her son had gone beneath the ground her grief had stayed above it. She had given up the worldly, her job, her home, her wealth, but not her sorrow—that she had worn to the convent like a second habit. And the novices had been her children. She knew that now. Each of them a grain of sand to balance in the scales against the stone of her loss. But a mother is the root of the family and the strength, and the mother to so many must be stronger than most can imagine. Her weakness, her taint, had been to care for each instead of caring for the whole. So she set the title Reverend Mother aside and became the abbess. Her care was for all of them and it must be singular, it must be iron.

"Abbess," said Sister Kettle. Somehow in her mouth it still sounded like Mother.

"Sister Apple pushed you into the shadow, Kettle. You did not step into it yourself and from where you stand you can still see the light. I believe the Ancestor will take you in when your work is done."

Kettle had been a waif when she joined them. So quiet you might have thought she lost her tongue rather than her mother. But children have resilience. Children scar and those scars remain across the years, but children grow too. Kettle grew around her hurts and learned to laugh again—learned wickedness as they taught her scripture—learned the swiftness of her body and the sharpness of her mind. She grew into a woman and learned to love and to be loved.

"I've read your report, sister. Exceptional work, once again."

Kettle twitched a smile, shadows rising across her throat like a blush spreading. Sometimes they danced around her, sometimes they lay quiet, a drifting smoke of them into which Glass's imagination would pattern horrors of her own making.

Some would call it a corruption. Some would say that the darkness spoke inside Kettle now and soon she would start to listen to it. But corruption knocked at every door, and power often invited it in, the power of emperors, of high priests, even of abbesses. Glass would back Kettle to turn a deaf ear to corruption's whispers where many of those who might accuse her would be seduced.

Glass set the report down and laid her hand upon the papers, each covered with Kettle's neat lettering, curled tight across the page. "Should we fear Adoma?"

"Mistress Shade teaches us to set fear aside." Kettle looked at her hands.

"Sister Apple is correct, as she so often is." No Grey Sister had come as close to the Scithrowl battle-queen as Kettle had. As much as she wanted to know Adoma's plans Glass wanted to know the woman more. Plans were one thing, but what a person would do when the ice pressed depended more upon what lay inside them than on what they had written on parchment about the future. "Caution is wise, but fear is seldom of help and should be set aside. What do we need to set aside for Queen Adoma?"

Kettle smiled, a hint of the mischievous novice who had once dusted Sister Wheel's habit with a sneezing powder so powerful that the nun had blown her own headdress off. "The queen is a very passionate woman. Nothing seemed to motivate her so much as being denied. I was never close enough to touch her, but I heard her hold court. She speaks well and knows it."

Touch. Glass suppressed a shiver. For a Grey Sister "close enough to touch" meant close enough to kill. Kettle hadn't been instructed to put an end to Adoma but any Grey took pride in coming close enough for the touch, whether they then made that touch or not.

"You did well to reach the black ice, sister." In Scithrowl, not far from the border, the black ice touched the southern wall of the Corridor. Few from the empire had ever seen it, though. Glass flipped pages to reach the relevant section of the report. Here the writing grew tighter, smaller, as if unwilling to let go of its information. "You did well, but I found the account of your experiences there somewhat confused. You lost track of Adoma and her priests in the outer chambers?"

"It is a difficult place to account for, abbess." Kettle hunched on her chair, cold with memory. "In places the black ice lies beside the clean ice, like ink on a white page, running through it. But when you approach from the Scithrowl margins you pass through tunnels and chambers where the ice greys, grows darker, and shades to black over the course of several miles. It is a taint. A pollution that clouds thoughts just as it clouds the ice. Something lives in it. Or at least there is something in there that is not dead."

"How did you lose Adoma's party?" Abbess Glass traced her finger along the text.

"The tunnels are narrow and she left numerous guards in her wake." Kettle frowned. "But the truth is I didn't lose her. I lost me."

"You lost your path?"

"I fell into . . . nightmare. The ice took me." Kettle's mouth became a snarl, perhaps remembering the mask she wore in the world outside. "I would not have lived if I weren't . . ." She held her hand out and shadow ran between her fingers. ". . . like this."

"Then I am glad that Mistress Shade was able to save you twice." Glass smiled. "You have done the Church a service of some significance, sister. Your report concerning Adoma's gathering of both the Scithrowl shiphearts to herself is of particular interest. Also you have placed flesh on the bones of these rumours about the battle-queen's explorations beneath the ice. Some even doubted the existence of black ice."

Sister Kettle reached into her habit. "I can lay those doubts to rest." She produced a vial filled with inky liquid. Glass found her eyes fascinated by the blackness of the stuff. "I chipped some free. It melted." Kettle returned the vial to an inner pocket. "Apple thinks it is related to the Durns' sickwood."

Glass pursed her lips. The Durnishmen built their barges from sickwood. Some claimed the stuff lived even when cut to timbers and planks, imbued with its own malign spirit and harnessed to the Durns' cause by their shamans.

"The forest in which the sickwood trees grow is fed by meltwaters. The rumour is that the ice in that region is grey. Sister Rule once showed me the works of Alderbron, the archon who was brother to Sister Cloud. They hint that it is some work of the Missing that taints the ice."

Glass turned the pages back and set her hand to the topmost. "Is there anything else I should be telling High Priest Nevis when I report to him next seven-day?"

"I would be more worried about *whether* you'll get to report to him, abbess. I came through Verity on my return and I took the time to listen at several important corners . . ."

Glass knew that meant places no nun had any right to be. "And . . ."

"The Inquisition is coming to Sweet Mercy."

11

---◆---

NONA HOBBLED DOWN the rock-hewn steps to the Shade chamber. Parts of her that she did not remember being struck had stiffened and now protested at each movement. She took the last steps with both hands to the wall, teeth gritted, sweat sticking her undershirt to her flesh.

All of Mystic Class looked towards the door when she entered, some stares narrow-eyed and accusatory, others wondering.

"Nona, good of you to join us." Sister Apple watched her without expression from the front of the class. She had a hat and scarf in her hands. "Your tardiness has volunteered you to spend your study period on third-day helping me with Red Class. We're brewing retchweed."

Nona knew better than to argue. She hobbled across to sit by Darla. Retchweed distilled to a liquid that could rapidly induce vomiting and diarrhoea. The smell of the stuff sometimes had the same effect. It was always a messy lesson.

"You look like you fell off the Rock." Darla shuffled up.

Nona looked around. Neither Elani nor Joeli were there. Crocey sat hunched over her notes, one eye black and swollen to a slit, a bruise covering most of the other side of her face.

"Today we're returning to the subject of disguise, Nona." Sister Apple held the hat aloft, a shapeless thing of dark felt such as a market stallholder might wear. "Which is particularly appropriate as you're up next for the Shade Trial."

Nona started to open her mouth in protest then clamped it shut. Each Mystic novice took the challenge every year; nobody graduating to Holy Class without a successful trial could entertain hopes of becoming a Sister of Discretion. Without a shadow Nona had no chance of that really, so it was good that she'd set her heart on the Red.

"Disguise," Sister Apple said, "is as much about changing your mind as about changing your appearance. I was taught by Sister Pepper. Yes, you've heard of her. Sister Pepper could, with nothing more than a simple grey tunic, or brown if you turned it inside out, pass convincingly at the gates of a dozen high houses and guild halls in Verity. I suspect she could have gained admittance to half of them wearing a sack. Sister Pepper knew in her heart of hearts that she belonged in each of those places. She knew who she was, why she was going, what to expect inside, and precisely how much attention to pay to those whose job it was to stop her. The body speaks its own language and Sister Pepper could use hers to say whatever she needed it to."

Nona stared at the hat, which was moving with Sister Apple's hand as she made her points. Nona had never had a talent for acting or imitation. Ruli could sound like any of the mistresses. She zeroed in on their particular affectations and habits, exaggerating them to a degree that made novices laugh hard enough to wet themselves. It was like an ear for music. Nona lacked the talent.

"We will speak of fuller disguises in later classes. Learning how to maintain an outfit or uniform and how to wear it is as important as getting the colour and number of buttons correct in the first place. However, even if you disguise yourself with a sufficiency of paint to resemble a section of wall, down to the smallest detail . . . a nervous wall that thinks it does not belong will be discovered, and stabbed, whereas a confident wall that knows her place and duty, that thinks wall thoughts and loves her bricks, will be fine. Trust me on this."

Sister Apple began to demonstrate a variety of gaits, from shuffling to bold. "As a Sister of Discretion, novices, a limp can save your life. People, as a whole, see very little and remember less. Imagine you limp your way through a market and stray close to a certain high official out in his furs and chain of office, his guards close at hand. Say that magistrate pats his inner pocket for the ninth time, checking on the important papers he is to bring before some still higher authority.

And they're gone! Suddenly he remembers the woman who stumbled against him—the momentary brush of contact. "Stop her!" he yells. Stop who? He struggles for detail. And all he can remember, all any of them can remember with surety is . . . 'She had a limp!' And of course now you don't. You're strolling away bolder than brass, head up. And not directly away but at a tangent that says you haven't a care in the world."

Nona's thoughts wandered away rather like the hypothetical novice in the market and led her to Thaybur Square. On at least a quarter of seven-days the Shade Trial kept the novices of Mystic Class from the chaperoned distractions of Verity's markets or family visits, hemming them instead into the broadness of Thaybur Square. By all accounts it wasn't too harsh an imposition. The square was popular with the merchant classes and many a well-dressed couple would promenade there, browsing the small number of licensed stalls and exchanging pleasantries. Older folk with good coin would play dominos or chess on hired boards at tables around the perimeter.

Nona's goal would be to reach the spreading pine at the centre of the square without being challenged by the novices on patrol. Reaching the pine would be nigh impossible. If she made it everyone on guard wouldn't get to eat for two days. But the novices couldn't afford to just challenge anyone who approached. An incorrect challenge lost everyone on guard a meal. Reaching the tree would be enough to continue being considered as a candidate for the Grey. For top marks though you had to not only reach the tree unchallenged but recover the puzzle-box hidden high in its branches. If you did that the guards missed meals for three days. The full task was to open the box as well, but you would have to be invisible to sit in the tree fiddling with the box long enough to open it and still not be challenged so Nona was not surprised to hear that none of the Poisoner's graduates had managed it.

"Zole can be first." Sister Apple's voice cut through Nona's imaginings.

Zole got to her feet, scowling, as the Poisoner beckoned her to the front.

Sister Apple offered her a smile in return. "Now, Zole, tell me how much you love to dance." She raised a hand to forestall the objection. "And while you sell me the lie, also convince me, without using words, that you're a native of Verity born to a merchant family of moderate wealth." In that moment the nun's accent so mirrored that of Zole and Yisht that Nona could believe her born on the ice and raised for thirty years without sight of green.

"I live to dance." Zole spoke through gritted teeth, tightening each word into something that sounded more like a Durnish sailor in pain than any subject of the emperor, let alone one of Verity's moneyed class. "Dancing is my . . . pleasure."

"Hmmm." Sister Apple nodded. "And do you favour the chattra or the mouse-step?"

Darla elbowed Nona while the ice-triber ground out her replies as though they were death-threats. "Even Zole stands a better chance than you in the Shade Trial." She pointed to her eyes with index and forefinger. "Joeli is going to organize a defence around that tree that a Noi-Guin couldn't get through, and with those peepers of yours two street kids would be enough to spot you before you got within ten yards."

"Pay attention, Nona, you're next." Sister Apple snapped her fingers. "And, Zole—that was terrible. You may never have an ear for accents but you can at least learn to lie more convincingly. Next class you *will* convince me of your love for dancing or *I* will convince you that your defences against poisoning are still inadequate. Here's my tip. In your mind substitute something that you love for the thing you hate. Clearly you're not a devotee of music and self-expression, so when you come to me again be thinking of something else every time you say the word 'dance.' You like punching people. When you're telling me how you connect to the music and let it speak through you tell me instead about blade-fist: map that love onto the words coming from your mouth. This is how honest people lie."

Zole pursed her lips, gave a short nod, and returned to her seat.

"Nona, you're from the House Namsis and you're disgusted that you have to have the peasants on your land resettled if you want to site a hunting lodge on their village. Make me believe your outrage. Go."

The door to the Shade cavern opened. The mouths of a number of novices did too. You knocked at the Poisoner's door, and then you waited, you did not just push on through.

The man who walked in had to stoop to avoid cracking his head against the doorframe. He wore white robes.

"Inquisitor." Whispered among the class.

"Well, girls." Sister Apple pointed Nona back towards her desk. "We are honoured to have an unexpected visit from a Brother of Inquiry today." She turned and raised her head to face the man. "How may we help you, brother?"

"I am Pelter from Verity's Hall of Questions. I am simply here to observe."

"Alata, get Brother Pelter a chair." Sister Apple indicated a spot by the door.

"I prefer to stand." Pockmarks from some childhood illness marked one side of the man's narrow face. He was perhaps fifty. The scrawny length of his neck, the prominence of his throat, and his greying hair, tufting up like the wool of a badly shorn sheep, would have made him comical if not for the brittle blueness of his eyes. Nona felt they were the eyes of a man who had witnessed horrors, and approved. She sat, grateful to join the others.

"Well." Sister Apple frowned and brought her hands together. "Let us return to the art of disguise . . ."

The tall inquisitor set a long-fingered hand to his throat. "I believe you were discussing the business of lying." He pointed to Nona. "Perhaps the girl could convince me that she is a Sis. A daughter of Elon Namsis. And that she wishes to clear peasants from her lands."

Sister Apple motioned Nona to her feet.

Pelter's gaze travelled the length of her, a sharp inspection that made Nona's skin crawl. Beneath her habit Keot circled away to the small of her back. The inquisitor's gaze met hers and she felt something new, a rustling of old memories, the focus moon through the starkness of bare branches, the Corridor wind through the wooden bars of a cage. Thread-work! Nona bit down hard, imagining the fist of her will closing around every thread that anchored her to the world and holding them fast. Her glance fell to the man's hands, down at his sides now. There was little to betray him, just the slightest twitch of his fingers, but she knew it then. A quantal thread-worker running the dirty fingers of his mind through her thoughts. She raised the blackness of her eyes to him and saw a moment's hesitation in his own. The inquisitor's lip curled and the tugging on her threads grew stronger, but she held them. Denied, Brother Pelter narrowed his gaze, the blue of his eyes turning to ice like that advancing from north and south to swallow the world. His smile held only winter.

"Come then, girl," he said. "Lie to me."

12

⸺ ✦ ⸺

NONE OF THE novices could tell Nona why the Inquisition had installed itself at Sweet Mercy. Inquisitor Pelter had four watchers with him and placed them in all the classes that he did not personally observe.

"Sherzal sent them because of Zole." Ruli spoke with the total conviction she reserved for all guesswork.

"Sherzal doesn't own the Inquisition, Ruli." Jula continued to sew the tear in her habit.

"She's prime instigator." Ara stretched out catlike across her bed. She patted for Nona to sit on the edge. "That means a lot. When Jacob sold her the role on his way to getting the high priesthood it was mostly an honorary position, but her archivists dug into the scrolls and found all manner of associated rights and duties the Church seemed to have forgotten about."

Nona crossed from the doorway and sat on the end of Ara's bed. She missed moments like this, lying boneless beside Ara after the heat of the baths, complaining together as they wrote essays for Academia or Spirit class, just spending time. She already felt like an interloper in the Grey dormitory. Wincing, she lowered herself slowly: she still had an ache or three from the beating Joeli's friends had dished out. "If Sherzal's so hungry for power why doesn't she set the Inquisition on her brother? Or can't emperors sin?"

Ara grinned. "Emperors are famed for their sinning, but be careful where you say it! *However*, the only place the Inquisition can hold the Lansis to account is in their palaces. All the most highly placed people have rights about where they can and can't be put on trial."

"So Sherzal should send the Inquisition into Crucical's throne room?"

"That's where the emperors got clever. Their line is the only one that can refuse admission to the Inquisition. So unless Crucical invites them in, the Inquisition can't touch him," Ara said. "That's what keeps Sherzal's sister, Velera, safe too."

"The emperor should just disband the Inquisition. I've heard how they get their confessions." Nona shuddered.

"The Inquisition keeps us pure," Jula said. "Someone has to see that the faith doesn't slip away from its foundations."

"Who keeps them pure?" Nona asked.

"Anyway this isn't about Zole," Ara said, returning to Ruli's assertion. "This is about the whole thing. The Grey and the Red. The emperor wants control. He wants to send the sisters against his enemies, not have to beg High Priest Nevis. That's what my father says. The emperor will be doing the same with the monasteries. They'll have inquisitors up at Narrow Path too, trying to find fault with the abbot. Crucical will want the Red Brothers and the Grey too."

Nona watched Jula sew, fingers quick, stitches neat and accurate. The tear in her habit had outlasted her memory of what had caused it.

"Why would Sherzal do anything to help her brother?" Ruli asked, reluctant to let go of her theory. "Wouldn't she take the Red Sisters for herself?"

"The emperor wouldn't stand for that. His legions would be at her door within the week." Ara shook her head. "There's been bargaining. A trade. Sherzal will get something she wants—but not Sweet Mercy. Not all of it anyway."

"We should go back to the caves." Nona reached over to set her fingers to a second tear in Jula's habit. "Who knows how many more chances we'll get if they set watchers on us?"

Only Ara acknowledged Nona had spoken. "I don't want to."

The rest carried on as if no words had passed her lips.

Much of Nona shared Ara's desire to avoid the caves from now until the moon finally fell from the sky, but other more stubborn parts refused to agree. Sherzal had sent the Inquisition into Sweet Mercy and yet her hands were stained with Hessa's blood, whatever Safira might claim. Yisht was Sherzal's weapon, she was responsible for what that weapon cut. Nona owed it to Hessa to undertake her own inquisition. To see if her friend had left her any clue or message in the place where she died. Added to this was the fact that Nona had been driven from those caves, fleeing in terror, her friends' minds altered. It was not in her to let such a challenge go unanswered. The Ancestor didn't value pride but Nona had never quite managed to let hers go, and it drew her back to the scene of that disgrace, more strongly with each passing day. And if vengeance and pride were not enough, Yisht had stolen the shipheart, striking at the abbess's reputation, robbing Sweet Mercy of its most valued treasure, walling its inhabitants away from their magics. It had to be recovered, and where better to start than at the beginning?

Nona held silent, watching the others. It seemed that time was only hardening their denial into fact. Patience would not solve the problem, and in any event time was running out.

Fix them yourself.

How?

Experiment.

And if something goes wrong?

Peh. Keot managed to convey an air of complete indifference. *Are you not here to learn? Mistakes are how you learn.*

"How did this tear?" Nona asked, lifting the sleeve towards Jula.

"I caught it on something." The stitching continued, a little faster, a lot less neat.

I need help, Keot. It needs two people.

I'll help—

Thank you.

But you would have to let me use your body to kill someone.

No! And who?

Anyone, I don't care. Joeli if you like.

No!

You weren't so squeamish about Raymel Tacsis. You enjoyed it. That's why I'm in you. Keot sank down her back, burning as he went. *Think about it. Otherwise you'll need two minds for both the silly trances you think you need. Perhaps Joeli will help you.* He settled into a sullen silence.

Nona sat back. She needed a friend, and who was there

who wasn't sitting before her? Only Amondo, and that had been the foolishness of a lonely child. Zole could help but Nona had no clue where her loyalties lay.

Jula had returned to her stitching. Nona watched her, letting her eyes defocus and reaching for her serenity. The lines of the old song ran through her: *She's falling down, she's falling down, the moon, the moon.* She reached for her clarity. Mistress Path had never spoken of entering more than one trance at a time, as if it made no more sense than riding more than one horse at a time, but to Nona it seemed akin to juggling. The slow and certain motion of Amondo's hands filled her mind. She had watched them with a child's eyes so many years ago that it seemed little more than a dream, and yet those days and the moments of them were written into her and no part of them had ever left. To reach clarity Nona watched a flame then turned to the shadow and watched the memory of the flame's dance. Lacking a flame she drew only on memory. And now she ran the song and the dance together without one tainting the other.

> *The ice will come, the ice will close,*
> *(the memory of flame dancing on the darkness*
> *to a music all its own)*
> *No moon, no moon,*
> *(two hands making their own pattern, catch and*
> *throw, exchanging speed and potential)*
> *We'll all fall down, we'll all fall down,*
> *(a single petal of flame dancing on a dark*
> *ocean)*
> *Soon, too soon.*

The song, the dance, the sure hands of a juggler keeping it all in the air.

Nona saw the world with new eyes and through each part of it the Path ran, burning and binding. She looked away as Sister Pan had taught her, to the halo, the pale nimbus of threads about each of her friends.

"We should go back to the caves." Her voice sounded impossibly distant, as if she spoke from the bottom of a deep well. But they heard her. She saw it in the aura of threads shrouding each girl. "Something chased us out. We don't run. Not here."

Nona saw how her words pulled on the vast web that connected them all, each to the other, and to everything else too, saw the vibrations spread, transmit, cross the space between them . . . and die. She focused her clarity on the place where her words failed to reach Jula. "We should go back." A tremor. Something knotted . . . Nona raised her hands, struggling to see the minute detail where the harm had been done. She pulled on a darker thread. "To the caves, Jula." She pulled again and the knot unravelled, momentarily too bright to look upon.

Nona understood the holothour's work now. It had tied a knot in each girl's threads, linking the caves to the very worst and oldest of their fears so that their minds would step around the memory of the holothour and everything associated with it, denying it space in their thoughts. "We should go back," she repeated.

"We should!" Jula looked up, her face eager. "What in the Ancestor's name was that thing? We should take knives. Swords if we can."

Jula seemed perhaps a little too enthusiastic: Nona worried she might have erased rather too much of the fear, or imposed her own desires on her friend. She resolved to use a lighter touch on the others. "Ara? We should go back to the caves. Don't you think so?" Nona struggled to maintain her twin-trance, feeling the edges of her serenity slip away as a sense of triumph pushed in.

"We'll have to be careful." Ara was easier to free, the knot more obvious and less tight.

"Ruli? Don't you think?" Now Nona's clarity was escaping her: the threads fuzzed before her eyes. A headache knifed its way in past her forehead, trying to make a reality of the splitting of her brain in two. Even so, she found the damage done to Ruli's threads and unwound it, not needing such sharp focus now that she had effected the repair twice before.

"I don't know." Ruli hugged herself and shivered. "That thing that chased us! I nearly wet myself when Darla got stuck in front of me at the exit."

"Well think about it." Nona pressed a hand to her brow and

staggered towards the doorway, teeth gritted. The pain made her want to throw up.

"Are you all right, Nona?" Ara made to follow her.

"Fine." Nona stumbled out into the hall. "Tired."

By the time she reached the top of the stairs she was crawling. She managed to get to her feet again for the passage across Mystic dorm to her bed. She glimpsed Joeli at her bed, knee splinted and bandaged, a walking stick across her lap, then collapsed into her own.

Darla looked up from her desk, quill in hand, fingers inky. She said something but Nona had fallen too far into the black agony of her headache to separate the words. She buried her face into her pillow and vowed never to try thread-work again.

THE WAKING BELL brought Nona from the confusion of a dream, something to do with spiders and with webs. The first thing she realized as she rolled from beneath her blankets was that her head no longer hurt. The second thing she realized was that the morning would be spent in Spirit class with Sister Wheel, and immediately a twinge of the previous night's ache returned.

"You're all the colours of the rainbow," Darla observed as her head re-emerged from the habit she'd pulled over it.

Nona craned her neck to look down over her shoulder and side. The bruising was still deep purple in some places, yellowish green over her hip, faded mauve on her thigh. Across the dormitory Joeli leaned on her stick, swinging her stiff leg to advance on her desk where against convent rules she kept a mirror. She spent several minutes each morning brushing her hair in it and Nona always felt less jealous of how good the girl looked when she remembered the effort Joeli had to put in.

"We're going below tomorrow. You in?" Nona looked away from Joeli, now busy with her brush.

"Ancestor! I hate Spirit class." Darla shook her head. "Couldn't we just spend the morning working in the laundry instead? Shovelling manure at the vineyard stables would be better."

The holothour's mark is still on her. Keot rested across her collarbones.

Nona pursed her lips. She wasn't in any hurry to try to untangle the mess Keot's monster had made of Darla's threads. A twinge of the previous night's headache echoed behind Nona's eyes and in that moment she decided that she would rather face the caves without Darla than undo the holothour's knot and suffer like that again.

SISTER WHEEL HELD that novices of Mystic Class should be awarded the honour of having their Spirit lessons before the statue of the Ancestor. In practice this meant standing in the cold and draughty space beneath the dome rather than sitting in the snug classroom off the foyer. Sister Wheel got to ease the ache in her legs by striding around as she read scripture from her scrolls. The novices had to remain still, their attention on the Ancestor's golden face.

Today's lesson was different only in two regards. Firstly, Joeli managed to get herself a chair, claiming that Sister Rose had forbidden her from standing until her knee had healed. Secondly, Inquisitor Pelter came to watch, standing at the base of the Ancestor statue as still as the stone behind him and showing no more expression. Only his eyes moved, studying one novice then the next.

"The bonds of family are holy." Sister Wheel stalked before them. "The links that bind you to your father and mother are repeated time and again, back through the years. These links form the chains that meet in the Ancestor. Each part of that unbroken chain is forged from the divine. A direct connection between you and the origin of all humanity. As the Path joins all things, the bonds of family join all people."

The novices stood in four rows of three so all but two were on the perimeter, any inattention apt to cause an ear to be twisted as Mistress Spirit passed by.

"Why?" The nun paused at Nona's shoulder. "Why does Sweet Mercy admit penniless strays from child-takers? Why does Abbess Glass reach into the Church's own coffers to pay the confirmation fees for peasants?" She moved on. "Because it is a sin that any parent should sell their child. Some might hold that this same sin taints the child themselves, but Abbess Glass points to the convent's own name and shows these children mercy."

"Also," Inquisitor Pelter spoke into the pause, "a sold child belongs to the Church in a way that a wanted child cannot."

Sister Wheel scowled, pressing her lips into a bitter line. She kept her eyes on the novices and resumed her circuit around their perimeter, a sheep-hound hemming in her flock. "The false precedence of the Church's claim on children in its care over that of their parents' is one of the pillars upon which the foul edifice of the Scithrowl heresy stands. It is clearly stated in the Book of the Ancestor that a parent's wishes are prime. The bonds of family, holy as they are, allow any parent to withdraw their child from service at convent or monastery, even if the high priest himself should object. In Scithrowl the Church claims a divine right to any child in their care. This is why they must burn—to purify them of their sin."

"And," Inquisitor Pelter slid his narrow voice into another gap, "it is why Abbess Glass buys girls. She would rather not lose control of trained novices should a father or mother demand their return. She avoids rather than defies the law."

Nona furrowed her brow, keeping her gaze on the face of the Ancestor, the golden features so simplified they could belong to anyone. Abbess Glass had always told her she was free to leave, that the convent was a home not a prison. It seemed that the Church might disagree with that assessment. She glanced across at Zole. Of all the Mystic Class novices Zole was perhaps the only other sold child. She hadn't been sold to Abbess Glass, though. Sherzal had acquired the girl from the ice. Zole had never seen fit to share the details of that transaction.

The lesson continued, Sister Wheel making her predatory circles and droning on relentlessly about the minor differences in the interpretation of scripture that made the Scithrowl Church of the Ancestor an unholy evil, worse than the Durns with their pantheon of battle gods, or the raiders off the grey ice who were said to eat babies and wreak untold horrors on their prisoners.

Nona occupied herself by studying Joeli. Slipping into the clarity trance, she could see how the fractured bone in Joeli's knee was thread-bound to several areas of the girl's head. Nona lacked the expertise to identify the areas individually, except for the pain centre, which was obvious. However, she had little doubt that one of the other areas the injury connected to was memory and another specialized in revenge. For her part, Joeli returned the inspection, watching Nona with an annoying half-smile.

At last Bray rang out and Sister Wheel released the class. The novices hurried from the dome, trying to rub the chill from their arms.

"Bleed me, that was dull, even for Wheel." Darla stamped alongside Nona, trying to get some life back into her legs.

"She's showing the inquisitor that we're well educated in the ways of heresy here," Nona said.

"It is surprising," said Zole behind them. "That surrounded by unbelievers on all sides, and even among your own peasantry, so much effort is spent on hunting down and torturing those who agree with your faith almost entirely."

Darla turned round, blinking. "She speaks!"

"Our faith," Nona said. "Not 'your' faith."

Darla glanced back at the inquisitor, now following in their wake. "The shrimp's right. Not a good day to be expressing doubts." She frowned. "Who do you pray to on the ice then?"

Zole shrugged. "Any god who answers."

They walked for a moment in silence, aiming for the novice cloister. Nona pursed her lips, then decided to see just how talkative Zole was today.

"It looks as if the abbess is going to let you on the ice-ranging."

Zole shrugged again.

"Are you going to run if she does?"

"Run?" Zole shot Nona a dark, unreadable look.

"Back to your tribe."

"Would you run with me, Nona Grey?" Zole asked. "I am told that the 'Chosen One' should not abandon her Shield."

"To your tribe?" Nona couldn't help smiling at the thought.

"Or to yours?" Zole said. "But I thought you had murder in mind. Revenge. A shipheart to recover."

The smile left Nona as quickly and as involuntarily as it had come. Of all the things that lay beyond the Rock, whether it be in the Corridor or on the ice, Yisht was the one that called to her. Yisht's blood, waiting to be spilled.

"We will visit the ice together, Nona," Zole said. "I will show you another world and how to live in it."

Nona met the ice-triber's gaze, surprised. "I'd like that." And for the briefest moment she could swear she saw a smile tug at Zole's lips.

IN THE NOVICE cloister Nona sat with her friends from Grey Class. Darla came over too but wandered off when talk turned to the caves.

"What's up with her?" Ara frowned at Darla's broad and departing back.

"The creature in the caves did the same to all of you. It's thread-work. The fear it put in us knotted something up in your heads. It was supposed to stop any of us coming back. It was something deeper than fear—you couldn't even hear me talk about the caves."

"That's not . . . true . . ." Ruli trailed off, echoing Ara's frown. "Is it?"

"It is. I saw the damage it did." Nona bit off any further explanation, not wanting to explain how she avoided the same fate.

"Why hasn't it worn off with Darla?" Jula asked.

Nona shrugged. Explaining what she'd done would just invite more questions. "Maybe it takes longer when you're that big."

The wind swirled hard for a moment, whipping up dead oak leaves and making the girls shield their faces. Seconds later the squall passed, the ice-wind returning to its steady north-south roaring.

"Ketti won't talk about it either," Ruli said.

"Maybe she's got boy-fever again." Nona shrugged. "So tomorrow then?"

"Yes." Ara nodded.

"I'm not going without a spear," Ruli said. "A knife at the least."

"I'll bring you a knife," Nona said.

At last she wants to kill something! And what she chooses to cut cannot bleed . . .

Give me a better plan then! Nona demanded, but Keot fell back into his silence.

"Is this sensible? Is it worth it?" Jula asked. "What if it's got teeth as big as my arm? Weren't there bodies in that cave?"

"Dozens of them," Ara said.

Nona's gaze found Joeli across the cloister amid a circle of her friends, almost hidden behind the trunk of the centre oak. "This is the Rock of Faith. The cave that thing was in is practically beneath this convent. In four years we could be Red Sisters. If we don't even dare explore the holes under where we live . . . what use are we going to be out in the world?" She bit her lip, remembering their escape. "Besides. If it were some monstrous creature, what does it eat? Flooding your prey with fear so that it runs away and never returns isn't a very good strategy for filling your belly. This thing seems more like a stink-fox to me, spraying its foulness to scare intruders off."

"But the bodies!" Jula said.

"I saw skeletons," Nona said, trying to see them again. "Covered in flow-stone like the ones in the niche. They had to be centuries old . . ."

"I saw all kinds of horrible things." Ara pressed the heel of her hand to her forehead. "They couldn't all be true. So maybe none of them were?"

Nona nodded. Even if the thing was as big as a bear and had teeth like swords she needed to see where Hessa died. With the shipheart so close Hessa might have worked miracles. There could be a clue. Missed by the nuns but waiting for one who was thread-bound to her. And with thread-work you start at the beginning. "We're going then?"

Ara and Ruli nodded. Jula frowned then nodded too.

"I hear you're up for the Shade Trial," Ara said, breaking the mood with a grin.

"Yes." Nona glanced back towards Joeli's clique with narrowed eyes.

"No chance." Ruli shook her head.

"What?" Nona turned her stare on Ruli.

The girl held her hands up. "I'm just the messenger."

"She's right, Nona. There's no way Joeli will let you get to that tree." Jula shook her head. "Even if they liked you they wouldn't go hungry just to let you pass. And you're not hard to spot."

"I can put on a headscarf or something!" Nona found her voice raised and struggled to push her outrage back. "I'm not useless."

"Can you put a shadow on too?" Ara offered an apologetic smile. "And it'll take more than a headscarf. Suleri went in with a long white beard, warts, and a cast in one eye. They challenged her before she got halfway to the tree."

"She overdid it." Nona sniffed. "Less is more."

"Well." Ruli grinned. "You've certainly got a lot of that!" She rolled back under the swinging slap Nona aimed her way and ran off shrieking with laughter.

Nona stood to give chase, then stopped, reminded by a dozen bruises that perhaps sitting back down would be better. She tried to imagine crossing Thaybur Square with all of Mystic Class on the watch for her. She let her gaze rest on the skeletal forest of the centre oak's branches, leaves tight-wrapped against the ice. "I'm lost, aren't I?"

Ara nodded. "It's not like you wanted the Grey. Just punch your way to the pine and claim it as a spoil of war."

13

---+---

NONA BUTTONED HER range-coat tight and hurried from the refectory, still chewing on a heel of bread. Ara, Ruli, and Jula were waiting for her to join them on the Seren Way, ready to dare the holothour's cave once more. And she was already late!

"Novice!" A nun, black against the sun where it rose between Blade and Heart Halls, called to her. "Walk with me." Sister Apple's voice.

Shielding her eyes, Nona hurried over. "Mistress Shade?"

Sister Apple motioned with her head and led off across the square. Nona followed, bowed against the ice-wind and hoping she wouldn't be kept too long.

On reaching the shelter of the steps down to the Shade classroom, Sister Apple turned and beckoned Nona closer so she too would be out of the wind. "Your Shade Trial will be next week, Nona."

"Next week? I'm not ready!" Nona's mind started to race. She could get a Mensis house-guard uniform from Terra . . .

"And it has been decided that it will be held here in the convent."

"But . . . Thaybur Square is . . ."

"Too dangerous. We will use the novice cloister and put the puzzle-box up the centre oak. I'm sorry, Nona."

"The cloister?" Nona tried to picture it. "That's madness. Everyone there is in a habit. We all know each other! The defenders would just challenge any stranger . . . not that I can make myself look like a stranger in a habit!"

"Even so—"

"I've no chance! This was Wheel wasn't it? She's always hated me." Nona hardly felt Keot burn across her tongue, rising with her rage. "Wheel and that bitch Rail. Revenge for Joeli! Namsis money bought and paid for this—"

Sister Apple's slap rocked Nona on her heels, setting the side of her face aflame. She had been too deep in her outrage to see the blow coming. Which, even as she raised her hand to her cheek, Nona realized was a good thing. If she had seen the blow and blocked it some unwritten rule would have been shattered, and Nona's exit from the convent would have been a likely consequence.

"*I* made the decision." Sister Apple fixed Nona with a hard stare. "Safira told you the Noi-Guin still want their revenge. Do you want Kettle and the other sisters out in Verity risking themselves so you can take the trial?" Her voice turned from angry to bitter. "It's not as if you stand a chance. You cut off your shadow, Nona. You cut yourself off from the shade. The Grey isn't for you."

Sister Apple turned and unlocked the gate. She locked it behind her and a moment later descended into the caves, leaving Nona standing before the steps, too full of conflicting thoughts and emotion to do anything but stand some more.

"THOUGHT YOU WEREN'T coming!" Ruli stepped out into the track from where she had been sheltering with Ara and Jula.

"It's hard to slip away with inquisitors all over the convent." Nona had crept out quite easily, but that had been quick feet and luck. Mainly luck.

Ruli nodded. "I walked the shadows with Ara." The other two emerged behind her. Ruli only had a touch of marjal, half-blood at most, but she showed a talent for shadow-work. "Jula just strolled out. The Inquisition know how holy she is and don't bother with her."

Jula snorted at that. "Did you bring a weapon?"

Nona pulled out the knife they'd discovered on their last exploration.

Ara frowned at it. "That's the same as before . . . you know, the one they tried to assassinate you with. It's Noi-Guin!"

"It's the same as the shadow-poisoned one that got stuck in

Kettle," Nona said. "One very persistent assassin, three knives. I must have hurt their pride by surviving."

"Do you think the . . . monster . . . scared the Noi-Guin away too?" Ruli shivered, then hugged herself as if to show it was just the wind.

"I'm guessing so." Nona put the knife back inside her habit. "What did you bring?"

"Half a quarterstaff!" Ara reached back into the crevice they'd been waiting in. "I guess that's an eighth-staff?"

Nona grinned: she recognized it as one she'd broken when Joeli's friends caught her.

"I got a hammer from the cooper's stores." Ruli let it slip from her sleeve into her hand.

"This." Jula sheepishly produced a frying pan. "It's all I could get."

"And Sister Coal won't beat you as hard if she catches you stealing from the kitchen as Sister Tallow would if she caught you stealing from Blade stores!" Nona nodded.

"Are we being stupid here?" Ara frowned at her broken staff. "There's a monster down there we know nothing about, and Jula has a frying pan."

"Maybe." Nona put her knife in Jula's other hand and folded her fingers around the hilt. "But they're going to send us out into the world soon enough and we'll be expected to deal with whatever we find. If we can't even face up to something on our own doorstep . . . *under* our own doorstep . . . what use are we?" She flexed her hands and brought the flaw-blades into existence shimmering briefly. "And I brought my own weapons."

THE FISSURE WAITED for them as it had always waited, hidden before there were people to hide from. Ara led the way into the corridor, lantern held high. The entrance held that faint rankness of old bones, damp stone, and rotting vegetation. A few dozen yards took them past the point where even the most shade-loving plant could cling to survival using whatever light bled through the entrance and soon the only smell was that of wetness on rock. They retraced their steps, a familiar route now, none of them speaking. Nona felt the weight of stone above her, the walls pressing in, the heavy silence. In places their footsteps echoed, elsewhere an emptiness, like that of the Ancestor's dome, swallowed the sound.

"I've worked out why I like this place so much," Jula said.

Nona looked back from her inspection of the long scramble up towards the chamber with the three exits. "Yes?"

"It's the wind."

"There isn't any."

"Yes. And it's not just that. There's no wind inside at the convent, but you can always hear it. Here, there's nothing."

"Serenity now." Nona let the lines of the children's song run through her head. "It will work. That girl at the Academy tried to make me run with her shadows. Serenity kept them from me.

"She's falling down, she's falling down . . ." Nona muttered the words beneath her breath and her serenity rose around her like the sides of a deep well.

Beside her Ara, Ruli, and Jula each walked their own path into the serenity trance.

"Let's go." Ara began to climb.

Ten minutes later the tunnel that led to the holothour and its cave of horror yawned before them. Ara walked on without a word. Nona and Jula followed, Ruli at the rear.

"I can feel it." Nona's skin prickled as if a thousand eyes watched her from the dark.

It can feel you. Keot rose across the back of her neck like a scald and her anger rose with him, darker emotions too, palpable through the thick velvet wrapping of her serenity.

"Me too." Ruli sounded calm, almost sleepy.

The light from Ara's lantern reached out across stone walls smoothed by ancient waters. Thick, glistening deposits of limescale coated every surface, like treacle frozen in mid flow, somehow organic, as if they were advancing down the gullet of some vast beast.

Nona wore her serenity as if it were a protective bubble, extending yards past the reach of her arms, beyond even the limits of their illumination, with the fear pushing at its borders a distant thing. Ahead, shapes loomed among the shifting shadows, the rock-bound skeletons of the holothour's victims.

The four girls pressed tight together, calm but seeking the

comfort of one another's warmth and a side from which attack would not come. The ancient night of the cave began to roll back before the lantern's advance, leaving calcified skeletons behind like rocks revealed by retreating waves. Shadows swung.

"It's coming." A whisper.

Nona felt it, like a squall racing across the flatness of open fields, something big, something vast that would carry her off. The walls seemed to pull away, the touch of her friends fade to nothing. Every fear she owned hurtled towards her out of the night at terrifying speed.

Then it struck.

The bubble of her serenity collapsed in less than a heartbeat, from something wide and confident to the thinnest skin moulded to her body with the holothour's unclean touch scratching dry-fingered across every inch. In a moment Nona hung high above herself, seeing her body in the small patch of illumination, a tight circle around her, and beyond that an endless void both wholly empty and full of implacable hate.

Run!

It wasn't Keot's command that set Nona turning to flee, it was the sound of running feet. The sound of being abandoned. She glimpsed Ruli's white face, stretched into a scream, horror in every line. Jula shrieking, dropping her knife as she started to run. Ara crashing into the nearest wall as she ran blind. The terror breached Nona's barriers and flooded through her. She tore off after Ruli, Keot demanding she run faster.

Ruli leapt Ara's sprawled body. Nona followed. Ara's collision with the wall had left her on the ground, blonde hair fanned around her head, one arm stretched out as if pointing the way.

Run! Keot fled into her eyes and suddenly the passage ahead revealed itself to her as if the stone itself were glowing with a reddish light.

Nona got five more steps, each slower than the last, before Jula overtook her, habit flapping.

Run! The voice that filled her brain rang with terror as the holothour's fear infected even the devil. *It's an old one. Too powerful!*

"She's my friend." The words brought Nona to a halt as effectively as a rope about her neck. She turned. Ara moved her head, groaning, the lantern lying on its side close to her hip. Keot retreated from her eyes, unwilling to see what followed them.

Take the lantern and run!

Nona took one step back towards Ara, then another, bowed as if braving a headwind. It wasn't that her fear had gone, simply that a greater one drove her, the thought of Ara's bones lying with the rest, slowly devoured by stone, a constant silent accusation that the foundation of her own existence lay as hollow as the Rock of Faith.

"No . . ." A whisper. Trembling in each limb, Nona stepped over Ara for a second time and faced the darkness. "No!" A shout.

She stood in an invisible wind. At the back of her head Keot hung, bleeding out into the air, trying to free himself from her skin and flee back to the Path. The intensity built: the cave's empty night reverberated with it, skins of stone shattered from the walls, warm blood ran from Nona's eyes and nose. She sank to her knees beneath the weight of it, every nerve screaming to run.

The rocks around her began to bleed. An awful rasping breath shuddered through the blackness. And out there a howling hate, condensing. A darker clot of night. The stench of decay surrounded her. Screams of pain worse than the abbess had made when they'd burned her. A novice emerged into the trembling illumination, thin limbs, rotting skin, dragging a withered leg, lifting up her face. Hessa!

RUN!

"No." A whisper.

And suddenly the fear blew out. From one moment to the next it had gone. The darkness was again just darkness. Nona fell forward onto all fours and vomited everything she had in her.

JULA AND RULI came back, patting their way along the walls. They emerged pale-faced into the light to find Ara kneeling by Nona, holding Nona's hair back as she wiped drool from her mouth.

"Where is it?" Ruli bent to pick up the hammer she'd dropped. It shook in her hand.

"Gone, I think." Nona spat and rose to her knees.

What does she mean, where is it? Keot sounded weak, distant, he shivered over the very surface of her skin.

She means, where is it?

That was it. Holothour have nothing so primitive as flesh.

"I think it's gone." Nona helped Ara up, raising her fingers to the scrape on Ara's forehead. "You're all right?"

"You should see the other girl." Ara managed a grin. It was an old joke.

"I see what you mean." Jula tapped her frying pan to the wall where Ara had collided with it, and more layers of stone cracked away.

Ara scooped up the lantern. "Come on."

She led them back.

"Where are all the bones?" Ara held the lantern high. The cavern floor lay clear of anything but rocks and stalagmites. Further back something large and circular loomed.

"Were the skeletons part of it? Like the fear?" Ruli whispered. "In our heads?"

"There's one here." Jula pointed at a limed skeleton sprawled between two rocks. "Just the one, like those two in the niche. The rest were illusion?"

Nona turned towards the object at the limits of the lantern light and advanced with Ara. It was a ring, four yards across, standing upright with the lowest part of it buried in the stone floor. The ring itself was the thickness of a roof beam and covered in flowstone, stalagmites and stalactites decorating the top of the arch.

"What is it?" Jula stopped and they all stopped with her.

"Something the Missing left," Nona said.

"No?" Ruli looked at her, round-eyed.

"Anyone could have put it here," Jula said. "The people who built the pillars."

"Sister Rule said it takes two hundred years for a stalactite to grow an inch," Nona said. "How long would you say those were?"

"Two feet? Three?" Ruli stepped closer.

"That's the best part of ten thousand years since someone

knocked them off last." Nona advanced too, her voice a whisper. "We should push on." She looked past the ring to the back of the cavern where two tunnels led off, one rising, one falling. "Which way, Jula?"

"Shouldn't we . . ." Jula returned her gaze to the ring.

"It's been there forever. I *need* to see where Hessa died." She saw the others' doubt. "It's the key to finding Yisht and recovering the shipheart," she added, with more confidence than she felt.

"That one." Jula nodded towards the tunnel heading up.

Ara led off, touching her fingers to her forehead every now and then. "Did you . . . come back for me?" she muttered as Nona came close.

"I tripped over you."

They walked on in silence.

Your friends will get you killed. I don't understand why you need them. Keot ran along the veins of her right arm, faint and petulant. *Especially the other two. They're weak. There's no gain.*

Nona thought about it. About the ties that bound her to those she had named her friends. Sister Pan's words returned to her, how she described the Path and the threads that bound each thing to every other thing, a web of influence and dependence, invisible, eternal, ever-changing.

I've been at this convent five years, Keot, and I've learned to believe in something more than myself. All this time Wheel has been banging on about the Ancestor, about all those who came before and have gone beyond. But the larger thing I believe in is what's here and now. Those novices are my friends and I would die for them. I would face a terror for them that I haven't the courage to stand against on my own behalf.

EVEN WITH JULA'S instinct for finding her way below ground, making progress still proved a difficult business. Time and again they had to double back, seeking alternative routes where a passage grew too narrow or too steep or turned and led away into the depth of the Rock. It felt to Nona like days, and was perhaps hours.

"I think we're getting close," Jula said.

"I think we're running out of oil." Ara held the lantern up and shook it to hear the slosh.

"Five more minutes." Jula pointed ahead with her Noi-Guin knife. "We risked our lives to come this far! We might not get another chance."

"If we lose our light we can still die down here," Ara said, but she followed on.

At the limit of their illumination the tunnel before them narrowed then opened into what might be a sizeable chamber. Nona had no idea where they were with respect to the convent but Jula's talent for navigation had proved trustworthy so far.

The sound of running water greeted them, the air thick with the smell of earth and rot.

"What are those?" Ara raised the lantern and stepped into the chamber.

"I don't know." Nona stared at the ceiling. Strange stalactites hung in twisting profusion, like nothing they had seen before.

"They're roots," Ruli said.

"We're below the centre oak."

Nona kept her gaze on the mass of roots. Towards the rear of the cavern they stretched to the ground and snaked across it. Just feet ahead of her roots reached so low she could almost touch one with a raised arm. For years she had walked the novice cloister, chased the others, sat on the benches chattering, and all that time this void had waited in darkness only yards beneath them. Perhaps people were like that too: a void had waited behind Clera's smile, a dark space where unspoken thoughts had festered and grown into betrayal.

"Look . . ." Ara stood at the side of the chamber beside one of five round, dark openings. Now she held her lantern closer Nona could see that the opening looked hand-hewn and that corroded iron bars blocked it off. The novices gathered beside Ara.

"It's a cell." Ruli pulled on one of the bars. Her hand came away thick with rust.

"Check the others," Jula said.

They were all cells. Each a space hewn just two yards back into the rock, sealed with bars and a locked gate. The second and third held bones, complete skeletons, blackened with age.

"This is a prison," Nona whispered, remembering the recluse, the cave where she and the abbess had been kept before their trial.

"An oubliette." Jula's voice was a whisper too. "They put people here to forget them."

"Those skeletons we found . . ." Ruli frowned.

"Might not have been people who came into the caves and got lost. They might have been novices or sisters who escaped the cells but never saw the light again." Nona tried to imagine it. Rotting away down here just yards beneath the novice cloisters where girls ran and laughed and played. Nothing but the stillness of rock and root. She suppressed a shudder. A place to forget. Did anyone in the convent still remember it existed?

To one side of the cavern in a low-roofed alcove a pool nestled, fed by a small stream escaping a crack.

"In the ceiling." Nona pointed. A circular shaft led up.

"What's in it?" Ara squinted. She crouched at the pool's edge holding the lantern above the water. The light's reflection on the rocky ceiling made a wonder of slowly shifting patterns.

"Is that . . . a bucket?" Nona frowned and squinted at something hanging in the shaft.

"It's the well!" Jula said.

"The well?" Nona didn't know of a well close to the novice cloisters.

"In the back of the laundry. That little room . . . They get the washing water there when the rain barrels are dry."

Nona wondered if those trapped in the cells might sometimes have heard the outside world echoing down the well shaft. She shuddered again.

"We need to go now," Ara said. "Or we'll be feeling our way in the dark."

With new meaning attached to the old bones along the way, the novices needed no further encouragement. They left without a word.

14

---◆---

ABBESS GLASS

ABBESS GLASS STOOD in the shadow beside her study window, watching the novices of Red Class hurry towards Academia Tower, clutching their slates. She rubbed Malkin behind the ears. The old cat tolerated this and watched with her. At the back of the class little Elsie, just eight years old, scurried to catch up. She had been given over to the convent by her mother, a metalworker recently widowed and struggling to keep her younger children housed and fed.

A sigh escaped her. Able had been eight when he died. Her son would have been a man now, perhaps with children of his own. It still hurt to think of it, a physical ache in her chest. Glass struck her breastbone, willing the pain away, and turned from the window.

Sister Tallow waited before the portrait of Abbess Mace, she of the miracle. Abbess Glass had forgotten the nun was there and noticed her with a start. Tallow showed no more motion than the portrait. If not for the wisp of her breath escaping in the cold air she might have been just another painting. Though it would take quite an artist to capture her hardness and the dark intensity of her eyes.

"It won't be long before the inquisitors want to read the Grey reports, you know that." Sister Tallow glanced towards the door. "I'm surprised there's not a watcher in your house yet."

Abbess Glass gave a grim smile. "Brother Pelter has suggested it. I declined."

"And the Grey reports?"

"I doubt they will prove of much use to the Inquisition."

"Encryption's no good. They'll just demand the cipher," Sister Tallow said.

"Even so." Abbess Glass spread her hands.

"You could appeal to Nevis. He could still get them out of here," Tallow said. "Before they get their teeth into . . . anything."

"Ah, sister." Abbess Glass reached out to pat Tallow's shoulder. The nun stiffened but let the familiarity pass. She wasn't much different to Malkin in that respect. "Don't you teach the girls that sometimes you have to let your opponent get a good tight grip before you can use it against them?"

"As a last resort, abbess. It's better to get the grip yourself."

Abbess Glass shrugged then shivered. "The Durns are landing again, in force, spreading along the southern margins. The Scithrowl armies are at both their borders, though more of them at the one we care about. The ice has advanced another mile since last year's ranging, on both fronts. The emperor is squeezed on all sides. Our options are running out at a startling rate, old friend. All we need now, as they say, is for the moon to fall!"

"And Sister Kettle?" Sister Tallow moved to the window. She stood, staring across the convent. "She's not safe here. Pelter will snap her up. I'm surprised he hasn't already. And what Apple might do then I couldn't say. Only that it would not be pretty."

"I need Kettle here."

"But—"

"Too many of the Greys are on missions. The things I've set in motion . . . The uncertainties . . . Sister Kettle is my reserve. Her skills are too valuable to waste, her condition a good excuse to keep her close."

"It's her condition that will see Pelter take her off to the Tower of Inquiry in chains, abbess!"

"The operative word there is 'see,' Tallow dear. He will not see her. She will remain hidden but close."

"And this business with Nona? Shade Trial in the cloister?"

"Nona is Red to her core. She was never going to pass the trial, not in Thaybur Square, not here. It will do her no harm to fail at something. We all have to get used to that. Even me."

A knock at the door.

"Come."

Sister Spoon leaned in through the doorway, the Ancestor's tree dangling from her neck in the form of a silver pendant, branches above, a single taproot reaching below. "Sister Rock says there are pilgrims massing on the Vinery Stair, calling for the Argatha."

"I'm sure Novice Zole will be delighted. What do you mean by 'massing,' sister?" Abbess Glass waved to Sister Tallow, letting her go; there would be a class of girls wanting instruction on how better to beat each other senseless.

"Hundreds, abbess." Sister Spoon stepped aside to let Sister Tallow leave. "There are said to be food riots in the Verity slums. People want reassurance. They want the Argatha!"

"Unfortunately we have Zole." Abbess Glass folded her arms across her stomach. "Have Sister Wheel go down and preach at the crowd. An hour or two of that should clear them." She chewed her lip. "Send some bread down to feed any that are in real need. Children first. Take it along the Cart Way and serve it out on the Verity Road. That way the food's associated with leaving rather than with waiting on our doorstep."

"Yes, abbess." Sister Spoon withdrew. Malkin slinked out at her heels. An appointment with a rat somewhere, no doubt.

The door closed and Abbess Glass found herself looking at the portrait that she had for a moment imagined Sister Tallow might be part of. "Abbess Mace." She hadn't seen the faces of any of the portraits in this room for a long time. Years maybe. They had become part of a fixed background, something for the eye to slide across. There were lessons to be learned there. Though little time remained for lessons. She had told Sister Tallow that all they needed was for the moon to fall. Of course the secret whispered in the corridors of power was that it had been falling all her lifetime and that fall was only getting faster. "What we need from you now, Abbess Mace, is another miracle." She made a slow turn, taking in the dozen former abbesses whose faces watched her from the walls. "Anyone?"

Abbess Glass returned to her post at the window. Brother Pelter stood at the doorway to the Ancestor's dome, letting the ice-wind gust past him into the foyer while he stared up at the abbess's house.

"Come along, brother." Abbess Glass set her fingers to the cold panes before her in their leaded diamonds. "Play your part."

15

———————— ✦ ————————

"WHAT ARE YOU reading?"

"Kettle! I didn't hear you come in." Nona turned from the heavy tome, grinning. She'd worried that Kettle had gone off on another mission without saying goodbye. There had been no sign of her around the convent for days.

"I can be light on my feet when I need to be." Kettle leaned over Nona's shoulder. "Saint Devid?"

"It says here that he travelled the whole circle of the Corridor." Nona placed her bookmark on the page. "That was five hundred years ago. It was over two hundred miles from the northern ice to the southern ice back then!"

"Not one I've heard of." Kettle raised her eyebrows. "Impressive though!"

"He visited three cities left abandoned by the Missing too! The ice has swallowed them now though . . ."

"Sister Wheel will hate him." Kettle grinned. "She can't abide stories about the Missing. She says they were animals, nothing more. The Church's official position is that they had no links to the Ancestor's tree. Which makes them animals in a technical sense. But you don't find many horses building themselves a city!"

"Saint Devid came from the Grey too, like me. I don't mean like a Grey Sister . . . the same place as me. And it wasn't the Grey back then either, it was some of the best farmland in the empire and they had a city there—a big town anyway called . . ." Nona started to turn back in search of the name.

"Have you thought about how you're going to pass the Shade Trial, Nona *Grey*?" Sister Kettle rolled Nona's last name around her mouth as if savouring it.

Nona snorted. "You know it's happening in the cloister, yes? I've got to sneak past Joeli and the rest of Mystic Class unchallenged. Perhaps if I wear a hat and cape . . . And then climb the centre oak, unchallenged, and reach the puzzle-box. After that all I have to do is hide in the branches with every leaf tight-wrapped against the ice wind, and sit there long enough to open it. Unchallenged."

"Sounds difficult."

"Sounds impossible. Even if I could still work the shadows."

"There's more to the Grey than wrapping yourself in shadow. Apply yourself to the problem, novice." Kettle smiled and patted Nona's shoulder. "I have faith."

NONA STAYED AT the library taking notes on Saint Devid, absorbed by the tales of his wandering. Somehow Bray's voice contrived to wash over her without breaking her concentration. As a result she arrived at Blade inky-fingered and late.

"Novice, nice of you to join us." Sister Tallow looked around as Nona creaked the doors open, icy-gusts lifting her habit around her. The rest of the class were paired on the sands, swords at the ready. "Novice Joeli can shave your head after the bell. I feel she should get to wield a blade this lesson." She nodded to where Joeli sat on the sidelines, her cane to one side, golden hair boiling around her shoulders, brushed to a high shine.

Nona gritted her teeth and ran for the stores to get a weapon.

The rest of the lesson passed in a flickering blur of swordplay, Alata gratefully surrendering her place opposite Zole to Nona. The pair of them fought with dedication, Zole precise, relentless and without mercy just as usual, Nona finding her instinctive fear of sharpened steel pushed out by anger at the humiliation waiting for her under Joeli's hands. With the prospect of the Namsis girl holding a cut-throat razor inches from her face, Nona found Zole armed with a sword a less intimidating prospect.

"Good." Sister Tallow's voice inserted itself into a gap in their sparring.

Zole and Nona paused, both panting. Mistress Blade used the g-word so rarely that the moment required witnessing. Nona realized she was dripping with sweat and saw that Zole's blade-habit was stained red around the site of her last thrust, the blunted point of her blade having penetrated deep enough to make the ice-triber bleed. Looking down, Nona saw she sported two similar injuries.

"Hah!" Zole launched another attack.

Nona dived into the space between heartbeats, deep as she had ever been. Even so the fight seemed blindingly fast, swords clashing, parrying, twisting, the sharp adjustment of feet, the stuttering advances and retreats. Their blades met perhaps twenty times before Zole dropped into an unexpected leg-swipe. Nona jumped it, almost. They crashed together, snarling, blades crossed between them, both pressing close. And leapt apart, feet bracing to rush in once again, sand piling up behind them.

"Break!" Sister Tallow called.

All around them the other novices watched amazed. Apart from the dropping of jaws none of them had had time to move.

"Good," Tallow repeated. "Changing rooms."

"There." Zole heaved in a breath. "Was that a bell?"

Nona hadn't heard it either. She grinned. An echo of it showed on Zole's lips. The ice-triber pushed back sweaty hair and turned for the changing room.

"Nona." Sister Tallow pointed to the chair that Joeli had vacated. "When you've finished here, Nona, have Sister Rose look at those injuries." The nun walked across to Joeli, now standing beside the chair, and handed her the razor. "If you cut her, Joeli, you'll be her sparring partner next lesson."

Sister Tallow relieved Nona of her training sword and went to stow it away. Nona took her place in the chair without a word, staring straight ahead.

"A close shave will make it easier to wear a wig for the Shade Trial." Joeli held the back of Nona's head, lifting the razor to Nona's brow, the steel cold on her skin. "You might get past us as a blonde . . ." The razor scraped and a chunk of black hair fell into Nona's lap.

Slice her throat. Say she tried to kill you. Keot flowed along the veins and tendons in Nona's wrist.

No. For a moment the idea tempted her. Keot's violence bleeding through. At least Nona hoped it was just that.

Yes! Keot moved across her down-turned palm, a scarlet scald. He twitched in her fingers, trying to take control.

No. Nona forced him back.

Joeli worked quickly with a sure hand, and although Nona kept her teeth gritted, her body tensed to spring into action, it was only hair that came down rather than blood.

With a surprisingly gentle touch, Joeli tilted Nona's head forward to scrape away the last of the hair from the base of her neck. Nona's head felt cold and strange.

"Of course you've no more chance of passing the trial than you do of taking the Grey." Another scrape of the blade. "Any more than you stand a chance of catching Yisht. It's been what, almost three years now? Your little peasant friend will just have to go as unrevenged as she was unmourned."

Nona snarled and thrust her head back, intending to get herself cut if that was the price of a sparring session with Joeli. But the razor was no longer there.

"I don't have to be fast if you're going to be predictable, now do I?" Joeli stepped away, laughing that same tinkling laugh that Ara and Terra had shared in the Mensis mansion, something as artificial to Nona's ear as it was ugly.

16

---◆---

"YOU WANT ME to throw you into the sinkhole?"

"Yes." Nona followed in Darla's wake, out across the fractured stone towards the yawning mouth of the Glasswater.

"In an ice-wind!"

"Yes."

"You'll freeze to death."

Darla had a point: the wind howled around them. Nona's head was already starting to feel like a solid block of ice.

"It's a risk I'm prepared to take. At least I won't have to dry my hair."

Darla barked a laugh at that and ran a hand over Nona's baldness.

"Why do you want me to throw you in?" Darla peered over the edge at the dark waters forty feet below.

"Because you're the strongest." Nona looked up at her friend. At fifteen Darla stood a good six-foot nine inches, broad in the chest, her arms thicker than Nona's thighs.

Darla sighed. "Let's get this over with." She reached for Nona.

"Not from here!" Nona skipped away from Darla's hand. "Over there!" Pointing, she ran to her chosen spot ten yards back into the wind.

Darla walked after her. "I know you're a shrimp, but I'm not sure I can throw you *that* far, even wind-assisted."

"I'm going to help you," Nona said. "Put your hands like this, down low." She cupped her hands together. "I'll run at you, step in your hands, and you boost me over your head."

Darla spread her arms, palms out. "That's insane!"

"You said you'd help me out!" Nona hugged herself against the wind's cold.

"But . . ." Darla shook her head and spat out a piece of ice. "What's this for?"

"Can't tell you. Conflict of interest. I'm protecting you."

Darla pursed her lips, frowning. "Do we have to do it this far back? What if you fall short?"

"If I fall short then I'll probably hurt myself."

"Can't we start closer?" Darla looked over her shoulder, judging the distance.

"We *are* starting closer. Next time we'll add five yards. And there's only so many times I want to jump in today." Zero was the true number.

"Ancestor!" Darla spat again. "You're crazy. You know that?"

Nona grinned. "Ready?"

"No." Darla knelt and put her hands into a stirrup, ready for Nona's lead foot.

Nona started to back off.

Darla called after her. "Let's at least practise the last few steps!"

And so they did. Nona took the last five steps of her run in, set her foot into Darla's hands and Darla launched Nona over her head. Nona landed two yards behind her, the force of the impact concertinaing her into a tight hunch about folded legs. They repeated the move four times.

"Good." Nona rubbed her aching ankles. "You've got to be even quicker this time. I'll be coming in fast and I need to keep the speed. Hold your hands higher . . . here . . . I'll jump."

Nona backed off ten yards and stripped off both shoes then her range-coat, placing them in the lee of a boulder.

"You want me to steal a tub of kelp juice?"

"Yes." Nona followed Ruli towards the vinery.

"Nasty stinking half-rotted seaweed?" Ruli stopped and peered at Nona as if she might be unwell.

"Yes. You can do it. Everyone knows Sister Oak is sweet on you."

"Sister Oak," Ruli sniffed, "appreciates my ledger-keeping skills and the nose I have for wine."

"Whatever." Nona pushed Ruli back into walking. "You can get me a tub."

"Of course I can." Ruli grinned over her shoulder. "There's scores of them at the vinery. Best fertilizer money can buy. Plus we don't pay for it. It's harvested on the beach at Gerran's Crag. I bet the Holy Sisters have a ball at that convent. My pa says most of them stink of seaweed and the ones that don't smell of fish."

"Good. Hide it for me somewhere easy to get at and let me know." Nona turned away, stifling a sneeze.

"Wait! You're not coming?"

"Got things to do!"

"You only love me for my rotten seaweed juice." Ruli pouted. "What do you want it for?" She brightened. "You're going to tip it over Joeli, aren't you? Do it! Do it! It'll turn her hair green. You can't wash it out!"

"Something like that!" And Nona ran off across the courtyard before stopping and calling back. "Oh, and I need a net. A big one, like the ones they use to keep the barrels in the carts."

Nothing to say, Keot?

The devil remained silent, sulking across her ribs. The discovery that being submerged in truly icy water distressed him so much was a useful one that Nona vowed to investigate more thoroughly at a later date.

"CHALLENGE!"

Nona raised her hands. "You got me!"

Zole scowled. "It was not difficult."

Across the novice cloister members of Mystic Class were converging on them, weaving through the other classes who stood chatting in their usual groups, huddled on benches or strolling beneath the galleries.

Nona unwound her headscarf. "Got to try!"

"You're the only novice wearing a headscarf," Zole said.

"And now you're the only bald novice," Alata said, drawing up to them.

"Also you're the only novice with huge black eyes like an insect." Joeli came up behind them from her patrol of the gallery.

"And with no shadow," Crocey sneered. Though with the

scudding cloud overhead there were few chances to check for the presence of a person's shadow even if Nona hadn't still been in the shade of the cloister walls when challenged.

Elani came across, her sneer echoing Crocey's, her arm still splinted from Nona breaking her elbow in the dormitory attack. "It's a pity you'll never reach the tree. I would enjoy watching you try to hide in it." She waved her good arm at the stark branches that stood like a thousand black fingers raised against the sky.

"Good!" Mally was one of the last to arrive. "We can go and eat at last!"

Normally the trial was held in Verity on seven-days and each candidate got to try her luck across a whole seven-day from dawn to dusk, with the sixth fail ending the matter. Since the novice cloisters were all but deserted on a seven-day Nona had managed to get Sister Apple to agree that she might try at any non-lesson time between breakfast and dinner, one attempt per day for the six days leading up to the seven-day. If she hadn't succeeded by dinner on six-day then the trial was over and she had failed. This meant of course that none of those on guard duty could get lunch without weakening the defence.

"Couldn't you just try before lunch?" Mesha trailed in behind Mally, rubbing her stomach. "Everyone knows you're not going to make it. So be a saint and fail early!"

"On the bright side. Only three more days to go." Joeli led the rush for the nearest exit. "Challenge you tomorrow, Nona!"

THAT NIGHT, IN the dark wake of the focus moon, Nona slid from her bed. She took her clothes and crept from the Mystic dormitory. On the stairs she hurried into her habit, tying her shoelaces blind. She stood, struggling into her range-coat. Dressed, she went down into the main corridor and stopped outside the Grey dormitory. She gave the lightest pull on a thread visible only within the clarity trance and using a quantal's eyes. Ara opened the door moments later and handed over the lantern and rope they used on their caving trips. A moment later she fetched the hooded lantern kept for trips to the Necessary and closed the door while Nona lit the first lantern from the second. Ara retrieved the hooded lantern and returned to her bed. Neither girl spoke during the whole exchange.

Nona left the building with the lantern trimmed so low that its glow barely reached past the smoky glass. She crossed the convent, keeping to the walls, avoiding the places where nuns were most likely to patrol.

In the bushes outside the sanatorium windows Nona recovered a heavy rope net and a wooden tub of kelp juice, five pints at least. She could smell the stuff as she picked the tub up. Burdened by her load, Nona made her way next to the novice cloisters, taking the path along the west side, a narrow alley between the laundry rooms and the low winery building.

"And where might you be off to, young lady?"

Nona froze. She turned her head slowly, seeing nothing in the darkness.

"Pssst." The hiss made Nona look up. Kettle watched her from the winery roof, crouched low, darkness wound around her in sheets, untouched by the wind. "What are you up to?"

"No good," Nona said.

"Be on your way then." Kettle grinned and melted into the night, as if the dark had swallowed her then poured from the roof like oil.

Nona hurried into the novice cloister via the arch through the laundry rooms that filled the south wing. First she positioned the net then went to search through the laundry for the well. She found it after trekking through the washing and airing halls. It lay at the bottom of a short stair. The door to the well chamber had been locked but the device was simple and Nona soon found the necessary thread to pull in order that it be unlocked. It was a trick Hessa had showed her years before.

Nona secured her rope to the well-head, tied her lantern to her belt, and started to descend. A person of Darla's size would probably not fit. Even Nona felt distinctly trapped as the sides rose around her, dark with slime and nitre, the lantern scraping on stone while she slid down the rope. The faint sounds of running water rose from far below.

Do you never sleep? Keot grumbled, stretching out along her arm, almost as if yawning. *What hole have you found to crawl around in now?*

Nona continued down the rope not bothering to reply. She became aware of the shaft opening up around her without needing to see it, something about the quality of the sound.

She shinned another yard down the rope and looked out across the pool beneath her. The lantern's glow reflected all around her, the light moving across rock walls capturing the ripples. Where the cavern opened out beyond the pool the forest of the centre oak's roots swallowed all illumination.

Nona started to swing. Once, twice, three times. On the fourth swing she released the rope and arched her back. She landed in two feet of water and stumbled up onto the rocky border. There, she unslung the kelp tub, uncorked it, then took out the cloth she had stuffed in an inner pocket and wetted it with the juice. The stink of the liquid took away her breath.

"Ancestor!" She spat on the stones. "This had better work."

Nona approached the nearest root that came low enough to reach and wiped the cloth across it, leaving dark smears of the kelp juice along its length. She moved to the next. Then the next. She kept to the fringes, the younger roots. They emerged in sheets from any crack that would let them through the rock. In the midst of the cavern the thickest and oldest roots reached the floor and sprawled out across it, but those were stone-clad.

Within half an hour Nona discovered that, however much fighting you might do, any work that required you to hold your arms above your head soon became exhausting. Added to the fatigue in her arms was the fact that no matter what care she took the kelp juice still managed to drip on her. One drop stung in her left eye, another found its way into her mouth and filled it with a sour foulness.

Keot made no further comment, perhaps having fallen back to sleep.

The lantern had started to gutter by the time Nona let up. She had used most of the kelp juice and all of her patience. Stinking and bone-tired, she took herself back to the pool, put the lantern down and steeled her nerves.

"Seven ice-baths in a day . . ." She plunged in and thrashed about, gasping, hoping to rid her habit of the kelp-stink. Keot's wordless howls of outrage provided just enough warmth to keep her from freezing. After that, the long climb back up the well-shaft nearly defeated her, but it did at least get her muscles working and her blood flowing once more.

Nona hauled herself over the low wall surrounding the well and slithered to the floor where she lay gasping. After a minute she picked up her lantern, recovered her rope, and set off to brave the ice-wind one more time in a wet habit.

"ATISHOO!"

"Sounds nasty!" Darla rumbled from her bed, just a mound beneath the covers.

"Atishoo!" Nona repeated herself. Grey fingers of morning light reached across the dormitory.

"It's your own damn fault." Darla rolled over, muttering to herself.

"Part of your next disguise?" Crocey called from across the room. "You're going to sneeze your way past us today?"

"I'm certainly going to try." Nona levered herself up and groaned. It felt as if she'd slept for three minutes rather than three hours. On the floor beside her bed her habit lay in a heap, water pooled around it.

Nona hung her clothes up to dry and went to breakfast in Darla's second habit, which was more of a tent than a garment but warmer than her own second habit which had been patched to the point at which there was more replacement material than original.

Sister Rail devoted the morning's Academic class to a history of Durnish invasions and the occasional ripostes from past emperors. Although she lined up a host of complex political reasons behind each act of aggression it seemed to Nona that the root cause was the same in every case. The ice kept advancing. If you squeezed any nation north and south it must expand east and west, or spend so many lives trying that the land remaining to it is sufficient.

"Atishoo!" Nona tried to hold the next sneeze in, she focused her will, reached for her serenity, gritted her teeth. "Atishoo!"

"Cover your mouth, girl!" Sister Rail stalked towards her.

Nona lowered the hand she'd had covering her mouth, biting back both her retort and the desire to wipe that hand down the front of the approaching nun.

"How many battle-barges were beached in the Durnish invasion at Songra Beach?" Sister Rail peered down at her.

Carry her to the window and throw her out!

Nona couldn't help but smirk at Keot's suggestion.

"You find this amusing, novice?"

"No, Mistress Academic. I was trying not to sneeze." Nona pressed her lips together. "And it was three hundred."

"When?"

"Uh . . . the thirtieth year of Emperor Tristan?"

"Nonsense." Sister Rail turned and stalked back towards her desk. "It was the thirty-first year."

When Bray tolled the class made for the door with indecent haste. Only Zole, Darla and Nona took their time. On each day of the Shade Trial two novices were allowed a day's respite from guard duty. Four-day was Zole and Darla's day off and no penalties incurred by the guards on post would fall upon their shoulders.

Zole walked out after the others. "Good luck today."

"What have you heard?" Nona fought back a rising panic.

"Heard?" Zole turned. "Nothing but footsteps in the night. But it is enough to know you. You will make your move today. You would not strike against a friend, Nona Grey." She shrugged and left.

"Better get on with it," Darla said. "This is insane, though. I did mention that?"

"You did." And Nona led off after Zole.

They went directly to the novice cloisters, the icy gusts swirling around them as the Corridor wind struggled to reassert itself. Mystic Class would be arrayed within the cloister now, ready to challenge Nona the moment she set foot inside. Darla followed Nona into the laundry wing, ignoring the main archway into the cloister. They went through the washroom, past Sister Mop and Sister Spear, one scrubbing, the other at work with the mangle.

"Where do you think you're going?" Sister Spear looked up as Nona started to climb the wooden stairs to the second storey.

Nona paused and met the woman's sharp stare. "I'm on Shade Trial, sister."

"And the big girl?" Sister Spear had recently joined from Gerran's Crag in the west and struggled with names.

She's old. Beat her and leave her bleeding.

"She's my prisoner," Nona said.

"Prisoner?" Sister Spear frowned.

Nona nodded. "Mistress Shade has instructed us at length on the value of hostages. I can't afford to let her out of my sight."

Sister Spear waved them away, shook her head and returned to her mangle work. "Novices . . ."

The floor above had been given over to the storage of linens, salt for the wash, and unspecified crates of the type that looked too important to throw away but too boring to open. Nona ignored it all and went to one of the outer windows. The shutters protested with a squeal of rusty hinges.

"I don't like this bit." Darla peered out at the drop.

"I won't let you down." Nona patted the rope at her hip then slipped out onto the window ledge. A quick jump and scramble saw her onto the roof, one flaw-blade skewering a roof tile to gain purchase. Crouching low, Nona hurried towards the chimney above the boiling room. She kept below the roof ridge and looped her rope around the narrow smokestack. Returning to the roof's edge, she dangled the rope for Darla.

"Come on." She sneezed and swore.

Darla made a meal of the climb, sending more than a few tiles crashing to the flagstones below. If the Mystic Class guards had truly believed Nona stood even a small chance of success they would have recruited eyes among the other classes and stationed them outside. But Nona had chosen the least overlooked side of the building and the ice-wind kept novices from lingering outside; and neither Joeli nor her friends seemed to consider her a threat.

Darla came to lie beside Nona, peering around the chimney and over the roof ridge into the cloister yard.

"How in creation . . ." Darla's mouth hung open. "The tree . . ."

The centre oak stood decked in green, the thick multitude of its leaves tossed this way and that by the blustery wind. The evening before it had been a stark cluster of sticks, every leaf wrapped tight against the cold.

"It's called horticulture," Nona said. "A smelly business."

"So. When do we do it?"

"Wait."

They held at the roof ridge, waiting.

"How long for?"

"Not long. Look." Nona nodded across to the less-used west entrance.

A novice came running through, hair covered by a nun's headdress, face down, weaving past the first girl in her way.

"Challenge!" Mally gave chase. The novice kept running. "Challenge!"

Crocey surged into the girl's path and seized her shoulders, shaking her. "She said 'challenge' you stupid—" The headdress fell away revealing Jula, nervous and flushed.

"Incorrect challenge. They all miss a meal," Nona said.

A second novice came in at a run, through the main entrance this time, steering all eyes from Nona's side of the cloister. Darla started to rise. "Shouldn't we?"

"Wait." Nona pulled her down.

Down below Joeli's shriek cut the air. "It's a trick!" She raced towards the new intruder. "Check her eyes! Check the eyes!"

The new girl wore a headdress and a scarf bound around her face. She moved like lightning.

"It's her! It's her!" Meesha cried as the girl dodged past.

"Challenge! Challenge!" Joeli reached them. "Got you!"

Her triumph proved short-lived. Ruli pulled her scarf aside, grinning beneath eyes that showed no white.

"How?" Darla whispered.

"Blackwort drops. It lasts a day or two," Nona said. "They all lose another meal."

A third girl burst from a window in the east range, headdress in place, scarf across her face.

"Wait! Wait!" Joeli screamed. "Let her get in the sun."

Mystic Class novices closed from all sides. "Watch for a shadow!"

As the new girl broke from the shade of the gallery half a dozen challenges went up as one. "No shadow!" "Challenge!" The girl skidded to a halt. Elani snatched the headdress from her. Golden hair spilled out.

"Lose a meal," Nona whispered.

"How?" Darla sounded exasperated even though it wasn't her meals being cut.

"Ara's great at shadow-work," Nona said. "She just sucked it up into her eyes making them like mine." Nona rolled to the side and started to retreat down the slope of the roof. "Get ready."

Screams went up. It would be the four Red Class novices Nona had recruited. With heads and faces covered they were to rush in after Ara was caught, one from the west entrance, one from the main entrance, one from Ara's window and the last ten yards behind the first, all of them screaming like banshees and weaving to avoid capture. In the chaos the defenders might not notice how short the decoys were.

Darla stood up and bent over with her back to the chimney and hands cupped almost a yard above the tiles. "This is *still* insane. You'll die."

"In service to the Ancestor, death is but a kiss." Nona quoted Sister Wheel with a grin, and from the edge of the roof she began to run at Darla with all the speed she could muster.

Nona let the world slow around her even as she accelerated up the slope. The high screaming of the little novices tumbled down the registers. She leapt for Darla, lead foot aimed at her cupped hands. Shoe met fingers and Darla heaved upwards as they'd practised, lifting with all the power of her back, shoulders and arms. Nona bit down on the terrified yell that so badly wanted to escape her and flew through the air, arms pinwheeling.

Below her, struggling through the moment, the novices from Red Class tried to evade the Mystic guards. Perhaps more challenges rang out in the chaos, Nona couldn't tell. Sister Apple would know. Nobody had seen Apple but they knew she was there, watching.

With their attention on the running novices at the far side of the cloister none of those in the square looked up to see Nona's flight. The green wall of the centre-oak's foliage rushed up to greet her, along with a hundred opportunities for being impaled. "I've missed! I've missed!" Nona could see nothing but leaves. "Ancestor protect me!" She had no time to say the words but they ran behind her lips.

In the next moment Nona was crashing through twigs and greenery. Perhaps she added her screaming to the mix in the cloister. She was too scared to know. The net took her by surprise even though she had been trying to aim for it the whole time. Her arms shot through the holes. The ropes lashed her face. The branches to which she had secured the corners the night before now creaked and groaned in protest, swaying all around her.

For what seemed an age Nona lay entangled in the net's embrace, panting out the panic that had filled her during the plunge. Gradually she became aware of the shouts and screams in the surrounding cloister, dying away now. Somewhere close at hand Joeli was cursing.

". . . the bitch. Four wasted challenges."

"Watch everything! She'll try again."

"She'll be in the next wave!"

"This is cheating!" Joeli again. "She's supposed to be disguised as other people, not have other people disguised as her!"

Nona lay high in the arms of the great oak, cocooned in green.

This is a stupid game.

Shut up, Keot.

Well it is.

Very slowly, Nona began to untangle herself. The puzzle-box lay where Sister Apple had placed it that morning, low down in a fork of major branches. The leaves that close to the ground were not thick enough to hide her. It sat there, taunting her. A cubic box maybe six inches on a side, a thing of black and white, perhaps a bone body inlaid with ebony, a handful of small locks and catches on each side.

Even if you could get it unnoticed they would see it gone before you had time to open it and then they would just challenge the tree.

I thought you weren't interested in my silly game?

Keot didn't reply. But clearly he hadn't been paying as close attention to Nona's doings this week as she had imagined. She wondered what else he had to occupy his time.

Nona fished from her habit the box Ruli had fashioned for her. "Damnation." The impact with the net had splintered one side, breaking away some of the fire-blackened washers that Ruli had used in place of locks. The body was bleached box-wood, the black design painted on with a tarry mix. It bore only a passing resemblance to the puzzle-box below, but if Sister Apple had taught them anything about disguise it was that people saw what they expected to see.

Nona looped her string around the hook at the corner of her fake box then clambered through the branches, keeping high. It took a while and she was thankful for the wind, for without it her passage through the branches would have been betrayed by the localized motion of the leaves.

At last she reached a position five yards above the box where the foliage was still thick enough to conceal her. Anchored by one hand, she used the other to dangle her second string. This one ended in a noose, with a lead fishing weight hung just above the loop; something from the endless mystery of Ruli's pockets, suggested to stop the string fluttering to the wind's tune.

Without the unrelenting grapple-tossing on their caving expedition Nona would have lost heart, believing that if you didn't manage to snag something on the tenth attempt you weren't ever going to do it. It took an age before the loop encompassed the box and didn't slip away when she pulled.

Go on!

If it slides out and falls it's all over.

Do it!

Before she could raise the string Nona felt a familiar tickle at the back of her nose. *No!* She screwed her eyes tight, bit down hard, concentrated the formidable power of her will so hard on not sneezing that her face hurt with the twisting of it. Still the tickle grew. *No! Damnation! Keot! Do something!*

What will you give me? He burned along the veins of her neck, stretching out across her cheek.

Anything, just stop the sneeze!

Anything? You'll kill for me?

What? No!

Keot retreated. The sneeze rose, unstoppable, coming to summon a barrage of challenges.

All right! I'll kill. But I choose who!

Keot hesitated then burned into her nose and down her throat. It hurt, but when he surfaced the sneeze had gone.

You should kill the one called Jula.

Yisht. I'll kill Yisht.

Keot made no reply but she could feel his disapproval. Even so as he retreated across her shoulders the devil felt more deeply bedded in her flesh, and it wasn't a good feeling.

Nona pursed her lips then returned her attention to the box, still lassoed despite how much her hand had trembled when she fought the sneeze. She pulled gently, then with more force. The box shifted, twisted, lifted. "Yes!"

As it rose the box began to spin, the kind of motion that would draw the eye. Ara had been waiting for this moment, Ruli too. Ruli, lounging inside the cloister, stood and ran across the main entrance. Ara, waiting outside, charged in once more, head covered.

"Just stop her!" Joeli yelled. They weren't supposed to lay a finger on anyone, only to challenge. The person on trial had to stop when challenged. They would all lose another meal over it, probably, to be added to the two hungry days they had yet to find out about, earned when Nona reached the tree.

Nona lifted the box. "Three more days, not two, Joeli." And began to lower the substitute.

By the time the novices had wrested Ara's headscarf from her in a struggle that put several of them on the ground, Nona had lowered the fake box into place and slipped the doubled string free of the hook. It looked deeply unconvincing to her and she turned her attention to the real item, certain that she would have only moments before a challenge rang out, aimed at the tree.

"Keep hold of her!" Jolie was presumably tired of catching the same imposters over again. "And the other one—Rula is she?"

The box was surprisingly heavy. It didn't rattle, and didn't even seem to have hinges. Each of the six faces bore three locks. Nona clambered to a more secure position where she could sit with both hands free, secured by her legs. She called on her clarity and defocused her vision to bring her thread-sight to the fore. A billion green threads laced the tree itself, every branch and twig joined to every other, every leaf, every *part* of every leaf, interlocked in a web of life, joined with slow, sure, vegetable certainty.

Nona focused on the first lock, a keyhole set into a disk of black iron not that dissimilar to Ruli's charred washers. "Locks I can do." Novices were introduced to locks in Shade during their Mystic Class years, though younger novices often acquired sets of picks and practised around the convent. Nona had never had the money for picks or the inclination to spend time on the fiddly business, but she knew a few thread tricks.

The first lock surrendered quickly. Finding its thread took a little hunting and a lot of concentration but once pulled the satisfying click followed immediately. The second lock proved a nightmare. It had two threads, connected in some complex way Nona couldn't fathom. Pulling one unlocked something, pulling the other unlocked a different thing and locked the first thing . . . Eventually she managed to pull both together in a way that sounded as if it did the job.

"Only sixteen left to go." Nona looked out into the leaves seething around her. Down below the cloister sounded almost deserted. How long did she have before Bray rang out for Shade class? She could only work on the box between breakfast and dinner, and outside class time. The prospect of another blind leap into the tree did not appeal, even if the distractions could be made to work again.

You'll have to leave the tree for class. They'll spot you then anyway.

Nona said nothing, only curled her lip, but the devil had it right. She hadn't imagined she would get so far and her plans had extended no further than securing and replacing the box.

Nona turned the box in her hands, seeking a lock that looked easier than the rest. Across the rooftops Bray sounded, calling out from the Academia Tower. "Blood!"

Nona started to climb down. If the guards left the cloister before she did then the contest was over. More than over, her achievements so far might no longer count. She paused for a moment low among the branches, struggling with the box one last time. In the next moment rather than be caught trying to creep out, she stuffed the box into her habit and dropped from the tree, landing in a crouch some yards from the trunk.

"Ancestor!" A handful of novices were still making their way out and the cordon of Mystic Class guards were beginning their retreat towards the exits. "It's her!" The first girl to speak wasn't even one of the guards.

"You got me." Nona straightened and stepped towards the little novice. "Elsie, isn't it? Red Class?"

"Challenge!" Joeli shrieked it, shoving Mally and Meesha aside as she stormed towards Nona.

"Too late." Nona turned to face her. "I've finished."

"Challenge!" Joeli looked ugly with her face twisted and red. She had both hands raised as if about to strike her enemy.

"Finished?" Sister Apple stepped out from behind the tree. Quite how she could have been there unseen Nona couldn't fathom. True, her range-coat was bark-patterned, but you couldn't hold a feather over your head and expect people to believe you were a hen.

"She's lying!" Joeli shrugged off Elani who sought to calm her. "She's a lying peasant bitch!" Her arm, raised in accusation, swung to point at the puzzle-box nestled in the fork of the tree. Nona peered up at it. From down below it did look quite convincing.

"That's not the box," Sister Apple said. "But to be *finished* you would have to have opened the real one, Nona. And that does sound unlikely."

Mystic Class crowded round now, Darla and Zole joining them.

Nona drew the puzzle-box from her habit, holding it carefully. It sat across her cupped palms.

"Still locked!" Joeli spat.

"It's a difficult box to open." Sister Apple smiled. "It was a marvellous effort to retrieve it."

Nona flattened her palms out a fraction and the puzzle-box fell into four sections along the lines that her flaw-blades had cut through it. The thing was a solid block of bone with no space inside.

"Is that open enough?"

17

---◆---

THE LAST DAYS leading up to seven-day proved rather tense ones. No one in Mystic Class save Nona, Darla, and Zole got to eat. Mistress Shade totalled the failures of the Shade Trial guards at seven days without meals. The abbess decreed that seven-day be an exception, presumably concerned that an unbroken fast of such duration might do physical harm to some of the leanest novices. The class did not take their punishment with good humour.

Sister Wheel devoted a lesson to the sin of pride. "We are none of us more than a twig in the great tree of the Ancestor. The gifts the Ancestor has given us are for the benefit of all, not the aggrandisement of the individual. Pride is a poison that corrupts." She turned her watery eyes on Nona. Nona resisted asking if the Chosen One was just another twig.

Sister Rail directed Academia lessons back towards algebra as if knowing how much Nona hated it. Of those without rumbling stomachs Zole was the only one able to cope with the scrawl of letters and symbols the nun covered her board in.

Sister Apple devoted two lessons to a dissection of Nona's tactics in the trial, keeping the resentful focus of the class on the origin of their distress.

"If you can't disguise yourself as someone else, then disguising others as you is sometimes an option. Keep this fact in mind. If you're set to trailing a target you might be tempted to fixate on one marker they can't discard. Perhaps their height. Perhaps they've lost an arm. These can be reliable when the target doesn't suspect they are being followed—but if they are suspicious then these seemingly unique markers can be the very thing they use to make you fail. You might find yourself pursuing another very tall man, another one-armed woman, offered up to take advantage of your laziness." She concluded with the box. "The box is there to teach a lesson. Its secret is revealed when sisters take the Grey. We will need a new way to teach that lesson now. At least for enough years to outlast the convent's memory. It's there to teach Sisters of Discretion that whilst there is a time to be subtle, a time for stealth, deception, and the lightest touch, there is also always when the seconds are running out and we come to the sharp end of things the possible need for violent and direct action. Never be so focused on picking a lock that you forget kicking down the door is also an option."

In Blade sword training continued but Sister Tallow took half a lesson to talk about the upcoming Ice Trial. "Sister Egg will be staying with us for four weeks to instruct you on surviving the ice. You'll need more than range-coats and convent shoes out there. You'll need to learn the nine basic types of snow, how to spot and traverse a crevasse, how to build shelters, cook food . . . four weeks will just scratch the surface. More novices have died on the Ice Trial than any other, so pay attention! Even if you take the ordeal of the Shield you will have Sister Rose on hand to try to fix whatever holes might get put through you. On the ice you will be alone, no matter how many novices are with you."

Nona's days rolled by: lessons amid the sullen regard of her classmates, nights in a dormitory full of rumbling stomachs, breaks in the cloister where her victory was replayed by Ara and the others over and over. And through it all Joeli Namsis watched her, with just the hint of a mocking smile on her lips. She didn't have to say it. *Hessa.* Nona could triumph in as many convent games as she liked. The real world lay outside, and on the one occasion that world had reached into Sweet Mercy Nona's friend had died. Yisht walked free out there. Sherzal had the shipheart. Nona's success meant nothing.

WHEN THE SUMMONS came to present herself before Abbess Glass Nona had no idea what to expect. She took herself to the door of the abbess's house and her knock was answered by Sister Pail who led her to Glass's office.

The abbess sat behind her desk with a welcoming smile and eyes that took Nona's measure. In a convent full of women honed into athletes by Blade training, and deadly with their hands, it often surprised Nona that ultimate authority rested in the palm of a motherly woman, somewhat overweight, hair streaked with grey, who wouldn't last more than moments against the youngest hunska half-blood. But then Nona would remember how that old lady's palm came to bear such a mass of burn scars and her question would be answered.

"Nona, have a seat."

Nona sat and waited.

"Your performance in the Shade Trial was a triumph."

Nona waited for the "but."

"But I want you to think about what role awaits you in the wider world, however narrow it might be when you leave our convent. Out there you can't always win. No one person, no matter what amount of physical skill they might have, can change the tide of a war, or deflect the uprising of a political movement. Not even the most famed of Mystic Sisters, with the power of the Path running through their veins, were single-handedly responsible for defeating nations or able to steer the populace.

"From the outside Sweet Mercy looks very small. Our job here is to teach you to deal with failure as much as it is to teach you to win. We have failed to teach you about failure. I tell you this as I fear time is running out and simply hearing the lesson may have to stand in for being shown it."

Nona opened her mouth to explain how she had learned that lesson when she failed Hessa, but her lips couldn't shape the words.

"You're powerful Nona, and you've come into your power at an early age. The understanding that power corrupts is an idea older than the language we repeat it in. All of us in positions that afford authority over others are susceptible, be we high priests, prime instigators, even abbesses."

"Or emperors," Nona said.

The abbess winced. "Some truths are better left implied, dear." She glanced at the door then continued. "The Church has power and the Inquisition is intended to keep it from corruption. The Red and the Grey are a power and among the high priest's tasks is to ensure those who direct them are not led astray from the righteous path. Each member of the Red and the Grey is a power in themselves and it is my job to ensure they remember their strength is a gift intended for service. And of course there are the shiphearts. Each a source of vast potential . . . but do they corrupt the ones who direct that strength?"

Nona said nothing. She didn't know the answers, saving that she was already tainted and the stain upon her had his own name.

"I tell you this, Nona, because difficult times are ahead for us all and I want you to have faith in what we've taught you here. What I've taught you. When strength is in your hands there is a temptation to lash out against what looks like injustice. But our rules are all we have to stop everyone lashing out, each to their own sense of justice. Battles are better fought within the system, even when it seems broken." The abbess sighed. "You're young and I'm boring you. Run along. But don't forget what I've told you."

Nona ran as instructed, but it wasn't boredom that snapped at her heels, but a host of worries, unused to such young prey.

"READY?" THE FOUR of them stood around the well-head in the laundry room. It was now the safest route into the caves. Seven-day trips into Verity had been suspended to allow the Inquisition closer observation of the convent and its inhabitants. Brother Pelter's watchers numbered eight now, swelled by new arrivals from the Tower of Inquiry.

"Ready." Ara held the lantern.

"Ready." Jula peered down the well.

"For Hessa." Ruli nodded.

"For justice. I'm going to get Sweet Mercy its shipheart back. I'm going to kill Yisht. And Sherzal is going to bleed for her crimes." Three impossible things, but passing the Grey Trial had seemed impossible just days ago. The abbess had cautioned Nona about failure, but she had also told her to have faith.

Nona clambered over the guard wall and began to climb down the rope. Even if escaping through the pillars unseen was no longer an option the well got them where they wanted to go much more swiftly. They'd dropped any pretence that they were respecting the abbess's edict against the undercaves. Even Jula hadn't blinked. It was for Hessa.

A short while later all four of them were standing wet-legged at the pool's edge in the oubliette beneath the novice cloister.

"Saints' teeth!" Jula covered her face. "It stinks in here!"

"A gallon of kelp juice will do that." Ruli went to get the empty tub that Nona had failed to return and placed it beside the pool.

"Let's go!" Jula took the lantern and led the way.

Although the distance from the novice cloister to the Ancestor's dome couldn't be more than a hundred yards it took nearly an hour of twisting passages and tight crawls until Jula stopped them.

"All I've got to go on is what you've told me. But if the shipheart was under the rear of the dome . . . we want to go up there. It shouldn't be far." She pointed up at a fissure in the tunnel's ceiling, three yards above their heads and fringed with stalactites.

"Tough throw." Ara frowned. She pulled the grapple from her back and twirled it around her hand. "Better hope there's a good edge at the top." She sped the twirling and with a grunt of effort released the iron hook vertically, trailing rope. A moment later the novices jumped back as it clattered down the fissure again.

Thirty throws later each of them had taken a turn and not once had the grapple caught even enough of a ledge to support its own weight.

"It's probably smooth. Coated in flowstone." Ruli took another throw and stepped away to let the hook fall.

"We need to go back. We can try again another seven-day," Jula said. "Oil's low."

Stealing oil was another thing that had become far more difficult since the Inquisition had tightened their noose. Not only were the watchers watching but the convent's ledgers were all under scrutiny, as if a nun might be selling off supplies to fill the pockets of her habit with silver.

"We can try a little longer." Ara reached for the grapple. Nona shot her a thankful glance.

"Not unless you want to try to find the way back in the dark." Jula held the lantern up. "Next time we'll get here quicker. We know the way now."

Nona looked up, biting her lip, glancing first at one wall, then the other. They stood too far apart to touch both let alone brace for a climb. The distance to the fissure was too high to jump, even if Darla were there and Nona stood on her shoulders.

"Let me try . . ." Nona backed against the left wall then launched herself towards the right, leaping as high as she could. When her hands hit the rock the flaw-blades sheathing her fingers sunk into the stone.

The rest of her crashed into the wall, her feet dangling not much more than a yard above the rock-strewn floor.

"Impressive," Ara said in a distinctly unimpressed voice. "Are you stuck now?"

"I may have broken both knees," Nona hissed. Certainly they both hurt. A lot.

"Should I help you down?" Ruli asked, not quite able to suppress a smirk.

Nona ignored her, instead hunching her body and walking her feet up the wall until all of her was bunched just beneath her hands. If her claws slipped free she would fall ten feet and her head and shoulders would hit the ground first.

Pushing with her legs, she angled up then launched herself again, backwards this time, releasing her claws. She turned as she flew towards the opposite wall and managed to dig her flaw-blades in again. This time before her body crashed into the wall she braced with her feet. She'd gained nearly a yard in elevation.

On the fifth leap, with every muscle burning, Nona caught the edge of the fissure in the tunnel roof and hung beneath it by her blades, swinging.

Jula applauded.

"Of course, now you really are stuck," Ara observed.

Nona dangled.

She's right, you know. Keot ran beneath her hair.

Nona scowled. Air escaped her in short breaths. She had nothing to push against. She released one set of her blades and dangled by one arm. The three novices below hurried into place to try to break her fall. Snarling, Nona swung, lunged upwards, and managed to dig her blades in six inches higher. A few panted breaths then she repeated the process with the other hand. Slowly, by degrees, she climbed into the fissure. Three times she hung, sobbing with the pain, her arms growing weaker with each moment, ready to drop, but against the darkness she saw Yisht, from Hessa's eyes, Yisht as she loomed over Hessa's broken body, knife in hand. "I am not given to cruelty, child," the woman had said. "But you reached into my mind, and a violation like that cannot go unanswered." The strength came from somewhere, and Nona climbed.

Once Nona had her feet inside the fissure and could brace herself against both walls climbing came easy, or would have but for the weakness of her trembling arms. A few minutes later she hauled herself onto flatter ground and lay there gasping.

"How are you going to see anything?" Ara called up.

"We haven't got time for us all to climb up—even if we *can* get a rope to you." Jula's voice.

"I don't need the lantern," Nona called down. "Just give me a minute or two to feel around."

"Feel around?" Ruli, incredulous.

"It's too dangerous," Jula called. "You'll break an ankle. Or probably vanish down a hole!"

"One minute!" Nona called.

Now do it.

What?

Make me see, like you did when you were scared.

I am Keot! Fear has no meaning to me!

Whatever you say. Make me see. Nona pushed Keot towards her eyes. For a moment he resisted, then, perhaps curious, he flowed into them. The pain made her gasp and brought tears running down her face. She hadn't noticed the pain the first time: the holothour's fear had left no room for such things.

Immediately the rocks took on the glow of coals deep in the fire. Nona looked at her hands and found them utterly black, her habit almost as dark with hints of deep grey here and there. The water-carved passage she had climbed into led in two directions. She chose the best one and scrambled off along it. Within twenty yards she stood where Hessa had fallen, at the foot of the shaft Yisht had dug up towards the shipheart's vault.

Your friend died here?

Yes.

And you still want to kill the one who slew her, as you agreed to?

Yes.

Good. Keot relaxed and the glow of the walls brightened. *Hate is good.*

"She died here." Nona crouched amid the scatter of broken rock. Yisht, a marjal with a rare talent for rock-work, had brought down part of the ceiling.

"Nona! Nona?" Distant cries from below.

She touched her fingers to the floor beneath the shattered stone. Had Hessa's blood spilled here? Had the nuns washed it away when they took her body? They had buried her down by the vineyards but left no marker. *We are all one in the Ancestor, our bones are nothing.*

"Nona?"

Nona reached for her clarity, watching the dance of an absent flame in the shadows of her mind. She looked for the Path and rocked back upon her heels. With Keot's vision the Path blazed red, written through everything, filling the air, diving into the rock and filling the hidden space beyond, writing itself across the surfaces and bringing each to life. Refusing to be distracted by the wonder of it, Nona strove to look past the Path's beauty to the periphery where threads stray. There in the depths of the earth she found a thread-scape that competed with Zole's for sparseness. Sister Pan said humans themselves drew threads from the Path, all life did. In the darkest and loneliest cave within the Rock, in places no person had ever seen, or would ever see, where no rat had scurried, no worm crawled, the Path would lie pure, bound tight. If that cave were broached then the mere act of gazing upon its secrets would set tendrils of thread straying from the Path, just as a foot set into a clear pool will raise silt from the bottom to cloud the waters.

"Nothing." The word tasted bitter. A faint hope can be nursed so long that when it dies the shock outweighs all reason. "Hessa would have found something in my place. *She* would have read something in the threads."

Keot remained silent.

"Nona!" The others sounded increasingly desperate.

"Coming!"

She almost missed it. Something at the corner of her eye as she turned. Perhaps without Keot she would have seen nothing. "What?" She turned back, reaching. A single black thread, so thin she almost thought herself mistaken even as her fingers tried to close around it. A black thread, leading from the spot where Hessa died, up along the shaft Yisht cut.

"There are no black threads." Nona reached to trap the thread between finger and thumb. Sister Pan said that using your hands was unnecessary, a childish affectation, like moving your lips when you read. Even so, it helped. Nona pinched the thread from the ground. "Ancestor!" Immediately a familiar energy trickled into her. Fingers first, then into her hand making it tingle. A fullness, a potential. It felt like . . . the shipheart?

That is not a thread from a corestone. Keot sounded interested though, moving entirely into her eyes, the pain so bad she had to grit her teeth against it.

What is it then? Nona pulled on the thread and immediately felt a peculiar sense of disquiet. Nana Even would have said, "Someone just walked over your grave." Nona leaned around the corner of the shaft, trying to see where the thread led, and picked it out easily now that she held it. It vanished into the rock. "That's where Yisht went!" The murderer had sealed the passage behind her as she went, her rock-working power amplified by the shipheart. Nona had hoped that her disembodied shadow had killed the woman—a hope that had survived only until she returned to the convent from the ranging with the other novices.

Are you so stupid? It's your own shadow . . . That is why you found it where others could not.

It's my shadow's thread? Nona stared at it. *Why does it feel like the shipheart, then?*

For that Keot had no answer.

"Nona!" Anger mixed with anxiety in the distant voices now.

"I can't just leave . . ." she whispered. "With the Inquisition here we might not get another chance for ages."

Take it with you.

What?

It's your thread. Take it with you.

So Nona did.

18

———— ✦ ————

ABBESS GLASS

HEART HALL HAD always been a lie, more so now the convent no longer housed the shipheart that had been entrusted to its keeping. Abbess Glass placed her hand against the door and frowned. Entrusted to *her* keeping. Abbess Mace they called "She of the Miracle." Glass knew what they would call her if her portrait ever joined the others. "She of the Lost Heart."

The abbess pushed through into the long hall where her sisters sat around the convent table. Tonight they waited beneath the watchful eyes of Brother Pelter and two of his assistants. Three inquisitors to witness eight nuns at table.

"Abbess Glass." Pelter inclined his head.

Glass took her chair. The seat beside it lay empty. Kettle's place. Sister Rail would have to take the notes this time. She exhaled and the air clouded. Every breath contrived to remind her of the shipheart's absence, of her failure.

"First item on the agenda?" Glass looked along the table. Rose, Wheel, Tallow, Rail, Apple, Rock, and Sister Pan huddled in her furs, dark eyes aglitter.

"I have delivered the Grey reports for the last five years into Brother Pelter's keeping, as requested." Sister Apple looked as if she would rather have poisoned the man.

"Thank you." Glass smiled. "And the ciphers?"

"And the ciphers."

The reports were fakes. Apple had for years been producing a copy of each report, altering, excising, and sanitizing.

The encryption she used differed from that employed on the true reports and the ciphers had been designed to be devilishly time consuming to apply. Glass wished Pelter and his subordinates much joy of it.

"Next?" Abbess Glass glanced towards Sister Wheel; she always had something to raise.

"Heresy." Brother Pelter stepped up behind the abbess's chair.

"Heresy, brother?"

"This whole convent is treading dangerously close to heresy, abbess. Your buildings may stand upon the edge of a cliff but your faith teeters at the brink of a far deeper chasm!"

"Indeed?" Glass steeled herself neither to rise nor look around. "These are grave charges, inquisitor. Perhaps you could elaborate?"

Pelter began to circle the table, staring at the back of each nun's head. "It is more a matter of attitude and atmosphere at the moment. Something rotten in the state of Mercy."

"Hearsay and heresy, though they may sound similar, are very different things, Brother Pelter." Glass set her elbows to the table and steepled her fingers before her. "A crime is built of specifics. Have you any of those?"

Pelter paused his stride. "The worst example so far has been in Spirit class."

"Spirit class? You amaze me!" Glass didn't have to pretend surprise. The idea that Sister Wheel might fall short in any measure of piety or protocol stretched her belief.

"There have been some questionable choices in the selection of saints to be studied." Brother Pelter looked grave.

"The novices make their own choice of saint for the Spirit essay." Sister Wheel looked outraged. "There are no works by or concerning heretics in *my* library. The Ancestor's library that is." She thumped the table. "I defy you to find even one."

"One of your novices is even now writing about Devid," Pelter said.

"Devid?" Sister Wheel opened her mouth but no further words emerged.

"Perhaps you could enlighten us, sister?" Abbess Glass asked. "I'm not familiar with the man."

"I . . ." Wheel's frown became a scowl. "I'm not . . ."

"Few people have heard of him," Pelter said. "Raised to the sainthood in the Onian period."

"I've nothing from the dark ages in the library!" Wheel shook her head.

"And yet there are books in Sweet Mercy that do not reside in your library," Pelter said.

A knock at the door forestalled any reply Sister Wheel might have to that. Sister Pail's head appeared.

"There's a novice who says she has important information for the table and that it can't wait."

Unexpectedly Sister Pan turned in her chair. "Tell her that it *can* wait and *will* wait."

Abbess Glass nodded. It paid to listen when the old woman spoke. "Tell—"

"She has Watcher Erras with her, abbess," Pail interrupted. "He wants Brother Pelter to hear her."

Abbess Glass sighed. "Send her in." Pelter would demand it. Better to give it to him and not lose face.

Sister Pail opened the door and Watcher Erras, a short man whose pot-belly strained his tunic, strode in. Joeli Namsis followed, looking demure, her gaze on the floor.

"Joeli? You had something urgent to tell us?" Glass fixed the girl with a hard stare.

Joeli nodded, biting her lip as if unsure.

"Well do tell us, novice." Glass motioned with her hand.

Joeli hesitated, a show of reluctance. "A trip-thread in the undercaves has been triggered."

"Intruders?" Glass closed the hand upon the table into a fist. But it wasn't outsiders. Sister Pan had wanted this kept quiet. "I hope it's intruders, Joeli, and that you have not interrupted the important business of the convent table to tell tales on fellow novices." She knew Brother Pelter would make his move sooner or later but this was too soon for anything usable to be placed into his hands. The abbess put every ounce of her will into the stare with which she pinned the girl before her. More woman than girl, truth be told, and far too beautiful for her own good. *Shut your mouth, novice. Shut your mouth and go away.*

On almost any novice Glass's stare might have had its desired effect but Joeli, full of earned grievance, natural spite, and the confidence that a rich family engenders, shrugged it off. "It's only, abbess, that I remembered how strongly you emphasized that the undercaves were off-limits. After, you know, the shipheart was taken. You said—"

"I remember what I said!"

Joeli proved relentless. "You said that anyone wandering there without permission would be banished from the convent."

"This sounds to be a serious act of defiance." Brother Pelter crossed the room to stand before Joeli. "How do you come to know of such a crime, child?"

Abbess Glass paid no regard to their play-acting. Pelter had started his career as house-priest to the Namsis family. He would have known Joeli as a young girl and still have close contacts with her father.

Joeli turned her wide green eyes towards the inquisitor. "I helped Sister Pan place the trip-threads and several of them are attuned to me." She paused as if waiting for a question. "So I know if anyone other than a sister crosses them, and who that person is."

"Who was it?"

"A novice, brother. One of our order, Nona Grey."

"And, Sister Pan." Brother Pelter approached the nun. "Did you not know of this too?"

"I did," Sister Pan replied testily.

"But you didn't think fit to mention it at table?"

Abbess Glass beat Sister Pan to a reply, well aware that her Mistress Path had been quite capable of levelling buildings in her prime and might still be able to turn an impertinent monk inside out. "We were only on the first item of business, Brother Pelter! You yourself interrupted the order to talk of heresy before we reached the second."

"There are no bad times to speak against heresy, abbess." Pelter folded his arms. "And the novice that was wallowing in it with her ill-advised writings on the dark-age saint known as Devid was none other than this Nona Grey we have just heard about." He resumed stalking around the table. Glass felt the jaws of the trap close around her. "And the punishment you prescribed for transgression was to be banished from the convent?"

"Nona is a three-blood! We can't send her out into the

world. That's madness." Glass drew a deep breath and released it slowly. "When I made that ruling it was a week after the theft. A novice had died down there. I said what was needed to keep others from getting themselves hurt."

"I agree with you." Brother Pelter nodded. He rounded the head of table, footsteps echoing in the cold air.

"I'm glad. Flexibility is what's needed." Glass forced herself to unclench her fist.

"I agree that we can't allow the child out into the world. She's too valuable. Others will seize her and turn her talents against the Church and against the emperor. Flexibility though? Flexibility is a toxin. The ally of heresy. It's flexibility that allowed this child to get hold of unsuitable histories in the first place. Rules must be iron. Decisions must be kept to. Decrees obeyed."

"We . . . I suppose we could strip her of the habit and keep her at the convent as a lay-worker. Perhaps a labourer in the vineyard," Glass offered. All along the table her sisters watched with mixed expressions, outrage from Tallow, horror from Rose, satisfaction twisting Rail's smile, confusion making something almost comical of Wheel's face. "Or in the pigsties."

"No." The inquisitor held his hand up. "Banished. That was the word. You cannot be banished and yet remain. And you cannot banish someone who can become so deadly a weapon in an enemy's hand."

"An impasse," croaked Sister Pan from her furs.

"No impasse, sister." Brother Pelter smiled. "We drown the child then throw her body off the cliff."

19

"GET YOUR COAT on!"

Nona looked up from the desk beside her bed. All around the dormitory novices stopped their preparations for sleeping or laid down their quills. Sister Kettle stood in the doorway, pale-faced, darkness smoking off her skin.

"Me?" Nona stood up, touching a hand to her chest.

"You." Kettle stepped into the room, glancing left and right. "You have to come with me." The points of a throwing star glimmered from the closed fist at her side. "Now!"

Nona glanced down at her feet. The slippers she had on were a gift from Ara, lined with blue-squirrel fur. She stepped out of them and reached for her shoes.

"What's the matter?" Darla rose from her bed, towering over the approaching nun. She rolled her neck, clicking bones.

"Gather what you need for a journey." Kettle knelt and started to rummage in Nona's cupboard. "We're leaving in two minutes."

Zole raised her head from between her bed and Mally's, abandoning her press-ups. "There is a problem." Not a question. "I will help."

"You have your own problem," Kettle said, still stuffing Nona's possessions into a hemp sack. "Tarkax is here to escort you to Sherzal's palace."

"No!" Nona had one arm into her range-coat and was struggling with the other. "Zole's one of us now!"

Kettle stood, tying the sack closed. "Not if her mother disagrees. Church over parent is Scithrowl heresy. The abbess can't afford to argue the case."

"Can't afford!" Nona realized she was shouting. "Can't afford?"

"I have no mother," Zole said. "And I wish to remain here." She stood by her bed now, a solid six-foot of killing machine, hard-eyed and ready.

"You stay there then." Kettle reached for Nona's hand and began to pull her towards the door.

"Wait." Darla stepped forward. "Where are you going?"

"Away." Kettle swept the room with dark eyes and shadows swirled. "I wasn't here." She set a finger to her lips. Her gaze settled on Crocey and Elani beside Joeli's empty bed. "There are worse things, novices, than the Inquisition. Consider that." A tug of her hand and she had Nona stumbling towards the door.

Together they hurried down the stairs. Nona dug her heels in as they drew level with the door to Grey Class. "What's going on? I don't want to leave!"

"We can talk about it outside." Kettle started towards the main door.

"Can't I say goodbye?" Nona jerked her arm free. She couldn't just go. "What about Ara and the others?"

"Ara and the others aren't in trouble." Kettle cocked her head as if hearing something. "Quick, come here!" She backed into the corner behind the main door, gathering shadows to her.

"Trouble?" Nona went to join Kettle and the nun drew her close, both arms tight around her as the darkness clotted.

"You were in the undercaves," Kettle whispered. "Joeli had trip-threads there."

"But . . ." A cold realization reached into Nona. "The shipheart wasn't thread-guarded . . . It washes those magics away."

"The shipheart isn't there any more."

Kettle put her hand to Nona's mouth as the door opened. Four watchers marched in, boots loud on the stone floor, a freezing wind whipping around them. They carried on up the stairs, not bothering to close the door.

"Stay close." Kettle tossed something out through the doorway. Nona heard it clatter on the flagstones off to the left. "Now." Kettle moved with hunska swiftness, wearing darkness like a robe. They slipped from the doorway, veering to the right, then pressed themselves to the wall. With the sun having set and night having fallen most of the way the two of them presented little target. "Over by the scriptorium," Kettle murmured. Nona saw a fifth watcher there, tight against the corner of the building. Her head turned towards the spot where Kettle's noise-maker had landed.

That one at least you should kill. Keot rose with the pounding of her heart.

"Move slowly. Keep close," Kettle instructed. "If I tell you to run then run. Get off the Rock. Don't come back."

"Don't come back?" Nona felt lost. "I need to say goodbye . . . to Ara."

Kettle pursed her lips in sympathy but shook her head. "They mean to kill you, Nona."

Let them try! Keot attempted to force her blades into being.

"Can't the abbess—"

"The abbess isn't in charge here any more, Nona. You have to go. Hide. Make a life somewhere else. Change your name." Kettle started to edge along the wall.

"Change my eyes?" Nona kept her place.

"If you stay here you will *die*."

Kettle moved off, the shadows flowing with her. Nona followed.

They reached the pillar forest before Bitel began to ring atop the Ancestor's dome, its voice harsh with accusation. Kettle led through the towering stonework, Nona close behind, eyes slitted against the wind-borne grit. The Corridor wind was re-establishing itself after the longest ice-wind Nona had ever known.

Neither spoke as they descended the long back and forth of the Seren Way, treacherous by day, foolish by dark. Nona slipped at the last turn, scattering loose rock over the fall. Kettle caught her hand. "Got you."

Nona regained her feet and shook free. "And now you're kicking me out?" The trail before them led down to level ground where field and forest stretched away from the Rock of Faith. The rising moon tinged it all with blood.

"They're after me too, Nona. Everything is falling apart. The abbess can't help us."

"We can fight them!" Nona rounded on Kettle. "They're just nine against us. I've killed more men than that by myself."

"And I wish you hadn't had to." Kettle looked down. "We can't fight them. They're the Church."

"*We're* the Church!" Nona shouted. "The Inquisition is nothing."

Kettle shook her head. "It's all one. All joined. What do you think Abbess Glass did before she came to Sweet Mercy? She ran the Inquisition. High Inquisitor Shella Yammal. That was before her son died . . ."

"No! I don't believe that." Nona backed away.

"We can't fight the Church." Kettle followed her. "What else would we have left?"

"Each other?" Nona said, eyes hot and prickling.

"Nona. You will always be my sister." Kettle reached out and caught Nona's shoulder. "The convent could fall from the Rock. Every holy book could burn. That wouldn't change." She put her other hand to the side of Nona's face, angling her eyes towards her. They were almost of a height now. "I'm going to try to make a shadow-bond between us."

"It won't work." Nona had seen Kettle call to Apple through her bond. The Noi-Guin used them too. "I lost my shadow."

"I'm going to try. And if you need me . . . you could call."

"Let's try." Nona attempted a smile. She couldn't twist her face right though.

Kettle took Nona's hand and interlaced their fingers into a tight grip, dark eyes determined. She frowned with concentration. The night thickened around them, blackening away the sky, swallowing the stars, leaving only the red eye of the moon. Kettle squeezed, hard enough to make the bones creak in Nona's hand. The darkness became a physical thing, masking even the moon. Nona felt it washing over her but sensed no deeper connection.

"It's not working," Kettle moaned.

"Try!" Nona stared at the place she knew their hands were joined. She stared until her eyes burned and the Path sliced through the blackness, everywhere at once, infinite, complex, filling the space, defining the surfaces, shaping Kettle from nothing with a multitude of glowing veins, a light that no darkness could touch. Nona stared harder still, seeing past the Path's brightness to the shining shroud of threads whispering through everything, strands freed from the unity of the Path.

"It's not working . . ." Kettle tried to release Nona's hand but Nona gripped back with all her strength.

A warmth rose around her. The focus approaching. They must have been locked in this embrace for hours! Anyone could find them. Inquisitors must be on their trail by now? Nona pushed away the sudden panic. The focus moon swept away Kettle's shadows and the Grey Sister cried out as if scalded. Nona wouldn't let her pull free. She remembered another focus, the heat bathing her and Hessa on the scriptorium steps on the night Hessa had thread-bound them both.

"It will work." Nona seized the threads around her wrist and Kettle's, without delicacy, taking all of them together, bundled in her left hand. She made a fist, and squeezed as hard as she could. And in that moment the focus moon blazed so bright it took the world away.

"WHAT HAVE YOU done?"

Nona opened her eyes to see Kettle kneeling over her, her face hidden in darkness.

"I . . . don't know." Nona struggled to sit. "I thread-bound us."

"Only two quantals can thread-bind. You have to share the blood." Kettle helped Nona to stand.

Nona put a hand to the cliff where the Rock rose from the plains. She felt too tall, as if her feet were twenty yards below her. "We do share a blood. We're both hunska."

Somewhere above them a scattering of rocks rattled down the slope.

"They're coming! Go!" Kettle shoved Nona towards the Verity Road.

"Come with me!" Nona heard the pleading in her voice and hated herself for it.

"I can't. Appy and the abbess need me. The convent needs me." Kettle bit her knuckle, hard. "I just can't."

Nona started to run into the night.

"I'll delay them," Kettle called in a low voice. "Stay safe, little sister. Be careful."

Moments later Nona was jogging along a rough track towards the Verity Road, everything she owned in a sack bouncing on her back, everyone she knew, everything she cared about, retreating behind her.

An hour later, running through rough fields of rain-lashed mud, she came to the margins of a wood and halted among the trees. The cold wrapped her, her stomach growled, her feet ached. An emptiness gnawed inside her, a sense of loss, of failure. She set her back to the trunk of a pine and the tears came. Racking sobs that hurt her chest.

She cried for an hour.

You should have killed her when I said.

Nona didn't have to ask who. Joeli had played her from the start. The girl had pulled her strings, her threads too, perhaps, but Nona wasn't sure of that. Joeli had goaded her into those caves, taunting her about Hessa, knowing the punishment, and knowing all the time that the moment Nona set foot in the place where her friend had died her intrusion would be known. Nona had been a fool.

You should have murdered her that first day.

Yes. Nona wiped her eyes and set her mouth in a grim line. *I probably should have.*

20

———◆———

W*HERE WILL YOU go?*
I don't know. Nona had no idea. Crouching in the margins of a damp forest wasn't a good long-term plan. It wasn't even a good short-term plan.

You'll need to steal food.

Probably.

You'll have to kill them.

Who?

The people you steal the food from. You don't want any witnesses to lead your enemies after you. Keot sounded quite cheerful about the whole thing.

Just a line of corpses to lead them instead?

You should go to the city. Keot had enjoyed their trip to Verity.

That's where the Tower of Inquiry is. I'm not difficult to spot. Sister Rose had tried to reverse the effect the black cure had on Nona's eyes several times, but none of her potions had any noticeable effect. Nona had been disappointed at the time but now those failures were taking on more importance. *There's nowhere I won't be discovered.*

In the east dawn made a sullen approach, shading the black sky towards grey. Nona's legs hurt, she was tired, cold despite her windbreak and range-coat, and her stomach had started to grumble even though she wouldn't have had breakfast yet.

"I'm going to have to leave the empire. I could take a ship to Durn . . ." She wriggled her fingers in the pockets of her coat, remembering that such things cost and that she had no money. "Or cross over the border into Scithrowl."

Or go back to kill Joeli, and then her friends, and the inquisitor, and his underlings.

Nona felt cold and tired rather than murderous. Joeli had been the architect of her downfall, but it was Nona's own stupidity she had used to do it. Still, given the chance, Nona felt she would enjoy breaking Joeli's other knee.

With the world revealing itself around her, Nona set off eastwards, cutting across country in case the Inquisition had guards on the roads. She dug a heel of bread from her coat pocket—she always kept some supplies against the possibility of night-time hunger pangs—and chewed as she walked. The world might have narrowed but it was still a big place and somewhere in it there would be a spot for her.

She looked back just once, towards the Rock where Ara and her other friends lay sleeping. "I *will* come back."

FOR THE FIRST day Nona kept off any track larger than a deer trail. She walked due east beneath a grey sky with the Corridor wind at her shoulders. At one farm she stole eggs from the nest box, quieting a mean-eyed hound with the whispering trick that Ruli had taught her. Some work of marjal empathy no doubt, though Ruli never mentioned the blood, just saying that the power was in whispering the right kind of nonsense.

Later she took a whole hen from the yard of another farm, wringing its neck and running when a fieldhand came shouting from an outhouse. She sat in her bivouac that night beneath a roof of branches and heaped bracken, staring at the bird.

You don't want it now?

I don't want it raw.

You ate those eggs raw.

I didn't want to. And this is different.

So cook it. Keot seemed disinterested but her hunger did appear to annoy him, as if he felt an echo of it.

Nona looked away from the heap of feathers, scanning the trees and the shadows gathering amid the undergrowth. All day she'd had the feeling she was being followed, but she was unused to such open spaces after years spent within the convent and it was likely just nerves that set the skin between her shoulderblades crawling, even when Keot was not sitting there.

Nona dropped her gaze to her open hand. The dark thread

that now bound her, however tenuously, to her shadow lay in the groove that her life-line made across her palm. The old women in the village had read palms. All of them except Nana Even who said it was superstitious nonsense, and read the entrails of rabbits instead. Nona knew that such threads could be followed. Sherzal's men had somehow followed the threads to discover Nona as a child, their thread-worker leading troops almost to her doorstep. But how someone pursued a thread Nona had no idea. Her shadow's thread didn't run through the forest like a trail of string unwound behind a cautious explorer. Instead, like every other thread, it led off at curious angles to the world, requiring steps that no feet of blood and bone could take if it was to be followed. If she were still at Sweet Mercy Nona would have asked Sister Pan and been taught the techniques required. But the convent lay miles behind and forbidden. The thread in her hand was less the solution to a problem, and more a reminder of what she had lost. Still, she would try to be open to whatever pull the thread might exert, to let it guide her. Perhaps it would steer her choices and take her by strange paths to where she wished to go.

SISTER TALLOW HAD taught the novices how to make fire with stick, twine and kindling, and Nona with her hunska speed had always been good at it in the convent. Out in the dampness of the forest though, with the wind complaining through the trees, it proved impossible to reproduce her success. Finally, with one of Clera's favourite curses, she threw down the stick, one end steaming gently, and let the wind steal what leaves and moss she'd gathered.

Find a peasant and take their fire.

If the last hut she'd seen were any closer Nona might just have followed Keot's advice. Instead she crouched and wondered what the others were doing back at Sweet Mercy. They would have eaten by now, stuffed themselves with stew and bread. In Grey dormitory Ara, Ruli and Jula might still be wondering about her. In Mystic dormitory Darla would be stomping around and Zole would be sitting silently as if nothing had changed. And Joeli . . . Joeli would be in her corner surrounded by her friends, laughing and joking about how she had got that stupid peasant run off the Rock. Anger flooded through Nona, sudden and unexpected in its ferocity, a red tide rising.

"I think I *will* have a fire."

Nona narrowed her eyes in a stare that looked past the world. The Path blazed before her as broad and clear as she had ever seen it and before her heart took another beat she threw herself at it. She struck the Path and ran its course as she had run once before when Tacsis soldiers had her trapped in a cave. The shock of the first contact rang through her as if she were steel, and on every side the glowing skeletons of trees lit within her mind, the entire forest caught in a flash, every twig and bough and branch, every angle, every tight-wrapped leaf. Before she knew it she had taken half a dozen strides and Keot howled across her back as if he were set upon the coals of a fire.

The sudden fear of what might come after sent Nona stumbling from the Path. You must own what you take, Sister Pan always said, and Nona had taken far more than she needed to light a fire, far more than she had ever taken save for that one day in the shadow of the Devil's Spine when she painted the rocks red.

Nona found herself sprawled upon the forest floor, the cold mud bubbling beneath her outstretched hands, her skin bleeding light and every bone in her body vibrating as if it desired nothing more than to shake free of the flesh restraining it. She thought of heat rather than strength, the same way they warmed the training room at the Path Tower, pushing the energy into the form she needed.

"Uh." Too small a sound for too large an amount of pain. Nona felt a heartbeat away from rupture, from having her insides very quickly become her outsides. In a sudden ugly gesture that Sister Pan would have roundly scolded her for, she wrenched the Path-given power from herself, ejecting it towards the nearest tree, a large screw-pine.

Something bright passed between them. The tree shuddered, a ripple ran along its length, shredding bark, and then in one moment of heat and light the forest giant exploded. The blast knocked Nona flat despite the shield of residual power around her. She might have lain there for a heartbeat or five minutes: time passed strangely and she couldn't tell. Keot was howling but her ears rang and, even though she didn't need them to hear him, his words passed through without her comprehension.

When Nona raised her head nothing remained of the tree and none of those closest were anything more than blackened trunks studded with the shattered stumps of branches. Further back, in the area into which Nona had been thrown, the forest burned in dozens of spots where blazing fragments had peppered both branches and undergrowth.

Don't. Keot sounded as if he were wheezing. *Do that again. Ever.*

Nothing of Nona's bivouac appeared to have survived. She glanced around for her chicken.

What are you going to do now? Keot demanded.

Nona spotted the bird's carcass, hanging in a tangle of briar, feathers smouldering.

She narrowed her eyes. "Pluck it."

21

◆

NONA ROSE WITH the light and left her shelter licking chicken grease from her fingers. She'd made a breakfast of the remains, taking the last of the meat from the bones. The Corridor wind fought its way through the trees, and on the boughs of frost-oak and elm leaves started to unfurl, eager to snatch up what the red sun had to offer.

The forest stank of char. In some places the wind had carried the fire a score of yards before the damp finally defeated it. Nona rubbed the cold from her bones and stretched her stiff back. In time she came to a woodsman's trail and followed it, bound east.

So you're still running away?

"I'm going home." Nona didn't know it until she said the words but at some point in the restless night her subconscious must have decided the issue for her and had set to waiting for her lips to part to let her know. "Back to the village where I grew up."

You're not grown up yet.

"Where I lived until I came to the convent." Nona strode on, unruffled by Keot now that she had a purpose once more.

BEFORE SHE HAD walked far enough even to lose sight of the forest Nona's thoughts returned to the fire she had made. Walking the Path had not come so easily to her since the day she killed Raymel Tacsis and Keot came to live beneath her skin, not since Sweet Mercy held the shipheart. She could have put it down to the depth of the anger that propelled her onto the Path this time, but there was more to it. She felt it in her bones.

Immediately before Nona walked the Path back in the cave where Raymel's men had them trapped she had been with Hessa, drawn along the bond threaded between them. And Hessa had been in the undercaves back at the convent, just yards from the shipheart. Somehow Nona had shared in that proximity and her quantal skills had been boosted by the stone's power. And now, once again, since she'd taken up her shadow's thread from the undercaves, Nona felt that connection to the shipheart's power. Just a trickle of it, but enough so that left untapped the potential would build and could be spent to magnify whatever strength lay in her blood.

Nona mused on the connection as she trudged between the cart ruts on the narrow lane she'd found. Somewhere out there the shipheart rested. Wherever Yisht, or more likely Sherzal, had placed it. To the east, she felt, not the west. And somewhere close by her shadow waited, trapped in some way, for unattended shadows are apt to wander.

IT TOOK DAYS for the land to grow familiar. Days travelling by back-roads, crossing fields and patches of woodland, but always she kept her back to Verity, to the Rock, and to the Tower of Inquiry. Whether there might be a search for her and how large it might be Nona had no real idea but she imagined they would likely be satisfied with simply having her gone, no longer polluting the faith or antagonizing the daughters of the Sis. She told herself that being forced to leave the convent now for breaking some silly rule was far preferable to being exposed as devil-tainted a year or two later, shamed in front of her friends, with all hands turned against her. She told herself it was a good thing, and tried to believe it as she walked the lonely tracks that would take her back to the village where her story began.

A dozen times every mile thoughts of the convent would slip into Nona's mind. What lessons the others might be taking now, what the nuns would say about her, how her friends would remember her when they came in sweaty and tired from the sands of Blade Hall. Each time the invaders came she drove them out with thoughts of the here and now, of the muddy ruts before her, the rustling hedges, the quick-wheat springing up even before the last ice-drift had fully melted. She watched the lone farmhouses, poor things huddled on slopes or in front of the treelines, as if expecting disaster at any moment. Twice she came to towns and skirted them.

The traffic Nona met consisted mainly of tinkers and farmers, the former carrying their skills in their hands and on their backs, the tools of their trade, the latter bearing the produce of their fields, be it on four legs following along behind, or stacked as bales on a cart.

Few of them passed a word with her and most of those few words were warnings. Warnings of Durnish fleets, their sick-wood barges packed so tight in the Marn that a man might walk across the sea from the southern ice to the northern without ever getting a foot wet. Warnings of the heretic hordes of the Scithrowl gathering behind their borders, whipped to a frenzy by their battle-queen. Nona nodded her thanks each time but robbers on the road and lack of food seemed more pressing concerns than distant armies.

She walked for half a day with an old woman who went from town to town sharpening edges—on knives, on plough-shares, on scythes, even on swords if such a thing were hung rusting above the elderman's hearth. The woman, Gallabeth, hardly reached Nona's shoulder, bent with age, all bones and uncomfortable angles. It took her three miles before she noticed Nona's eyes.

"'Cestor's Truth! Ain't you got no eyes, sister?"

Nona suppressed a laugh. "They're not holes, they're just black. It was an illness. And I'm not a sister." Not even a novice.

Gallabeth made the sign of the tree. "Thought you had the devil in you."

Nona opened her mouth then closed it.

Gallabeth shuffled another ten yards before ceasing to suck at her few remaining teeth and offering another opinion. "It's good you're a nun, child." Another shuffled yard. "Don't have to worry about a husband."

Nona had forgotten the uncompromising honesty of the ancient. Sister Pan had a touch of it but perhaps she still retained too many of her wits to let her tongue wander into unintentional cruelty. But Gallabeth was right. Joeli and her friends had delighted in telling Nona how ugly her eyes made her. How no boy would ever want to gaze into them. The old woman knew it too. "I'm not a nun." Nona made a mental note to cover up the sign of the Ancestor's tree seared across the back of the coat she wore, branches spreading above, taproot reaching for the source below. "Not even a novice."

Gallabeth waved the denial aside as if a convent range-coat and a glimpse of habit were impervious to dispute. "Husbands are overrated. I had one once. Oh yes. I was a pretty thing, long brown hair, good legs." She slapped them for emphasis. "Was married for twenty years, till the flu took him. He was still a young man, not far past forty. Didn't give me any children mind, or leave me much. Just a cottage too busy falling down to be much use, and this." She rummaged in her skirts and produced a dull grey object, like a river stone, dark and specked with glints of crystal perhaps, longer than it was wide.

"What is it?"

"What is it? Best whetstone in the empire is what it is!" Gallabeth returned the object to its place. "My John didn't leave me much, but this," she patted her hip, "was how he made his living, and how an old woman like me is still welcomed up and down the Corridor. His grandfather found it under the ice. Harder than nails. Can put an edge on a diamond, he said, though I ain't seen one of them . . ."

Kill her and take it. Keot flowed towards the hand nearest Gallabeth.

Why, what is it? Nona flexed the hand and kept Keot from passing her wrist.

Something old. A piece of the Missing.

A piece of them?

Ark-bone, not ship-bone, something older. Familiar. I can taste it.

"A useful thing to have," Nona said.

"Keeps me fed, long as I can move my legs." Gallabeth nodded. "And when I can't walk the roads I'll up and sell it to some youngster in Verity. Then I'll see how long I can buy a place by a warm hearth. I won't need long." A grin. "My John always wanted a child so they could carry both his name and the stone. A son or daughter to have it and walk the Corridor. Keeping it sharp, he called it. Keeping us all sharp."

Nona nodded. *If it's ship-bone or Ark-bone then it's not from the Missing.*

You don't know anything: you're too young to remember last year. Keot made a rush for her hand.

Nona held him back. *And unless you start making sense I have to assume you're too old to remember yesterday.*

Keot sulked after that, only twisting her last farewell into a snarl when Nona finally managed to leave Gallabeth behind at a farm that needed her services, or at least needed her stone. Nona didn't pursue the matter. She knew from experience that more than two questions in a row just set the devil talking nonsense. She'd come to think of him as a broken thing, part of a mind perhaps, filled with fragments of knowledge, occasionally useful as the shards of a pot can be, offering a sharp edge but no good for holding soup.

NONA'S RECOLLECTION OF the wider Grey, past the Rellam Forest to the west of the village and the bone-mire to the east was, like Keot's memory, a fractured thing. Giljohn had taken them back and forth across the Grey and out beyond, chasing rumour when rumour showed its tail, then returning to some long-established if tortuous circuit when the well of gossip ran dry. What remained with Nona were slices. A town skirted here, a hillside there, a ruin, a lake.

Eventually, following directions from another village almost as small as hers though bearing a name, Nona found her way to the Rellam Forest. The old man who had known of the forest, apparently by its ill-repute, also knew of her village and, miraculously, had a name for it too.

"Rellam Village. Aye. Ain't heard tell of that place for years though." He gave Nona a peculiar look, as if she might be testing him. But then everyone Nona met gave her odd looks. Your eyes might occupy only a tiny fraction of what you present to the world but they are what each stranger seeks when they meet you, as if needing reassurance concerning the person that watches through them. When you present two wells of darkness to the world the world makes the sign of the Ancestor's tree, or points a finger up across their heart to the Hope hidden above cloud-scattered skies, or makes the horns to summon the protection of the small gods who watch from between moments and under shadows.

Nona found that the unfamiliar track she had been directed along turned into a familiar one and led her through the arboreal gloom of the Rellam Forest where once she had run in the red mist of a focus moon. That time she had been chasing Amondo, her first friend and also a man who had betrayed her before they had even met. She paced the track with the woods whispering on both sides, remembering the juggler, the quick magic of his hands and the strangeness he'd brought with him into her life, a splash of colour, proof of a world beyond the boundaries of the Grey.

Nona had once told the girls at the convent a lie. On the first day she met them she had claimed that the bloodshed that saw her given to the child-taker was wrought by a wood-god upon the Pelarthi who captured her. There had been no Pelarthi. Nona had never seen a Pelarthi mercenary, only heard of them in Nana Even's tales. There had been no wood-god either—though she *had* seen one of those, a year before, watching her from the Rellam, his face almost like those twisted into the bark of trees. Almost.

The shadows on the forest path lengthened while the distance to open ground shortened. Nona fought to keep her pace from quickening. Around her the wood grumbled at the wind, creaking, groaning, always in motion. Nona felt eyes watching her and wondered whose they might be. A wood-god perhaps, ragged, leaf-clad, crouched in the boughs of an oak. Or perhaps just an owl, shaking off sleep.

Somewhere along this path she had murdered half a dozen soldiers. The troop Sherzal had sent with her quantal thread-worker, to guard him as he sifted through the world's threads in search of bodies in which more than one blood ran. The men who had hired Amondo to coax her from the village. How much had they paid? How much had it been worth to them to keep their business quiet? If Amondo had proved too expensive the soldiers would have just come in to take her. Their time was worth more to Sherzal than the lives of a few villagers.

Ahead, with the shadows of the trees slanting across the trail like cage bars, the green arch opened and the land lay exposed to the sky. Nona left the Rellam, still feeling the eyes upon her back, and followed the path up through the moor towards the fields and huts of her village.

IT'S BEEN TOO EASY. Keot burned across the back of her neck and she lowered her hood to let the Corridor wind cool him.

It wasn't easy. Though as she said it Nona realized that it had been. A walk through the empire's garden lands and into the Grey.

She said they meant to kill you. The dark one said it.

Nona shrugged. *Kettle was probably just trying to scare me into leaving more quickly and not coming back. They would certainly have whipped me and sent me from the Rock.* She frowned. Perhaps the inquisitors might even have thrown her into the Glasswater to add her bones to the bottom. But why would they pursue her once she'd gone?

Only as she closed the last mile did Nona's thoughts wander to the kind of reception she might find waiting. In her head the village had been an indivisible object, a ball of memories tight-bound, all or nothing. Now long-banished thoughts of her mother intruded for the first time in an age. Would she recognize her daughter? Would she be angry? Would she pull back from the blackness of her eyes, or open her arms with the mother's love that haunted Nona's most vague and distant recollections, soft, encompassing, safe, and forgiving?

You'll see it now. My village. Nona crested the low rise that the village knew as Heddod's Ridge. Her heart suddenly took to pounding as the land opened out before her. Her eyes tried to make sense of a scene that should have been familiar. At first it looked as if she had been mistaken and the village must lie over the next rise. The houses were gone. But here a spar stood, black and alone, there a scattering of tumbled stones, and everywhere the ghosts of pathways, covered now with grass and bushes, but clear enough if you knew where to look.

TURN AROUND! Keot's voice exploded into her skull.

Nona found herself obeying without question, but sluggishly, as if her mind were an anchor her muscles had to drag, still mired in the scene before her. With hunska speed Nona's body wrenched itself through the degrees, fighting inertia. Her head led the turn and out of the corner of her eye she saw the projectile's glimmer as it sped towards her back. Confused, shocked, Nona felt her grip on the moment slipping. She drove her flaw-blades out from the fingers of the hand she was reaching over her shoulder. The missile held her focus, thin as a nail, long as a hand, flighted, spinning, some kind of disk around the shaft an inch back from the tip, as if the bolt had pierced a copper penny on its way through the air. Somewhere back behind it a blurred figure stood in the roadway.

Nona reached for her speed. Even if she got her fingers to the spike she doubted she could slow it enough to stop it skewering her shoulder. It became a race, a yard left for the bolt, ten inches for her fingertips to intercept its path. Only her hand and the bolt moved. No heartbeat, no breath, no sound, no chance. The bolt came too fast for her to grasp it. Instead Nona turned the tip of the flaw-blade extending from her index finger, presenting the flat and angled side of the invisible blade to the bolt. Deflected, the bolt carried on, its path slanting upwards. It tore into the material of her range-coat a thumb's width above her skin, and came to a jolting halt there, stopped by the ridge set an inch behind the point.

Nona's eyes adjusted, bringing the figure on the road into sharp focus as she completed her turn. He stood twenty yards back, having emerged from the thicket of dendron bushes that flanked the lane. A tall man, grey-haired, gaunt in his heavy coat, a crossbow raised and bolstered against his shoulder, one eye staring down its length at her. He didn't need to close the other: the socket gaped empty, divided by a scar that travelled to his cheek.

"Damn." Giljohn lowered his crossbow. "I always knew you'd be fast."

22

---◆---

NONA TUGGED GILJOHN'S bolt from her range-coat and glanced at it. The disk was to stop the shaft penetrating too deep, angled so as to allow it to fly straight though. She wondered what venom it had been smeared with.

She looked back at the man. "Not going to run?"

Giljohn shrugged. He looked older than she remembered. "I had one chance. It should have worked. Now I have none." He frowned. "How did you know?"

Nona's turn to shrug. "Magic." She hadn't heard of any magic that would give you eyes in the back of your neck, but marjals had been known to manifest all manner of odd powers. She walked towards the child-taker.

Kill him!

"Are you going to kill me?" Giljohn shared Keot's interest. He looked resigned rather than worried. He made no attempt at a defence. The child-taker knew enough about hunskas to understand it would do him no good. "Well?"

"Honestly?" Nona closed the gap between them. "I don't know."

She stabbed him with the bolt, punching it into the meat of his pectoral muscle as far as the collar would allow. She had to reach up—the man was still a head taller than her.

"Ahhh!" Giljohn slapped a hand to the puncture wound. "Not like that you won't."

"No?"

Giljohn wobbled and sat down. "Groton paste. Fast acting."

"Where were you going to take me?"

Giljohn waved an uncoordinated arm to the west, shook his

head, and collapsed. He lay with eyes open, pupils dilated, watching nothing in particular.

Nona knelt to check the child-taker's breathing and pulse. It looked odd to see the man who had ruled over her, Hessa, and the others lying there like that, hair in disarray, cheek to the cold ground. For so many miles his rule had been absolute as he sat, his back to the cageful of children, Four-Foot plodding ahead of him. She relieved him of his pack and coin purse, then tied him hand and foot with the rope he had on him.

"That was foolish," she muttered, standing.

Yes. You should have cut him open!

I should have asked my questions before testing his own venom on him.

"Well." She looked down at Giljohn. "If you weren't going to kill me, then you must have a horse nearby. Probably a cart too. You weren't going to carry me over your shoulder."

Nona hefted Giljohn's pack then shook his purse. It hung limp with hardly a jingle of coins. She remembered it as ever-full, Giljohn emptying it with maddening sloth as he purchased a child here, a child there, for a scatter of copper pennies.

NONA SET OFF back along the path looking for any sign of tracks just as Sister Tallow had taught her. But in the end she saw not so much as a single hoofprint and found both horse and cart by exercising common sense and checking in the places she would have hidden a cart if she'd arrived ahead of a target she wished to waylay.

Giljohn had left his transport along the last of a dozen old charcoal burners' trails that led from the main track through the Rellam Forest. He'd made no attempt to disguise it, just taken it far enough to be hidden from the track. She stopped as she sighted the mule, grey and unkempt, and behind it the cage in which she had travelled, huddled between Saida and Hessa. Her friends. Now dead.

Nona untied the mule, pulling her hand away swiftly as it tried to bite her, and led it on, dragging the cart through the unwilling undergrowth. In time she found one of the charcoal burners' clearings and turned the cart before returning to the track.

Hefting Giljohn into the cage nearly broke Nona's back,

but she'd gained a lot of muscle since they had parted company at the Caltess almost six years before, and the years had pared the child-taker closer to the bone. Nona pushed his feet through the gate and closed it on him, knotting the rope to hold it in place. The mule snorted once then fell silent. She leaned back and stared at the ruins of the village with no thoughts, just the open fields around her, overgrown and turning wild, tugged by the damp wind. Above, the grey sky racing eastward, far to the south the smokes of Morltown smudging the air. The idea that her old home no longer existed wouldn't seem to fit in her skull no matter how she turned it. She might not have liked the place, but it was her foundation, the roots of her. She straightened and walked down the slope towards the spot where her mother's house had stood.

To call the remains of the village "ruins" was over-generous. "Traces" would be more accurate. In another five years it would be hard to tell the site where the people had lived from the spaces where they had grown their crops. Grey Stephen's house was a pile of rubble, soon to be swallowed by the rising turf. The stones of James Baker's home still showed; the lintel beneath which his wife, Martha, used to scowl at the world lay half-buried.

Little more than a stain amid the nettles marked where Nona's own home had stood. The wattle-and-daub walls had gone to nothing and the thicker timbers lay in ashes and rot among the grass, falling apart at a nudge of her boot.

It took another hour before Giljohn cracked open an eye. The Grey Sisters brewed groton venom from the gallbladder of a rare fish that seldom emerged from beneath the ice. It wouldn't have been cheap, or easy to obtain. As well as a rapid descent into unconsciousness the victim could look forward to a period of disorientation followed by days in which concentration would prove impossible. The Sisters used it if they needed to capture a quantal or marjal. No drug would safely render a victim unconscious for a week, but a dose of groton could deny an Academic the use of most of their magics for nearly that long, or keep a quantal from the Path.

"Where's my mother?"

"I . . . don't know." Giljohn blinked, spat, and tried to sit up.

"What happened here?" Nona waved an arm at the place where the village had stood.

Giljohn was too occupied with the rope around his wrists to reply, staring at it in fascination as if it might be made of gold and braided with gemstones. Nona repeated the question and he spat again, as if the venom had left his mouth sour, and laughed. "You happened, child."

"Me?"

"She probably would have done it just for the soldiers."

"Soldiers?"

"You killed five of Sherzal's household guard!"

Nona said nothing. The hunters had brought her back to the village wearing blood, almost enough to drown in.

"It was Onastos Hadmar that she did this for though."

"Who?"

Giljohn looked vague as if forgetting where he was.

"Onastos who?"

He shook his head. "Hadmar! Up in that convent of yours you forget how rare any sign of the tribes is. Quantal's the hardest of all to find. Not one in a thousand, girl. Onastos was a prime, wearing Sherzal's scarlet and silver. And you cut him up like meat. Sherzal's guard must have destroyed this place while we were on the road. That's all I know. It's the first time I've been back. I got here last night."

"So why didn't they come after me? Catch us on the road?" Nona's fists tightened at the thought, nails biting palm. *Let them come now.*

"I'm sure they . . ." Giljohn rolled over, trying to free his hands. "I'm in my own damn cage?"

Nona banged the bars. "Why didn't they chase us?"

"Damn!" Giljohn hit his head against the cart deck. "It's good stuff, this groton. Feels like I'm swimming through the world."

Nona banged again.

"They did chase us! I'm sure they did. But Sherzal got wind of a better prospect. Something Onastos had pointed her at, I'll bet. And she set all her guard on that instead."

Zole. That was Nona's guess. The Chosen One, saving her life before they'd even met.

"Who sent you, and how did you find me?"

"A number sent me."

Nona shook her head. The groton had his tongue.

"One hundred sent me. A hundred golden sovereigns."

"They posted a reward?" The size of it staggered her. Giljohn had filled his cage for less than one sovereign.

"Too big a number for me to ignore, girl. Old Giljohn's fallen on hard times. Yes he has. You and your little friends were the richest lot I ever hauled. Never found another like it." He rolled to his back, staring at the sky with his single eye. "And who better to hunt you? I knew where you came from. Knew you'd go back. The runners always do. Spent my last coin on something to keep you quiet, came here, waited. Thought my best chance would be when you saw what had happened. That moment of shock. Thought I'd be enough. One shot. One captive. One hundred divided by one. I gambled . . . I lost."

Kill him.

Nona frowned. Giljohn had rolled to her side of the cart and had the bars in his hands. "Where am I?" Confusion in his voice, the drug taking hold again. "I'm in my own cage?"

"We all are," Nona said.

"If you let me go I won't say that I saw you." Giljohn met her eyes. His clarity seemed to come and go in waves.

"You will if there's money in it," Nona said. A sadness rose through her. The village and the child-taker weren't things she had placed value in, or even liked, but they were *her* things, part of her own story, and you couldn't choose those, not when you were a child. Now they both lay ruined, each in their own way. Something had gone out of Giljohn. Perhaps it had left the day the high priest humbled him and beat Four-Foot to death. Perhaps it had left a little each year starting before he came into her life, maybe it had begun the day the Scithrowl took his eye.

Giljohn clutched the bars and stared at her, less than a yard separating them now.

Kill him! Even you should be able to see this one needs killing. He'll betray you without a thought. He was going to give you to your enemies!

You're right.

Nona focused and four flaw-blades shimmered momentarily as they sprung from her fingers. "You would have seen me killed, child-taker, just to put coin in your pocket."

With a snarl Nona lashed out. The bars before Giljohn's face fell away in sections.

"You won't hunt for me again."

The child-taker made no reply, only watched her as the blood dripped from a cut across the tip of his nose. Nona bent and scooped up one of the sections of bar, a wooden disk, narrower than her finger and about two inches across. She took the child-taker's purse from her pocket and put the disk in as if it were an oversized coin.

"Yours." She tossed the purse into the cage.

With that she walked away.

You're just leaving him?

Yes.

He would have sold you! Again!

Yes.

You're insane!

Maybe. Nona shrugged. *I do hear voices in my head.*

23

---◆---

ABBESS GLASS

"THE GIRL'S SAFE?" Even in the study of her own house Glass would no longer name her. They called the rank below inquisitor "watchers," but in truth they were more often listeners, and they were good at it.

"Safe's too strong a word for it," Sister Apple said. "But she's gone. My friend assures me that the girl left the Rock in one piece." Behind Sister Apple Sister Tallow said nothing but her shoulders relaxed a fraction. To Glass the fraction spoke volumes.

Glass nodded. Kettle would report to Apple from now on, and Apple would bring word to the big house. Nona would have the sense to run, though her instincts would tell her to fight. Kettle would have made sure the girl ran. Of course, she would run back to whatever collection of muddy sticks the child-taker had purchased her from. You didn't need to see much to see that. Even Pelter would guess as much. It would take the Inquisition a while to find the child-taker though—too long probably—and without him they'd never discover the village.

Sister Tallow coughed, bringing Glass back to the moment. "Abbess, you need to take action. Brother Pelter won't leave here until he's brought you down. If he can't find anything concrete he'll make his case out of innuendo and gossip. It won't matter."

"I am taking action, sister." Glass stayed at her window. "I'm watching the watchers." She smiled at the old joke. "I can see two of them from here. One is following Sister Chrysan-themum in the direction of the Necessary. I fear he may be disappointed if he hopes for any secrets to be dropped."

"I mean *action*! The high priest—"

"The high priest is struggling to hold on to the Church," Glass said. "The ice is closing, the emperor feels it. In such times trust is squeezed out and we gather power to ourselves. It would take no great leap of imagination for Crucical to take Nevis's mantle and declare himself high priest as well as em-peror. Nevis would rather lose Sweet Mercy than lose it all. He'd lose a dozen convents and monasteries and count himself ahead."

"Direct action then." Sister Apple tucked a red coil into her headdress, thoughtful as if choosing the right weapon for the job. "Pelter's just one man we could—"

Glass shook her head. "We must have faith, Apple."

"I pray to the Ancestor at the four corners of every day."

"Faith in me." A smile. Glass turned from her window and put a hand to Apple's shoulder, deepening her voice theatri-cally. "Grey Sister, you may pass unseen and drop poison in a cup, but my intentions are hidden deeper than any shadow goes. I can place *my* venom in any ear where words may echo." She reached for Tallow's shoulder and brought both nuns to her side. "Red Sister, you might punch through a door but when my blows are struck no castle wall will stop them, no miles will keep you safe." Glass spoke with a confidence she didn't feel, but she needed them strong. In any game of bets and forfeit the bluff was always of more importance than whatever might be written on the cards held tight against your chest.

"We have faith in you, abbess," Tallow said. Tallow always had faith.

"Be cautious though." Apple still looked worried. "Spend too long watching the long game and the short game will kill you."

DAYS PASSED, THE ice-wind broke, the fields shaded from white to green. It had been the best part of a week since Nona had run. Abbess Glass watched from her study window as she did every day. Her gaze settled on Novice Zole standing in the shadows by the base of the Dome of the Ancestor. "Come on, girl, what are you waiting for?" Glass spoke to an empty room. Zole should have made her move by now.

Glass shook her head. She seemed to do more watching than Pelter's watchers these days. It had been her first post in the Inquisition as a young woman: Shella Yammal, watcher. At first she had been tasked just to bring tales to the tower, whatever snippets of information passed across and around her father's market stall. But Brother Devis, her handler, had seen the talent she had for the work and had made her a watcher, an official appointment, recorded in the great books.

Zole stepped from the shadow now, intent on something. Glass followed her gaze. "Brother Pelter, Sister Rail, and Novice Joeli, a holy trinity." The three emerged from Academia Tower, heads bowed in conversation.

Three sharp knocks on the door behind her and Sister Apple came pushing through before the "come" was fully past Glass's lips.

"Mistress Shade?" Glass raised her eyebrows. Apple looked as if she had run all the way from the undercaves, hectic red blotches across both cheekbones.

"Kettle's gone!" Apple drew in a breath. "Something happened to Nona. Something bad."

"She went after Sherzal?"

"What? No! I told you. She's gone after Nona."

"I was asking if Nona had gone after Sherzal." Glass glanced back out of the window. Everything still looked calm. It wouldn't last.

Apple blinked. "Nona? Why would she? And how could she imagine she could do anything to Sherzal?"

Glass drew a slow breath, willing her impatience away. She couldn't expect Apple to think clearly where Kettle was concerned. "What kind of trouble was Nona in?"

Apple shook her head. "Kettle left a ciphered note. No details. She knew I wouldn't let her go alone."

"Kettle is a Grey: she doesn't require your permission, sister." Glass smiled. "Besides, that girl is death on two legs. Worry for whoever gets in her way."

Apple looked down, frowning.

"Additionally," Glass said, "it's probably safer for her out there. Sister Rock reports Inquisition guards and seekers approaching the Vinery Stair."

"Guards?" Apple met Glass's gaze, her frown deepening. The seekers would be to hunt out Kettle—rumour had it she still haunted the convent, and rumour was bread and butter to the Inquisition. But the guards, that one clearly puzzled Apple. Why did the Inquisition need its shock troops for Sweet Mercy?

"Think it through, dear." Glass pulled out her chair and sat at her desk. There were papers that would need signing. She paused, arm extended for her quill. Apple's intelligence had never been in doubt but the woman applied it too narrowly. "Imagine Pelter is making one of those poisons of yours. He selects his ingredients. He assembles them. He adds them, in the required order and in the required amounts. Not all at once. Some watchers first. Let things simmer. Some more. Stir. Wait. Then the next."

"But what's he brewing?" Apple's fingers moved as if imagining mixing ingredients of her own.

"I told you," Glass said. "Poison."

24

---◆---

I T TOOK LESS than two hours to reach White Lake. Back in
the days when her mother first left to go there Nona had always imagined it as distant a place as the moon. "It's too
far," her mother would say when Nona wanted to go. "Much
too far." In the end though she'd taken her curious child to a
handful of meetings at the Hope church and likely Nona
would have been confirmed in the light soon enough. But the
juggler came and everything changed.

For each mile Nona walked, her mind raced a thousand,
back and forth over the same questions, the same hopes and
fears. The people would have run from the village. Soldiers
would have fired the buildings but it would mean more if people ran to spread the news. To lift a hand against those in the
scarlet and silver meant your home would burn.

Her mother would have run. And she would have run this
way, towards White Lake.

During all the days that Nona had travelled to reach the
village her mind had refused questions about her mother. The
old hurt had scabbed over, been sealed beneath scar tissue,
and Nona refused to pick at it, not until it was time. But now
there might not ever be time and Nona's questions queued for
their turn on her tongue. Accusations too. But behind all that
lay the oldest memories of safe arms, warmth, love without
condition. Memories that Nona treasured, however indistinct
they were. A taste of something that she still sought.

The trail thickened into a track, the track into a road, and
she came around the margins of the White Lake, watching the
town on the far shore grow closer with each stride. Perhaps

two hundred homes hugged the water, scores more stepping up the slopes behind. Quays reached out, questing fingers probing the lake's secrets. A score of boats lay tied, half a dozen more heading in from the day's fishing. Here and there a light burned in a window, the first of many that would rise as the night fell.

Nona spotted the Hope church on the outskirts of town, a stone-built structure that should have carried a peaked roof but instead stood open to the sky. As she drew closer she spotted rooms adjoining the back, sheltering under tiles and timber. Presumably Preacher Mickel liked to sleep in a dry bed.

The light had all but failed by the time Nona came to the church doors. They stood twice her height and were supported by scrolling iron hinges. It had always seemed odd to have doors on a place with no roof. Nona listened but heard nothing save distant cries from the quays, and laughter on the road, perhaps at the sight of a novice of the Ancestor knocking on the doors of Hope. She dismissed the thought. Few in White Lake would recognize her range-coat as part of the order, and surely not from the road. She had smeared dirt over the sign of the tree scorched into the leather across her back, and it would take close inspection to see it for what it was.

She knocked. Nothing. Above her the sky was almost dark, ribbed by the red edges of clouds. Nona climbed the wall, using her blades only twice where the stonework offered no hold. She straddled the top and looked down into the church. A slate-flagged floor supported an altarstone at the centre; otherwise the place lay bare. At the services Nona had attended the altar had sported a strange globe of brass bands, something to do with pointing to the Hope when the skies were veiled.

She eyed the door at the back. *Must be where he lives.*

Keot made no reply. He'd kept silent since Nona spared Giljohn. Disgusted, she presumed. She felt him moving from time to time, sliding across her skin but going no deeper.

Nona hung off the wall and dropped down into the church. The memory of incense haunted the place despite the wind moaning in through window slits. She straightened and approached the rear door. Before she reached it Preacher Mickel bustled out, carrying in both arms the brass device Nona remembered. He kicked the door shut on the warmth and light behind him and crossed half the distance to Nona before registering her presence and startling to a halt. The bands of the globe slipped from his fingers. On instinct Nona leapt forward and caught the device before it could hit the floor. She straightened and held it out to him. It was heavier than she thought it would be given it was mostly air enclosed by just half a dozen strips of metal bent into interlocking hoops.

The preacher took his globe, his mouth working but no words emerging. Shock had replaced the fierceness Nona remembered. Mickel stood an inch or two taller than her. He was perhaps thirty years of age now, his dark hair still thick but receding in a widow's peak. "I'm looking for Myra from Rellam Village." It felt odd to give both her mother and the village a name. "She worshipped here."

"Who are you?" The preacher backed away to put the altarstone between them. "A demon?" He set the heavy globe before him.

Nona puzzled for a moment then raised her fingers to her face. "No, just a normal person. A poison made my eyes dark. Do you know if Myra Grey survived? What happened . . . at the village? Sometimes she goes by Myra Reed."

The preacher narrowed dark eyes at her. "You didn't move like a normal person. Hunska, are you? How did you get in?"

"I climbed."

The preacher snorted his disbelief and opened his mouth before glancing around. Perhaps lacking any more believable explanation he stopped short of calling her a liar. "You're looking for a woman?"

"Myra from Rellam."

"Rellam?" The fear in his eyes when he had thought her a demon had now entirely made way for suspicion. "What interest would this Myra be to you?"

"That's my business." If he didn't recognize her then Nona had no desire to identify herself.

The preacher touched the amulet hanging from his chain, a flat ring of grey metal, set with runes. "If this Myra worships here then she's my business. The Hope's business. What right do you have to ask questions here?"

Nona's temper lashed her tongue. "Right of blood. She's

my mother!" Subterfuge had always been a faint hope, marked as she was, and having shown her speed.

"Ha!" Preacher Mickel drew himself to his full height. "Now the truth comes out! Don't think I didn't know you, Nona Reed, standing there in your nun's coat with talk of blood-rights on your lips. The Ancestor-worshippers have schooled you well." A sneer now as if remembering the child reduced the warrior before him. "When we humble ourselves before the Hope we join a greater family than any founded on seed and grunting in the dark."

"The Ancestor-worshippers taught me that the Hope is just a star like any other, only younger and still burning white. It's not coming to Abeth. It won't save us from the ice." Nona flexed her fingers before her. "And they taught me how to beat a grown man to death with my bare hands if I need to. So, I'll ask again, where's my mother?"

"She has given up her spirit to the Hope." He said it with such poorly disguised satisfaction that Nona had to fight not to follow through with her threat. Had Keot seized his chance he might have tipped her into violence.

"She's dead?" Realization hit home and Nona's anger blew out, leaving her hollow.

The preacher's eyes flickered towards the door to his chambers. "You should go, nun."

"She's in there? You've got my mother in there?" The conviction seized her, the truth suddenly obvious, denial easy. Her mother couldn't be dead: there was still too much unsaid between them. They could speak now, as adults, not separated by that gulf between a child's ignorance and a grown-up's sorrows. She started towards the door.

"What? No! Of course not."

Nona was through the door before Mickel started after her. "Wait! That's forbidden!"

A corridor ran for twenty yards, three doors to the left, two to the right, and one at the far end. Nona glanced around, took the lantern from the wall, then ran for the second door on the left, which was heavier than the rest and bound with iron straps.

"She's not in there! Don't be stupid!" Mickel came flapping through the church door after her. He sounded as though he were hiding something.

Nona reached for her serenity so that she could pull the lock's thread but waves of emotion pushed her back, a turbulence she couldn't still. With the preacher closing on her she punched a flaw-blade into the heavy lock, once, twice, three times, then turned it. The ruined mechanism surrendered with a squeal and, shrugging off Mickel's grasping fingers, she pushed through.

The room beyond was a small one, windowless, with a broad shelf set at waist height running around three walls. An image of the Hope returned the lantern light, sparkling in a thousand pieces of glass, mirror, and crystal. Scores of objects covered the shelf, arranged with reverence rather than scattered.

"I thought—" Nona let the preacher wrestle her back into the corridor. Her mother was dead. Her denial had been stupid. "I'm sorry."

"Sorry?" Mickel shoved her back against the wall. "You've defiled the Hope's sanctum! And broken my door . . ."

Images of Nona's mother filled her mind. The hurt was worse than a wire-whip. She needed something, anything, to drive the memories out. Questions might help. "What *is* all that stuff?" Nona tried to see past the preacher's shoulder.

Pieces of the old world. Keot broke his silence.

"Treasures." The preacher tried to push her down the corridor towards the rear exit.

"I saw black-skin . . ." Red Sisters made their armour from black-skin, the oily sheen of the stuff was unmistakable. Even the scrap among Mickel's treasures would be worth more than the building. "And . . ." Nona didn't have names for the rest of the things but some of them had the same grey glinting quality of old Gallabeth's precious whetstone. "Ark-bone."

The preacher had her by the hood of her range-coat, pulling her to the back door. He lifted the bar and kicked it open. "They are parts of the ships that carried our tribes here across the black sea between the stars, and parts of the works they built here. When the Hope comes he will make them whole again just as he will bind flesh to bone and raise the dead from their graves to live once more."

He pushed Nona out into the blustery night. She put her foot against the door as he tried to haul it closed.

"Where does it come from?"

"It's the gift of the Hope." Mickel tugged the door again. Nona held it open. One more tug and Mickel relented, hanging his head. "The Sis build their homes over the best of what remains in the Corridor. The emperors themselves built their palace above the Ark and bind the Academy to them with its power. We pay explorers to hunt beneath the ice."

"My father—"

"Your father sold my predecessor much of what we keep here."

Nona blinked and in her moment of surprise the preacher pulled the door free and slammed it between them.

Nona turned slowly from the doorway. The wind came laced with a cold rain. A graveyard lay before her, scores of headstones black in the moonless night. Her mother was dead. Her bones buried, waiting for the Hope. They would never speak again. Nona would never ask whether her mother truly sent her child away to save her from Sherzal's revenge. She felt nothing, only an emptiness that reached up from her chest to constrict her throat. She stumbled between the headstones, dazed, trembling with a hurt that had no centre to it.

Where are we going? You said you'd kill someone. That was the deal when I helped you win your game with the tree and the box.

Nona straightened. The headstones were thinning out now, the ground overgrown with bramble. A few buildings lay ahead, lights at their windows, more behind them, their number building rapidly towards the town. The hurt and loss that had taken her breath contracted into a tight ball of rage. "I *am* going to kill someone." She spoke it to the night and to the dead. "Perhaps a lot of people."

Yisht? Is she first? How will you find her?

"I'm going to Sherzal's palace and when I leave the emperor will only have one sister living."

Something punched Nona in the shoulder. She turned and stared back into the darkness of the graveyard, trying to find her opponent. Her fingers discovered something like a narrow stick standing proud from her coat and she yanked it clear. A black shaft similar to Giljohn's, but thinner. Another hit her just below the collarbone. Too late Nona dived for cover behind the nearest headstone. She could feel a stiffness in her muscles already, lock-up, the same toxin that Clera had jabbed her with on the day they parted company.

Did you see them? Keot asked.

No. The attacker had to be close: the darts couldn't be fired more than thirty yards with any accuracy, but Nona hadn't seen anything save blackness and hints of the graveyard. *I can't stay here. I need to kill them while I can still move.* Was it the preacher? Or had Giljohn followed her for a second bite at the hundred sovereigns? If she were properly prepared she would have a dozen antidotes in her habit, but she had fled the convent empty-handed. *Help me see!*

Keot needed no encouragement. He poured into her eyes and when the burning sensation dulled enough for her to un-screw them Nona saw a world on fire. She gathered herself, ready to spring. Belatedly she pulled out the second dart and stared at the yellow line of it for a moment, trying to focus her thoughts. They refused to order themselves.

Something . . . different . . . on this one . . . groton? Was it really Giljohn again, after she had spared him?

With an oath Nona flung herself from cover, the graveyard revealing itself in shades of orange. She could see no attacker, only a clot of darkness beside one of the larger tombs sporting a winged Hope.

Darkness? Keot saw through darkness . . .

A third dart came hissing towards her out of that impene-trable inkiness. This one at least she could see. She reached for it with the remnants of her quickness, muscles screaming in protest. Darla had once described her father coming home drunk from a military banquet. Nona felt as if she were re-enacting Darla's mimicry of her father's uncoordinated stag-ger. The dart slipped past her grasping fingers and sunk into her flesh just above her left hipbone.

"Oh." And she pitched forward into her own midnight.

25

———— ✦ ————

ABBESS GLASS

WITH SISTER KETTLE gone from the convent Abbess Glass had to rely more heavily on Mistress Shade's network of Grey novices for information on the inquisitors' activities. Apple used her most trusted and promising candidates for the Grey to observe Brother Pelter and his watchers. However well trained the inquisitors might be nobody knew the convent better than the novices who grew up there, and it was easy enough to keep an open ear in most corners.

"Here comes trouble." Glass watched Sister Spire cross the square, habit flapping around her legs, her walk close enough to a run that it might be called either. The abbess's window comprised a dozen panes of puddle-glass, their unevenness lending a flowing quality to the nun's approach. Sister Spire vanished around the corner of the building and Glass went to her desk to wait.

The knock came a minute later, evidence of Spire's urgency.

"Come."

The mistress of Mystic Class hurried in, her blunt face flushed, headdress tugged down across her forehead almost hiding the puckered burn there. Glass had discovered that the young nun had earned her scars carrying children clear of a house fire. The information had arrived the previous week in Archon Kratton's report on the mission to the Meelar territory. Spire had spoken of the blaze when asked, but made no mention of returning for children.

"Ancestor's blessings, abbess."

"And to you, sister."

"Novice Zole is missing!" Spire blurted out the words as if it were her failing.

"I see." Glass folded her hands, elbows on the desk. "Do we know where she might have gone?"

Spire shook her head. "She's taken her ranging equipment. Nobody saw her leave. One of the watchers asked me where she was this morning."

"Well, if the Inquisition didn't manage to watch her I doubt there was much you could have done, sister."

Spire pursed her lips. "You don't seem very surprised, abbess."

"I'm surprised that she stayed this long."

"You . . . expected this? You think she's safe then?"

"Safe? I doubt that very much. But she's a dangerous young woman. I'm sure she'll make a good account of herself when trouble gets in her way."

"Well *I'm* surprised. Zole was making such fine progress with all the mistresses. Even Sister Wheel! And she seemed very happy to have your permission for the ice-trial. Well, happy for Zole. She even smiled when I told her!"

"That I would like to have seen!" Glass picked up the papers before her, then looked up. "Is there anything else, sister?"

Spire looked surprised. "Well. Aren't we going to do something? We could send someone after her. Bhetna, I mean Sister Needle, has just taken the Grey. She could . . ." Spire hugged her arms across her chest. "I just hate to think of her out there all alone. I know they say she's the Chosen One, but she's still just a girl."

"There are many girls out there all alone, Spire. The empire is awash with children, lost, abandoned, orphaned. We will tell Brother Pelter. I'm sure he'll know soon enough either way. Doubtless he'll be keen to send agents of the Inquisition after Novice Zole."

Spire nodded, turned to go, paused and opened her mouth as if to speak, then closed it and left.

NIGHT FELL BEFORE they came. Sister Tallow preceded them, bursting into the abbess's office without knocking. "Pelter's at the door, he has his guards with him!"

"You're to allow him to go about his business, Tallow."

Tallow's eyes darkened at that. "They can only take you if you let them." She looked old, too thin, her habit loose around her, iron in the black of her hair now, but Glass knew what she was capable of. "Just speak the word."

"To set any nun in this convent against the Church, in my own defence, would confirm the worst suspicions whispered into the emperor's ear. If I were to use the Red and the Grey as my personal army it would only encourage Crucical to take them for his own."

Glass remained in her seat, watching the door. She knew how the Inquisition worked. Once it had been hers. Old Devis, the man who had recruited her as a watcher, had been ten years a watcher himself. Then fifteen as an inquisitor. After Shella Yammal came to work for him Devis's star rose swiftly. He rode her shoulders to the deputy's chair before she jumped him to become high inquisitor with Devis as her second. Had Able not died she would still be there, watching the world from the highest room in the Tower of Inquiry. But the loss of a child tears something from any parent. Often what is ripped from a mother's chest leaves her broken, a husk waiting to be gathered to the Ancestor. Always it will change her. But sometimes the person who sets aside their mourning blacks is a better one.

Three knocks at the door. Sharp, precise.

"Come." Glass knew a moment of fear. She had seen the horrors of the Inquisition up close. Nothing is as cruel as a righteous man. She had been righteous in her time.

Brother Pelter strode in, two Inquisition guards clattering at his shoulders, three more behind them, all gleaming in their armour, polished steel plates overlapping from neck to elbow.

"Brother Pelter, how may I help you today?" Glass returned her quill to its holder and stoppered her ink.

"Abbess Glass, I'm placing you under Church-arrest on the charge of heresy. You're to be taken to the Tower of Inquiry for interrogation."

"Heresy?" Glass pursed her lips. "Am I allowed a little more detail?"

"I've told you the charge." Pelter waved his guards on and they advanced around him.

"*I* would like to hear more." Sister Tallow stepped into their path. At her hip she wore her sword, a cruel strip of Ark-steel.

Pelter's guards stopped. They might be hard-bitten and well-used to violence—the woman on the right had a gerant touch and stood well over six foot, broad-shouldered with it—but all of them had heard of Mistress Blade at Sweet Mercy.

"There are questions to be asked and answered, Sister Tallow. Asked and answered in the Tower of Inquiry, a place that admits no lies." Brother Pelter stepped back to open the door. "A novice under sentence of death ran from the convent within minutes of that decision being reached at the convent table."

"That's hardly heresy!" Tallow spat.

"Holding any law above that of the Ancestor is heretical. And the novice had been encouraged to write in praise of past heretics whose histories have no place in any convent library." Pelter waved the matter away. "More importantly Abbess Glass placed her authority over that of the parent. Zole Lansis was to be sent to the ice against her parent's express instruction—expressed, I may say, through a judge of Verity's highest court." He turned his gaze from Tallow towards Glass. "And now the child has gone missing, an absence I suspect you to have arranged in order to keep your heretical control over someone you consider politically important at this time of heightened tension. The bonds of family form the branches of the Ancestor's tree. No cleric can take to themselves the authority to overrule a parent. Such practice is an abomination before the Ancestor, a crime worthy of the Scithrowl."

"Step aside, Tallow." The abbess stood. "You're to let Brother Pelter carry out his duty and arrest me." She raised her wrists.

The guards stepped forward, the oldest of them taking a symbolic silver chain from his belt and using it to bind the abbess's wrists.

"Abbess Glass." Pelter stepped forward now with his warrant scroll. "You are a prisoner of the Inquisition. Come with me."

"Let the sisters know, Tallow." Glass came around her desk, dwarfed by the guards around her. "And of course the Martial Sisters and Sisters of Discretion will need to take action if I *am* questioned in the Tower of Inquiry."

Sister Tallow frowned. "But you just said—"

"Ignore that, sister," Pelter cut across her. "Clerics of the rank of abbess, abbot, or above are entitled to refuse questioning in Inquisition outposts and indeed in most other locations, but the Tower of Inquiry is sanctified and sanctioned to put any cleric to question, even the high priest himself. Abbess Glass needs to improve her research."

Abbess Glass shook her head. "A high inquisitor, former or current, may not be put to question on Inquisition property. It's an old ruling passed after a succession of high inquisitors were removed from office following interrogation by their deputies. It appeared to be being used as a form of self-promotion. Fortunately the 'former' was added to the ruling in order to defend past office holders such as myself from having the Inquisition used against them to settle old debts. And as an abbess I am of course subject to Church law rather than secular law, so the judges' courts are not a fit place either."

Pelter, wrong-footed, began to bluster. "Where, pray tell, can an individual such as yourself be made to answer to heresy? You don't expect me to believe there's no place fit to host so eminent a person!"

"Of course not." The abbess smiled. "Take me to the emperor's palace."

"I'm taking you off this rock, that's for sure," Pelter snarled. He waved the guards forward.

"Have the sisters watch from a discreet distance, Tallow dear," Glass called over her shoulder as they led her out.

The inquisitor and his guards ushered the abbess down the stairs and along her own entrance hall to her front door. Glass drew a deep breath, preparing to face the day. Many at the convent had seen her paraded in an iron yoke by their own high priest. As humiliations went the silver chains of the Inquisition were not the worst.

She stood while the guards tied her outdoor robes around her shoulders. If Pelter took her to the emperor's palace it wouldn't guarantee Glass's safety but there was no place within those walls that rumour would not spread from. Rather than have Sherzal hand him both a confession and control of the convent, along with an excuse perhaps to seize any monastery he liked, Crucical would have the whole business unfold under his own roof before the disapproval of the high priest and the archons, before the Sis and the Academy. To Glass's knowledge Crucical wasn't even aware what was happening. It was one thing to grumble about not having the Red and the Grey answer your every whim, quite a different thing to wield the Inquisition as a political knife to carve out what you wanted. The latter required a stomach for blood. Lots of blood.

26

---◆---

IN THE BLACK and rolling confusion into which Nona woke she found nothing to hold on to. Her limbs refused to obey. Her eyes found nothing to see. Keot's words were distant, muted beyond understanding. The world moved and creaked and jolted and swayed around her. Something contained her. A box? And she was in motion. Captive and being taken somewhere?

Nona discovered herself unable to form sentences or coherent thoughts. Everything swirled around in her mind with nothing constant. When, in all that shifting chaos, she stumbled upon a way out, she took it.

Nona left the maelstrom of her poisoned thoughts to sit mute and watchful in the quiet place into which she had fallen. The eyes through which she gazed were not hers and looked where they wanted to, but they were sharp enough.

I've done this before.

Nobody answered, though she could feel another's thoughts all around her, pulsing back and forth between memories. Some thoughts spiralled towards action, others were discarded and began to fade.

I'm inside Kettle. We're thread-bound.

Nona watched a disjointed series of images roll past. Scenes from the Seren Way, nightfall in a forest, roads thick with travellers, wagons and carts queuing at a bridge. Sunrise over a river, watched from the prow of a boat.

While she tried to make sense of it Nona reached for the memories closest at hand, letting them run through her. It seemed that the memories around her were . . . *about* her.

Reading lessons in the scriptorium; the day she arrived and Sister Apple made her wash in the bathhouse, how small and skinny she'd been; the sight of herself jumping from one loop of the blade-path to the next—scores of others . . .

Nona took another memory, this one feeling fresher, still buzzing with energy. It jolted into her, filling her mind with sound and light.

"Kettle? Kettle, are you even listening to me?"

Kettle sat up, holding the sheet to her against the cold of the undercaves. Apple stood above her, a pewter cup in one hand, salt-glazed flask of the convent red in the other.

"What?"

"Did you want any more wine?"

Kettle glanced up at Apple, in her nightdress, red hair unbound and coiled around her shoulders. A moment later it was all gone, Apple, the bed, the cave, and Kettle was reliving Nona's fight in the graveyard at White Lake. The shock of the attack had drawn Kettle along their thread-bond to experience it with Nona.

Nona discarded Kettle's memory of the attack before the third dart that had brought her down. She worried that, if she let it, the memory would drag her back into the darkness and confusion she had so recently escaped.

Nona left Kettle's memories alone, feeling guilty for trespassing, both nervous and intrigued about what she might accidentally happen upon. Instead she concentrated on what the nun was looking at now. Concentrating inside Kettle's mind was easy, as if somehow Nona had left behind the poisons that kept her prisoner wherever her body was.

A boat. Kettle was on a boat, watching the bank pass by, bushes, stunted trees, fields beyond, low hills rising, the line of the ice in the distance, a white underscore beneath the clouds, so faint it could be imagination and nothing more.

"Nona?" Kettle's voice but Nona could "hear" the thought too, directed at her where she lurked in the darkness behind Kettle's eyes.

Nona tried to answer but found herself mute, perhaps not as free of the poisons as she thought, allowed to watch through

Kettle, a passive passenger, but unable to take any action, or speak with a voice of her own.

Kettle frowned. She knew something had changed. The bond that Nona had made between them was not something she understood but it was something she could follow. Kettle had been trying to shadow-bond when Nona had taken over and thread-bound them. Some element of the shadow-bond had become woven in and shadow-bonds were something Kettle could follow. She had shadow-bonds with Apple, with Bhetna—whom she must learn to call Sister Needle—and with Sister Frost. Kettle's bond with Safira had been cut years ago, the severing more painful than the knife that Safira had stuck her with. But no shadow-bond is ever truly broken. Since Apple had pushed her into the dark Kettle had started to hear whispers along that old bond with her former bedmate, hints of emotion, tugs of wanting.

"Nona?" she asked again. Nothing. But she felt the girl's presence. "Be strong, Nona. I'm coming for you."

Kettle glanced upstream. The river had been narrowing all morning and the first hint of rapids foamed white in the distance. The boat she'd hired wouldn't get much further. Part of her regretted not disembarking at Feverton that morning, but with the Corridor wind filling the sail the skiff could eat up the miles faster than the alternatives, even heading upstream.

"Here! Stop here." The River Ganymede fed the Swirl which in turn emptied into White Lake. Kettle had learned nothing in the town that she had not already seen when the sharpness of Nona's fear had torn open the bond between them, channelling her experience into Kettle's mind. It had been a revelation, far more intimate a connection than the shadow-bond.

Kettle pressed her lips together and hoped that details of her own private life had not been slipping back along the bond into Nona's mind without her knowledge. She pointed to a shingle beach at the outer curve of the river. The Ganymede had been angling away from the route she needed to take for some miles now.

"Right you are, sister." The fisherman and his girl set to grounding their craft.

"Ancestor's blessings on your journey." The girl brought a

loaf and cheese bound with cloth out of a wooden box at the stern.

"And upon your family." Kettle took the food with a smile and vaulted out onto the stones. "Safe return!" A wave and she was hurrying up towards the track that paralleled the river.

Kettle hunched her coat around her, not the range-coat of a nun, just the weathered garb of a traveller. As she walked, her fingers counted through the vials in their straps against the coat's inner lining, poisons on one side, antidotes on the other. She checked her weapons from sword and throwing stars to the smallest knife and envenomed pin. Her eyes stayed on what lay ahead. She kept her mind empty of worry and of speculation. She had already considered who might have taken the girl and reached no firm conclusion. To dwell on things, to circle them over and over on the road as she might at the convent, was to invite death. The Grey Sister lives in the now. Thinking ahead was something to make space for, to do in as safe a space as possible, not something that would push you away from the moment. Whoever had taken Nona could easily have covered their back trail, left a friend or two watching from the boughs of a tree, or beside the road, or standing behind the counter of a pastry stall in some market town, just waiting for someone to kill.

KETTLE WALKED FROM before noon until late into the night, pushing her body to maintain a fierce pace.

"I'll find you, Nona. I swear it to the Ancestor. I'll find you and make an end of anyone who seeks to stop me." Images of cut flesh swarmed forward from a score of memories, quickly pushed back into their places as Kettle focused on the road ahead. A moment's lapse and she centred herself in the now once again, watchful, taut, ready.

The nun slept that night in a farmhouse not far from Honour. A clipped halfpenny proved adequate compensation for rousing the tenants and bought her a room, a bed with fresh linen, plus a meal with meat and mead into the bargain. With her body fuelled, Kettle took to her chamber and set her traps. Finally she arranged the bolster under the sheets, then curled beneath her grey cloak, settling to sleep in the corner the door would obscure if opened.

A little later when the focus moon turned the blackness of her shutters into narrow bars of blazing crimson Kettle felt Apple's pulse along their shadow-bond. Kettle sent her own pulse beating back to Sweet Mercy, letting Mistress Shade know that she was safe.

Nona stayed watching, even when Kettle closed her eyes. She didn't want to retreat into her own darkness, to the confusion and nausea, the blindness and the pain, and yet, as the stuff of Kettle's dreams began to rise around her, Nona released her hold on the nun's mind. For though we may share some dreams, others we don't speak of, even to ourselves, and no one should look that deeply into another person without permission. Maybe not even then.

Kettle's dream rose, red, curling around her, and Nona fell, loosening her grip, dropping away into the chaos of her own mind.

27

⬩

NONA ROLLED ACROSS rough planks and fetched up against a wooden wall. Everything swayed, everything heaved.

A box. I'm in a box.

The darkness stank of her own waste; her mouth tasted vomit-sour. Light leaked in between the planks, razors against her eyes. Without instruction her body rolled the other way, one rotation before another wall stopped her. Someone had bound her hands behind her back.

I'm at sea.

You're being carried. Keot sounded deeply annoyed.

"What?" Nona tried to sit up and banged her forehead against the planking just inches above her face.

You're being carried in a small box. You've been in it for two days.

Nona screwed her eyes shut and tried to see the Path. Nothing. She flexed her arms and gasped at the agony flooding up them. She couldn't feel her hands, though everything else from her shoulders down screamed in protest. Her wrists seemed to be chained together. She tried to will her flaw-blades into existence, but whether anything happened she couldn't tell.

The light dimmed and Nona heard footsteps on stone, the sound of the people carrying her box, several of them. The noise had an echoing quality. Nona felt herself slipping away into the darkness again. She ground her teeth against the drugs, their poison rising through her like nausea. "I'll kill them. Every last one."

That's the first reasonable thing you've said. Keot's voice followed her into the muffling blackness. *Perhaps ever.*

NONA CRACKED OPEN her eyes an unknown length of time later. They had her on her belly, two of them at least, in a dimly lit room. One was clasping some kind of collar around her neck, the other putting restraints on her ankles. Nona twisted her head as fast as she could, lunging to take a bite of the nearest wrist, but her teeth snapped shut on nothing, the hand withdrawn too swiftly. Another hand pressed her head to the hard floor with awful pressure and the first person returned to fixing the collar.

"It is done." A soft voice without urgency.

Someone knelt on Nona's back, struggling with something. A sudden snap and a rattle of chain. Nona's arms slid to her sides, lifeless but no longer bound together at the wrists.

The three of them retreated a few paces. Nona tried to rise but her arms hung limp, the pain of returning circulation just beginning as pins and needles, running down her veins.

The first bucket of water took her by surprise, ice-cold and sudden. She hauled breath back into her near-paralysed lungs and had begun to curse when the second bucket hit her with the third a fraction behind it. Somewhere in the middle of it all it occurred to her that she was naked.

"Roll over." The same soft voice, empty of mockery or compassion.

Nona lay where she was, shivering around her pain. She didn't think she could roll even if she wanted to.

One of the shadowy figures approached, bending low. Nona willed her blades into being to lash at the person's leg, but all that happened was that her arm flopped out from her side. Her captor stepped over it and, seizing her opposite shoulder, rolled Nona onto her back.

The figure stepped away again and several more buckets of icy water followed. When the last one had been thrown and Nona's spluttering had calmed she could hear the water gurgling away down a nearby drain.

"Stand."

Nona tried. With minimal help from her arms and unbalanced by waves of nausea and confusion she ended up pitching to one side whilst still on her knees and lay there shivering uncontrollably. Two of her captors pulled her to her feet. Both were dressed in grey robes with long sleeves, their hair shaved to a finger's width. Nona found it hard to guess their age or sex. Perhaps the one to the left was a woman, perhaps the one to the right a man, neither of them young, but neither old yet.

The third approached with a white linen smock that they worked to get Nona into. She noticed as they did it that she had metal bands around her wrists, her ankles too, presumably matching the collar at her throat.

Nona shook her arms, trying to get more life into them. She couldn't see much of the chamber. The only light filtered in through a barred window in the door. From what hints the gloom offered, the room seemed to be fairly small and bare, maybe a washroom.

For people who had gone to great lengths to abduct her and keep her incapacitated Nona's captors didn't seem to be particularly wary. She puzzled. They must know of her Pathwalking, and likely they would know of her blades too. If they had taken the trouble to find her they would have taken the trouble to find out about her first.

"Come." The tallest of the three walked to the door, knocked, and led through when it opened.

Nona followed, flanked, and occasionally supported, by the other two. A fourth person, similarly shaven-headed and robed, waited in the corridor and joined the escort. Nona supposed they knew how the drugs must still be affecting her and thus felt safe enough from any display of violence on her part.

Single candles burned at irregular intervals in niches along the corridor, just bright enough so that at the darkest spots a hint of the surroundings could still be seen. The doors that they passed looked like cell doors, heavy, each set with a small barred window and a large iron lock. Nona gave silent thanks to Hessa for showing her how to deal with those. Mistress Shade taught classes on overcoming the various mechanisms with a dozen curiously shaped picks, or a vial of acid, but Nona had never fared too well at these, perhaps lacking the motivation of those who can't open a lock by pulling its thread.

A sewer-stench hung around the corridor. Nona knew that she had smelled worse before they sluiced her. The stink put her in mind of Harriton gaol, whose bars she hadn't thought of in an age. Smells will do that for you, reach out and pull you back across the years. She remembered being walked along to the cells with Saida, two little girls, only one of whom would come out again with her neck unbroken.

"Here." The woman at the front—Nona was sure she was female now—stopped at a door no different to the previous half dozen. A key appeared from the woman's robes and once the door stood open she led the way inside. In the blackness against the back wall somehow the woman found a chain and locked the clasp at its end into the cuff around Nona's ankle. Nona considered kicking her in the head and making a break for it but she still felt weak and ill. Better to escape in private later.

Her four captors left without further words, locking the door behind them. Nona supposed that at least one of them must be a marjal touch with some shadow-weaving skill in order to perform their task in such gloom.

You're in trouble. Keot moved across her collarbones, stinging like an old scald.

"First I need to get this chain off." Nona tried to force her flaw-blades into being but nothing happened. "Bleed me! I'll try later. Unless you can do something to clean this muck out of my blood."

It won't make any difference. The collar and the bands are sigil-worked. I can't move under them. They must be to disrupt your abilities . . . such as they are.

"Hells." Nona felt the metal cuffs around her wrists. The sensation in her fingers had returned. The cuffs were heavy pieces of metal, hinged, locked, smooth except for where the sigils had been engraved in deep, swirling lines. Sister Pan had told her that to permanently imprint power into a sigil was an act that required far more than just marking the correct symbol. A marjal full-blood would have to train at the task for half a lifetime and even after such training the setting of a single sigil could take anything from hours to days, months for the most potent sigils. Sigil-marked armour and swords lay beyond the pockets of even many of the Sis. Such things were passed from lord to heir as treasures of the house. "If I get out of here wearing these I'll be richer than Joeli Namsis."

Nona leaned back against the wall, finding it cold and uncomfortable. Her body appeared to be made entirely from aches connected by pains. She retched then gathered her will and tried to find the Path. Her eyes saw nothing but darkness. She tried to defocus her vision, to look past the world to the network of threads that underlie all things, including darkness. Again nothing.

"I'm going to have to do this the hard way."

The bravado was for any ears that might be listening. It was also a lie.

"A LONELY TRAIL, sister. Are you lost?" The man stepped into the path from the treeline and Kettle's heartrate doubled from one beat to the next.

In a dark cell miles from the forested foothills of the Artinas Ridge Nona's head snapped back and what Kettle saw replaced her blindness.

"I'm neither lost nor your sister." Kettle ignored the woodsman, though her eyes continued to point in his direction. She drew in the halo of peripheral vision that surrounds what we see, searching for any hint of motion. Her ears opened to every whisper of the trees, every creak, rustle, or scrape, hungry for the telltale crack of a twig.

The one that allows you to see them is the distraction. The one that will kill you is hidden, waiting their moment. That was how Apple always opened the first lesson on ambush. It wouldn't take long for a novice to ask why they both didn't stay hidden and attack together. "Because in conversation you may reveal information that they are interested in. But mainly because you will be more vulnerable with your attention on the one before you," Apple would say, and she would lift her hand, wriggling her fingers in a puzzling motion. At that moment her assistant, Bhetna for the last few years, would rise behind the curious novice and lay a blunt knife across her throat. "As we have demonstrated," Apple would conclude.

"So, where would you be heading?" The trail behind the man lay thick with evening shadow.

Kettle spared him a moment's attention. He had pallid skin, short brown hair, pale eyes. His garb was convincing enough, but it didn't suit him. The hand-axe at his hip gleamed as if sharp enough to shave with.

Sometimes you need to wait for an enemy to reveal himself, sometimes you need to take the initiative. Knowing which to do, and when, makes the difference between those who live and those who die.

"I could give you directions?" The man seemed relaxed enough but his questions were too pointed.

"I've been invited to dance naked for the battle-queen," Kettle said. A nonsensical statement can create a moment of confusion in which the Grey Sister acts. A flexing of her wrist dropped an envenomed throwing star into her cupped fingers, the edges slightly dulled to avoid poisoning herself. Kettle was already turning as she released the star. She dived between the nearest trees, closing off as many angles as possible, scanning the confusion of undergrowth, the lines of the trunks, the branches interlocking against a purple-grey sky.

Kettle heard the thunk of her star hitting home: she'd aimed for his upper arm. There was always the chance he was simply a woodsman, and if not, she would want someone to question. Either way she didn't want him dead.

Two bolts hissed above her as she dived. Heavy bolts, not the knitting needles Nona had been hit with. The killing kind. Poor shots though. Hunskas could move with great speed but they couldn't fall faster than anyone else: the shots should have been on target and required Kettle to deflect them both.

Crashing among the undergrowth, Kettle saw flickers of motion between the trees, and not in the direction the bolts had come from. At least five attackers then!

Under the canopy the light was so poor that it would leave most blundering, but pushed into darkness as she was Kettle had no problem seeing. She scurried around the bole of the thickest tree on knees and elbows, a throwing star in each hand.

They came fast, silent, knives in both hands, weaving between the pines with hunska-speed. Kettle was faster. She rose, launching herself to her feet from her knees, spinning both her stars towards the nearest two attackers, waiting for them to get almost close enough for blades. At a separation of three yards and driven with the speed of a hunska full-blood Kettle's throwing stars allowed no opportunity for evasion. The left one would hit the closest woman somewhere in the neck; the right one would take the other woman in the right eye. Kettle was more accurate with her right arm.

Kettle fell backward, ripping two of her knives from their hidden sheaths over her upper arms—not her best pair for close work but the easiest to reach. She let herself drop since it was likely to be the last thing her opponents expected. Unseen attacks could be coming her way and the only defence was not to be in the place they expected her to be.

The first of Kettle's remaining attackers came at a flat sprint, daggers bared, showing some skill and remarkable night vision by avoiding tripping on any root or briar. Kettle could see the confusion in the man's eyes as she fell away from him. Her outstretched foot hit his knee. He toppled forward, blades stretched out towards her, the pain from his shattered joint not yet having reached his brain.

Kettle, her back thumping into the forest floor, extended her knives, points reaching for the falling man. She thrust between his arms, pushing them wider with her elbows so that his daggers drove hilt deep into the soil, missing her shoulders by an inch on each side. Her own blades punched into his neck, grating over each other as they met in his spine.

Both knives came free with a spray of blood and Kettle rolled aside. She was clear before her victim had dropped half the remaining distance to the ground. She saw the last two attackers closing as she twisted onto her front, facing them. Both were fast, and both had abandoned their crossbows in favour of swords. If they weren't hunska Kettle could have got to her feet and brought them down with throwing stars, but their speed promised they would hack her to death on her knees if she tried that. Hunskas would very rarely be shadowweavers, though. They would see little but confusion in the forest gloom. Kettle banked on their blindness and rolled to use the nearest tree as cover.

Both ambushers veered unerringly towards her. Prone, the advantage of Kettle's greater speed was considerably lessened. One ambusher swung to split her head but branches blocked the arc of his blade. The other, wise to the limitations of a longsword in woodland, thrust to skewer her. Kettle rolled onto her back again, bringing her knives up to deflect the thrust. She barely managed it and the blade sliced through her coat before driving into the ground.

In desperate straits, Kettle focused on the only opponent she could reach. Taking advantage of the momentarily trapped sword, she sliced one knife across the wrist of the hand holding it. The other she stabbed up into the man's groin.

The last attacker stood revealed as his companion doubled up, an ugly grin on his face, the point of his sword less than two feet from Kettle's chest. On her back, arms extended, she knew she had no real chance to avoid or deflect this thrust. But she gave no space to fear or regret, only gathered herself to try.

At the back of Kettle's mind Nona knew the nun had no hope. The man had moved with the speed of a half-blood at least. Nona, unable to help, or leave, or even scream, tensed for the blow. She would share the pain. It would be the last thing she could ever do for Kettle.

Nona knew that, even for those without hunska blood, at the sharpest edge of things the world would slow to a crawl. It might not offer you the opportunity to act but the inevitable happened slowly. Nona watched the point of the sword. It filled Kettle's vision, finding glimmers in the gloom. She watched the killer's face, met his stare, and knew those eyes would see the death of one of the few people she treasured and of her last hope.

When the man's face began to distort, bulging outwards, Nona could make no sense of it. When blood suffused his skin and began to erupt from eyes, nose, and mouth, both Nona and Kettle stared in vacant disbelief. Suddenly, as if their terror had released its hold on time's flow, the face exploded and a red fist emerged from the tumbling gore.

Moments later Kettle was on her feet facing a figure so wrapped in shadow that even her dark-sight struggled to make out any detail. The pair of them stood for a moment in silent regard. Kettle became aware of the moans from the groin-stabbed man by her feet, and of his hand reaching into his jerkin. She stamped on his neck, breaking it with a detachment that startled Nona. Her gaze never left the figure before her. "Who are you?"

The darkness smoked away by degrees. The newcomer stood of a height with Kettle, clad in a range-coat.

"Sister?" Kettle cocked her head, staring into the midnight still gathered beneath the hood.

The figure made no reply, only stepped back, shaking the blood from her fingers as the last of the shadows left her.

"Zole?" Kettle saw it before Nona did.

Zole pushed back her hood. She looked at her hand in distaste and wiped it on the nearest tree. "I do not think there are any others close by."

"Zole? What are you *doing* here?"

"Following you." She blinked as if the answer were obvious.

"Why?" Kettle glanced around at the trees that pressed on all sides, as if expecting more novices to emerge.

"Because you are following Nona."

"How do you—" Kettle abandoned the question in favour of "Why do you want to find Nona?"

"We planned to visit the ice together." Zole almost shrugged, turned away as if embarrassed. "She is the Shield. I am not supposed to lose her."

"I didn't think you believed in all that Chosen One stuff?" Kettle crossed to the first two attackers and stooped to recover her throwing stars with the aid of a knife.

"I do not."

"Why then?" The second star came loose with a wet noise.

Somewhere behind Kettle Zole spoke in a voice almost too quiet to hear. "She is my friend."

28

———— ✦ ————

NONA CLUNG TO Kettle's thoughts, refusing to let them slip. The surge of tension that had dragged her along their thread-bond now seeped away but a dark cell waited, and sickness, and boredom, and fear. She wanted to be with Kettle, out in the world, hunting down those who had captured her. Also, there was Zole.

Between them Kettle and Zole had dragged the supposed woodsman from the trail and off into the woods, taking him in the opposite direction to where the bodies lay.

The union between Kettle and Nona was weakening. Nona could no longer hear Kettle's thoughts or touch her memories, but she could watch through her eyes, feel through her hands, and listen with her ears. It was enough.

Night had fallen and Kettle had made no fire but both she and Zole wove shadows well enough to see in any natural darkness. Kettle secured the man to a tree using cord from her pack. She sat him with his back to it, hands tied behind the trunk. His head flopped on his chest. The throwing star had been coated with a resin based on the boneless brew that rendered its victims limp and unable to move. She removed the star from his biceps and bound the wound.

"You punched through that man's head." Images of the act flooded Kettle's vision. In a distant cell Nona winced.

"I walked the Path," Zole said, standing behind Kettle as she attended the captive.

"You could have just stabbed him. Or punched him more . . . gently." Kettle stood up and turned around.

"I did not know how many I would have to deal with. And I have not got a knife."

Kettle presented Zole with one of the daggers from her belt, a hefty piece of iron, nine inches long and honed to lethality. "Now you do." She smiled. "And thank you. I think he had me."

Zole said nothing, just scowled and flexed her fingers.

"You've not killed someone before." Not a question.

"No."

"You're right to feel it. It's not something to be taken lightly." Kettle put her hand to Zole's shoulder. The girl flinched but made no move to push Kettle away.

In the distant cell a frown creased Nona's brow. She tried to remember her first. One of Sherzal's soldiers that night in the Rellam Forest. She had been eight, perhaps. She had worn the blood of those soldiers into Giljohn's cage but any trace of guilt had washed off long before.

"Well." Kettle gave Zole's shoulder a squeeze then removed her hand. "We should find out who our friend here is and what he knows."

Kettle crouched and studied the man. The others had been similarly dressed in grey jerkins, dark trousers. Nona had little doubt they were the same order that held her captive. They had the same short hair, the same quiet dedication.

"I don't really have to ask what he is," Kettle said. "He's one of the Lightless. He's shadow-threaded, like me. I can sense it now I have a moment to concentrate. You can see it in him."

Now Kettle said it Nona could see it too and wondered how she hadn't before. The darkness moved around the man, a subtle thing, as mist would move around any other person.

"Lightless?" Zole asked.

"The Lightless are servants of the Noi-Guin," Kettle said. "Most of them candidates who survived the training up to some point but failed to prove themselves. They outnumber the Noi-Guin considerably. You don't often find them out and about though: it indicates that Nona has been captured by a

Noi-Guin. Also that either this Noi-Guin took Lightless with him and left them to guard his trail—which seems unlikely. Or that they guard this trail habitually. Which would indicate that we are near the Tetragode."

Zole had no more questions.

Nona had plenty but none of her efforts to get Kettle's attention met with any success. Nobody knew where the Tetragode was sited, though it was rumoured to relocate every two to four years in any case. But wherever it was the place would be impregnable. The Noi-Guin had survived many enemies over the centuries, a good number of them emperors. Remaining hidden might be their primary defence but it was far from being their only defence.

"I'll give him the antidote and we can see what he has to say for himself." Kettle reached into her pocket.

"Is there any point?" Zole kicked at the ground. "He will be sworn to silence. I do not know what tortures they teach a Sister of Discretion but will it be enough to break him, and quickly?"

"I know how to hurt someone." Kettle's voice was grim. She took out her boning knife and used it to cut a rectangle from the bottom of the man's trouser leg, enough to cover two splayed hands. Next she showed a pill between thumb and forefinger. "Antidote first." Lifting the man's head she put the pill into his open mouth, closed it, and raised his chin. She turned the man's head so she could stare into his eyes. "In a short while you'll gain control over your muscles again and be able to speak." She picked up the rectangle of cloth and waited.

Control came to the man's eyes first. A twitch, another twitch, and then a frenzy of darting this way and that.

"Your friends are dead," Kettle said.

Next his mouth recovered. He spat a dark mess at Kettle who caught it neatly in the patch she'd cut from his trouser leg. She moved back. The man kept spitting and gagging as if he had the foulest taste in his mouth. At the back of Kettle's mind Nona puzzled. The antidote to boneless tasted of nothing . . . perhaps a little salty.

"How far from here is the Tetragode?" Kettle asked.

"Ten miles." The man slurred the words, his muscles still

weak from the boneless. He blinked, a look of horror and astonishment coming over his face.

"We're looking for a girl who has been captured. Tell me about anyone who has passed this way in the last few days who might have had her with them."

The man's face contorted with effort but his mouth betrayed him. "Tellasah came through two days ago, she was leading a mule, the box on it smelled as if it held a prisoner, or a body."

"Who is Tellasah?" Kettle asked.

"She is a Noi-Guin, second order." The man struggled to raise his hands to cover his mouth but the ropes held him.

"Describe the entrances to the Tetragode and their defences," Kettle said.

"The main entrance is a cave at the foot of cliffs in the Grampain Mountains, half a mile west of the ri—" With a scream the man bit down hard and blood sprayed from his mouth. He gargled through it as if he were still answering the question but Nona couldn't make out the words.

Kettle glanced down. Between the man's gore-spattered legs lay a chunk of flesh. A large piece of tongue. Nona felt Kettle clench her jaw. A moment later her knife jutted from the man's left eye, his pain over.

"You gave him Mistress Shade's truth pill along with the antidote?" Zole asked, her voice as flat and free of emotion as ever.

"I did."

"How many more do you have?"

"None." Kettle pulled her knife free and wiped the blade on the man's sleeve. "It's not just a matter of rare ingredients, a powerful enchantment has to be used to bind them. Apple swapped favours with an Academic named Hanastoi, but no help from the Academy is ever cheap . . ."

"No point trying to capture another one then." Zole knelt and started searching through the man's pockets. "They must have a camp near here. What is your plan?"

"I don't have one." Kettle started back towards the trail. She paused. "How did you follow me without my noticing?"

"Carefully." Zole looked up, pocketing a few coins. "Do not feel too bad about it. I *am* the Chosen One, after all."

Although there was no hint of a smile Nona suspected that she might have witnessed Zole's first joke.

"We should take their robes." Kettle led the way back to the track. "If we can find any that aren't obviously bloody. And cut our hair like they do. You're almost there as it is." She glanced back at Zole's black and bristling thicket.

"You should," Zole replied. "You are shadowed like they are. I should be your prisoner."

"They won't buy it." Kettle reached the first of the fallen Lightless. The woods were thick with the smell of death, clinging despite the wind. "The guards will know this lot by sight. I can't believe there are so many out here that they wouldn't. And if there were that many then there would be passwords and such. Besides, we'll probably be spotted hunting for the entrance. I doubt it's obvious . . ."

"If we can get near I can make them believe we belong there." Zole flexed her fingers.

"Really?" Even detached from Kettle's thoughts Nona could feel the Grey Sister's doubt. "This isn't like Pan's classroom you know. These Lightless are—"

"Go home." Zole's narrow gaze rocked Kettle on her heels.

Kettle paused as if struggling with some reply, then without a word she turned and strode back to the track. Once clear of the trees, she turned to the left and walked back the way she'd travelled. Overhead the red stars bore witness and in the east the white eye of the Hope began to rise. It took perhaps fifty yards before Kettle's confident stride faltered. She glanced back, saw Zole following, and came to a halt.

"What . . ."

"I changed your mind," Zole said.

Kettle turned to face her.

"It was not easy, but a large part of you wants to go back to the convent anyhow, and I just helped it."

"Thread-work?" Kettle asked.

"Yes."

"Don't do that again." Kettle shivered. "At least not on me. What makes you think it will be easier on a Lightless?"

"Because they are not you, sister," Zole said. "You have a strong mind and it is well-trained. If you really did not want to do something I could not make you do it. But making a guard believe that you are a Lightless who is new to the order, or that the person next to them recognizes you should be easier."

"Should be?"

"Some people hold their threads more tightly than others." Zole shrugged. "I can also do this." She thrust an open hand at Kettle, who burst into laughter.

Even at the back of Kettle's mind, shielded from her emotions, Nona felt the echoes of it and in the darkness of her cell she smiled.

"Marjal empathy," Zole said over Kettle's snorts and giggles. "Sherzal had Academy tutors train me before I came to Sweet Mercy."

"I . . ." Kettle fought for breath, bent double. "You'll never need a punchline . . ." More laughter, before she forced herself to stand, still grinning.

"It works on you because you trust me," Zole said, no hint of a smile on her. "But with less guarded minds I can have quite an effect."

"I don't trust anyone." Kettle dropped her smile. "Not out here. Not on a mission."

"'Trust is the most insidious of poisons.'" Zole quoted Sister Apple. "But you do trust me, and you are not on a mission—nobody told you to do this."

Kettle frowned and glanced to the west, through the treetops. The moon's focus would be sweeping across the Marn by now, making the sea steam. Time was slipping away. "So that's the plan? Present myself at the gates as a Lightless with a prisoner and hope that because I walk in shadow it won't take too much of a push for you to make them believe it?"

"Yes."

"And then what?"

"Then we see."

"They're dangerous, these Noi-Guin," Kettle said. "They're like us, like Grey Sisters, but worse because killing is all they do. If just one of them spots us we're done for."

"The Noi-Guin are even spoken of on the ice." Zole rolled her head, clicking the bones in her neck. "They come after people in the night and murder them in their sleep. We are going into their home, where they believe that they are safe. If they find us we will see what they are made of. And show them what we are made of."

Kettle grinned. "And what's that?"

Zole did not smile in return. "Sweet Mercy."

29

------ ✦ ------

ABBESS GLASS

THE CARRIAGE THAT Brother Pelter had waiting for Abbess Glass proved to be quite luxurious. She had expected one of the usual black wagons with barred windows normally used to transport suspects but this one looked rather like the sort some lesser lord might own to bear him to the palace, although if the doors had ever sported a coat of arms the evidence had been expertly removed.

"For me?" Abbess Glass pursed her lips. "I'm impressed."

Brother Pelter climbed in and one of the Inquisition guards helped Glass into the opposite seat before joining her, another climbing up top. The other guards remained at the pillars as the carriage rattled away across the Rock.

"Two guards is all I warrant, brother?" The abbess inspected the silver chain wrapped half a dozen times around her wrists. "I'm not sure whether to be offended that you think me so lacking in threat or complimented that you have such trust in my good behaviour."

Brother Pelter made no reply, only watched her, cold-eyed. He had sent a rider on ahead, clutching a message-scroll, presumably to forewarn of their arrival.

"I suppose it might be of considerable help to some parties if I did escape." Glass sat back. "Nothing makes the Inquisition's job quite as easy as when someone declares their own guilt by running."

"Like the novice in the caves," Brother Pelter replied. "Nona Grey."

Glass shrugged. "Nobody was arguing over her guilt, brother, just her punishment."

EVEN THE EXPENSIVE suspension of the inquisitor's carriage proved unable to provide much comfort over bare rock and they bounced and jolted along. Beside Glass the overlapping plates of the Inquisition guard's armour rattled to the point of irritation. It proved something of a relief to begin the descent of the Vinery Stair where a layer of earth softened the road.

Glass leaned over and, with bound hands, adjusted the slats of the window shutters so that she could gaze out across the vineyards. Beyond them, farmland stretched until distance and rolling hills devoured the detail, merging the patchwork fields into a blur. The sky above lay pale and strewn with streamers of cloud running west to east. Sweet Mercy was said to have been built upon the Rock of Faith to raise the sisters above mortal concerns and let them focus their adoration upon the Ancestor. Now the everyday world had reached up its hand and plucked Glass from her eyrie. She settled back and sighed. She would have to see how well she remembered the ways of the worldly and whether she still had that old fire in her. She would most certainly need it.

Once on level ground the carriage began to bump along the Verity Road, past the hedgerows and farmhouses that Glass had so often looked down upon from Sweet Mercy's heights. A mile rumbled beneath the wheels, another followed, and Glass retreated into the ordered chaos of her mind. She had from an early age practised the memory arts often employed by Holy Sisters. The nuns used them when engaged within the scriptorium or required to recite lengthy portions of the family tree at ceremonies sponsored by some or other Sis family. Some archives of useful information she recalled using nonsense songs, often lewd, or rambling stories associating one fact with the next in unexpected ways that anchored them into her memory. For the disposition of the clergy and of the Inquisition however she kept a map, hung upon the back of her mind and ever-glowing. Each report that arrived at her desk brought certain players into sharp resolution, their location at a particular time and place assured, their current whereabouts diffusing along likely routes and towards likely destinations as time blurred fact into speculation. The abbess received far fewer updates than she once had when the highest seat in the Tower of Inquiry was hers, but information flowed into Sweet Mercy at a rate that would have surprised many a lord's spymaster. It came on feathered wings, on holy writ, on Grey feet and on Red; it came through shadow-bonds and thread-links; through couriered parchment in cipher or merely whispered watchwords; and it came through open ears in Verity, many patient and attentive ears, some devout, some mercenary, and all passing word to the Rock. Always it arrived unseen, often borne by the return of carts that carried the barrels and bottles of Sweet Mercy red to the great and the good up and down the length of the empire.

The carriage rumbled to a halt, jolting Glass from her inspection of imaginary maps. She frowned, wondering if the road ahead were blocked. The driver rapped four times on the roof and the guard beside the abbess leaned forward to open the door.

"Abbess Glass, how wonderful to see you." Lord Thuran Tacsis clambered in as Brother Pelter vacated the opposite seat to squeeze beside Glass.

Thuran shared little in appearance with his sons, being neither golden and handsome as Raymel had been, nor dark and lean as Lano was. A portly man of no great height, he would barely reach his elder son's ribs. A florid face, that seemed unlikely ever to have been handsome, gave over to a thick grey beard. He was smiling as he took his seat. A second man climbed in behind Thuran, a man in his forties with a thick head of dark blond hair and a luxurious blue robe. Taking his place beside Thuran, he fixed the abbess with glacial eyes.

"Joen Namsis." Glass made a politer nod than decorum demanded. "You're a long way from home." Joeli's father kept estates close to the coast and was rarely seen in Verity's social circles save at the grandest of Tacsis flings.

"On my way to another engagement I received word that my daughter had been severely injured whilst in your care, abbess. High Priest Nevis suggested that I visit Joeli before deciding whether to remove her from the convent."

Glass nodded. "A broken knee. A nasty injury. And not one sustained during training." She offered her most sincere smile.

The girl's class mistress, Sister Spire, reported several of Joeli's friends injured on the same day, and Nona covered in bruises. The truth of the matter was pretty clear, and Nona must have been heavily outnumbered for Joeli not to report the incident, painting herself as victim. "Imagine, all that time practising punching and kicking and stabbing and slashing . . . and then poor Joeli hurts herself falling down the dormitory stairs." The carriage lurched back into motion and Glass peered through the slats. "Though if you're wanting to visit your daughter at the convent you'll find we're going the wrong way."

"We're only riding a short distance with you, abbess." Thuran Tacsis spoke up now, still full of apparent good humour. Glass didn't allow the mask to fool her. She knew the Tacsis lord as a cunning operator. He wielded considerable power at court on account of the family's wealth, but he had also inherited and possibly improved upon many of the skills his distant ancestors had relied on to make that fortune in the first place. "Joen must get to the convent and see his daughter. I've asked him to draw up plans for the running of the place in the emperor's name. In anticipation of Crucical taking Sweet Mercy from the Church, as he surely will once your guilt has been established."

"It never hurts to be prepared." Glass nodded. She wouldn't give the man the satisfaction he was so obviously trying to squeeze from her distress. "And will you be visiting the convent, Lord Tacsis?"

"I have other business to attend to." His smile broadened. "You should have let that child hang, abbess. It would have been a quick and easy death. Less than she deserved after leaving Raymel for dead."

"On that we disagree." Glass kept her tone light.

"I hope your chains are more comfortable than the last time you faced trial, abbess. I heard that they put you in an iron yoke and burned the flesh from your palm."

"It was me that demanded the candle and held my hand to it." Glass met Thuran's eyes.

"And again you kept the girl from an easy death. Drowning is not so bad, I'm told. Takes no longer than a bad hanging and hurts less. The assassin's knife would have been quick too."

"I didn't believe she deserved death, easy or hard."

"No. You had her trained to kill instead." A flicker of anger now. "And she killed my son!"

Glass kept her mouth shut, her gaze darting to the inquisitor and finding him peering through the window slats, studiously ignoring the conversation.

"And in the end, oh delicious irony"—Thuran forced the humour back onto his face—"it is your own order that she breaks and which sees her driven from your protection." He raised a hand to stroke his chin. "Imagine if she were captured out there somewhere in the Corridor . . . Do you think she would meet an easy death then, dear abbess?"

"I would think anyone who tried to capture that girl would be taking their life in their hands." Glass fixed Thuran with a hard stare, backed by a confidence she didn't feel.

"Imagine if she *were* captured," Thuran repeated, his voice soft now. "Do you think they would invite me to watch her die?"

"The emperor forbid you—"

"The emperor will never know." He lurched forward, roaring his words, flecks of spittle peppering Glass's cheeks. "Do you think *you're* going to tell him? Do you think it's Crucical's palace the inquisitor here is taking you to?" Thuran's face was now red and twisted, the rage he'd been holding back all this time let free in a sudden rush. "Did you think you'd won again with your forgotten laws and petty little rules? Did you, abbess? Did you?"

"I cannot be tried at the Tower—"

"You'll be tried in a palace, you sorry hag! You'll be tried in a palace, found guilty in a palace, and burned in a palace! Just not Crucical's. Pelter here is taking you to Sherzal! How do you like that? And while you're getting your just desserts I will be making sure that a certain young novice of your acquaintance is wishing with all her black heart that you'd let her hang or drown or even that Raymel had taken his pleasure, because she won't die easy, abbess, she really won't!"

Glass bent her head to hide the emotion she couldn't keep from her face. She stared at her hands and at the silver chain wrapped around her wrists but what she saw in her mind were dominos falling, endless lines of dominos, one toppling the next, lines splitting, splitting again, everything in motion, the complexity doubling and redoubling, the clatter swelling into a roar, the speed increasing, everything out of control.

It seemed so long ago when Judge Irvone had pronounced, "This is a poor decision, abbess," and she had replied, "Even so." And had with two words toppled the first domino.

30

———— ✦ ————

NONA SLIPPED FROM Kettle's mind into her own dreams, and from those into a fitful state halfway between sleep and waking. Gradually her eyes found focus on a single point of brightness and her body made sense of itself. She realized that the cold beneath her cheek was that of a flagstone and raised her head. She uncoiled slowly, groaning to herself.

A single small candle had been placed on the ground just beyond the sweep of the door. Already it had burned down to less than a thumb's length. Its only purpose appeared to be to illuminate the knife set before it on the floor. Nona squinted then sat back against the wall. A single object had answered most of her questions. A throwing knife of modest size, its pommel a plain iron ball, the grip bound from pommel to hilt with a thin strip of leather. The Noi-Guin had left the weapon. The same Noi-Guin who had failed to take Nona's life on her second night at Sweet Mercy, the Noi-Guin who had stabbed Kettle in the wilds while hunting Nona two years later and been hurt in turn, the Noi-Guin who had tried to re-enter Sweet Mercy by the caves; the Noi-Guin the holothour had driven away.

Was it a woman who captured me in the graveyard?

Yes.

The same one who came to Raymel's side after I sliced his neck? The same one who was sent to kill me?

Yes.

You didn't think to mention it?

How would it help?

Tellasah, that was what the Lightless had named her with the bitter taste of the Poisoner's truth upon the tongue he had bitten off moments later. She might well have been waiting close to the Rock, waiting for any whisper of her prey. How far had she followed Nona before making her move? Maybe for days. Nona had been headed in the right direction after all, and what better way to get your target to your lair than have it walk itself there? It must have been when Nona started talking to people in White Lake that Tellasah had decided to strike, worried that the novice would find companions or guides there and gain safety in numbers.

Keot circled Nona's neck, trying to find a weakness in the collar that would let him slide beneath. She ignored his efforts and found her gaze returning to the knife. It had been left there as a message. To put fear into her.

And it was working.

How ARE YOU going to get out of here?

Nona had been staring at the candle, and now as it guttered into darkness, wax consumed, Keot broke into the emptiness of her mind.

"I don't know." Prison cells and chains were much the same all the length of Abeth's Corridor. Simple and effective. Nona had no sudden inspiration as to how to defeat them. With the band off one wrist or the collar removed from her neck she would make short work of the rest of her restraints, but the things were made not to be removed without a key.

Why do you think they haven't killed you yet?

"Whatever the reason, it can't be good." Nona slammed her wristband against the wall. Despite her effort to hold her hand back it hit the stones too, skinning her knuckles. In the darkness she could barely see her arm, let alone any detail, but the wristband revealed no damage beneath questing fingertips. She checked the chain, first where it attached to the wall, then each link until she reached her ankle cuff. She tried twisting, pulling, swinging the chain against the ground. All with no result. She attempted to thread the chain beneath the wristbands but the links proved too thick and the fit too snug.

Animals in traps often gnaw their foot off to escape.

"I don't think I would get far hopping." The Poisoner had

taught them that all bonds could be slipped, but Nona suspected she had meant those on wrists rather than ankles, and with the bands fitting so tightly it seemed unlikely they would come off over her hands without taking most of her skin and breaking bones. Perhaps not even then.

Nona stared at the slightly darker patch by the door, all that she could see of the knife now that the candle had burned out. It would be a useful thing to have, but at the full extension of the chain and lying flat she was still yards short of reaching it.

"Tellasah left it there, and me here, so I would try to reach it. So I would know who had me and so that the fear would grow inside me."

Nona pulled off the smock they'd put her in. Immediately she felt the cold, as if invisible hands were touching her in the dark, pinching away her body-warmth. She felt more vulnerable too, which she reminded herself was ridiculous, given that she was chained in the dungeons of the Noi-Guin. She could hardly be more vulnerable and a linen smock would not preserve her.

Nona knew without trying that the garment wasn't long enough to reach the knife, but artfully torn it might be. She would normally slice the thing apart with an invisible fingernail. Robbed of her abilities, she resorted to brute strength. At first the material resisted her, but once she found a seam it ripped quickly. Within a minute or two she'd made the thing twice as long as she was tall and had torn additional holes in it, hoping one would encircle some part of the weapon.

The flagstones were gritty, grime-covered, and cold. Lying naked, flat out, Nona began to flail with her torn smock. Experience trying to grapple hidden and possibly nonexistent edges in the dark of the undercaves had schooled Nona to persistence.

A score of tries brought no success. Twice Nona thought she had snagged the dagger, only to gently increase the pull and find her smock returning to her without the scrape of metal on stone.

Again! Keot urged.

Nona threw the material out, drew it back, threw it out, drew it back. She threw again. It snagged! She pulled. The knife's weight resisted her. It seemed well entangled. She pulled harder. Somewhere outside, close at hand, something fell with a clatter . . . a small bell perhaps?

The door began to open almost immediately. Nona pulled harder. The knife resisted. She pulled harder still . . . and the smock came free with a tearing sound.

A figure stood in the doorway, one of the Lightless, framed by illumination that had seemed barely enough to see by when Nona had been escorted down the corridor, and now made her screw up her eyes.

The man bent down and picked up the cord that tied the knife in the cell to the bell that had rested just outside the door. He looked at her, lying there before him, his face too shadowed for any expression to be read, then backed out, closing the door behind him. A key turned in the lock.

A game. He was sitting just outside all this time. Waiting. Keot sounded grudgingly appreciative.

Nona opened her mouth to curse her gaoler, or Keot, or both, and finding she had no words sufficiently vile, closed it again. She levered herself to her knees and retreated to the wall, wrapping herself in failure, misery, and the tatters of her smock.

"A CORD." NONA wondered how she had missed seeing it. Even disguised and in a darkened room the cord shouldn't have escaped her. She had been trained to see. She sat up straighter, shrugging off self-pity, and applied her training, focusing on the memory of a flame, the start of the route into her clarity trance. Not every discipline she had learned could be forbidden by sigil-marked iron.

Clarity settled upon Nona, frosting across her skin, cleansing the darkness of ambiguity, and bringing every faint sound into focus as if the instrument of her being had been tuned to perfection. Nona isolated one sense then the next as Sister Pan had taught her, then brought all five together. She could hear the man outside the door draw breath, exhale, draw breath. The dark still hid what it hid, but those shapes it did offer were extracted and given meaning. Nona ran her fingertips across her restraints, learning all their secrets, from the sigils cut into the curved iron to the details of hinge and clasp.

"Nothing."

The iron peg that anchored the end of the chain attached to her ankle cuff had been driven between two great stones in the wall, held there more by the weight pressing on the stone above it than by the mortar filling the joint.

Nona moved the chain to one side and pulled, bracing her legs against the floor and tugging slightly upward.

Every prisoner tests their chains. If they came loose then the gaolers would replace them with stronger ones. An untold number of desperate men and women have tested these cells before you and helped refine them.

Why don't you help me then? Nona replied. *When I die you're going back to lurking on the boundary where Raymel found you.*

There's nothing I can do. I can't make you stronger.

Nona put her head back against the cold stone wall. They had taken her blades, taken all of the marjal skills she had been working on in private. Her flame-work was still remedial, her rock-work hardly enough to fracture a pebble, but both might have been useful. They had shut her off from the Path and threads. All they'd left her was her speed.

With a lever I could turn this pin. Work it free. Nona imagined a steel rod narrow enough to slide through the eye of the pin alongside the last link of chain. With a long enough lever and a fulcrum a person could move the world.

You don't have a lever.

It doesn't have to be a lever. Anything that could wrap it, grip it, allow her to apply her strength further out to twist it. If she held the pin in her fist and tried to rotate it she could break her bones and not move it a degree. If the pin were fixed at the centre of a cart-wheel she could grip the outer rim and twist it with little effort no matter how tightly it was anchored.

You don't have anything else. Keot sounded as if he were already thinking of his return to the chaos he came from and of his next escape. Nona doubted opportunities came along often. Perhaps there wouldn't be another chance for Keot before the ice closed and the moon fell.

Nona began to wind the chain around the wall pin. After one turn the second layer of chain started to slip off the first. There wasn't enough pin exposed to wrap one turn next to the other, and no point to that anyway. She needed to build out.

Slowly and with enormous care she managed to wrap three turns around the pin, each layer of chain resting on the one below, but inevitably the whole lot began to slide, then collapsed and fell off the pin.

She knelt, the gritty stone hurting her knees, racking her brain for other ideas. How many prisoners had done the same before? How long had it taken before they resigned themselves to failure and sat helpless, shivering in the dark, waiting on the mercy of the Noi-Guin?

"I was in that convent five years . . . They must have taught me something useful."

They taught you to reach the Path. That's the only true power.

Nona frowned. "Actually they didn't. They told me to go slow, serene, approach it gently. I didn't have any success until I learned to use my anger. To run at it. Use my speed . . ."

She wrapped the chain around the pin again, slow, thoughtful. It slipped off.

I need to use my speed.

Nona threw herself into the space between heartbeats. In the darkness of the cell nothing changed save that the chain went from flexible to stiff, resisting motion at the speed she demanded of it. She began to wrap it around the pin again, forming an ever-widening coil against the wall. Unable to slip, because she gave them no time in which to slip, the layers of chain spiralled out to six inches on each side before Nona ran out of chain. She threw herself at the circular coil, with the wall pin at its midst, and gripped the outer edges, hauling to try to rotate the whole lot. With no time to slip, the links locked together and for one small fraction of a second the whole coil acted as if it were a solid, unbreakable body. A moment later the mass of links fell away from the wall, a shapeless weight of chain hanging from her fingers.

Did it move? A note of interest from Keot now.

Nona didn't know, but she got ready to try again. Struggling with a hopeless task in a dark cell might offer little comfort, but it beat thinking about that knife and what was coming.

31

THE GRAMPAIN MOUNTAINS rose in a ridge that crossed the Corridor. North and south the range marched into the ice, buckling the sheet for scores of miles until at last the ice grew deep enough to drown even the peaks. Many referred to them as the Empire Wall, tacit acknowledgement that it was the terrain more than the legions sent by successive emperors that took most credit for holding back the Scithrowl hordes for the last century.

"Sherzal's palace is not far from this place." Zole paused to scan the snowcapped ridge. She had abandoned her range-coat in favour of the jacket worn by the Lightless who had been pretending to be a hunter. They had managed to wash most of the blood spatters off and to disguise the rest with mud. "I'm sure I know these mountains."

Kettle raised a brow. "I've not visited the area. I crossed to Scithrowl through Windsong Pass, twenty miles north of here." Her gaze roamed the landscape of fractured rock ahead of them. Lightless watchers could be stationed anywhere.

A minute earlier a mountain goat had broken from the shadow of a boulder on the slope just above them. The shock had set Kettle's heart pounding, and the moment of panic had allowed Nona's awareness to push along the bond they shared. Kettle could feel the girl, watching from her eyes. Why they couldn't speak to each other she couldn't say. Perhaps the Tetragode had barriers that limited their contact. Either way, she hoped Nona would draw comfort from their approach. She tried to bury the thought that even with all the Grey Sisters and all the Red she would not be confident of breaching the Noi-Guin's stronghold.

"That peak, with the snow pluming off it." Zole nodded towards it. She couldn't point: her wrists were bound behind her, tethered to a rope Kettle held. "I am sure it can be seen from the palace."

"How sure?"

Zole paused before answering. "It is hard to say. It might just be similar, or appear very different from a new angle. But Sherzal's palace is on the western flanks of the Grampains and you can see the southern ice from her towers. It cannot be too many miles from here."

Kettle bit her lip, continuing to hunt the slopes. Even if Sherzal were only five or ten miles away it could take a day or two to cover the distance across the cliffs and ravines of the Grampains. It seemed unlikely that her troops would patrol the mountains in any number. The Scithrowl threat was always met at the passes. The invasion game was just a question of whether the enemy would try to force passage through the lowest and easiest pass, contending with the strongest defences, or pit themselves against the elements to risk a high pass and lighter defences.

"Let me concentrate a moment." Kettle stopped walking. She had been pursuing the thread-bond she had with Nona. Where a shadow-bond would give a sense of direction as the crow might fly or the shadow points, the thread-bond seemed to remember the path taken. But in the folds of the mountains' roots it had proved hard to follow, like sniffing out the vague trace of scent where someone had passed. Now though, with Nona sitting in the back of her mind, Kettle found it easier to discern her path. It wasn't really a sniffing, or a seeing, more of a knowing. Kettle felt her way through the options before her and let the right one draw her to it. "Down there."

KETTLE SPOTTED THE first watch-point a mile on. Then a second and a third. The Lightless observed her advance from rock shelters on the slopes above. Another mile of hard climbing brought Kettle and Zole to a series of steps so artfully made as to almost appear natural. They led up to the dark mouth of a cave at the base of a sullen cliff of grey stone.

From a distance the size of the cave mouth proved impossible to judge. The mountains offered nothing by which to gain a sense of scale, not even a stunted tree. As Kettle came closer she realized that the opening was actually a modest one, through which a carriage would have to scrape its way.

The ground at the base of the cliff proved fairly level, a shelf in the mountainside, carpeted with broken stone, frost-shattered from the cliff above. They trudged up towards the entrance, Zole stumbling from time to time to make herself appear more prey than predator.

"Stop!" Five figures broke from the cave mouth, grey-robed Lightless, four with crossbows. In the midst of her clarity-trance Kettle took them all in, down to the heavy bolts in the bows of the two to the left and the fanned needle-clusters in the bows of those on the right. A shot from either of those crossbows would launch a funnel of a dozen or more poisoned darts, making evasion or deflection near impossible. "Who are you?"

Kettle had been wishing, ever since the Lightless who pretended to be a woodsman had bitten out his tongue, that she had asked the names of his companions. Her knowledge of the Noi-Guin was substantial compared to the rumour and myth that most people laid claim to, but it didn't extend to knowing if their servants adopted new names and adhered to any particular convention.

"Mai," she said. It's easier to lie when you're telling the truth. "I've brought this prisoner for Tellasah to interrogate. She has information about the convent." Kettle raised her head to dispel any suspicion that she was hiding beneath the hood of the robe she'd taken from the Lightless. She reached out to shove Zole's shoulder, sending her stumbling forward, getting the girl closer so that she might work the magic she'd claimed would make this ruse succeed.

Four crossbows lifted, four fingers tightened on triggers. Back in the cave, that looked to broaden as it went on rather than to narrow, Kettle caught other motion.

"Come here, you!" Kettle pulled on the rope, making a show of holding Zole back whilst at the same time letting her close another yard on the five Lightless immediately before her.

"One more step and I'll have her shot, then you." The man

in the centre of the five watched Kettle with pale eyes set in a broad face. He overtopped six foot, his solid build apparent despite his robes. He bore no obvious weapon but darkness smoked around his hands. Kettle could sense the shadows around him. This one had been pushed further into the night than his companions, further than her too.

"Mai of the Lightless is taking me to Tellasah." Zole kept her face down and her voice was quiet but it seemed to burn through the air. Nona sensed it buzzing in Kettle's skull. "I am her prisoner."

Kettle felt the words building up, spiralling around her, demanding that she accept their truth. It was almost true, after all. It would be easier to believe it.

"Tellasah will want to see me," Zole said, her voice resonant.

"Tellasah *will* want to see her." The officer nodded. His pale eyes never left Kettle's face. The lack of malice in them worried her. Cruelty bred stupidity but the quiet dedication of the Lightless promised only efficiency, and success in attaining their goals. "Escort Mai and her prisoner to the holding cells."

The man indicated the cave and at his signal four more Lightless came forward. The first of them had a slightly puzzled look. "I'm to take this woman to the cells, Arthran?"

The man looked down at his subordinate, a frown creasing his forehead. "Yes, take Mai and her prisoner to the cells."

Kettle could see the tension in Zole's jaw as she stood, head down, some mutter on her lips.

The woman nodded and indicated that Kettle should follow her. Two of her companions moved to flank Kettle and Zole, the third bringing up the rear. "Come."

THE ENTRANCE TO the Tetragode opened out beyond the cave mouth into a natural cavern of impressive dimensions. A score or so Lightless occupied the space, some busy with a stack of barrels and crates near the centre, others armed and ready in natural galleries along the rear wall. Kettle tried not to look around too obviously but set that desire against the need to understand the challenges attendant on leaving again. She wondered briefly how the supplies came to be there. If they were brought in by foot across the foothills then the cost would be stupendous and the trail left for any curious party to follow would be hard to miss.

Kettle was glad of the escort in as much as it meant that the woman in front of her was leading the way. They had soon passed enough junctions for it to grow clear that becoming lost was a real possibility. She was less glad of the audience. It made little sense to her that her prisoner needed three extra guards here when the ideal time to escape would have been out among the foothills with just one captor.

The tunnels were natural, cut by ancient rivers, but shaped here and there by pick and hammer. The floor, where not level with the hard-packed sediment of those vanished rivers, had been evened out with rubble or well-secured planks. Wooden steps allowed easy passage up the steeper inclines.

The spread-out and labyrinthine nature of the Tetragode was perhaps as important a defence as the strong points, but did mean that most of the complex lay empty at any given time. The long galleries returned to darkness once Kettle's party had passed through and silence stalked them. The nun felt a sense of familiarity, having explored the caverns beneath the Rock of Faith at length, and behind those thoughts Nona added her own appreciation of deep places.

The first major checkpoint came as a small fortress built around the exit from a cavern that could have housed a large fortress. Lightless watched from the battlements and raised a portcullis when hailed.

In the long, stone-clad tunnel that led through the fortress a single Noi-Guin waited, seated at a desk set in their path. A score of murder-holes pierced the ceiling and the walls for ten yards before and behind the desk.

Where Kettle's attention focused discreetly upon the walls, Nona drank in the details of the Noi-Guin. Echoes of Kettle's memories informed Nona that the assassin who had tracked her on her ranging had been similar in appearance. Additionally, Sister Tallow's report to the convent table had described the two she fought outside the novice dormitories years before to be clad in the same manner.

The Noi-Guin's most striking feature was the black-skin mask that covered his face, with just a slit exposing the eyes and perforations at the nose and mouth. Taken from the hull of a tribe-ship, the stuff was as flexible as silk unless some object tried to move it too swiftly, in which case it became rigid and tougher than steel.

A close-fitting leather hood, descending to spread out over the shoulders, prevented Nona from telling how far the black-skin extended. Red Sisters who were hunska primes or full-bloods, as most were, would wear black-skin only over their torso as otherwise it could resist their fastest movements with unfortunate consequences. Also the stuff, being fabulously rare, was often in too short supply to be used more widely. The rest of the Noi-Guin's outfit was black leather, variously ridged or reinforced with iron plates. The dark grey cloak was presumably a concession to the enduring chill of subterranean life and shed when action was required.

"Where are you going?" The Noi-Guin studied them, his eyes like black beads within the slits of his mask.

"Arthran received this woman at the west-cave. He instructed me to escort her and the prisoner to the holding cells." The Lightless stepped aside, leaving Kettle and Zole fully exposed to the Noi-Guin's scrutiny.

"I don't—"

"I'm Mai of the Lightless." Kettle interrupted the assassin. It was better to break decorum than let someone state their opinion out loud. Once anything was spoken it became harder to change. "You know me, surely?" She stepped up beside her prisoner.

"You know her." Zole's whisper buzzed through the air. She stood, head bowed, the tendons in her neck rigid with the effort of working her geas.

"I know her." A whispered reply from all four of the escort. Kettle heard it echoed behind the walls too, coming down through the murder holes above them. "I know her."

"I don't know this woman." The Noi-Guin stood, though slowly, puzzled.

"You *know* her." Zole's whisper came more intense, bleeding through the air. Kettle had to restrain herself from shouting it out.

"I know her!" One of the escort yelled it, proud of the fact.

"No." The Noi-Guin raised an empty hand, as if fending

off the suggestion. The fingers of his other hand quested for the hilt of the knife at his hip. "I don't know you."

Zole changed tactics. She raised her head and her voice. "Your watch is over. Go to your beds. Now!"

Kettle couldn't help but glance at her. The ice-triber's face had grown pale, her eyes black wells. Her whole body trembled with effort and a trickle of blood ran from one nostril.

The Noi-Guin stood, seeming to struggle with the concept. Behind Kettle the four Lightless turned on their heels and began to walk away. From the sounds behind the walls, footsteps, doors opening, closing, others were also following the suggestion.

Seconds passed and still the Noi-Guin stood there while his servants walked away.

"Leave." Zole spoke the word through gritted teeth. The sound sunk into the stone, the command hanging between her and the assassin in the silence that followed.

The Noi-Guin closed his fingers around the hilt of his blade.

An instant later, without warning, as if something snapped, Zole slipped her bonds, snatched out the knife hidden beneath her jacket, and threw herself over the desk at the Noi-Guin.

Even Kettle, who had seen Zole training on dozens of occasions, was taken by surprise, shocked by the girl's swiftness. Both feet struck the assassin's stomach, driving him back. By the time Kettle had drawn her sword Zole had one hand around the Noi-Guin's wrist, controlling his knife while driving her own up into his armpit.

The Noi-Guin brought his arm tight to his body to trap the blade bedded in his flesh, and drove his forehead forward towards Zole's face. She twisted her neck to avoid the head-butt and, hooking her leg behind his knee, drove the man backwards to the floor.

Kettle lost sight of the conflict as she turned. Three of the four Lightless were still walking away. Their leader had halted in confusion. Kettle drew her knife in her off-hand and hoped that the Lightless hidden by the walls were already out of their compartments. With doors closed behind them they would be shielded from being distracted by the sound of the fight.

Moving fast, Kettle sliced the woman's throat from behind

and strode past without a second glance. Back along the tunnel an awful screaming started, so agonized that Kettle couldn't tell if it was Zole or her enemy. A moment later the nun caught up with the rest of the escort. She sliced two more throats and buried her knife between the vertebrae of the third. In the darkness behind Kettle's eyes Nona winced at the brutality of it. Without her own heart pounding, and without the imminent threat to life and limb, she found such killing much harder to watch.

Kettle spun around. The first of the Lightless had her hands to her neck, blood welling between her fingers, but she had yet to fall. Kettle raced past her towards the desk that stood amid the murder-holes. Behind it Zole and the Noi-Guin were still entangled, but the oak bureau blocked all save the flailing of legs.

The scene that greeted Kettle as she ran around the desk was a grisly one. Zole had trapped the Noi-Guin's knife-arm, scissoring it between her legs while she forced her thumbs into his eyes. His screaming ended suddenly.

Behind Kettle the first thump of a body hitting the ground echoed along the tunnel. Three more followed as Zole regained her feet. She wrenched her dagger clear and stood back from the spreading pool of blood in which the Noi-Guin lay.

Kettle blinked. "You killed a Noi-Guin."

"His mind was confused." Zole reached up to squeeze her forehead, wincing as if she had a headache beside which all other considerations, such as the gore her thumb was smearing across her temple, were secondary. "Do we have time to take his clothing?"

"Take the mask if it will come. But we have to move. The others will be coming. They'll have felt him die."

"How many?" Zole stooped to wrestle with the black-skin mask.

Kettle stared down the tunnel, all her senses open wide. Noi-Guin were shadow-bonded, not to a few closest to them, but each to the other in a great dark web.

"All of them."

32

---◆---

ABBESS GLASS

THE EMPIRE HAD always rested against the Sea of Marn. The roots of its origin lay tangled as much in myth as in history, but most scholars agreed that from tough and independent fisherfolk a tightly knit confederation of ports and coastal towns had grown. The midst of this proto-state had spawned the founder of the empire. That man, Golamal Entsis, had forged eastward, overland, despite his naval power and the saltwater in his veins. In fact, apart from short-lived strongholds established at vast cost on the Durnish shores and never held for more than a generation, the empire's history had always been one of driving east along the Corridor.

At its height the empire stretched seven hundred miles east, through all of what later became Scithrowl, and deep into the Alden, the federation of city-states that was now the Kingdom of Ald. The reversal had been swift. In the space of forty years and six weak emperors the border had fallen back against the rocky spine of the Grampains, and there it stayed, immovable.

Some now declared "empire" too grand a name for the territory currently held, and "emperor" too lofty a title for the men and women who took its highest seat. To Abbess Glass's mind, both titles had been earned through centuries of greatness. Even so, she had to agree that when the Corridor wind picked up its feet and raced eastward then the empire could be crossed at such a speed that it really did feel quite small.

Brother Pelter exchanged the carriage horses at various stops and had them driven hard. Along the spine of the empire lay metalled roads, built in the reign of Golamal the Fifth for swift movement of troops in time of war. They had been well-maintained ever since. Along such routes the carriage devoured the miles before it. Twice they took to the rivers, pressed upstream by the wind's hand, swapping to new carriages at the Patience Monastery and at the estate of the newest archon, Hedda. Glass felt at each stage as though they were fleeing something rather than just hastening towards Sherzal's palace. Perhaps Pelter worried that Red Sisters were in hot pursuit, bent on freeing his prisoner. No such rescue would come, though. Glass had forbidden it and, though she might never quite understand why, the loyalty that had grown around her came coupled with an obedience that was just as deep and enduring.

During the long days of travel Glass made conversation, or at least one half of it, and slowly the boredom, and the pressure of questions unanswered, eased Brother Pelter into supplying the other half. Glass sensed that the Inquisition guards, Melkir and Sera, who rotated from duty atop the carriage to duty beside her, would have liked to join in too. But Brother Pelter, whilst not following the stricture himself, had made it clear that nobody was to talk to the prisoner. And so Glass was left with only Brother Pelter to speak to.

She found the man to be almost exactly what her research had indicated him to be: ambitious, focused, easily flattered, and whilst deeply versed in the points of heresy on which most Inquisition trials hinge, his knowledge of the faith in a broader sense would not compete with that of any novice that Sister Wheel had passed as fit to move up to Grey Class.

"Do you know who the Inquisition's prime instigator was when I was high inquisitor, brother?" Glass lifted her voice above the clatter of the wheels and the drumming of rain on the carriage roof.

"No." The inquisitor frowned as if his ignorance on the matter bothered him.

"There wasn't one," Glass said. "The last holder of the office was Juticar, cousin to our current emperor's grandfather.

Juticar died holding the title. According to Inquisition records he attended three meetings in thirty-six years, although he was quite a regular at executions."

"Why are you telling me this?" Pelter fixed Glass with those eyes of his, perhaps his greatest asset, holding as they did something truly chilling, usually only to be found in the reflection of a brittle blue sky in deep ice.

Glass shrugged. "By my reckoning we'll be at Sherzal's palace sometime the day after tomorrow. So the office of prime instigator seems at least topical. It was a paper title, you see, an invention to please some emperor of long ago, an office meant for royalty, so that the Crown could feel . . . if not a sense of ownership . . . at least some illusion of control of the Inquisition and some more solid feeling that it could not be wielded against them. The raft of regulations protecting emperors and their siblings from the sharp edge of the Inquisition was part and parcel of it. Similar to those laws protecting high inquisitors."

"And *former* high inquisitors." Brother Pelter took on a sour look, reminded of the fact that such details had him crossing half the empire rather than hauling the abbess the five miles from Sweet Mercy to the Tower of Inquiry.

"Well, we can hardly make such a fuss about heresy, which is after all the business of following the details of the faith, if we're not prepared to follow our own rules elsewhere, can we, brother?" Glass smiled. "If you're happy to set hot irons to a man to establish the degree of his piety then at least you can endure a few days' ride to ensure you yourself follow the letter of the law."

"You'd do well to practise your penitence, abbess." In the light slanting through the carriage shutters Pelter's pock-marked face took on a somewhat monstrous aspect. "It's over for you and your convent. The Lansis will have what they want. You should apply yourself to the question of what state you will be in at the end of it. Ashes perhaps. Sherzal is fond of burnings. Not as a spectacle, but as a neat end to problems."

"Does High Inquisitor Gemon know what you've done yet, brother?" Glass ignored the threat. "Did any part of this come from his desk? Does the Tower even know where you're headed?

Or was this all Sherzal's bidding? The prime instigator . . . the office is well named for her."

"I've indulged you on this journey, abbess, but you will speak of the emperor's sister with respect! Hers is the voice the Inquisition listens to. Gemon's time is coming to an end."

"He didn't sanction my arrest, did he?"

"Sherzal's sanction is sufficient."

"So . . . Gemon hasn't sent any senior inquisitors for this trial I'm supposed to have? There should be three judges. I hope you're not thinking to adjudicate, brother? You're neither senior, nor threefold . . ."

"Sherzal isn't about to let Gemon send his favourites." Pelter smoothed down the grey tufts of his hair, a nervous habit. "We will recruit inquisitors of the required rank and number from the environs."

"Environs?" Glass asked.

Brother Pelter glowered at her.

"Oh," Glass said. "You mean you'll be picking my jury up along the way?"

Pelter gripped the seat, thrusting his face towards her. "We will present ourselves to the honourable Sherzal with a trio of senior inquisitors, abbess, and when they put you to the question it will be me who employs the iron, be it sharp, or hot, to discover the truth. So you would do well to rid yourself of any hint of mockery."

Abbess Glass pressed herself back, away from the fierceness of the man's face and the rank cloud of his breath. "Of course, brother."

As NIGHT FELL Pelter had the carriage put in at Treytown, a settlement of modest size, perhaps five hundred homes, many dependent upon the tin mines for a living. The place boasted a church of the Ancestor considerably larger than most such towns could afford and was able to provide lodgings for the inquisitor and his guards, along with a penitent's cell for the abbess.

Come morning the local priest unlocked Glass's door and she bore his disapproval as the yawning guards escorted her to the carriage.

"We're making a diversion today." Brother Pelter handed her the prisoner-ration, a brick of black bread that was supposed to last the day.

"Indeed?" Glass accepted the bread into her chained hands. She had been tightening the rope on her habit daily. If the journey had been all the way to the empire's old boundary out in the Alden she might have arrived with the figure she'd had at twenty, though she wouldn't have counted it a good exchange for all those hungry days. "Where to?"

"The shrine at Penrast," Pelter said. "I had Melkir and Sera do a little investigating around town last night. It seems that the Inquisition is following reports of heresy at the shrine. An investigation led by senior inquisitors . . ."

"Who will be useful in judging at my trial," Glass supplied.

"As I said, from the environs." Pelter nodded.

"And who is leading this inquiry?"

"Brother Seldom and Sister Agika. Friends of yours, I believe?" Pelter allowed himself a narrow smile.

Abbess Glass folded her hands across her diminished belly and pressed her lips into a thin line. Seldom and Agika had been trusted subordinates during most of her tenure in the Inquisition's highest seat, but the estrangement that had preceded the announcement of her departure had been the talk of the tower, and famously bitter. "It's when your power is taken, or given, away that you discover who your friends are, brother. There's a lesson for us all in that."

THEY REACHED THE shrine by noon. From a distance Penrast looked like a toy discarded by some lordling child. A silver cylinder rising from the broken hilltop at a drunken angle, thirty yards tall, maybe twenty yards across. Its walls were a yard thick, a weight of silver-steel that to purchase would beggar empires greater than the one it stood in. Except no fire could melt the stuff, no blade could cut it. Abbess Glass had it on good account that an Ark-steel blade couldn't scratch the mirrored surface. And so, by having the properties so valued in Ark-steel, but to an even greater degree, the thing moved from priceless resource to worthless curiosity.

Steps led down into the underchambers via a tunnel hewn

into the bedrock. Until the Church of the Ancestor took the site over it had been claimed by the smallfolk that the Missing had fashioned the tower, or the "titan's ring" as they called it. Now the official line was that the tribes had brought it with them from the stars.

"You'll come with me, abbess." Pelter gestured her down from the carriage. "The face of an old 'friend' will help motivate the inquisitors to step up and do their duty."

Abbess Glass, with Sera to steady her, emerged into the cold bluster of the day. After a short transit, huddled against the wind, the three of them escaped into shelter again, now bowed over to avoid scraping their heads as they descended the steep, rocky stairs.

The Missing, or whichever of the four tribes built the place, had not bothered with building material. The walls were either bedrock, sheared away with miraculous precision, or the soil itself, fused into a smooth marble-like substance as hard as stone.

Whatever inquiry had been underway appeared to be in the end stages. The Inquisition guards on duty had a bored look. Inquisitors Seldom and Agika were not among those who favoured the more brutal methods of extracting information. Agika was a marjal touch with a gift for coaxing the truth off unwilling tongues, and Seldom had come to Glass's way of thinking on the subject of interrogation, namely that the information came more swiftly and more accurately if the questions were presented as a concerned attempt to reduce the subject's final punishment.

Glass waited with Sera while Brother Pelter went to speak to the inquisitors. Sera quickly fell into conversation with other guards at the doorway, men she'd not seen in months, leaving Glass to twiddle her thumbs or study the room.

The chamber held benches for the faithful during services or contemplation or whatever it was they did at the shrine. Of the original occupants, though, there were no signs remaining save for one symbol carved into the glassy surface of the rear wall. To Glass's eye it had much in common with sigil-work, though it didn't twist the mind as sigils did. If the marking held any magic it was of a deeper kind, too deep for Glass to touch.

Glass was tracing the symbol's curves with a finger when another guard arrived and thrust a peasant into the room. At the doorway Sera looked up then returned to her conversation. Glass had the room's only lamp in one hand, using it to illuminate the symbol. She abandoned her inspection and crossed over to the new arrival. The young man looked worried enough without being left in the dark.

"Sit, conserve your energy." Glass gestured to the nearest bench. The man gave her a look as blank as it was scared. Glass rephrased. "Sit, you need to rest."

"Thank you, sister." The man slumped in the wooden pew. His jerkin looked to be made of sackcloth and mud, he had dirt along both cheekbones, and smelled of pigs. "I don't understand what I've done."

Glass took a seat and made a smile for him. "Perhaps you've done nothing?"

"I don't understand." The man shook his head, looking at his knees. "In my uncle's village the old men leave the first cut of the harvest for the corn god. I heard they have a stone church to the Hope down in Whittle. Why are they arresting people here? The Ancestor's own children? For what? They took Master Root. Said he was reciting the Ancestor prayer wrong. And the rector, they took him too, because he said this place was here when the tribes came. It's madness . . ."

Glass shook her head. It was a confusion she had heard many times before, most often at the edges of the empire. "The greatest threat to any faith is not other faiths or beliefs but the corruption and division of its own message. When the Durnish sail on us beneath their banners we band together and become strong. Nobody begins to wonder if they should worship Orm or Gataar or the triple-headed goddess. But when we're left to our own devices it's not long before someone, often greedy for power and influence, takes it upon themselves to change the Ancestor's teachings, just a little bit, but in a way that makes that person more important or special or allows them privilege. And before you know it you have four different churches, four high priests at war, a legion of archons arguing. This has happened time and again. More blood has watered our fields as a consequence of such internecine wars . . ." She stopped, seeing the man's incomprehension. "We present more of a danger to ourselves than do the Durns or the Scithrowl, and even the Scithrowl wars can be said to have been over interpretations of the faith."

"But in my uncle's village—"

"The ice closes and it brings together many people and many faiths. The emperor has sanctioned the Hope Church: its holy texts are about the future and do not dispute the Ancestor's teachings. The Ancestor's Church itself has declared that those who follow the small gods may do so unmolested in the more remote corners of the empire. Only in the cities, and those towns declared as church towns, is such practice forbidden." She raised a hand to deflect the next question on his lips. "The thing for you to do is wait and see whether the clerics who taught at this shrine have been found guilty of heresy. Answer any question truthfully. If it turns out that they are guilty and that you were part of their flock then you must do the penitence placed upon you and attend a sanctioned church to learn the true teaching. After that you will be without taint and of no further interest to the Inquisition."

Glass had given that speech or one similar an untold number of times. She had repeated it so often that, like a word repeated again and again, it had lost its meaning for her. In the end she saw only the immediate consequences, the victims in the here and the now, rather than those postulated casualties from the wars of a divided church. She had begun to lose heart for the work before her boy died. And when Able choked out the last of his life before her, her heart had broken entirely. She had never returned to the Tower of Inquiry.

New figures arrived with lanterns at the doorway and Sera gestured for Glass to approach. Glass got to her feet, aided by the peasant who for the first time noticed the chains around her wrists.

"Thank you, sister," he said, gaze still held by the silver chain.

Brother Pelter bustled into the room. At his shoulders stood the hawk-like Seldom and the slender Agika, dark-eyed and sceptical. "The senior inquisitors have agreed to accompany us to Sherzal's palace, abbess." He rubbed his hands together, unable to contain his enthusiasm.

Glass acknowledged the inquisitors with a curt nod and

turned back towards the field-worker. "Remember what I've told you, young man. Honesty and penitence." She glanced towards the waiting inquisitors. "You'll be fine." She meant it too. He likely would be. Of her own prospects she was far less certain.

33

———————— ✦ ————————

ZOLE RAN BESIDE Kettle, the Noi-Guin's black-skin hanging from her hand, twisting strangely as though it were a live thing.

"We have to lose ourselves." The tunnel ahead held Kettle's attention. The most obvious of the side passages had been blocked off but any cave system is riddled with fissures and holes. "The lost are hard to find." They ran another fifty yards, Kettle slowing to investigate an opening low in the wall. "Two days and two nights. Then we make our move."

"We should separate," Zole said. Her left hand bristled with cross-knives stolen from the dead assassin.

"We should not!" Kettle abandoned the narrow opening and moved on, veering down the smaller fork where the passage split. "You're in my care, novice. And how would I find you again?"

"I found you before. I can do it again. I will make a diversion. You can rescue Nona."

"This is the Tetragode, Zole! The Tetragode! You're a novice! You shouldn't be here! Neither should I . . ."

Kettle took a right turn down a narrow passage delving steeply into the mountain's depths. The floor fell in uneven, muddy steps, a steady trickle of water spilling down them.

"I am the Chosen One." Zole stopped by a fissure in the wall, a vertical slot wide enough for an arm but not a shoulder. "That is what they say. So either have faith in me, or stop worrying. If the Argatha's prophecy is a piece of nonsense then I am just a child from the ice, of no particular value." She reached into the crack beside her, the nitre-caked walls scraping her arm.

"You're of particular value, chosen or not." Kettle clasped the girl's shoulder, knowing anything more affectionate would unsettle her.

Zole twisted her mouth into an almost-smile. Her hand was empty now, the black-skin and cross-knives stowed away. She slid deeper into the crack and laid her palm against the rock where it gripped her. "Worry about yourself, sister. And Nona." Her brow furrowed and, with obvious effort, she pushed. And somehow the rock moved. The whole fissure widened, the wall bulging to accommodate the displaced volume, as if the whole thing were semi-liquid.

"How—"

"Yisht was my mentor." Zole eased her way into the crack. The blood began to trickle from her left nostril again as she taxed her powers. "And there is a shipheart in this place. Can you not feel it?"

Kettle thought for a moment. She felt nothing specific, but it was true that she saw through the utter darkness of the caves with greater clarity than she had experienced before. And prior to Yisht's theft of the Sweet Mercy's shipheart Kettle's shadow-working had always improved when she neared the vault in which it was kept.

"Be careful!" she called after Zole.

"They will not find me." The fissure narrowed, rock groaning, as the novice moved from sight. "I will find them."

"Watch for traps . . ." Kettle stared at the crack, unremarkable now, with only a handful of fractures to mark Zole's passage. She wanted to call her back. Whatever her talents, however chosen she might be, she was still only a girl, a novice, and this was the Tetragode, a place where the most legendary of the Grey would fear to walk. Sister Cloud had done battle with Noi-Guin centuries ago and barely escaped with her life. Kettle had accepted when she understood her destination that she would not be coming back. She found it harder to accept the same for Zole or Nona.

"Ancestor watch over you." A whisper. And with throwing stars in hand, Kettle carried on down the slippery descent.

+ + +

EVER SINCE APPLE had pushed Kettle partway into the dark world to save her life Kettle had felt the shadow as something fluid, alive almost. Every shadow-worker experiences some element of that sensation but for those steeped in shadow it was more intimate, more real. The darkness was something that flowed through you, blotted into your skin, ran in your veins. In the depths of the Tetragode Kettle could feel the Noi-Guin's web of shadow-links all around her, alarms pulsing from one to the other. And something more, something dark and awful, like a spider lurking in the midst of that web, some many-legged monstrosity ready to scurry out to devour any foreign body trapped in its strands. Something singular. In charge.

Kettle continued to go deeper, taking care to leave as few traces of her passing as possible, choosing the narrow paths over the broad, winding her way down among the roots of the mountains. She wrapped herself in the clarity trance, filling every detail with meaning. Twice she found traps. The first barbed and rusty blades anchored beneath the soft mud covering an area of tunnel floor, the second a fall of rocks, ready to drop at the tug of a thin, black chain that crossed the stony ground. They marked the limits of the Noi-Guin territory, designed to thwart infiltration via any of the unknown ways snaking beneath the Grampains.

There are times to attack fast and relentlessly, allowing your foe no moment to regroup, but that is a tactic best suited to a place you know well or have studied in diagrams to the point at which you could navigate it blind. Having rung the Tetragode's doorbell, the best policy, the one Sister Apple would suggest from her study of the grey tomes, was to lie low, let the defenders expose and exhaust themselves, and then to learn what needed to be learned before striking and striking hard.

THE WAITING GAME is a difficult one, especially when a friend is in danger. The Noi-Guin would not know that Nona was the target of the intrusion—they had many enemies after all—but she would be high on the list of reasons for the attack. Probably they would move Nona, maybe even kill her and be done with it. Kettle didn't think so, though. If they thought Nona the target then Nona was also the bait. The Noi-Guin were vengeful. And even if they were not vengeful an attack on the Tetragode was an attack on their reputation and could not be allowed to go unpunished. If Nona were killed then perhaps the attackers would melt away, uncaught, and that could not be permitted.

Kettle thought that the most probable course of action for the Noi-Guin, if they believed Nona to be the likely target, would be to torture her in the hope of drawing the attackers out. They would consider the possibility that she was threadbound to at least one of her would-be saviours. The only other alternative would be to accept that the Noi-Guin who had brought her in had allowed herself to be tracked to the Tetragode by more conventional means, and that was unthinkable.

Kettle settled herself deep at the end of a chain of choices committed to memory and waited. She crouched in the chill, utter darkness of a passage where perhaps no person had ever been before in all the long millennia since the stream that carved it had found a different course. She wrapped herself in clarity, ears open to the smallest suggestion of sound, her mind touching the darkness, sensitive to any vibration that a shadow-worker's power might cause. She ate, chewing slowly on the trail-biscuit from her pack, letting the moments slide by and accumulate into hours. And Nona, summoned along the thread-bond by the terror that Kettle had experienced approaching the Tetragode, albeit suppressed and channelled into more useful forms by her training, now found her grip on the nun's perception slipping. As fear mellowed into calm, and boredom became the most immediate threat, Nona's place in the back of Kettle's mind became smaller and smaller. At the last she began to feel the cold of her cell and the shivering of her own flesh, which unlike Kettle's was wrapped in nothing but the torn remnants of a smock.

NONA'S EYES SNAPPED open. "Damn."

What? Where were you? Keot burned across her throat, just below the collar.

With Kettle. She's here with Zole. They killed a Noi-Guin and now they're hiding. Kettle thinks the other Noi-Guin will torture me to bring her and Zole into the open.

You had better escape then.

Nona uncurled, finding her muscles stiff, her arm and hip sore from supporting her on the stone floor. She stood and faced the wall, feeling for the iron pin that secured the chain leading from her ankle cuff. She didn't know if the winding trick had worked, or even if it could work, but it was all she had. With every ounce of the speed at her disposal she repeated the process, winding the chain around the pin so fast that the disc she built against the wall had no time to collapse. At the last circuit she gripped the outer edge before the links could shift, and applied all her strength to turning it.

Nothing. Just a double handful of chain dangling from scraped fingers.

Again! Keot flowed across her skin, trying to reach her right hand but finding himself blocked by the wristband.

Nona tried again. And again. She lost count of her efforts.

Any hunska, even a full-blood, tires quickly when using their speed at its limit. Eventually Nona slumped on the floor, exhausted, her fingernails splintered, hands sore. She lay, reaching for her serenity trance, waiting while her body gathered its resources for more bursts of speed. She heard people approaching, many of them, on soft feet. Her serenity shielded her from the jolt of shock but the fear still rose, a tide of it. She gained her feet and prepared to fight.

The door remained closed. Nona heard the newcomers arrange themselves outside her cell, exchanging a muttered comment or two. And then . . . nothing. Kettle was half-right perhaps. The Noi-Guin were ready for any attempt to free her, but not ready to hurt her. Not yet. Their reticence made little sense to Nona. What were they waiting for? Tellasah could claim the kill that had been denied her for so long. She could do it before her peers. If she wanted to torment Nona she could do that too. Why wait?

Nona sniffed at the water they'd left her, stale stuff in a mud-clay jug. If she broke it the pieces would be too brittle to serve as weapons, too crumbly to bear any edge that might cut an enemy or even her own wrists. The water might be laced with drugs, but if she didn't continue to drink it she wouldn't be much use. She took a sip and returned to her battle against the pin.

Hours passed. Many of them. Perhaps days. The guards outside changed shifts, Nona snatched fitful sleep, her stomach growled and true hunger, her childhood friend, returned to her for the first time in years. Nona wound her chain a hundred times, tried a hundred times to twist the pin to the left or right. The iron resisted her.

THE BANG THAT hauled Nona from the dark confusion of her dreams was the cell door being thrown open. Light streamed in. More light than Nona remembered being in the world. She flung up her arms, screwing her eyes tight behind them.

"Ice! It stinks in here!" A man's voice, cultured and full of good humour.

Nona sat up and squinted through weeping eyes at the dazzle of light. It came from a single lantern, held aloft by a tall figure. Two figures—one portly, one slim—stood beside that one, and robed Lightless stood to both sides, perhaps four of them, more filing in.

Nona pulled the scraps of her smock around her and retreated on her backside into a corner.

"And this animal, rotting here amongst her own sewage, killed my Raymel?" The humour left the man's voice. "Lano? Is it her?"

The slim figure leaned in, a dark-haired man in fine clothing. "It's her, Father."

"She is yours, my lord." The woman holding the lantern wore a black-skin facemask. A Noi-Guin. A belt laden with cross-knives hung over her shoulder, down to the opposite hip. "You may dispose of her as you wish. My contract has been fulfilled. The Tetragode regrets the delay."

Nona knew the two men though she couldn't see them clearly yet. She smeared away the tears that the light had filled her eyes with.

"It was not well done." Thuran's voice narrowed to sharpness. "But at least it has been done." He stepped back. "Secure her." And the Lightless surged forward.

Still half-blind, Nona tried to stand but the Noi-Guin, that Nona now knew must be Tellasah, hooked a foot into a loop of the chain and jerked Nona's feet from under her. The Lightless had her a moment later. They were not unskilled, having been trained for years in the Noi-Guin arts, and all of them had at least a touch of hunska. Nona broke someone's wrist and struck an unguarded throat, but dazzled, chained, and fresh from sleep, she couldn't fight them off.

Four Lightless pinned Nona to the stone floor, the two injured retreated, and Thuran Tacsis crouched over her, his son Lano, lean, dark, watching hungrily over his shoulder. Tellasah held a long thin cane tipped with a needle towards Nona. The Noi-Guin kept the needle point hovering about eighteen inches above Nona's hip, ready to jab her should she somehow start to break free, presumably with a fast-acting poison.

Nona stopped struggling and stared at the red, bearded face of the old man hunkered down beside her. A Sister of Discretion on a mission in which capture is likely often conceals two things in her mouth. First a waxed tablet of crail root powder, secured below the gum. Crail root stops the heart. It's not painless but it is swift. And second, requiring great skill to use, a needle in a leather tube. It's not possible to spit the needle without poisoning yourself, but anyone it hits will suffer the same fate. The needles are coated with chamon, a venom milked from eels that feed at the bottom of ocean trenches only accessible from rare spots where warm upwelling water melts holes in the ice. Chamon brings about a slow death: the victims bleed into their lungs and suffer nightmare hallucinations. Most of the poisons the Grey Sisters use are chosen for swiftness. Chamon is not swift, but unlike many of the faster toxins it has no antidote. Nona would happily have spat such a needle if she had one.

"I have a party to attend, Nona. A very important gathering filled with very important people, and I really must show my face. But I will be back to see you later." He took something from the pocket of his jacket, a disc of black iron maybe four inches across and almost an inch thick, set with raised sigils around the edge, one side having a leather cover held in place by a strap. Thuran Tacsis removed the cover with care, revealing a spiralling set of sigils, each like a twisted spider, something deeply unwholesome in the way they held the eye and seemed to writhe.

"This is the Harm. It has been in my family for generations. The pain it causes is said to be unsurpassed. Worse than burning or acid. Worse than any venom. And it doesn't leave a mark." Thuran held the device above Nona's stomach. He frowned. "It's very effective but I've never really enjoyed it. Pain should leave a mark. Pain should be ugly and irreversible. So when I come back from mingling with lords and ladies, the highest of the Sis, when I'm done with the wonderful music, the exquisite food, conversing with my peers, I will return to this cell and hurt you in more primitive and more satisfying ways. We will start with cutting pieces off you. Everything it won't kill you to lose. For now though . . ." A shrug, and he pressed the iron disc down onto Nona's stomach.

Pain filled her, spreading rapidly from the contact site. It felt as if the disc were red-hot, flowing out to cover her entirely. Somehow it combined the first awful shock of a burn with the lasting agony, maintaining both together. Each part of Nona's body made its own contribution as the effect reached through her. Bones snapped, fingers burst, teeth shattered, her tongue blistered, her eyes scalded. The torment lasted far longer than Nona could endure. She had no way of knowing how long and could do nothing in its grip.

When at last Thuran Tacsis lifted the device from her spasming stomach the pain lifted, leaving only nausea and tingling. Nona lay there gasping. The limbs she thought broken looked untouched. The eyes through which she looked were unharmed. Where the Harm had touched her she had expected a charred circle of raw flesh, but the skin there showed just faint impressions of the sigils that had been pressed against it.

"You see?" Lord Tacsis replaced the leather cover and returned the disk to his pocket. "No marks. As if it never happened. Cutting off a nose may not hurt quite as much, but there's a horror to it. Don't you think?" He smiled and let the Noi-Guin help him to his feet. "I'll be back soon, novice. I've paid more gold than you can possibly imagine for this and I intend to get my money's worth."

Lano paused, dark eyes still on her. "It's a nice toy Father has, but now it's back in his pocket you're not in pain any more, are you?" He held up his right hand, the middle two fingers crooked over as if he couldn't straighten them. "You did this to me."

Nona remembered. Lano had shed his disguise and attacked her on the abbess's steps, in front of the judge his father owned. She wished she'd done more than slice his hand. She wished she'd cut his head from his shoulders. She wanted to say it, to spit defiance at him. But pinned on the floor at his feet, her body still spasming with the aftershocks of the agony that had run through the marrow of her, she lacked the courage. And she hated herself for it.

A heartbeat later, with full-blood hunska swiftness, Lano was leaning over her, his face close to hers, the point of a thin blade inserted into her left nostril. She felt his breath on her lips. "Before you die I'll take your fingers, one by one, and then your eyes." He stood and at the last moment pulled his knife up through her nose. The sudden burning pain made her cry out. Hot blood spilled across her face, the taste of it filling her mouth.

"Back soon!" A grin and Lano hastened after his father.

Nona lay helpless and shaking for a long time after the last of the Lightless left her cell. She hunched around herself, soiled and weak, and made no move until at last Keot's voice sounded in her skull.

You have to admire their cruelty.

They're sick. Evil.

Those are just words. Thuran's desire is a pure thing. Just because it is at odds with your own does not make it lesser.

He's a monster. So is Lano. Nona rolled, surprised to find no lingering pain save the burn of her cut nostril. She levered herself to her hands and knees. *Why didn't you pass into him if you admire him so much?*

We're bound until death, Nona. But when the old one kills you . . .

The two of you deserve each other. Nona spat and started to follow her chain hand over hand to the wall.

So pious! You can't claim to be much different. You have felt that same desire to hurt, motivated by revenge. I found a home in you because of it, because of how you killed Raymel Tacsis.

Nona paused before replying. It was true that part of her had rejoiced in taking Raymel's life. There had been an unholy joy in plunging the knife into him over and over. She had told herself it was for Hessa. But in the moment it had been an end in and of itself. *People are complicated. We're all made of parts we like and parts we don't.* She tugged absently at her chain. *Zole said you were a part of the Missing. All of you devils. Parts they didn't want any more.*

It was Keot's turn to fall silent. He went so quiet while Nona returned to working at the chain pin that she wondered if he might have left entirely.

An hour later she abandoned the chain to let her muscles recover their speed. Her mind returned to the agony Thuran Tacsis had inflicted and to the threat of his return. The wound on her nose still throbbed and ached. So much hurt for so little a thing. She tried to distract herself.

What's Kettle up to? Nona couldn't understand how the nun could be inside the Tetragode and have the thread-bond between them remain so quiet. Kettle must have joined her when the Tacsis lord had used the Harm on her. Nona hoped Kettle hadn't felt the full horror of it. The idea that Kettle might suffer the tortures that Thuran Tacsis had planned for her filled Nona with despair. She hadn't thought you could add anything to being tortured that would make it worse, but forcing Kettle to watch and to share the pain . . . that was worse.

Finding her thoughts had once again returned to what awaited her, Nona forced them onto a new path. Clearly Kettle's plan to lie low was working. She only hoped Zole was hidden just as successfully.

Maybe the nun has run away. The girl from the ice too. Keot had tired of Nona's efforts against the wall pin, seeming to have abandoned hope and resigned himself to Nona's destruction. His ambitions now lay in the chance that she could at least maim one of the Lightless before they secured her for the Tacsis lord's next visit. If she were honest, Nona's own plans didn't extend much beyond that either. For Nona, though, what followed would end in pain and death. Keot had hopes that Thuran Tacsis would be his new home once the man finally put an end to Nona.

Unable to keep her mind from the Tacsis lord and his plans, Nona returned to her work. Coil, twist, coil, twist. One effort became the next, each consuming precious time, devouring the gap before Thuran Tacsis returned from his party. In a pause in which she gathered her strength Nona tried to imagine what social event could have drawn the Sis into the barren mountains she'd seen through Kettle's eyes. Her imagination failed her and she returned to her labour. Coil, twist, coil, twist. She stopped to examine the pin.

It's moved! It turned!

She tried to twist the pin by hand, and found no give in it.

Really? Keot sounded unconvinced.

Nona tried again, coiling the chain and twisting. She returned to the pin once more. *It's moved again. I can feel powdered stone on it.*

She tried again, first to the left, then the right before gripping the pin in her fist. *I can almost turn it . . .*

Again to the left. She knelt and seized the chain close to the pin. She yanked it to the right and it shifted minutely, grating against the rock. She repeated the effort, right, left, right, tugging from one side then the other, and suddenly the pin came free, dangling from the end of the chain in her hand. Impossible. A miracle.

Nona stood, panting. She held the chain taut against her hip, the length of it running up from her ankle.

What now? Keot asked.

It was a good question and one for which Nona had no answer.

A key rattled in the lock.

Another trick. Keot howled. *Like the knife. They were watching. Waiting.*

The cell door began to open. And suddenly Nona had her answer to "what now?"

Now I kill as many of them as I can before they get me.

34

⸺ ✦ ⸺

NONA SWUNG HER leg, flailing the chain, getting the feel of it. In the convent the novices' game of Step involved a rope looped around an ankle with a block of wood at the far end. The game was to spin it around one ankle while stepping over the rope with the other leg each time it came round. Naturally the novices most keen on earning the Red also made a fight of it.

The first Lightless through the door had a club raised above his head, a two-foot staff that Nona would struggle to close her hand around. She lashed out with her foot and the chain followed, snapping out to its full length. The last two links hit the Lightless between the eyes, breaking his forehead. He collapsed to his knees and toppled to the floor, facefirst.

Three Lightless stood around the doorway behind the fallen man, black silhouettes against the faint candlelight in the hall. Darkness bloomed around them like ink in water and Nona stood blind in her cell. She dived aside.

You have to let me see, or we're done for.

Trying! Keot's voice rose to a roar, echoing in her skull. Where he spread from her collarbone towards her neck it felt like the fresh brand of a hot iron. The devil knifed deep into the flesh of her neck to gain distance from the sigil-cut metal and forced a path beneath the collar. Once past it he poured upwards into her eyes.

Nona saw a club swinging down and jerked her head back with no time to spare. The weapon's end scraped her cheek. Two other Lightless were coming forward, drifting to either side. More in the doorway, dragging the dead man aside.

Keot's vision painted all the walls in fire-tones and the Lightless themselves as black-skinned, wearing robes of pale, shifting silver.

Nona, having evaded the club, punched the man in the eye. She swung her leg, wrapping the chain around his ankles, then stepped away, yanking his feet from under him. He fell heavily on his back.

Great, now you have an anchor.

Nona ignored Keot. She swayed out of the path of another descending club and elbowed the woman wielding it in the throat. The man attacking simultaneously from the other side swung horizontally. Nona kicked his wrist, sending his club flying. None of the Lightless so far had much more than a touch of hunska blood and they proved easy work.

The man on the floor in front of Nona kicked loose of the chain and started to rise. As he did so a Noi-Guin flitted across the doorway, releasing, with a crack of the wrist, a spreading cloud of needles. Keot's sight painted them as a score or more of glowing red dashes in the enchanted dark.

Nona turned side-on to minimize the target she presented and dove to the left. Hunska can't fall faster than anyone else. A hunska can rise faster, driven by swift muscles, but with the needles centred on her torso Nona couldn't jump clear without first crouching.

Think. It's a puzzle.

Nona saw the needles, envisioned their lines of flight, saw the voids between them. If she was fast enough she could adopt a shape that would evade many of them, but no contortion would permit all the needles to pass her by.

She fell, twisting, flexing her knees to allow one of the widest-spread needles passage beneath them. Still five needles would hit her square on, with perhaps three more that might catch her. The tatters of her smock wouldn't slow them.

The needles closed half the distance as Nona swept her arms up. She deflected the first on the wristband of her right hand. Her enemy had provided her armour. She knocked aside another with the back of that hand and stopped two more against the metal of her left wristband. The fifth she let hit her in the throat. It bounced off her collar.

Was the Noi-Guin Tellasah? Nona hoped so. The assassin

had stalked her for years and finally captured her for Thuran Tacsis's demented pleasures. If Nona had to fight a Noi-Guin she would rather it be the one she hated.

Nona hit the ground awkwardly, a bruising impact, her hands instantly hunting to see if she had been stuck by any of the other needles. Nothing. She rolled, kicking the Lightless she had tripped. The blow landed between his legs while still rising, and he lost all interest in continuing to get up.

The Lightless that Nona had disarmed now drew his knife rather than chase his club. Nona hauled herself around and up him, using his body to shield her from any further attacks from the doorway. The man hardly moved to stop her, mired in the moment as he was. She brought her elbow down in an overhead blow, hammering into the base of his neck. He started to fall.

The Noi-Guin came in fast, knives in hand, amid billowing darkness that even registered on Keot's sight like swirls of mist. Nona stepped around the falling man to meet the assassin, tugging the knife from the Lightless's hand as he dropped, and circled her ankle, swinging the chain towards the assassin's legs. The Noi-Guin, whose shape hinted at female, leapt over the chain's arc. Nona slowed the world to the limit her body allowed, exhausted as it was from constant efforts to free the wall-pin. The Noi-Guin came straight on without hesitation, stabbing both her blades towards Nona's chest. Nona turned the first on her stolen dagger and the other on her wristband, struggling not to let it slide off and gash her arm. They slipped past each other and separated.

No cross-knives.

Keot was right: Tellasah had been wearing a bandolier of cross-knives. This Noi-Guin had none.

Nona threw herself forward, still furious. Zole would have been coldly clinical. Kettle fought in the serenity trance. But Tarkax Ice-Spear had been the one to see Nona's true nature, reflecting his own. Rage drove them both at such times and only by embracing that rising fury could they approach perfection.

The clash of metal on metal punctuated the brief exchange that followed, as rapid a tempo as any drummer could beat. The Noi-Guin's attack left no time for thought. Nona sank into instinct, letting her muscles lead by memory. Once she slashed across the woman's torso, finding her blade unable to cut what lay beneath. Once the Noi-Guin's thrust came too close as Nona twisted, and scored a burning line across her upper arm.

Nona found herself pitted against a better knife-fighter; but she was a beat faster. She broke from their sharp engagement, pivoting on one heel, throwing her torso towards the floor and bringing her other leg up in a kick towards the woman's face, trailing chain. The Noi-Guin snapped back away from the kick, but the chain slammed across her mouth and cheek.

Nona went into a roll and came up onto her feet. The Noi-Guin staggered back towards the doorway. The black-skin across her face took the chain's force but the shock of the impact still rattled her brain. Behind her two Lightless took off running down the corridor.

Nona followed the assassin, knocking aside the dagger thrown at her. They met in the doorway, one knife each now. Nona kicked at the Noi-Guin's off hand, stopping her attempt to pull some new weapon or poison from her belt. They feinted, jabbed, slashed, Keot raging behind Nona's eyes, howling for blood.

The Noi-Guin seemed to have gone on the defensive, maybe still recovering from the blow to her head. Nona reminded herself that the Noi-Guin was the better knife-fighter and had only to wait for her to tire and slow. Also, the cut on her arm had started to burn, more than a cut in the heat of combat should. The Noi-Guin's knife had blade-venom on it, not useful in the scant seconds of a hunska fight, but if she slowed things down and drew them out, the venom would do her work for her.

Nona launched herself, releasing every piece of the rage and frustration that had built inside her since her capture and before, since her flight from Sweet Mercy. She slid through the air, knife angled for the Noi-Guin's heart, her other hand coming forward too. The Noi-Guin, knowing her centre was protected by the armour that had stopped Nona's earlier slash, focused on driving her blade at Nona's chest. At the last fragment of a second, as her knife point drove under the Noi-Guin's blade Nona angled it upward and tore a furrow from the base of the woman's palm, down through veins, arteries, and tendons towards the crook of her elbow. Her other hand caught the Noi-Guin's wrist before the blood had even begun to squirt, and pushed it up so that her thrust cleared Nona's shoulder by a hair. Nona's own knife-thrust carried on and hammered uselessly against the black-skin beneath the assassin's jacket.

The pair of them went down together, Nona on top as they spilled out into the corridor. She dashed the Noi-Guin's blade from her injured hand, sliding over her to control the other arm with both legs. The Noi-Guin hammered her knees up into Nona's side. The white pain of breaking ribs threatened to take her consciousness but Nona hung on, cursing. She reached down to cut the arteries in the woman's thigh. The Noi-Guin thrashed but Nona shifted her weight to keep her pinned. One surge nearly flipped her off, and then the assassin's strength was spent, pooled in crimson around her.

At the far end of the corridor the heavy door slammed and a key turned in the lock. The fight had taken only the time required for the two Lightless to run the length of the passage.

Nona pushed herself clear and made an end of her enemy, cutting first the black-skin's straps, then the pale throat revealed as she lifted it. The assassin made no cry, only gargled on her blood, then stiffened and went limp.

Painfully, Nona got to her feet. Her vision was blurred, her body weighed three times what it ought to, and her breath came laboured.

You are poisoned.

I know. It didn't really seem important.

Do something about it.

I didn't know you cared.

If you die here I have nowhere to go.

I might like you more if you were less honest. Nona felt herself floating up, out of her body.

Nona!

Almost with regret she fought the sensation. Inch by hard-won inch she clawed her way back into her heavy, painful flesh and found herself kneeling beside the Noi-Guin, knees in the blood-pool. She began cutting open the woman's leather tunic. A score or more steel vials with glass liners studded the garment's interior, arranged in a row of tight little pockets.

All identical, marked with raised symbols that meant nothing to her.

Nona took the only one that stood out, being larger than the others, which were all the size of half her little finger. She worked the stopper free and sniffed from a distance. "Thought so."

The cure?

Nona tried to laugh and ended up coughing, nearly spilling the contents. "No."

She held her wristband up and dribbled liquid from the vial into the lock. Immediately it started to smoke and the air filled with acrid fumes that set Nona coughing again. She tried to open the band but found it still locked. She dripped more acid in. The lock fizzed and bubbled, the metal protested . . . and then gave suddenly. A hot spatter of half-spent acid drops ate holes in Nona's smock and her skin. The wristband fell away.

"That took a lot." Nona shook the vial. Most of the contents had been used.

Make your blades.

Nona tried, straining the nonexistent muscle that sat at the back of the mind. Her flaw-blades pushed into being, shimmering out to their full length, vanishing, appearing again, unstable. In Keot's sight the blades were a blue-white that was almost painful to look upon.

Nona made to slice the other wristband off but the blades melted away from it, refusing to cut just as they had once refused to cut Raymel Tacsis. "Sigil protected."

Burn it open.

Nona shook the vial. *Not enough.*

Her fingers sought the lock on her collar, hoping it would be smaller. It wasn't.

She lifted the vial.

You will waste it. It is not enough. You said.

Nona's fingertips found the sigils on her collar. Three of them. She fell back across the assassin's corpse, tilting her head. Gritting her teeth, she spilled the acid across the sigil marks. Searingly hot trickles ran down onto her neck and Nona cursed, tearing pieces from her smock to wipe them away. She kept still though, letting the acid hiss and bubble, eating at the metal, pitting it.

The shipheart's presence reached her as the acid spoiled the sigils' deep-cut perfection. Not the full measure of it, but some of that old pressure she remembered from the convent, fingering in past the fractured wards. Familiar but different: this wasn't the Sweet Mercy shipheart but another, beating with its own rhythm.

Nona tried to see the Path but the collar's damaged sigils still blocked her way like a thicket of thorns. She felt the poison closing her throat, driving her heart into a frenzy.

Find the cure!

She looked down at the vials. Too many of them. She wasn't sure what had been on the blade. Fevercut would race the heart to destruction, bitterwode would strangle, redwort would paralyse with pain. It could be any of those, all of them, or something else, and to identify the antidotes by smell and taste alone . . .

Nona? Another voice in her skull, not Keot's. *Come to me!*

And as the pain from Nona's broken ribs turned from unbearable to incandescent, magnified by the venom in her blood, Nona leapt from her flesh to Kettle's.

35

---◆---

NONA FOUND HERSELF running. Awkwardly, careening from one side of the uneven natural passage to the other. She understood that she was in Kettle's mind once again, but not why Kettle was staggering as if drunk, nor why she couldn't hear even a whisper of Kettle's thoughts.

The unlit passage hid no secrets from Kettle's eyes and yet she still managed to stub her toe against a ridge of rock and go sprawling clumsily onto all fours. The pain from Kettle's foot was small compared to what Nona had left behind but she still swore at the shock.

"Bleed on it!"

Kettle remained on all fours, looking from one splayed hand to the other.

She wiggled the fingers of the left hand.

"I'm doing this!" She raised her head. "Me. Nona, Nona, Nona." Her voice echoed.

The sound of distant running reached down the tunnel into the silence that followed. People were coming.

"Oh hells." Nona stood Kettle up, finding the length of her somehow disorienting even though they were of a similar height now. She ran her hands . . . Kettle's hands . . . over Kettle's body. "Where are you?"

The sounds of pursuit grew louder, closer. Nona patted her unfamiliar body once more then set it running again, concentrating on the task of not tripping over "her own" feet, a task that had somehow become very taxing. Ten steps later on she tangled her legs on Kettle's scabbarded sword and fell again.

"Help?" Nona got to all fours again. Her legs felt too long, her top unbalanced. She spotted a sinkhole, a stone gullet just wide enough to take her. Kettle's dark-sight revealed no bottom, just a near-vertical shaft plummeting away.

Nona hesitated. Shouts rang out. Not far away, she thought, though the echoes could play tricks. "They're hunting me . . . where are you, Kettle?"

She could jump down and risk being trapped in a narrowing rock throat, a gift for the Lightless, who could either winkle her out or leave her to die. Or run on, slow and falling, to be overtaken and killed within minutes.

There's a paralysis in choice, especially when what's at stake is more precious to a person than what they own. Nona risked her own life with frightening regularity and without hesitation, but tasked with deciding how to save Kettle, from the inside, she found herself frozen. "Kettle?"

KETTLE'S WHOLE WORLD was pain, a white sea of hurt. With enormous effort she uncoiled and forced her eyelids to part. She blinked. The world looked wholly alien, the colours strange, stone alive with fire. Her eyes burned too, as if rubbed with pepper. She lay in a corridor, the floor awash with blood, the Noi-Guin who seemed to have supplied it close enough to touch. The assassin's flesh looked black, her black-skin mask dark but with glints of gold as if something brilliant swam beneath its surface.

Kettle struggled up and sucked a breath through a throat that felt narrower than a straw. The hands she used weren't hers. One wrist bore a metal cuff. The tatters of a smock hung around her nakedness. Her ribs screamed at her.

I'm in Nona. Somehow I'm in Nona as she was in me. Kettle raised a hand to her face. *I lifted her hand. I did that.*

A spasm clenched her stomach into a knot of pain, curling her around it, and her throat sealed completely.

Kettle clutched at her neck—Nona's neck—frantic. A moment later she felt something like a scalding hand that clenched her throat beneath her own useless fingers and somehow opened it again.

Get up. Do something. You are as useless as she was. A harsh voice, like that of an ancient, neither male nor female.

Nona . . . ? It wasn't Nona.

You are dying. Move!

Kettle drew a throttled breath and crawled to the Noi-Guin. Her jacket had been cut open, exposing the antidotes and poisons she carried. *Pain, weakness, strangulation. What poison? Think.* Kettle's memories surged, carried with her into Nona's empty mind. She heard Apple's voice, the lecturing tone she reserved for class. "You have close on a hundred of choices for blade-venom. Unless, of course, you want it to stay potent for more than a day. Then you have only a score. If you also want it to have a chance of disabling your opponent before the fight would have ended naturally then you have only a dozen. If you want it to be something people can't build up resistance against too, then you have fewer still. If you want to source the ingredients locally rather than bring them halfway around the Corridor . . . there are five."

Five choices. Pain. Strangulation. It has to be blue scorpion . . . but weakness? Varnish of boneless? You can build resistance . . . maybe that's why Nona can still move?

Kettle began opening vials in an ecstasy of fumbling, stoppers popping off, contents spilling. A splash of the wrong poison on her skin and her problems could be compounded. The Grey Sisters had ideas about the Noi-Guin scripts, theories, but the Noi-Guin rotated their ciphers and Kettle would rather die because she was failed by her senses than because of an error in translation.

The Greys had training in sniffing unknown compounds. Not just for a day, or two, or a week. Kettle had been drilled with her two fellow would-be Sisters of Discretion for a solid month. A month during which she came as close as she ever had to disliking, even hating, Apple. Two sniffs, one at a distance, one close. Then decide, and if you think it's safe . . . take it. The distant sniff gave a first and vital impression, and a chance to survive any trap. Noi-Guin in particular were known for packing a tube marked with some or other antidote (in cipher) with grey mustard, which when inhaled would eat away your lungs.

"Blind-eye." Kettle wheezed a breath and tossed the vial aside. "Cramps." Another tossed. "Blue scorpion." A sharp scent and the stuff inside looked viscous. Spread on a blade it would dry to a clear coating like a resin varnish. "White-blood." The first antidote but no use. Four more, three unpleasant poisons and an antidote to the blind-eye. Her throat tightened again so that each breath was sucked in with a wheezing rattle. Her heartbeat was now so fast it practically vibrated in her chest, and the effort of keeping her arm raised was starting to defeat her. And the pain. It made death seem welcome. If she had the air in her lungs for it, she would be screaming.

Hurry. The stranger's voice in her head . . . in Nona's head.

The next one had that sharp, almost lemon, smell that made Kettle's gut roil. Proper lemons, grown at vast expense in the orangery of some lord, had a smell that made her mouth water, but somewhere between "proper" and "almost" something went very wrong. It was the red cure. Kettle would bet her life on it. The mixture had to be prepared much like the black cure, but lacked some of the more dangerous ingredients, and included a couple of others specific to counteracting the scorpioid venoms.

Kettle bet her life on it. With the last of Nona's strength she lifted the vial to her mouth and tipped in the contents, trying not to choke as they leaked down the constricted passage to her stomach.

NONA LAY DEEP below the tunnel she had first found herself running through. The narrow sinkhole had swallowed her. Gravity had pulled her over yard upon yard of slippery rock, a sinuous near-vertical descent, weaving around harder intrusions of igneous stone, the passage growing narrower, starting to grip Kettle's body on all sides. Nona raised her arms and, just as she thought she might become wedged, her heels found a ridge. She'd slid down so far that the sounds of her pursuers no longer reached her. Nona held her breath and listened. She couldn't imagine any Lightless so dedicated to the hunt or so scared of failure that they would voluntarily lower themselves feet first into the stony throat and allow themselves to be swallowed too.

Nona stood, clutched by the cold rock, damp, shivering, alone in the deep blind dark, yet seeing. The darkness pressed on her and into her. Nona understood the power she held over it, here in this body. But more than that, she was vulnerable to it too, in new ways. The dark was neither empty nor kind. She felt the shadows flowing through Kettle's flesh in a way that she hadn't on the previous occasions she had shared her body. This time was different. Kettle had gone.

Given a moment to think, Nona remembered where she had fled from. Somewhere not so far away her own body lay poisoned. Dead by now, surely? She would go back if she could but there seemed no way to do it. She sensed no connection.

An awful suspicion rose through her. Somehow Kettle had taken her place along the thread-bond. Somehow Nona had allowed it when she had weakened the sigils that walled off her power. Nona reached for the echoes of Kettle's memories, hoping for some clue. She ground Kettle's teeth with concentration and forced the most recent recollections to the surface, sifting through them with the fingers of her mind.

Kettle had been hiding, waiting where she came to rest after her long flight from the fortified tunnel. Judging the passage of time can be hard when you're alone in a dark place, far from the sun and moon, but the Sisters of Discretion have their ways, and Kettle had sat her first day and night in silence. At some point she had slept, dipping into that feather-light and dreamless sleep in which those of the Grey are trained. Kettle had spent time remembering, without pleasure, the long, arduous weeks of her instruction on remaining alert. She had endured those weeks in the undercaves, as had a trio of other candidates for the Grey. It had been her first trial on reaching Holy Class. Safira was one of her three companions.

Sister Apple and Kettle's classmates had made scores of attempts to take her unawares, day and night, creeping to the cavern where she waited, coming at her from any of five entrances. She had to last six days. If anyone managed to touch her without challenge then the count was reset, the six days started anew. If she hadn't managed the six days before the month was up, she would never have worn the grey. Sometimes they came at her every hour, or twice in five minutes, sometimes they left two days. The longer gaps were the worst . . .

Nona shook herself out of Kettle's older memories, searching for something fresher and almost immediately found a memory of Kettle lifting from her shallow sleep. Eyes opening to the darkness. Clarity descending as she strained to hear

GREY SISTER · 279

again whatever had woken her. Some faint sound reached her. A pebble sent tumbling by an insufficiently cautious foot. Distant but not distant enough. Kettle had risen silently and started off down the tunnel she had scouted. She sped up. Started to run. And suddenly her head had split with incredible pain, a hot rush of fear flooded her, she saw visions of a burning world and knew Nona was in mortal danger. Forgetting her own plight, she had reached for the novice. And somehow . . . somehow this.

36

---◆---

ABBESS GLASS

BROTHER PELTER'S RAPID success in acquiring the services of senior inquisitors Seldom and Agika had been followed by frustration. Pelter chased one report of Inquisition activity after another, only to find the operations completed, the inquisitors departed, or the report exaggerated and the investigation lacking sufficient importance to have a senior inquisitor in attendance.

On their infrequent returns to the swift toll-roads, the paved thoroughfares that constituted the empire's spine, Glass had seen an unusual number of grand carriages hastening east. Great wheeled confections of ebony and silver thundered by, the devices of many of the greatest Sis families blazoned on their sides. On several occasions the abbess had managed to catch a good look at the coat of arms flying past her window slats. Black axes crossed before a red sun: the ancient house Rolsis, the tower and quill of House Jotsis, and the hangman's noose of the Galamsis, swift climbers and relative newcomers to the highest circle.

They had travelled on, ever east. From her carriage window Abbess Glass had seen more of the empire in that space of days than she had seen in the last fifteen years. She had always maintained good lines of information, from the Grey Sisters and the Red, but also from a dozen and more old contacts, people who had been her eyes and ears when she sat in the highest chair at the Tower of Inquiry. The tower overtopped all of Verity's spires and the view was a commanding one, but its mistress had needed to see further still. Even so, the carriage journey had reminded Glass that nothing beats seeing and hearing it for yourself. The gossip of trader and merchant, farmer and soldier, even subdued by the sight of Inquisition robes, offered up the pulse of the empire.

"We'll soon be there, abbess." Brother Pelter had taken to repeating the reassurance with greater frequency as the delays mounted. The white peaks of the Grampains dominated the skyline, lending weight to Pelter's claim. He sat between the senior inquisitors Agika and Seldom on the bench opposite Glass, no kindness in his smile. "Soon be there."

Pelter thought he was threatening her but Glass now hoped with all her heart that their hunt would end soon. The world held many kinds of magic but the greatest of them, it seemed to Glass, was timing.

"Do you think that Sherzal coming to power would be a good thing, brother?" Glass asked.

"She has already come into power," Pelter said. "And it is good for those who support her."

"Sherzal is hunting more than a seat at her brother's table. She's collecting shiphearts. The harm she could do—"

"To *others*!" Pelter snapped. "The harm she could do to others! Wisdom in such times lies in knowing who to follow when things fall apart. You, abbess, have been unwise."

"Wisdom lies in not allowing things to fall apart, brother." Glass's gaze flitted from Seldom to Agika. "We are all part of the Ancestor's tree. A twig that breaks free will, however advantageous the wind, fall and wither in time."

PELTER CALLED A stop in the village of Bru, at a ramshackle tavern named the Elusive Pig. He commanded that lunch be served for his party and placed another brick of penitent's bread before Glass. She sat, chewing the coarse slice that Sera, applying her guards' sword to the purpose, had cut for her. And while Pelter asked after Senior Inquisitor Hames, who supposedly was investigating the heretical reinvention of some would-be lordling's family tree, Glass listened to the chat at neighbouring tables.

Individuals, families, and whole clans had arrived in Bru, and in-lying villages all along the Corridor, in past months. All of them displaced from the margins by the advancing ice.

"More came in last night." The speaker two tables away had a rumbling voice that slid under the general chatter. Each word like a boulder rolled out for inspection.

"They says as how these beggars are coming in from the margins." A narrow-faced merchant opposite Rumbler, dark complexioned and sour. "They says it wrong though. *We're* the margins now!"

"We'd better toughen up then and protect what's ours," Rumbler said. "Harder than nails these frost-farmers are, poorer than Hope Church mice. What they going to do when they get hungry?"

"They're hungry now!"

"Well they won't starve quietly in the road. I'll tell you that for nothing."

At the table behind Glass the patrons were, with voices amplified by ale, discussing both the Scithrowl threat and the Durns.

"Piss drown the Durns. What do we care about empire ports three hundred miles west of us? They're closer to Durnland than they are to us! Let them fight it out on the beaches. Durns and their little boats!" The speaker spat mightily, giving her companion a chance to break in and air his opinions.

"Jace Leaner hunts white lion up on the east slopes. You want to listen to that man. See clear across the border from those slopes, you can. He says you can't hardly spot the ground in Scithrowl, there's that many battle-tribes gathered. Adoma'll have them over the passes before the year's out, mark me. Like a tide. A red tide. Beggars off the margins won't matter then. Durns won't matter then."

"She wants the Ark, they say." A third voice. *An old man,* Glass thought. "That's what the battle-queen wants."

"That's what they say. It's always about the Ark. Me, I think it's about land. They want acres. They want our acres, and they're happy to water them with our blood. Once they've got the land they won't give three whistles for Crucical peering out of the Ark at them."

Glass sat back, her gaze on the table, immune to the malice

in Pelter's glances, listening. Perhaps five minutes later the sea of voices, from which she fished her gossip, fell to near-silence. Glass lifted her gaze and turned, like almost everyone else, to see three large men in furs and iron come through the inn's main door. Juregs. Like the Pelarthi in the north, in the south the Juregs reigned largely unchallenged as the fiercest and most feared of the tribes that stalked the ice margins. Unlike the ice-tribes, they did not want to live out on the sheets nor could they survive there long. But they could certainly retreat ten or twenty miles onto the ice when empire troops threatened, then march east or west to reappear unannounced, weaving down between the crevasses on a glacier's back and abseiling from the heights where the moon's focus sheared off the ice's snout.

The Juregs scanned the crowded taproom, wolves eyeing the flock.

To either side of Glass, Pelter's guards, Melkir and Sera, quietly slipped hands to sword hilts. Agika and Seldom exchanged glances. Juregs were known for taking clergy for ransom. Even if a packed inn discouraged them from immediate action the chances were that they would follow the carriage when it left.

The Juregs ignored both bar and fire-pit, plotting a straight line for the inquisitors. The crowd of villagers, farmhands, and travellers standing in the main room melted out of the men's path. Melkir made to stand but found his chair wedged beneath his legs by that of a portly cloth merchant behind him.

The largest and eldest of the trio, a solid six and a half foot tall, broad in the chest and sporting a wild beard shot with grey, offered them a discoloured grin. "You're claimed. Come." He gestured to his companions, possibly twin sons. "Leave your guard and we won't hurt him."

Glass met Sera's eyes. The Juregs adhered to a bizarre patriarchal version of the Ancestor faith that relegated women to a menial status barely higher than that of slaves. They kept the trappings of those beliefs in the language they used with outsiders but sadly were not so committed to their principles that they would ignore armed females such as Sera. They would underestimate her, though. Even so, the life of an Inquisition guard was a soft one compared to one spent raiding on the ice margins. Glass would be tempted to bet on any single one of the three Juregs against both of Pelter's guards. Despite that, she would urge both guards to fight. She had a timetable in mind and the delays thus far had been welcome. But being ransomed by the Juregs would take weeks and ruin everything.

"Up!" The older man clapped callused hands together. As adherents of a heretical strain both Juregs and Pelarthi would set high ransoms for inquisitors, and harsh deadlines. Putting an inquisitor to a gruesome end was said to please a Jureg almost as much as being handsomely paid to let them go.

"I don't think the nun wants to go with you." A man's voice from behind the Juregs. He sounded gently amused.

The tribesmen turned together, the two sons reaching for their swords, the father with his hand resting on the haft of his axe. Glass saw that the speaker was a surprisingly young man, not as tall as the Juregs and of considerably lighter build. He wore a travelling cloak of good quality, held an ale tankard in one hand, and the strap of his travel bag in the other. The dark eyes beneath the scroll of his black hair mirrored the amusement in his voice, as did a crooked smile on his narrow lips.

"Not your business, lad. Dying will be your business if you don't step back." The senior Jureg spoke with rasping malice.

"Make me." The smile broadened, showing white teeth.

One of the sons stepped forward, drawing his sword. The man released his ale and bag, dropping as fast as they did and sweeping out a leg that took the son's feet from under him. The speed of it was breathtaking. The man surged up faster than the son came down, stepped inside the other son's sword blow and punched him in the throat. Somehow he had the father's knife out of his belt and pressed into the thicket of his beard before Glass properly formed the thought "hunska full-blood."

Two more Juregs appeared in the doorway, halting when they saw the problem. The young man walked the Jureg leader towards the exit. "I'm sure you gentlemen can find another tavern to drink in." He waited for the sons to pick themselves up and leave. The other two men backed out of the door and, once they were both through, the hunska returned his prisoner's knife to its scabbard so fast that Glass barely saw the flicker of his hand. The Jureg took the point and left without bravado. He could roust a tavern every day for the rest of his life and not meet another hunska full-blood. Pride was one thing but no raider got far on pride. Pragmatism was what kept you alive in the margins, and the Jureg had lots of it.

The young man spoke to a couple of locals by the door then returned to the table. There were no cheers: the villagers stared at him as if he might at any moment burst into flame or become a horse. Not until the last yard of his approach to the inquisitors' table, his half-smile fading as he spotted Glass's silver chains, did a weather-beaten traveller call out in sudden excitement, "It's him! I know him! From Verity! The ring-fighter! Regol!"

37

———— ✦ ————

ABBESS GLASS

"I'M SURPRISED THAT we met on the back-roads, given that you're bound for Sherzal's palace." Glass watched the young fighter, ignoring her bread. The inquisitors, even the guards to either side of her, had much finer fare on their plates. The town of Hurtil nestled among the Grampain foothills and, as the last civilized staging post for travellers visiting the palace or forging on through the Grand Pass to Scithrowl, it boasted several restaurants of passable quality.

"Those toll-roads will bleed a man dry." Regol took a forkful of beef from his plate. Despite his confidence, something in the action declared him an irregular user of cutlery.

"I thought ring-fighters were handsomely paid. Especially successful ones. And surely you must be successful to be known so far from Verity?"

"I win more than I lose." Regol shrugged, chewed, swallowed. "And I'm careful with my money. It has to cover a lifetime. Nobody lasts too long in the ring. There's always someone getting better while you're getting worse. And when the time comes to quit, many leave the ring unfit for other work." He cut more meat from the joint before him. The smell of it set Glass's mouth watering. "Besides. I wanted to see something more of the empire than what you can glimpse clattering along the toll-road." He paused, considering. "That village, Bru? I came from near there. Born in a barn. My parents sold me to a child-taker."

The inquisitors looked up at that. The Church of the Ancestor took a very dim view on any who would sever the bonds of family for as little as money. On the other hand the fruits cut from the tree in such a manner were invaluable to the church. Children given to the monasteries and convents by a parent could be taken back; those sold from their families and arriving later on the church's doorstep could not.

"Did you see them?" Glass asked.

"Them?" Regol looked up from his meal, flashing her a dark glance from beneath his brows. Glass made no reply. They both knew what she meant. Regol returned his gaze to his knife and fork, cutting his meat ever smaller. "My father died a few years ago. I saw my mother in the crowd that gathered when I rode in. She didn't recognize me."

Glass leaned back and let the young fighter pretend to concentrate on his food. Properly Regol should not be allowed to address a prisoner, but Brother Pelter had needed him. The inquisitor had engaged Regol as additional security, offering the promise of Sherzal's gratitude as well as a handsome purse. Glass welcomed the company. Regol for his part, once realizing that Glass had been the abbess of Sweet Mercy, had been keen to talk about the blade training, then the Caltess forging, and gradually, like an artist revealing their subject from a confusion of lines . . . Nona Grey.

With her trial jury watching on Glass knew she had to guard her tongue where Nona and her escape were concerned. She knew that keeping Regol happy and continuing to offer his protection was certainly among Brother Pelter's motives in letting him talk with her. But a stronger motive for Brother Pelter was doubtless the desire to give her enough rope to hang herself with. Even so, she told the ring-fighter as much of the truth as she dared.

Brother Pelter perhaps had never known the emotions that rule the young. He might claim that he was old enough to forget such passions, but Glass had as many years as Pelter, and her first loves still burned bright among the dusty archives of her memory. They waited around forgotten corners, waiting to surprise her at the strangest of times. Glass saw in Regol's careful dance around the missing girl an interest she recognized. She saw a domino standing, others lined behind it. She saw the time to push it. "We always hope that other people will see past the skin and bones we wear, Regol. These masks we've been given. We hope they'll see *us*. Some spark, some flame, something special, something that's of worth. Some people are born without that sight. Some mothers find they lack it even when they look at their children. They are as crippled as the blind. Worse perhaps. Your mother didn't see you when you returned because she had *never* seen you. I would know my Able after fifty years unseen, though he were old and grey himself." Her fingers still remembered her child's hair. The clean scent of him as a baby still haunted her at unexpected moments, causing her breath to catch and her heart to ache.

Glass watched Regol. He seemed still a boy to her—young man he should rightly be called but she could still see the lines of the child that Partnis Reeve had purchased for the Caltess. She had watched him, watched his sarcasm, the lightly mocking smile, the sardonic airs and assumed *ennui*. She knew armour when she saw it. And who wears such heavy armour if they are not vulnerable without it?

"All I know is my mother didn't see me. Just the clothes and the horse . . ."

"The fault isn't yours, boy." Glass picked at the penitents' bread. "She may lack that sight. But it's burning in your eyes. And you've seen the flame in others. In someone. In someone who could be precious to you."

Later Glass would speak again of Nona Grey. Of how she fled the Inquisition and of the manner in which Lord Tacsis had promised her life would end. Later but not now.

UNDER REGOL'S PROTECTION their luck had turned within the day and a third senior inquisitor, Brother Dimeon, had been located and won to the cause. It hadn't been hard for Brother Pelter to convince him. Brother Dimeon's antagonism towards the abbess was well known. Glass had kept him on a tight rein and at a low rank during her tenure. Since her departure Dimeon's star had risen swiftly.

With their party complete, Pelter had directed that they return to the toll-roads, and the carriage had made swift progress. Their driver promised to have them at the palace by evening.

"Come." Pelter placed a silver coin on the table and stood to leave. "Time we were going."

Glass rose slowly. She broke a piece from the brick of penitents' bread before her and began to chew.

THE GRAND PASS proved less grand than its name. Although the Grampains boasted no deeper or broader pass this side of the Corridor, the Grand Pass was neither deep nor broad. The road grew narrow and wound its way up slopes of frightening steepness to gain altitude. With the increased elevation the winds grew fiercer and colder. Ice clung to the rock and gathered in any hollow. The dark stone of the Grampains became white-clad, the carriage frost-bearded. They left the trees behind first, then the grass, until all about lay pale as death, unmarred by any sign of vegetation.

Small forts studded the pass at regular intervals. Not primarily for preventing passage—Blenai's Fist served that purpose on the eastern slopes—but to house the soldiers who made regular sorties into the peaks, patrolling for Scithrowl spies, or raiders, or the forerunners of any mass invasion. Smoke rose from behind their battlements and firelight bled between their shutters but still they looked bleak and isolated amid the vastness of the mountains, mere points of warmth and light scattered across an untold weight of cold stone. The wind ceased to moan and took up howling instead, running its teeth along the carriage's slatted windows. Ice fragments peppered the backboard and the stronger gusts set the whole vehicle lurching first one way then the other. Although all manner of perils lay ahead for Glass she found herself at that moment feeling rather sorry for Regol, leading the way on his painted mare, sorry for Heb the driver, hunched in his seat, and even a twinge of sympathy for Sera atop the wagon whose job it was to cut her down should she try to escape.

The sky above was a deep maroon, shading towards black, strewn with dark ribbons of cloud that looked like lacerations where jagged peaks tore the heavens.

DESPITE THE TWISTY narrowness of the route, the road they followed was not without traffic. The dim way-lights of carriages, carts, and wagons punctuated the sinuous length of the pass, snaking up towards the highest point and the long descent that followed. And there, cradled and largely hidden by the arms of a side valley, a glow that might have risen from a small town but instead hinted at the lights of Sherzal's lonely palace.

"I would say that anyone who secretes themselves so high in such a forsaken place must be plotting something." Glass continued to peer through the slats, speaking to nobody in particular. "But that might hold just as well for a convent atop a rock or an inquisitor in a tall tower."

The three senior inquisitors dozing on the seat opposite made no reply. Brother Pelter only curled his lip, but Melkir, though he stiffened his face into the guards' mask, couldn't help but twitch the corner of his mouth in the direction of a smile.

THEY ADVANCED IN fits and starts, seeming to halt at every second one of a hundred and more passing places to allow wagons and carts coming in the opposite direction to go by. Trade flourished across almost every border in the Corridor. Any closed border sealed off the world to the east from all nations to the west. The pressure that then built to reopen such a border grew rapidly and was exerted by a growing number of nations, starved of whatever delicacy or local rarity their people craved. And as conflict threatened trade boomed, merchants suddenly desperate to stockpile goods that might not be available again for long and bloody months, even years. Glass had no real basis for comparison but given how many heavily laden wagons they were having to stop to let pass, she guessed this might be a boom.

TO MANY OF the Sis, Sherzal's decision to isolate herself amid the Grampains had seemed like madness. Granted, the emperor's youngest sister had also taken herself to the very edge of the empire, but Velera's palace lay in the thriving port of Gerren, a city that had few equals in terms of wealth and society.

Sherzal's palace was, by necessity, more of a fortress, at least from the outside. In fact it had been a fortress before she took command of it and set her masons to work. The Grand Pass offered no hospitality, no concessions to the frailties of humankind. For grounds and gardens Sherzal had windswept rock. Her home's reply to the constant gales was to offer only slit windows, and few of those. The emperor's eldest sister lived behind thick walls of dark grey stone, quarried from the mountains themselves. Her palace squatted between the arms of a side valley, seeking shelter, with only three towers brave enough to push above the sullen bulk of stone.

High walls enclosed a courtyard in front of the main palace. Glass watched through the window slats as guards drew open the huge gates and ushered them within. No plumes and pomp for the hardy souls manning Sherzal's door or patrolling her battlements: these were soldiers, dark-cloaked, armoured veterans who had known both victory and defeat.

Wheels clattered over flagstones and crunched over gravel. The driver brought his horses to a stop. Sera opened the door and Brother Pelter stepped down into the swirling wind. Glass followed with Melkir holding her elbow to steady her on the step down. She took in the scene. Constructing a level area wide enough for the scores of carriages now lined up within Sherzal's courtyard must have been the largest feat of engineering involved in the whole project. The emperor's sister might have taken herself away from society but clearly she had intended from the very start that society should come to visit, and in numbers!

The emblems, resplendent in glowing colours beneath rain-beaded varnish, announced a gathered throng of unmatchable pedigree. Glass hadn't time to catalogue many before two footmen descended the steps from the grand portico and begged that the esteemed inquisitors follow them out of the wind. And so Glass, together with her guards, her accuser, and her judges, climbed Sherzal's marble stairs. They passed beneath the arched doorway, leaving the wild night behind.

The great door clanged shut behind them. For a moment inquisitors, guards, and prisoner stood blinking, adjusting to the sudden warmth and absence of wind. The brilliance of scores of crystal lamps bathed the vaulted hall. Statues lined the walls: members of the Lansis dynasty, proud, regal, dwarfing all members of Glass's party, emperors side by side with those who never sat upon a throne. Between one statue and the next lay a niche, each hung with a crystal lamp and displaying a single object fashioned by artisans, some ugly, some exquisite, all of breathtaking value simply on the basis of the kind and weight of the materials from which they were made.

Servants came forward to take the inquisitors' coats. Others went out to collect luggage while a butler, an older man with an impressive mane of white hair, established the credentials and business of the new arrivals. Inquisitors are seldom welcome at parties, even when the host is the Inquisition's prime instigator.

From what Glass could catch of the low-voiced conversation between Brother Pelter and the butler it seemed that their arrival was expected and that contrary to decorum they were invited to join Sherzal's gathering, immediately.

Glass knew that Sherzal's parties typically lasted a week or more to allow for the uncertainties of travel, her guests often being far flung. She would accommodate a sizeable fraction of the empire's nobility, providing scattered entertainments during the day with grand balls and banquets to crown each evening.

"We're road-stained and tired," Brother Dimeon grumbled. A big man with an unhealthy pallor and puffy flesh, the inquisitor had proved a poor traveller, clambering from the carriage at every pause to stretch his back. "I want a room, clean robes, and a rest."

"I concur." Agika nodded. Her hair was in disarray after dozing against Brother Seldom for the last two hours of their journey. She hid a yawn behind her hand.

The butler relented. "Leon and Noel will show you to your rooms, inquisitors." He paused. "But the honourable Sherzal was insistent that your prisoner be brought before her on arrival."

"I will present her," Brother Pelter said. With a motion of his hand he invited the senior inquisitors to follow the servants to their rooms.

"I'll come too," Regol said, showing his smile. "They'll expect a ring-fighter to look like a ruffian." His black cape sparkled with melting ice fragments and he smelled of wet horse. Glass imagined him striding in among the bejewelled throng in Sherzal's hall and found an echo of his smile on her lips. A glance in Brother Pelter's direction wiped all humour from her mouth. The palace opulence might make it easier to forget why they were here, but the narrow malice on Pelter's face allowed no doubt. He wanted to see her burn.

SHERZAL'S GUESTS WERE already gathering before their banquet. Scores of the Sis moved in loose groups between three huge reception chambers. In one a gallery held several musicians, and the gentle tones of harp, thinule, and flute drifted across the conversation. In another acrobats performed feats of balance and strength, largely ignored by the glittering crowd, and in the third dancers twirled, pulsing to the soft beat of drums.

The butler led Brother Pelter and Glass with deft surety, navigating the sea of silk and diamonds, gold and brocade. Sera followed with Melkir, their services wholly unnecessary but perhaps calculated to add an implication of guilt and danger in case any should miss the abbess's chains.

Any crowd can be a lonely place but Glass knew that those who have experienced a hostile crowd would choose loneliness in an instant. In such a place there was always someone at your back. Hard glances, sharp comments, laughter behind hands. The Church abjured its flock to be humble but it was hard to hold high office and not grow accustomed to the respect it brought. Glass had worn that authority and approval like a cloak for many years. It had grown around her, slow and insidious, but now it had been stripped away in an instant. She felt diminished. Naked. An old woman paraded for show and mockery. She kept her head high, but her body lied, a last defence against the humiliation Sherzal must have planned for her.

However, of all their party, it was Regol, following the two guards, who claimed the most attention. Glass was grateful to have the focus taken from her. It seemed that more of the Sis frequented the Caltess than anyone might suspect. But then again few families rose to such heights without having at least a little taste for blood. Recognition, greetings, and invitations rang out where the ring-fighter passed, though none would mistake them for friendship: he was a novelty, and winning his company would reflect well on the lord or lady who drew him to their circle.

"Regol!" A young woman's voice, raised in pleased surprise. "How fashionably late you are!" Glass glanced over her shoulder to see a tall young woman in flowing green satin insinuate herself into the hunska's path. "I came to protect your virtue in such company. Surely only the Durnsea has more sharks."

"But none with such white and even smiles." Regol made a half-bow while slipping to the side to pass her, a fighter's move, and left her in his wake.

Terra Mensis. Glass knew the family, though the girl had been eleven the last time she laid eyes upon her. Glass had hoped for the child's sake that she would grow into her nose.

"Abbess Glass?" A large figure loomed out of the crowd and Glass turned to find herself facing a great lord robed in imperial red with the snow-lion trim that only the head of a Sis household might wear before the emperor.

"Lord Jotsis." Glass inclined her head. She should have expected the Mensis to be near the Jotsis in such a gathering. Carvon Jotsis she knew of old. A good man, honest, bold, lacking in the subtleties his forebears possessed. Unfortunately it was those subtleties which court life required if a house was to flourish.

"It pains me to see you in such circumstances, abbess." Carvon bowed his leonine head. Brother Pelter hovered in the background, the irritation on his face not quite brave enough to escape as words of reprimand.

"Holy Mother." From around the broadness of Carvon Jotsis came Arabella Jotsis, hair a cloud of golden curls, a vision in blue silk and taffeta, neckline plunging, waist tight, presenting a softer aspect to the hard warrior's body beneath. The girl dropped into the lowest obeisance of the novice, one offered only when at greatest fault or to an archon, high priest, or statue of the Ancestor. Her skirts billowed then pooled around her. All around conversation fell away, Sis heads turning.

"Get up, Ara." Glass found her eyes misting. "Whatever are you doing here?"

Ara looked up, her own eyes bright with tears. But it was Lord Jotsis who answered. "Forgive my niece, abbess. My brother removed her from Sweet Mercy after the recent unpleasantness. Temporarily, I'm sure. I thought it too soon for a return to society, especially here, but the girl insisted and my brother has never managed to stand up to his women." Carvon coughed and glanced across the crowd, looking for his own formidable wife, no doubt. "Still, it sends a message, no?"

Glass nodded, and smiled as Ara rose beside her. The message sent—that the Jotsis fear no one—was rather undermined by the fact that many knew Sherzal's interest in Ara had evaporated on discovering that Nona filled the Chosen One's shoes still better, and then that Zole met all requirements. Perhaps the true message was one of peace rather than defiance, and by sending both Carvon's brother had demonstrated some of that necessary subtlety the lord himself lacked.

"Glass." Brother Pelter found his voice, staring pointedly at Sera and Melkir.

Glass ignored him. "Ara?"

"I came to be of service, Abbess Glass," Ara said. Although her maids had made her beyond pretty with all the arts of powders and rouge there was still something in those blue eyes that promised a world of hurt to any who crossed her. "You have only to ask. And I am not alone." She motioned with her gaze, pointing out Darla who towered above her father, the renowned General Rathon, newly promoted and surely just one more victory from his lordship.

Glass found herself oddly touched that the two novices had contrived to have their family connections move them to her destination as soon as they had discovered it. The delays encountered while Pelter hunted her judges had allowed Darla and Ara to overtake her along the more direct roads.

"Heretic." A vicious whisper, close at hand.

A glance found the source, decked in diamonds and lace. Joeli Namsis. Her whisper spread, giving licence to tongues held still in the moment. "Abbess Glass?" A malicious smile. "Were chains all you could find to wear that would get you past the door to so grand a home?" This girl wasn't seventeen yet but she could pass as a woman of twenty-one among the gathered heiresses. "And I had heard that you were supposed to be good at these games of empire."

"Glass!" Pelter again.

The abbess turned away from Joeli, nodded to Lord Jotsis, and pushed on before Melkir's hand quite found her elbow.

The butler pressed forward, employing some personal magic to forge a path through the assembled aristocracy without causing offence. Ahead the throng thickened as cattle will around a feeding trough, the conversations joining and swelling, each voice raising itself by degrees in order to be heard. Like a marjal water-worker the butler parted the vivid sea before them and, revealed at its midst, Sherzal, in flowing black.

"Abbess Glass!" Her already-wide smile widened. "Have you brought my daughter to me?"

"Novice Zole's whereabouts are unknown to me." Glass studied the woman. Sherzal looked younger than the thirty-nine years recorded against her name. Nobody would call her beautiful—perhaps striking would be closer to the truth. Undeniably, the energies that animated the emperor's sister created a personal magnetism about the emperor's sister.

"A disappointment." Sherzal managed to hide the alleged disappointment from her face. "And you come to us in chains?" All eyes save Sherzal's fell to Glass's wrists. "Are we to have a trial? How exciting."

Glass raised her wrists, palms turning upwards, and drew the crowd's gaze back to her face. "A trial without inquisitors would be impossible, I'm afraid. And it would be remiss of me not to note that Brother Pelter is here illegally, along with Brothers Seldom and Dimeon, and Sister Agika. They have entered a royal palace without permission and must remove themselves immediately to await punishment in the Tower of Inquiry."

Two vertical lines appeared momentarily between Sherzal's brows. "No matter. Their transgression is forgiven."

Glass kept herself erect despite the weight of the crowd's regard. "Forgiveness is admirable in one so blessed with position, but the fact remains that without invitation none of them can be beneath your roof. As law-breakers they lack the authority to hold me and these chains, however silver, become the tools of the abductor."

"I invite them," Sherzal snapped, the violence beneath her skin suddenly manifest. "All of them, welcome guests. We shall have our trial at midnight."

A man pushed by Glass, his robes lordly but a faint rankness swirling in their wake. "The trial will be something to

settle stomachs after the banquet and before the dancing."
Lord Thuran Tacsis reached Sherzal's side. He bowed low.
"My apologies, honourable Sherzal, for returning in haste and
disarray, but I heard our new guest had arrived and I had to
greet her." He turned to direct the blaze of his good humour
upon Glass. "I'm glad to see you here, abbess. Or perhaps it
should just be 'prisoner' now?" A huge grin. He patted the
ample belly beneath his robes. "I've been attending to that
matter we discussed back on the road to Verity, if you recall?"
On Thuran's snow-lion collar a small grey smear of mud drew
Glass's eye.

Sherzal clapped her hands, suddenly serious. "Enough. Inquisitor Pelter, take the prisoner away and let your jury know
they sit at midnight."

Glass found herself being bustled back through the press of
Sherzal's guests. She had no eye towards their faces this time,
and no care for any jibes. Thuran Tacsis had come to them in
haste from wherever Nona was being held. Glass knew the
smell he carried. Mud and shit. But more than that. It was a
scent she knew from her time beneath Sweet Mercy on the
night before another trial. The smell of deep places. Of a recluse or cell in caves far below the ground. Had the Noi-Guin
delivered Nona to Sherzal's dungeons? Glass had known the
emperor's sister was reckless but not so reckless as to allow
Thuran Tacsis to flout the emperor's ruling in her own palace.
Crucical had forbidden the Tacsis from pursuing Nona for revenge or justice. He had made it a capital command after Raymel broke the first declaration. Everyone involved in any
further contravention could be summarily executed.

Glass had been sure the Noi-Guin would take Nona to the
Tetragode and that if Thuran were to gloat over his prize it
would be there. There was perhaps no place in the empire so
far from the emperor's eye. Crucical probably didn't even
know where the Tetragode currently lay. It seldom remained
in one place for long: the assassins never stayed more than
four years and took almost nothing with them, erasing all evidence that the Tetragode had ever existed. They took only
their wealth, rumoured to be in diamonds of exceptional quality, their shipheart, and the Book of Shadows, the list of clients
and targets dating back over six hundred years. The Noi-Guin

and the Lightless would melt away one by one, regathering at some new location with the most extravagant care.

"Hurry!" Pelter snapped, and Sera gave a push to encourage Glass along.

The abbess raised her head. They were far from the great halls now, in a long corridor lined with quarters for the servants of guests. She paused. The others walked a couple of paces before Pelter spun around. "What are you waiting for?" The tone a mistress might use for a tardy novice.

Glass frowned. "There's a feeling . . . when you know something is there. You absolutely know it, and yet whilst you have all manner of evidence that implies it is there, you've nothing that *absolutely* demands that it is. Like a case built on circumstance. Or the next stair in a dark cellar after you've passed the point that you can see where you're placing your feet. There's a feeling you get sometimes in those situations, a crisis of doubt and faith. You step down, feeling for the next stair, you pass the point where you might pull back and still not stumble, and you keep going, with just faith and guesswork to keep you from breaking your neck in a black place beneath the ground." Glass lifted her foot for her next step. "I just had that feeling. That's why I was waiting."

38

---◆---

NONA PLUMMETED THROUGH empty darkness. She wasn't sure how long she had been falling for or where she had fallen from. All she knew was the terrible certainty that soon she would hit something hard and at a speed that would spread her across it.

The impact, when at last it came, jolted open eyes she had thought already open. She found herself staring at a wall just inches before her face, all her plunging speed arrested with just enough momentum remaining to jerk her forward and bang her head against the stonework.

"Bleed me!" The curse came weakly from a raw throat. Her eyes hurt and the world looked to be on fire.

Keot?

You're back. He sounded unsurprised. *She left you a message.*

Nona levered herself from the wall and rubbed her forehead, fingers coming away sticky with blood. Scratches covered the surface of the stone block immediately before her. Slowly her eyes found focus and the scratches gathered into letters, the letters into words.

They're breaking in. You've taken red cure. You're still sick. I'm coming.

Nona became aware of distant pounding. Actually, not so distant. Hammers or axes being applied to the door at the end of the corridor.

Why don't they just—

The nun jammed the lock to stop them coming back in. There are many of them out there.

Nona tried to get up and failed, her muscles too weak and too full of hurt to lift her from the ground. She fell back, one of Clera's worst curse-words escaping through clenched teeth.

The manacles on her ankles and right wrist remained in place, the collar still locked around her neck. She appeared to be just inside her cell. Rolling, she saw the Noi-Guin's sprawled remains. She dragged herself painfully to the cell door and looked towards the far end of the corridor. The first splinters were beginning to break away from the wood around the lock. The door wouldn't hold much longer.

Nona considered the door to her own cell, the timber two inches thick. She forced flaw-blades into being around the fingers of her freed hand. With one stroke she shaved off a curling sliver of wood. Then three more. Gathering her strength, she struck down at a steeper angle, muscles screaming, and sliced off a narrow triangle several feet in length, then a second chunk. Panting with effort, she bundled the shaving and chunks of wood into the Noi-Guin's cloak and shuffled on her hip towards the failing door at the corridor's end.

The bright crescent of an axe greeted Nona's arrival at the door. More blows fell as the weapon was levered out. Nona took a few moments to pit her blades against the pieces of timber she'd dragged with her, dividing them further. Using the wall as support, she reached up for the candle guttering above her, barely half an inch remaining to it. She lit the wood shavings and held the cloak above the flames until it caught. With the lengths of wood balanced against each other above the blazing material she retreated. More pieces splintered from the door. Those beyond would be smelling the smoke now.

It's not enough, Keot said.

The smoke followed Nona back, swirling a pale, luminous green in the altered sight the devil granted her. She heard coughing beyond the door and bit down on a cough of her own. Some heavy piece of the door fell, hitting the ground with a metallic clunk.

The lock.

Nona could see the flames, an ethereal scarlet, through the coiling smoke. The scene had an otherworldly beauty to it. It wouldn't keep the Lightless back for long. Maybe not at all. But it was all she could do. Shuddering and sweating as the red cure fought the blade-toxin in a battle raging all the length of her veins, Nona staggered to her feet to make her last stand.

"Hey!" A voice behind her. "Quick! Over here!" A woman's voice.

Nona turned from the corridor's end where choking and cursing now mixed with the splintering of timbers. A figure leaned out of the doorway of a cell on the opposite side to Nona's and three doors further back. A spiky-haired figure with a lantern in hand. In the devil-sight's skewed colour palette it was hard for Nona to know if she should recognize the person.

Keot drained from Nona's eyes, leaving her blinking, stumbling forward. "Kettle?"

The woman caught Nona as she fell, her strength spent. Back along the corridor the sound of advancing feet, coughing and confusion. The newcomer dragged Nona back into the cell, pushing the door shut, locking it as she struggled with Nona's weight. "Shit on a Scithrowl! You've got fat."

Nona managed to look up at that. Only one person cursed quite as colourfully as that. "Clera?"

"Come on! Help me out, it's like I'm dragging a whale." Clera grinned down at her, face pale and mud smeared. Behind her a small square door in the wall stood open. The kind that every prisoner dreams about, stone-clad, perfectly disguised, leading onto a narrow tunnel that stretched away from captivity.

Nona kicked ineffectually as Clera bundled her backwards through the door, pushing her headfirst along the crawlway. While Nona lay panting on her back, the stone ceiling just a foot above her face, Clera went to get the lantern. She joined Nona on all fours moments later, and reached back to pull the secret door closed behind them, setting several bolts in place.

"Ssssh." A finger to lips. "I'll have to go first."

Clera wriggled her way over Nona, a snug fit in the confines of the tunnel. When their faces drew level she paused, her nose almost touching Nona's.

"You look awful. You're not going to die are you?"

"P-poisoned."

"What was it? I've got some antidotes . . ."

"On . . . Noi-Guin knife. Took red cure." Nona's ribs

screamed protest against Clera's weight and her breath came in gasps. All of her hurt but it seemed as though she'd been hurting forever and after so long alone in such dire straits it felt good to be with a friend. Even with Clera who long ago had betrayed her to the Tacsis. Just having someone there, albeit on top of her, was a wonderful thing. If there had been space she might even have put her arms around the girl.

"Red cure? That should work. Let's just hope your eyes don't turn red this time." Clera grinned, licked the end of Nona's nose, and continued to wriggle past, as if for all the world they were playing some convent game, not escaping torture and death in the bowels of the Tetragode.

"W-what are you doing here?" Nona whispered, her words largely lost as Clera's chest scraped across her face.

Clera ignored the question. "I can't turn around here so if you can't follow me I'll have to go ahead and come back before I can drag you."

Legs slithered around Nona's head and Clera was clear.

"I . . . I can do it." Nona braced her heels against a lump in the tunnel floor and pushed. She inched forward, gasping.

"Too slow and too noisy," Clera hissed. From beyond the door faint shouts could be heard. "Wait here. I'll come back and drag you. Be quiet!"

Nona wanted to ask her not to leave but bit her tongue. She felt weak and tearful. The poison's doing, no doubt. Clera crawled away, the sounds fading. She had left the lantern, standing beyond Nona's feet, turned low. Nona hoped no crack of light would show around the hidden door, but she could do nothing about it even if she had the energy—the tunnel held her too tightly.

You should kill her when you reach a space wide enough that you don't have to cut through her body to advance. It will be easy if she's dragging you. Just reach up and cut—

I'm not going to kill Clera!

She's the reason we're here. If she hadn't brought you to Raymel then I would still be enjoying his excesses and you would be doing . . . nun things. Kill her and leave her body to rot.

Clera thought the Tacsis wanted Ara, not me, and not for killing. She doesn't deserve to die for that!

The convent would drown her if they caught her.

Nona closed her eyes. She couldn't deny that the Ancestor, or at least the Ancestor's Church, had some harsh rules.

THE FORCE THAT pulled Nona back into Kettle's head allowed no alternatives, but after so many unions of their minds Nona was starting to understand the process. When not half-dead with exhaustion and toxins, and with the sigil collar off her neck, Nona felt that she would be able to exercise some choice in any future calls. It would require her to intercept the process, to cling on to her own identity and the flesh that housed it, and to match Kettle's excitement or panic with a calm of equal weight. For now though she was plucked from her own head like an unfurled leaf before the ice-wind.

KETTLE HAD EXTRACTED herself from the vertical passage into which Nona had manoeuvred her body. Escaping Nona's pain had been a vast relief but a short-lived one as she began to appreciate quite how wedged in she was. There had been several moments of panic and cursing, the conviction that she would never escape pressing down with terrifying weight, but she had at last emerged, filthy and panting, into the tunnel above.

In all, a day had passed and a night and another day since Zole and Kettle had hidden. The vigilance of the Noi-Guin would be fraying. All that time at highest alert, scouring tunnels, guarding key points, extending their perimeter. Nobody, no matter what their training, could stay focused indefinitely. Kettle had eaten and drunk sparingly, counted away the hours, listened to the silence, and now it was time to act. Nona would be recaptured soon.

Kettle knew that to try to reach the cells was likely a suicidal venture. She had no idea of the Tetragode's layout and just a thread-bond to follow. And if the thread-bond were to guide her through the twists and turns of the cave system she would need to rejoin the tunnels that Nona had been taken through. This meant a return to the area just past the fortress where Zole had killed the Noi-Guin. That fact still sounded unreal. A novice killed a Noi-Guin. But Nona had repeated the feat.

Kettle cleaned off her Lightless robes as best she could, checked her weapons, then hurried back along the long convolutions of tunnel and cavern towards the fort. She wrapped herself in clarity rather than shadows, straining every sense for news of her enemy.

She was perhaps two hundred yards from the place where Zole had vanished into the wall when she heard approaching feet. What surprised her was that they were coming from behind, and fast, half a dozen or more people. Kettle picked up her own pace and kept ahead of them. Approaching the main tunnels of the Tetragode at speed had not been her plan. At last she spotted a fold in the rock wall where she could hide. Moments later seven Lightless came jogging by, the shadows swirling behind them. Kettle guessed they had been recalled to defend or breach the cells. Most of the Lightless seemed unable to use shadow-bonds over longer distances but in the confines of the Tetragode all of them appeared to be linked to some central will.

With the Lightless out of sight but still audible Kettle gave chase. More patrols might be converging on the cells from behind her, and if the one in front stopped for any reason then she might become trapped between them. In any event the forces arrayed against her at the cells would certainly be significantly beyond her ability to overcome. But choices, always slim, had now run out. Soon Nona would be recaptured and not long after that Lord Tacsis would return to exact his revenge. Kettle had suffered the agony of the Harm in what she had to assume was full measure. It was certainly beyond any pain she had experienced before. Dying in an attempt to free Nona seemed by far the better option than sharing her final hours through the thread-bond.

The patrol wound its way along what appeared to be a major highway of the Tetragode, the floor well-trodden, chasms and inclines tamed with bridges and stairs, even the occasional dim lantern burning in a niche. Other Lightless joined the general flow from side passages, mostly in groups but sometimes just singly. Kettle found herself dangerously close to a pair of Lightless up ahead, struggling with what looked to be a door-ram, a heavy timber two yards long, iron-shod at one end. She dropped her pace.

Seated at the back of Kettle's brain, Nona could feel the nun's unvoiced thoughts and regrets churning, struggling to break into her conscious mind and being relentlessly shut off. No part of Kettle wanted to die. She wanted to be back at Sweet Mercy, to hold Apple, to see another dawn. She wondered how many Lightless she could take down before they got her. She wept for the novice trapped and facing an awful death. She worried for Zole. But no hint of this maelstrom of fears was allowed to disturb her focus.

The hurrying footsteps behind Kettle drew closer and she considered her choices. She could sprint past the pair ahead of her and hope that burdened by the ram they wouldn't challenge her . . . but more likely they would demand her aid, then realize that they didn't know her.

A faint tremor ran through the mountain. Kettle felt it through the soles of her feet and it trembled in her chest. A moment later she felt the pulse along dozens of shadow-bonds. What message was imparted Kettle couldn't tell, and a shadow-bond usually allowed for only the simplest of communications, but enough of the emotion leaked out for her to get a taste of it. *Panic*.

The Lightless approaching from behind stopped, reversed their course and started to sprint away. The pair ahead dropped the ram. Kettle heard it hit the ground and pressed herself to the wall as the men who had been carrying it raced past her, robes streaming. They should have seen her but they didn't. Kettle followed them a short way until she found a side passage where she waited as a full dozen more of their comrades hurried past, swift, silent, determined.

Zole. It had to be. She had seen the Lightless head towards the cells and known that either Kettle or Nona was in trouble. This was Zole's diversion. *Panic!* How could even Zole panic the Noi-Guin?

Kettle emerged from her hiding place, listened hard, then carried on, tracking the thread-bond as swiftly as she dared. Twice more she had to backtrack and hide at the hurried approach of groups of Lightless and Noi-Guin. She passed areas where a greater density of caverns, together with hand-hewn connecting tunnels, made the Tetragode almost a subterranean town rather than a series of locations isolated by the twisting distances of an ancient river course. She saw signs of industry, forges whose smoke passed up great shafts to vent above the snowline, and of communal living, dining and sleeping areas, even what looked to be a temple of some kind.

On the temple steps a lone guard stood watch, armoured in what looked to be black glass.

"Stop!" The call arrested Kettle in mid-stride. "Show me your face."

Kettle turned and spun a throwing star at his head. He almost avoided it. The star caught him just below the left cheekbone rather than in the eye. He proved less fast after that and the second star took him in the throat just above the line of his breastplate.

Kettle ran on, wrapped in clarity. She entered a large chamber, her exit on the far side. The faint echoes of a door being battered reached her from the distance. And something closer, just the ghost of a sound, high up. Kettle swerved and a cross-knife sliced past her ear, rotating as it flew. Kettle kept running. She knew her attacker lay above and behind her, probably in some gallery over the tunnel through which she entered the cavern, probably a Noi-Guin. She jerked left, then right, running an erratic zigzag path, relying on her speed and the distance between them to not be where she was expected to be when the knives arrived. And arrive they did, a storm of them, hissing out of the dark, clattering against the rocks to both sides of her, striking sparks from the stones at her heels. A sharp line of pain scored her shoulder and another knife flew past. Without breaking stride, Kettle found the most likely antidote, kilm oat, and smeared it over the cut. If she was right and fast enough the venom on the blades wouldn't touch her. If she had to take an oral cure then the effects might overwhelm her before the antidote kicked in. She muttered a prayer to the Ancestor.

Two-thirds of the way across Kettle stopped dead and spun around, drawing her sword, and struck a cross-knife from the air. She was near the limits of the Noi-Guin's range now and wanted to exhaust their supply of the deadly little knives. Two more came and she avoided them disdainfully. Her shoulder burned where the small cut still trickled blood. She kept her vital signs in mind, alert for any signs the kilm oat hadn't solved her problems.

Back across the cavern the Noi-Guin on the balcony turned and ran through a tunnel, either to give chase or gather more of his kind. Kettle sprinted back. She knew the doorway they would most likely exit from and didn't want a Noi-Guin following her to the cells.

As she returned through the tunnel she had entered by she heard the soft impact of the Noi-Guin landing behind her. The assassin had also doubled back and vaulted from the gallery.

"Damn." Kettle turned back around.

"NONA! WAKE UP, Nona!" A hand slapped Nona's face. She opened her eyes and found herself being dragged across a rough floor. Flickering lantern-light painted the rock ceiling just inches above her face. One of the hands under her armpits pulled loose for another slap. "Bleed on it! Wake up."

"Kettle!"

"You're stuck with boring old Clera." Another grunt, another heave. Nona felt herself inch across the rock. "Little help?"

Nona began to wriggle her shoulders and push with her feet. Their progress accelerated markedly. "Kettle's in trouble!"

"We're all in trouble," Clera said.

Nona shook her head, trying to clear it of pain and confusion. "What are you *doing* here, Clera?"

"Besides saving you?" Another heave. "The Tacsis are my patrons. Lord Tacsis sent me to the Noi-Guin to get the same training his son got here. Lano, the younger one."

"And . . . they showed you a secret tunnel into their cells that they've . . . now forgotten about?" Nona jammed her arms against the walls to stop being dragged further. She felt stronger. Not good, but stronger.

"These caverns belong to Sherzal. She's hosting the Noi-Guin, but she hasn't shared all her secrets with them." Clera tugged. Nona stayed where she was.

"But she shares them with you?"

"Lord Tacsis is her main ally. I've spent time training at the palace too. And you know me. I dig out secrets." She tugged again.

"At the palace?" Nona struggled to turn to her front. She managed with difficulty, gasping at the pain from her ribs. "Training with who?"

Clera frowned, coughing on the lantern smoke building around them. "Safira."

"And Yisht?" Nona reached out, closing her hand around Clera's wrist. "A woman who stabbed Kettle and a woman who killed Hessa?"

Clera's face hardened. "I'm saving you here. Remember the torture? I'll be getting some too if they catch us."

"Get my collar off." Nona rotated the lock towards Clera and turned her neck.

"How?"

"They've been training you haven't they?" Nona tugged at it angrily.

Clera moved in closer, the lantern in Nona's face, her breath on Nona's neck. "I could try to pick it. Might take a while. It's more heavy duty than complicated. Applying the torque—"

"You have acid, don't you?"

"We'd both end up with holes in our lungs if I used it in here. We need space."

"I'm going back." Nona started to push herself back along the tunnel, feet first.

"Saving you is much harder work than betraying you!" Clera frowned, advancing after Nona's retreat. "Turn your head to the side."

"What?" Nona did as she was asked though.

A fuzzy sort of pain blossomed as Clera struck the nerve cluster at the bottom of Nona's neck. Nona fought to hold on to consciousness but lost her grip and pitched forward into a darkness the lantern could not illuminate.

NONA SAW, THOUGH whether her own eyes were open or not no longer mattered. Kettle's urgency had hauled Nona into her mind once more.

The nun crept along a tunnel, part natural, hewn out in sections. The stink of smoke hung in the air, stinging her eyes; her arm ached and the taste of blood filled her mouth. She used a tiny mirror on a thin metal rod to look around the next corner. Twenty yards away five Lightless and another guard waited before the ruins of a door. Beyond it figures moved in a smoke-filled corridor.

Noi-Guin. Kettle's heart sunk so far that even Nona felt it drop. However the previous encounter had ended, it clearly had not gone easily.

Kettle withdrew and began to set traps in the corridor behind her. First a scattering of envenomed caltrops: small, razored pieces of tempest-glass, tough enough to pierce any boot sole, small enough to be overlooked. Next she set a small sigil-marked piece of iron to the rock wall. It bound fast and she drew out the Ark-steel wire attached to it, pulling it taut and binding it to the opposite wall with a second sigil-marked fastener. The device would require a fortune to replace, and not a small one. Finally, with great care, she felt among her poisons and antidotes, removing a screw-topped steel tube. She undid the lid and extracted a leather tube from within. She coated the tube with a thick tar-based adhesive, holding it by the weak, untreated ends. Nona sensed the Grey Sister's anxiety . . . Without further hesitation Kettle threw herself at the nearest wall, kicked off, gaining height, stretched up, pressed the tube to the ceiling, and landed on soft feet. The tube stayed where she stuck it.

Nona knew she had to leave. She was no use to the nun as a mute watcher. She had to get back to her body, deal with Clera. Quite how to do that was another matter. Nona set to work.

Ducking under the near-invisible wire, Kettle returned to the corner with her mirror in one hand, a throwing star in the other. She peered around. The Lightless were beginning to advance, the Noi-Guin behind them. Soft feet had not been soft enough.

The nun took her enemy's measure, threw her star, exposing only her hand, and started to run away. A leap over the caltrops turned into a slide beneath the slanting wire. A moment later she was sprinting away down the tunnel.

Kettle turned on her lead foot, body spinning, her other heel scraping against stone as it absorbed her momentum, the timing a simple judgment call. The first of the Lightless were rounding the corner. Throwing stars spat from both her hands, the aim of less importance than the rate of fire. The Lightless, hunska-fast themselves, spun and twisted to avoid the incoming stars. Caltrop spikes pierced leather soles and found flesh, the ball of a foot, the soft instep, the heel. A point that's driven through leather is apt to have any venom wiped from it but the weapon-smiths who wrought these particular works of devilry for the convent included shallow wells along each spike, reservoirs where toxins might be smeared, waiting to be washed out with blood.

Some Lightless failed in their attempts to dodge Kettle's throwing stars, others lamed themselves on the caltrops. The first to pass these twin threats unscathed, a woman, ran into the wire. The effects were ugly. Ark-steel is reluctant to break. The wire cut in across her face, sliding down across the resistance offered by the skull beneath, cutting into her neck. The man hopping behind her hit the wire lower down. It sliced into his thigh. A third Lightless, tearing at the throwing star embedded in his pectoral muscle, stumbled into the pair before him and their joint weight at last parted the wire. The three of them fell in a welter of blood and sliced flesh.

The Noi-Guin came around the corner at a rush, batting away a throwing star that would have hit him. He wove between the remaining pair of Lightless.

Kettle had six stars left. She threw one high. So high that the Noi-Guin became suspicious at the last and lunged upwards with his knife, trying to intercept it. His effort came too late. The throwing star hit the tube Kettle had stuck to the ceiling. Grey mustard powder jetted out with the force of the impact, blooming into a cloud.

If the Noi-Guin hadn't been lunging upward, tracking the star, he might have been able to run on, avoiding all but the outermost edges of the cloud. As it was he dropped immediately, but not quite fast enough. Kettle allowed herself no pity. When the Noi-Guin tore off his black-skin mask with a blistered hand, reaching towards his mouth with the other, a steel vial in his grip, she threw another star at his fingers then drew back from the screaming.

Grey mustard spores become rapidly denatured by exposure to air with even a slight moisture content. Quite how quickly they would lose their bite in the dampness of the Tetragode Kettle wasn't sure, but she also knew she couldn't afford to wait long. She smeared mud from a nearby seep over her face, neck, ears, and hands, took a deep breath, drew her sword, and ran, avoiding the bodies of those still busy dying. She rounded the corner, praying to every aspect of the Ancestor that there wouldn't be another Noi-Guin lined against her, and slid into the turn, dropping to avoid the reflex-thrown cross-knives. There wasn't a Noi-Guin waiting for her. There were three. A dozen Lightless stood ready before them.

"Take her alive." The voice of the central Noi-Guin. She held a sword that looked like a ribbon of darkness. "You may injure her."

The Lightless came forward, fearless despite the fact that her sword overreached their knives. Kettle considered retreat but the tunnel behind her was strewn with bodies and blood, not to mention caltrops. Instead, she charged the foe, sword sweeping out at throat height in a wide arc.

It's perhaps not true to say that no amount of training or skill concentrated into one person will undo a determined group of fighters, but when space is limited and the opposition are themselves swift and skilled it turns out almost always to be true.

Kettle had time for two swings of her sword. Both killed and injured, but she could find no way through or around the Lightless nor could she retreat faster than they could advance. After two blood-soaked seconds she found herself tackled, grappled, stabbed, and brought to the ground, where she lay cursing, bleeding and struggling beneath several assailants with a knife to her neck. In that moment she had no regrets. She gathered her strength for the sudden lunge that would push the blade through her throat. Being taken alive wasn't an option.

It wasn't fear that stopped her: it was the light. It was so unexpected that Kettle turned her head and watched it from the floor through slitted eyes and a forest of limbs. Something impossibly bright was coming from the cell-block. First a metal ring, perhaps six inches wide, rolled out into the corridor, sparking. It wobbled and fell, dancing on its rim like a spinning coin that has almost stopped. The light grew and grew again. A figure stepped out of the cell-block, a figure wreathed in arc-bright streamers of crackling energy that snapped back and forth from one path across her body to another. She looked like the night sky in the worst of lightning storms, the land-breakers that rage on those rarest of occasions when a northern ice-wind meets a southern one above the Corridor.

Persistent lines of jagged lightning reached out from all across the figure, touching the walls, the ceiling, the floor, the burning points of contact wandering slowly over the stone. It looked almost as if the person were some strange and many-legged insect, propelled by a multitude of thin, brilliant limbs. Light shone from dazzling eyes, erupted from an open mouth, bled from their skin. The whole of their body pulsed erratically, brightening to a blinding intensity, dying away to leave Kettle watching a dance of afterimages. It seemed at any moment the creature's skin might lift with the brightening, and the flesh melt from their bones. The angle of its legs and arms, its uneven advance, spoke of agony, as if whatever energies it contained might at any moment tear the creature apart.

The leftmost of the Noi-Guin recovered first and, shielding his eyes behind a hand, reached for some weapon at his belt.

The explosion happened in that instant. A directed release, snapping the newcomer upright, arms splayed. A crackling bolt of white energy erupted from its chest, turning every body into a silhouette. The central horizontal column of power extended the length of the hall, surrounded by smaller threads or streamers that quested in all directions. It blasted through the Noi-Guin and Lightless as if they weren't there.

An agonizing shock ran through the Lightless holding Kettle, ran through Kettle herself, and leaked away into the floor, taking everything with it.

NONA COLLAPSED, DIMLY aware that her body was smoking. The stone lay scorched all around her and somewhere far off Keot was howling. A yard from her rested the sigil collar that she had rolled ahead of her entry to the tunnel, now charred almost beyond recognition.

"Ancestor!" Clera fell back on the simplest of oaths, taking her hands from her eyes. "I didn't know you could do *that*!"

"I didn't either." Nona lay where she had fallen. Steam issued with her words, drifting up in the lantern-light. The flame behind the cowl seemed pale now, weak though it had been turned to full. "Don't ask me to do it again any time soon." She felt hollow, cored, brittle. As if her arm might simply come away should Clera take it to haul her to her feet. "Go and find Kettle."

"She'll probably try to arrest me or something." Clera looked dubiously at the charred and smoking ruin of the Noi-Guin and the heap of their servants behind them. Some of the corpses were still twitching.

"*I'll* probably arrest you or something." Nona tried to make her blades form but failed.

Clera rubbed at her neck where four thin parallel cuts wept blood, and shrugged. She drew a knife and advanced on the fallen with caution. Nona watched as Clera tugged aside the dead and put holes in those who weren't yet quite finished with living. Nona's limbs twitched from time to time, like those of the Lightless, and the memory of how close she'd come to being torn apart kept returning, distressingly vivid.

Nona had extracted herself from Kettle's mind and woken inside her own flesh, still dimly aware of Kettle's progress. Opening one eye a crack, Nona had found that Clera had dragged her to a place where the tunnel pierced a small natural void. Feigning unconsciousness, Nona had waited until Clera drew near and had reached out for the girl's neck with all the speed she could muster.

"You're going to get this collar off me, and I'm going back for Kettle," Nona had said. The hint of flaw-blade along the middle of each finger had convinced Clera of Nona's sincerity. Clera had produced an array of square lockpicks, suited to the simple heavy mechanism on the manacles, and in short order the collar had dropped away to clang against the rocks.

"SHE'S HERE," CLERA called, standing up.

Nona crawled towards them. She lacked the energy to stand, though strangely her limbs seemed to be buzzing with the stuff, legs twitching, hands atremble, the occasional miniature lightning bolt arcing from one finger to the next. The Path's gift was raw power, to be shaped and released, as light, as heat, as a blast. Nona's rage had given the energies form as lightning. It seemed to suit the storm that had built within her over her captivity.

Kettle had been at the bottom of quite a heap of bodies.

First those that had been holding her down, then those around her who had been blown forward over their kneeling friends. In two places holes an inch or so across had been burned through her robes, the flesh beneath scorched.

"She looks dead," Clera said, failing to sound particularly sorry about it.

"She's not dead." Nona's whole body convulsed, nearly pitching her forward onto her face. "I would know."

Clera squatted again and held her hand against Kettle's neck. "She's not breathing . . . and . . . there's no pulse. That's pretty dead. Sorry, Nona." She turned towards the Noi-Guin. "I wish you'd left bigger pieces. I really wanted my own black-skin."

"She's not dead." Nona arrived at Kettle's side. The nun did look extremely pale. Some of the Lightless corpses looked more lively.

She's dead. Keot voiced his opinion.

"She's *not* dead!" Nona reached out to grab Kettle, intending to shake her awake if need be. But just before her hands made contact fat streamers of lightning arced from each finger, running into Kettle. The nun convulsed, arms, legs, and head jerking up with considerable violence. A heartbeat later she fell back, limp, and in the next moment drew a huge gasping breath as if she had been underwater for far too long.

"Kettle!" Nona touched her shoulder, tentatively at first, then finding no further shocking occurred, gripped it hard. "Kettle?"

Kettle rolled over, choking. Nona noticed that the dark material of the nun's leggings glistened with blood.

"Tear some strips of cloth, Clera: she's got a knife wound in her thigh." Nona returned her attention to Kettle. "Clera's going to get you out of here. I'm going to get Zole."

"You're what?" Clera stopped tearing.

"We can't just leave her here!"

"What's Zole even doing— Wait, I don't want to know. You can't go after her. Neither of you can walk. Even if you were fighting fit it would be insanity."

"Well *I'm* going." Nona edged to the wall and used it to get to her feet.

You're insane. Leave her! Keot sounded weak. Not only was he quieter than before, but the voice in her head cracked and trembled.

"We can't leave her!" Nona snarled, angrier at the truth than at Keot or Clera. A tug at her ankle drew her gaze to the floor. Kettle had reached out to grasp her.

"Zole can hide in the walls. Go where we can't follow." Kettle's voice still vibrated with the shock that had brought her back to life.

"That's right!" Clera sounded surprised but she jumped on the idea. "If Yisht taught her rock-working she can hide anywhere. We'd turn up and instead of finding her we'd just find half the Tetragode hunting the halls and thirsty for blood."

Nona wanted to shout, to curse, to grab the front of Clera's tunic and shake her for her cowardice. But it was true. Zole had made the diversion that had saved them. Whatever it had cost her would be a price wasted if they now staggered into the arms of the Noi-Guin.

"Nona?" Clera had started to bind Kettle's leg wound. "We fix Kettle, then we go."

Nona looked away to where the tunnel turned. Beyond it some of the Lightless brought down with the grey mustard were still bubbling out their pain.

"All right." She bit her lip, frowning. "We go."

39

---◆---

ABBESS GLASS

T HE LIGHT OF the focus moon found chinks even in Sherzal's shutters. Moonbeams lanced through, painting brilliant red spots on the far wall of Glass's small room. Outside the slopes creaked, ice melting, water steaming, even the rocks themselves giving voice in the heat. Glass rose with a sigh. Sera and Melkir would be coming any moment now to escort her to the trial.

When, decades before, she had first been tasked to speak in public Glass had found herself seized by a fear that made no sense. Why did words she would say to any single person without hesitation become so hard to force from her lips when all those single persons were seated side by side? She had, of course, conquered her nerves in time, but even now, after a thousand sermons, a certain anxiety gripped her stomach before every performance. And Glass had, in all her long years, never performed before a crowd so high, mighty, rich, and hostile as the one she faced at midnight.

In such trials, the judges would, on rare occasions, find the accused innocent and they would be free to leave, reputation unblemished. If it was decided there was a case to answer, the accusing inquisitor would be granted licence to put the prisoner to question, using either light, moderate, or severe methods. Light methods included beating and sleep deprivation and were reserved for those deemed probably innocent. Very few prisoners subjected to severe methods during questioning ever failed to confess to the charges against them. Of course a guilty verdict was more often reached, in which case proceedings would simply move swiftly to the execution of the sentence.

The knock came sooner than Glass expected, before the focus had fully waned. At least they *did* knock though. The two guards treated her with a respect wholly lacking in Brother Pelter.

"Coming." She rose. Fading spots of moonlight slid across her, and she let one play in her palm. Based on Glass's analysis of the reports from dozens of Grey missions, Sherzal's ambition was to hold the moon *itself* in her palm. Did Sherzal's belief stem from the fake Argatha prophecy or from the older tales that might have inspired it? What was clear was that the woman had set her mind to gathering shiphearts. Trusted documents held in the most secret of Church vaults hinted that the Arks could command the moon. Other more dubious writings claimed it as fact and offered instruction in the practice. They too were placed in vaults. In the whole circle of the Corridor there were only three Arks, and the emperor made his home in one of them. Glass suspected that very little discussion had passed between Crucical and his sister on this matter . . . a conversation long overdue.

The lengthy walk to the banqueting hall passed in silence, led by a different butler from the one who had guided them earlier. Brother Pelter followed the man, then Glass, with the two guards bringing up the rear, clanking. Glass turned to inspect Sera and Melkir over her shoulder, both of them resplendent in the full regalia of Inquisition enforcers. A momentary pang of sympathy ran through her. The pair's duties today would likely prove more onerous than either of them suspected. She hoped them up to the task and fast in their loyalty to the office they held. All had important roles to play today, be they abbess, inquisitor, or humble guard. Especially the three senior inquisitors, who had gone ahead to oversee the setting up of the courtroom in the middle reception chamber adjoining the banqueting hall.

Soon they began to hear the sounds of distant revelry. Sherzal's extravagantly costumed house servants waited by each door they passed. Glass's nerves began to sing as tension rose through her. She became acutely aware that she had worn the same habit for the best part of the last week, not even removing it to sleep. Opportunities to bathe had been severely limited. She missed the convent, every part of it, but the bathhouse most of all. Perhaps Pelter had planned that she should arrive stinking and that the high and mighty should wrinkle their powdered noses at the evident rankness of her offence.

A small crowd of lesser guests had already assembled in the newly instated courtroom by the time Glass arrived. Regol and Darla were among those standing to watch the abbess take her position before the court. Among the small sea of faces Darla's stood out both for being a head above everyone else's and for being dark with suppressed fury. Glass felt for the girl. Anyone who wore their emotions so openly was at a great disadvantage in every game that mattered beneath such a roof.

Glass set her chained hands upon the rail before her, and as she made contact with the wood a small tremor ran through her fingertips. She felt it in the soles of her feet too, as if some hefty statue had toppled in an adjoining room, or the mountain had shrugged its shoulders to slough off some huge weight of stone. Nobody else seemed to notice it.

Sherzal and the lords of the Sis kept the Inquisition waiting until well past midnight. Glass listened to the strains of music escaping the great doors to the banqueting hall, while the aroma of roasted meat reached out to rumble her stomach, waking her hunger despite her nerves.

A great fireplace stood behind her, stoked to a blaze, making her sweat, her habit becoming damp around the armpits. She imagined that from where the audience stood the flames would frame her, rising above her head, an intimation of things to come when Sherzal had her way.

A change in the tone of the chatter from beyond the doors heralded the start of proceedings. A minute later servants, three to a door, pushed the huge portals wide, and Sherzal emerged at the head of a broad column of lords, Tacsis behind her left shoulder, Jotsis the right, others of the great houses fanning out to either side, anxious to be in the first row.

Sherzal had changed out of her blacks into a gown of dazzling white. Silks from distant Hrenamon where somehow they still kept production despite the pressing cold, ivory buttons traded from the ice tribes, lace borne across the Marn.

The emperor's sister crossed to the chair that had been placed in isolation for her while the lords and ladies of the Sis took their seats, tiered as if in anticipation of some theatrical production, behind her. Two of Sherzal's personal guards flanked her, both black-clad, a dark-haired man to her right, Safira to her left. The former novice met Glass's gaze for a moment before letting her eyes drop. Was there a hint of shame there? Glass thought there might be.

Brother Pelter strode back and forth before Glass's rail the whole time, on guard, awaiting his moment and perhaps feeling his own dose of nerves at performing before such a crowd.

The audience took several minutes to find their places and settle but slowly the conversation died to murmurs, and when Senior Inquisitor Agika rose to her feet silence fell. "If we could have the honourable Sherzal Lansis take the stand in readiness?" With a pale hand she gestured to a second railing on the opposite side of the judges' bench, facing the lords.

Sherzal frowned. Her gaze darted to Glass, swept the judges, then fixed on Brother Pelter who echoed her frown.

Agika put a thin smile on lips unaccustomed to the burden. "Your complaint did initiate these proceedings, prime instigator."

Sherzal scowled, then apparently deciding not to start the trial off on a note of contention, she abandoned the chair that was to all intents and purposes a throne, and stalked across to take her place behind the rail, the whiteness of her dress making the noise that crisp new snow does when stepped upon.

Brothers Dimeon and Seldom flanked Sister Agika behind the judges' bench, the former almost as tall as Agika with her standing and him seated. Dimeon waved a hand at Pelter.

"The charges against the accused." Brother Pelter faced the lords, the words eager to escape his mouth. "Abbess Glass of Sweet Mercy Convent, formerly Shella Yammal of Verity, firstly you are accused of wilfully denying the rights of a parent in favour of those of the Church, a clear heresy in line with the Scithrowl abomination. Secondly, you stand accused of permitting and encouraging the teaching of heresy at the very convent placed in your charge by the Church of the Ancestor.

"The Inquisition's own prime instigator, the honourable Sherzal, sister to our emperor Crucical, is my first witness in this case. Additionally I have sworn testimonies from four separate watchers attached to the investigation at Sweet Mercy, which I personally supervised. And I will be calling upon the daughter of a lord highly placed among the Sis to give evidence relating to her years at Sweet Mercy under the abbess's care. Joeli Namsis will give us a first-hand sworn account of heretical practice witnessed within the convent over recent—"

Glass adopted a puzzled expression. As Pelter drew breath to express further thoughts on the subject of her guilt the abbess rattled her chains to claim the room's attention. "Isn't it normal for a *senior* inquisitor to lead such high-level investigations, brother?"

"It's *me* that asks the questions here, abbess," Pelter snapped. He brushed a hand across patchy grey hair on a reddening scalp. "Senior inquisitors are required for the judges' table. Any full inquisitor can lead an investigation."

"But it *is* unusual for the investigation of a convent or monastery to be led by anything other than a senior inquisitor." Sister Agika commented from the judges' table without looking up from her notes. "One might even call it unique?"

"Who gave the order for this investigation, brother?" Seldom fixed Pelter with amber eyes and a raptor's stare.

"The prime instigator initiated proceedings, as is her right." Pelter's glance flickered to Sherzal behind the second railing.

"Then she must have initiated them before the occurrence of any of the events that your charges relate to." Glass spoke into Pelter's discomfited pause.

"*I* ask the questions!" Pelter rounded on Glass, practically spitting.

"I didn't ask a question," Glass said.

"Enough." Sister Agika raised a hand. "Perhaps you could present your first witness, brother, and have her address these points as well as any others you feel pertinent." She nodded towards Sera, who came towards Sherzal, her hands glimmering with silver chain. As she reached out the emperor's sister pulled back, scowling.

"As the prime instigator undoubtedly knows," Sister Agika raised her voice, "all witnesses in an Inquisition grand trial wear the silver chains during their testimony to bind them to the Ancestor's truth."

Sherzal's gaze flickered towards the gathered lords. With a forced smile she presented her wrists to Sera and the guard dutifully bound the thin chain around the royal wrists, wrapping them half a dozen times before leaving the ends hanging loose.

"Now, prime instigator." Brother Pelter positioned himself before the emperor's sister. "Honourable Sherzal. If I may—"

"You didn't ask me how I plead." Abbess Glass raised her voice just as she would on seeing novices misbehaving in the cloister.

Brother Pelter rounded on her, mouth working but managing to articulate no words.

"It is customary." Sister Agika nodded.

Pelter gathered himself. "My apologies. I had assumed that you would try to cling to a claim of innocence and force us to the unpleasantness of putting an abbess of the Church to the sternest of questioning. Am I to understand that you wish to plead guilty and move directly to sentencing?"

Abbess Glass let her gaze wander from Pelter's flushed cheeks to the men and women on the lords' benches. Sherzal had done an impressive job to array such a large fraction of the Sis beneath her roof. Some of course would never place themselves in her power, but many had decided to entrust themselves, old allies, new allies, or just houses with sufficient confidence in their own power and in Sherzal's fear of the emperor's censure to keep them safe. The Sis have a saying: "Murder the wrong man and he'll kill you."

"I am not pleading guilty, no."

Pelter threw up his hands with a noise of disgust. "So you claim innocence and waste our time." He turned back to Sherzal, mouth opening to speak.

"I'm not pleading innocent either," Glass said.

Pelter didn't bother to turn but he did lift his voice. "Your grasp on Church law seems to be as feeble as your grasp on Church doctrine, heretic."

Some among the lords laughed at that. Glass spotted Arabella Jotsis and Joeli Namsis sitting just a few seats apart on benches to the left of the lords, Terra Mensis between them.

"I'm pleading special dispensation," Glass said.

"Special . . . ?" Pelter turned back to her with a bewildered smile, hands circling to bring forth some explanation.

"Special dispensation," Glass said. "I have permission from High Priest Nevis and High Inquisitor Gemon to practise heresy."

A rumble went through the crowd, heated muttering, glances exchanged.

"Why would—" Pelter abandoned questions in favour of accusation. "No you don't! That's a lie! You expect us to believe such nonsense just because you have the audacity to speak it?"

"I have written permission. Signed and sealed." Glass met the inquisitor's stare.

"No you do not!" Pelter shouted. Then more quietly, "We searched you!"

Agika struck the table before her. "Produce these documents or fall silent, abbess. Such claims cannot stand upon the word of the accused."

"My hands are tied." Glass lifted her wrists. "But if someone were to reach into my habit?" She pressed her hands to her left side. The document had spent most of the journey strapped high on her left thigh but in the seclusion of a palace privy Glass had placed it for more ready access just before coming to trial.

Sera clanked across, meeting Glass's eyes with a puzzled look as she retrieved the parchment, then passed it to the judges and returned to her station. Pelter eyed his colleagues furiously as if the offending article should have first been delivered into his hands.

The three inquisitors crowded around the parchment, holding corners to keep it flat.

"It bears the high inquisitor's seal . . ." Seldom said.

"A forgery." Dimeon dismissed it with a wave. "The abbess once held that office herself! She kept her seal and—"

"It's Gemon's seal," Agika said. "And his signature."

"I'm not so sure," Brother Dimeon rumbled.

"There is also High Priest Nevis's seal and signature." Agika raised her head and looked towards Glass. "Why would both men give their permission for heresy?"

Seldom stood up, staring at Glass in confusion. "And why would you keep it secret?"

Glass tilted her head and allowed herself a smile. "How else to get a full Inquisition trial beneath the roof of the emperor's sister and the woman herself in chains before the rail?"

Laughter rose from the lords' bench at this, some of it simple amusement, some shocked, some nervous and confused. Here and there a hint of realization dawned. Carvon Jotsis saw it and his eyes widened.

Sherzal shook her arms in an attempt to be rid of the silver chain.

"Judges!" Glass barked out the word. "Your witness has not been given permission to depart."

Agika stood now, then Dimeon, dwarfing her. "What is the meaning of this nonsense?" he boomed.

"Honourable Sherzal!" Agika ignored her fellow judge. "You will remain, please." She waved to Sera who, white-faced, placed herself in Sherzal's path. All around the margins of the great chamber members of Sherzal's personal guard exchanged confused glances.

Glass bowed her head. "I collected you three judges—"

"*You* did not collect them! I collected them!" Pelter shouted.

"I knew where they would be, and when," Glass said. "I chose the time of our departure. Thus I selected them."

"*I* chose the time of our departure!" A note of desperation had entered Pelter's voice. He looked to Sherzal for support. "*I* arrested her!"

Glass looked up. "And I chose when to take the action that made you arrest me." She had thought Zole might go after Nona immediately but the girl had waited until Kettle left, perhaps knowing that Kettle would not have let Nona go without some means of finding her again. Even then Zole had hesitated. She had come to Glass seeking wisdom, and Glass had told her to follow her instinct. "I wanted you to bring me here."

"But why?" Pelter, almost helpless now.

"No court of the Inquisition could ever be set up beneath the roof of the emperor's sister without her invitation," Glass said. "And neither the emperor nor the immediate members of his family can be put on trial anywhere but beneath a Lansis roof."

"But Sherzal is not on trial!" Brother Dimeon blustered.

"She will be once Sister Agika has her arrested and charged." Glass turned her gaze on Agika. "Sherzal's agent took the Church's only shipheart. The case for suspicion is simple and well documented. Under questioning she will admit her guilt and return what was stolen."

Glass had lied when she said that she had chosen the judges. Pelter had been slower to act than anticipated and their journey east more convoluted. However, Agika and Seldom had been high on Glass's list of possibles and she had prayed they would be found. She had also been aware that Brother Dimeon would be a likely inclusion since the last report on the man had him held by his duties on the path Pelter would almost certainly follow. In a minority, however, Brother Dimeon was an asset, his loyalty to Sherzal well known.

A decade earlier, after Glass had made her decision to leave her high office atop the Tower of Inquiry, but before she had announced it, she had set several acts of forward planning in motion. Prime amongst these acts was the fall from grace of certain of her most loyal inquisitors, Seldom and Agika among them. Their arguments and growing mistrust were both public and false, a deception agreed upon by both parties. Former holders of any high office were vulnerable both to their immediate successor and to all those subordinates who resented them. What better insulation against future extremis than to promote to the top of any list of enemies men and women who held secret loyalty to her?

"There's no evidence to base any such charge upon!" Dimeon thumped the table before him. Both Sherzal's bodyguards who had flanked her at the proxy throne now moved to stand behind Sera. Safira was the first to reach her, one hand resting on a sword hilt.

Glass ignored the open threat. "Evidence abounds, Brother Dimeon! Sherzal's own employee, placed at Sweet Mercy on her insistence, stole the shipheart. Were we talking about anyone other than the emperor's sister and the prime instigator of the Inquisition, they would have been arrested and put to the question years ago. Only the impossibility of doing so has prevented formal accusation."

"If this is true," Agika placed each word with care, as if thinking furiously, "why were we three judges not informed?"

"Yes," Brother Dimeon demanded. "We cannot be expected to put our host to the question without instruction from Gemon himself! It's nonsense to suppose he would desire such a trial and yet issue no orders."

Glass appreciated the judges' reluctance. Their authority might stand on firm legal ground but they had only the fact that a full third of the Sis stood witness to ensure their safety. Had the party been concluded by the time Glass was brought to trial, as she had begun to desperately fear that it might, then Sherzal would very likely have had Glass and the inquisitors quietly murdered rather than submit to their inspection and judgment.

Safira's proximity to Sera was a reminder of how swiftly the two Inquisition guards could be overcome. A warning not to take false comfort in the presence of two armed Church enforcers.

Glass motioned for the three judges to take their seats again, and to her surprise, they did. "No word of this possibility was sent out because Sherzal has too many ears among the Inquisition. Any communication would risk discovery. If even a hint of such an idea had reached the palace you three would never have received a formal invitation to enter the premises. Brother Pelter would have taken me to the emperor's palace instead and hoped for a swift conviction before the wider Church and the Tower of Inquiry became involved." Glass was willing to bet a very large sum that had Brother Dimeon received word of the plot then Sherzal would have known of it shortly after. Brother Dimeon would remain Sherzal's creature, but fortunately Inquisition judicial panels could conduct all their business with a simple majority. A unanimous vote was never required.

"And we are now expected to . . ." Brother Seldom stared at Glass. The falling out between Glass and her former disciples had been all about her safety in the years to come. Now she had stood them both at a precipice where it was very much *their* safety at risk. "You want us to—"

"You're expected to do your duty, brother. You have the opportunity to right a great wrong perpetrated against the Church. High Priest Nevis and High Inquisitor Gemon set seal and signature to the dispensation before you exactly to win you this chance to act. The Ancestor's eyes are upon you."

Sister Agika stood. She made a slow turn towards the outrage on Sherzal's face, and with reluctance, as if each word pained her, she said her piece. "Honourable Sherzal, you are hereby under arrest, a prisoner of the Inquisition, charged with theft of a holy relic."

40

━━━━━◆━━━━━

"THE HEARTBEAT IS changing." Nona stopped in the narrow passage, her hand raised before her, fingers spread as if she could feel the shipheart's pulse.

"You're sure?" Kettle limping up behind her.

"Why would it change?" Clera turned back, impatient, the lantern swinging.

Nona didn't know. The beat of the shipheart at Sweet Mercy hadn't changed from the moment she first learned to sense it to the moment it was taken. Without an answer she posed her own question. "You said these tunnels connect with Sherzal's palace. How are we going to get away?"

"There are entrances further down the Grand Pass. We'll get you past the guards somehow and you can be on your way. Bye-bye Tetragode, hello Sweet Mercy."

"Kettle's been stabbed in the leg. She can't walk down a mountain." Nona wasn't sure she could either, though her strength was returning slowly.

"She won't have to. If you get across the pass there's a road with plenty of traffic. You can get a ride on a wagon. You'll be back before the abbess." Clera started to walk away again.

"How steep is this pass? Can Kettle make it ac—" Nona stopped. "'Back before the abbess'?"

"It's pretty steep in places but if you choose your route carefully a three-legged donkey could do it." Clera quickened her pace, her speech quickening too.

"Clera!" Nona stood her ground.

Clera turned, face innocent, body guilty. "Yes?"

"What about the abbess?"

"Oh." Clera lowered the lantern, leaving her face in shadow. "She's at the palace."

"Doing what?" Kettle and Nona asked together. Part of Nona feared that Abbess Glass would be hunting her for the Church. She pushed the thought aside. The abbess had sent Kettle to help her escape.

"The Inquisition brought her," Clera said. "There's to be a trial tonight."

"We have to save her." Nona advanced on Clera, jaw set.

"Do I have to repeat everything I said about going after Zole?" Clera hung her head. "Look, I know it's bad, but I'm sure the old girl will wriggle out of it, and you can't fight your way through Sherzal's guard any more than you could fight your way through the Tetragode. She has an army gathered! A whole army!"

"To hold the pass against the Scithrowl," Kettle said.

"We have to go after her," Nona said.

Clera faked a cough. "Zole . . ."

"The abbess isn't Zole!" Nona shouted. "She's just an old woman. She must be fifty! We have to go after her. Tell her, Kettle!" She rounded on the nun.

Kettle, deadly pale where the shadows ebbed, frowned and said nothing.

"What?" Nona widened her eyes. "It's the *abbess*, Kettle!"

"I know." Kettle leaned against the rock, taking the weight off her injured leg, hissing in relief. "But she gave me this great long speech about how we weren't to fight the Inquisition, about how if we started fighting them then where would it stop? She said it wouldn't stop, and that the Church and the convent would be torn apart. And . . . that the Ancestor would weep to see it."

"That's just . . . words," Nona said helplessly. "We have to do something."

"Even if we could, Nona, the abbess wouldn't thank us for it. She would turn herself over to the authority of the Church at the first opportunity." Kettle shook her head as if imagining Abbess Glass's condemnation. "We have to go. It's what she would want for us. We'll keep her in our hearts." She offered the last thought as if for comfort, as if Nona were still a child.

"Our . . . hearts?" The corner of an understanding angled

into Nona's mind. She held out her hands, one back the way they had come, towards the Tetragode, one to the front, towards Sherzal's palace and the Grand Pass.

"We need to move." Clera shuffled her feet.

"Nona?" Kettle hobbled forward, shadows swirling.

"That's why the beat changed when we travelled." Nona spread her fingers. "I got more of one and less of the other . . ."

"What are you talking about?" Clera, curious despite herself.

"Hearts," Nona said. "There are two shiphearts, not one. The first is behind us, the other ahead." She looked at Kettle. "It's our shipheart, from Sweet Mercy. I'm sure of it!"

"How sure?" Kettle set a hand to Nona's shoulder.

"It doesn't matter how sure she is!" Clera threw up her arms, bashing one on the rock and cursing. "You're not going to get it back with a wounded nun and a sick novice!"

"I know it's there." Nona ignored Clera.

"Take us to the palace, Clera." Kettle advanced on the girl. "We can't leave."

"Not going to happen." Clera backed away.

"If we recover the shipheart the abbess will pardon your crimes, Clera." As Kettle spoke the shadows thickened around them, pressing the lantern's light back towards its source.

"But you won't recover it," Clera said, hand straying towards her hip. "At best you'll die. If you're captured they'll get my name from you, but it will be obvious enough who helped you even if you're killed quickly."

"Get me close to the shipheart." Nona remembered the awful power of the thing, seen and felt through Hessa. "If I lay hands upon it nobody will stop me."

Kettle frowned at that, almost spoke, but bit back the words. "We have to get it back. Any price is worth paying."

Clera made to skip away but Kettle proved too fast, seizing her arm.

"Please, Clera." Nona fixed her eyes on her friend's face. When Nona had shared Kettle's mind she'd felt the strength of the compulsion Zole used. Being twisted like that by Zole's will had woken in Nona an understanding of how to better use her own touch of marjal empathy. "We *need* to do this." Nona's guilt at manipulating her friend stood in the shadow of their cause and the memory of betrayal in another cave years ago. She let the strength of her conviction flow through the cracks in Clera's personality, cracks that she knew of old. Ambition, pride, and a need for challenge.

"I don't know where the shipheart is . . ." Clera started to weaken. "And Yisht might be with it. I don't want to meet her."

"We *need* you, Clera," Nona said. "Aren't you tired of being a tool for these people? I want you back."

Clera frowned. "Sherzal probably keeps it in her treasury."

"And you know where that is?" Kettle asked.

Clera's frown vanished. "Of course!"

HAVING GIVEN CLERA some semblance of conviction Nona found her own fading as they approached the palace. She couldn't reach the Path again so quickly. It would be many hours before she would be able even to see it. How they could hope to penetrate Sherzal's stronghold so deeply without being overwhelmed by her guards Nona had no idea. And without the shipheart there was no chance of saving the abbess.

"We're close now," Clera said. "There will be guards up ahead. They know me. You two they'll put chains on."

Nona frowned. She felt a little better, but hardly fighting fit. Pain and sickness had been replaced by tiredness, hunger, and a fierce thirst. Her ribs still troubled her but were perhaps only bruised rather than broken. Her nose stung where Lano Tacsis had cut her. That particular sting made her angry though and anger chased tiredness into the background. "How many? I don't want to kill them unless I have to."

What? Keot had held silent ever since the aftermath of Nona's Path-walking but now he spoke up. *Kill them! They're the enemy!*

"Normally four on duty with twenty more close at hand. They're quality too, veterans. Sherzal doesn't trust the Noi-Guin any more than she has to. There are sigils on the walls that they say can be used to collapse them if there's an attack."

"So we make our entry unseen," Kettle said.

"Because with all the Noi-Guin in the whole world connected to her palace's basements Sherzal won't have defences against stealthy intrusion?" Clera rolled her eyes. "It can't be done. I just brought you here to prove it."

Kettle and Nona exchanged glances, their faces shadowed, just the edges caught in the glow of Clera's lantern. They shared a nod. Even without a thread-bond Nona knew they both would have understood.

"We'll just have to kill them all," Nona said.

Yes! Keot flushed across her chest, rising along both collarbones. *Yes!*

Clera snorted. "You'd be lucky to take one down before they got you, Nona. And Kettle will be lucky to reach them at all."

"Did the Noi-Guin not teach you all that shade-work can do, Clera?" Kettle closed a pale hand into a black fist, night running liquid from her fingers. "I may be wounded but my shadow can still rend."

Clera shrugged. "Pray too, if you like. You'll still both be dead before the reinforcements get there."

Nona knew it to be true, and knew that Kettle shared the understanding. It didn't matter. With the abbess and the shipheart both in reach, no sister, Grey or Red, would abandon them. The nun took Clera's advice and bent her head to pray.

Nona resisted the urge to join Kettle's devotions, instead looking around the bare tunnel for inspiration. "What we really need," she said, "is a diversion."

Whatever Clera had to say about that Nona never had the chance to find out. The echoing thunder that reached down the tunnel from the palace above took the words from both their mouths.

41

✦

ABBESS GLASS

"YOU PROPOSE TO torture a confession from me? In my own house?" Sherzal's neck burned red above the white froth of her collar. She looked furious rather than scared.

"There are serious charges against you, Sherzal." Sister Agika aimed her dark-eyed regard at the woman, slowly warming to her new role. "Your employee stole an object of incalculable value, exploiting a position that she was only able to obtain at your insistence. Your implicit guarantee of her good conduct demands that you answer our questions. The same investigation would be carried out in any other case."

"You had best vote upon it then. I have pressing matters to attend to." Sherzal waved Agika on as if impatient. "A great many more guests are expected . . ."

"You've nothing to offer in your defence?" Agika raised a brow.

"No, and I don't plead guilty either." Sherzal leaned across her rail to look past the judges at Glass. "Nor special dispensation!"

Sherzal looked entirely too self-composed for Glass's liking, though she suspected that the woman's self-confidence was, like the colour of her eyes, a thing that could not be dimmed. Glass thought that Sherzal would wear that same look of utter confidence were she to topple from a cliff. She'd be staring down the rocks even as they rushed up to greet her.

"We will consider our verdict then." Sister Agika pushed

back her chair. "This court can find you guilty, innocent, or require that you be put to questioning."

To either side of Agika Brothers Seldom and Dimeon rotated their chairs so that all three faced each other. They leaned in close, heads almost touching. Agika began to address her two fellow judges, leading to a swift exchange of heated whispers. Glass had some sympathy: she had put them in a difficult position. Either follow their obvious duty and risk the ire of the empire's most powerful woman within her own walls, or ignore their duty and deal the Inquisition a crushing blow before the assembled leaders of the Sis whilst simultaneously losing the chance to recover one of the Church's most treasured possessions. Even arguing over their decision was a loss of face and authority. Dimeon would most likely opt for "innocent" whatever evidence was presented to him but thankfully a majority was all that was required, and there was no way that Agika and Seldom would not require further investigation.

Glass watched and listened, catching only the occasional word but getting a good sense of the direction of the discussion. As expected, Agika and Seldom were incredulous at Dimeon's refusal to agree to subjecting Sherzal to questioning and both sounded as if they were getting exasperated by their failure to persuade him otherwise.

Then something unexpected. Pauses from Seldom. Interjections where he seemed angry at Agika. And from her, disbelief.

A cold crawling sensation advanced up Glass's spine. Could Seldom somehow have been bought off? He'd always seemed the perfect inquisitor. No family to pressure, an ascetic's disdain for money . . . She'd staked her life and more on the man's integrity. How could he—

Glass looked away from the huddle of judges and scanned the audience. She found Joeli swiftly, the girl's golden hair unmatched among the crowd save in one place. Lines of concentration crossed her usually flawless brow, and her fingers, raised before her chest, twitched.

Glass couldn't see the threads haloed around Seldom nor appreciate the skill with which Joeli was changing the man's mind, but she knew what was happening.

". . . we should vote!" Seldom, his voice strained but decisive.

"We should!" Dimeon, almost crowing with victory.

Glass's jaw tightened, the cold shock of defeat washed through her. She would die here, after-dinner entertainment for these over-fed lords.

". . . but . . . wait . . . I'm confused . . ." Seldom lifted both hands to massage his temples.

At the far end of the guest benches Arabella Jotsis had raised her hands, plucking the air before her, face screwed tight with focused effort. The abbess knew from Sister Pan's reports that Ara's thread-working potential was smaller than Joeli's and her skills far less developed. However, undoing thread-work takes less talent than the original manipulation. The human mind resists tampering and is always trying to return to its natural state.

Among the glittering crowd, Joeli sensed the interference and redoubled her efforts, her jaw taking on a determined set, face darkening. Brother Seldom, caught in the storm, allowed himself to be turned first by Dimeon's arguments, then by Agika's, then by Dimeon's. Slowly though he seemed to be falling back beneath Joeli's influence.

". . . emperor's sister! We just can't . . ."

A loud thump and squeal of outrage snapped Glass's attention back to the guest benches. Joeli lay sprawled in saffron skirts and cream lace, too stunned even to draw breath for a proper scream. The spot on the bench where her bottom had so recently resided lay empty and gleaming. Darla was just straightening up after using her height to lean in from the back, crowding past several outraged matrons, and then to deliver a hefty shove between Joeli's shoulderblades.

"General Rathon, control your daughter!" This from Joen Namsis, rising from the lords' benches.

By the time Darla had been scolded and two palace guards had escorted her from the hall, while Joeli was restored to her seat by several fussing daughters of the Sis, the judging panel had reached their verdict. Sherzal regarded them with a face like thunder.

Agika straightened in her seat. Brothers Dimeon and Seldom pulled back.

"By a majority decision we find good cause for Sherzal Lansis to be put to moderate questioning by an officer of the Inquisition."

Brother Pelter blinked at that, as if unable to comprehend the scale of the change of direction so recently delivered upon him. He would get to use the skills and tools of his trade, just not against the person he had believed would be given into his care.

Sherzal leaned back from the rail, her anger replaced by a speculative look. Glass imagined that she was weighing up her options. She must have realized by now that all she had to do was hold out until her guests had departed—something that she could make happen quite swiftly. Then, with her lordly audience back on the westward roads, she could take matters into her own hands. Later a suitable story could be spun, one of innocence declared followed by a tragic accident involving returning judges. Quite possibly Brothers Dimeon and Pelter might survive such an accident and corroborate Sherzal's version of events . . .

"I have a second document." Glass raised both her voice and her right elbow, gesturing to her side with her head. "That will save the honourable Sherzal the distress of questioning under duress." She saw Sherzal's brows rise at that. Even a woman as redoubtable as the emperor's sister must have had some concerns about inquisition. Moderate duress extended to whippings of various types, along with the stressing of joints and the application of various mechanical devices to the hands and feet. It sounded unpleasant in theory and in practice was fairly horrific.

Melkir came across to extract the second parchment, which was tied with ribbons to Glass's side. A tiny muslin bag hung from the document, sewn to the lower edge. He took it to the judges who crowded together, devouring the words.

Agika pulled the bag free and tipped five small black tablets into the palm of her hand. She pursed her lips. "They look so insignificant . . ."

"A work of genius," Glass said. "The combined efforts of the Academy and the Church's own Mistress Shade. Sadly, they are frighteningly expensive and very time-consuming to prepare. It would be nice to believe that such wonders might one day remove the need for any to suffer in the Inquisition's quest for the truth."

Sister Agika straightened and addressed the lords. "High Inquisitor Gemon has set his signature and seal against this authorization to use these 'truth' pills in the trial of Sherzal. This will allow the Inquisition to avoid inflicting physical harm upon its prime instigator, which would be highly regrettable were she to prove innocent of the charges against her. Furthermore it will permit a swift and public resolution of the matter with the Sis as witness. And—"

"Poison!" Sherzal shouted. "I will not be fed poison from that woman's hand!"

Sister Agika picked a pill from her palm between thumb and finger. "The High Inquisitor's own seal attests to their safety but I am sure that the abbess will not mind taking one herself to set your mind at ease."

Glass minded very much. She understood Sherzal's objections perfectly. For a woman whose power was built upon secrets the compulsion to speak the truth was indeed poison. "I would be delighted, Sister Agika." She smiled and nodded.

Melkir returned with one of the black pills in his hand. He raised it towards Glass's mouth.

"I request that only Judge Agika be permitted to ask me questions, and only those that she plans to put to the prisoner. I know many of the Church's most holy secrets and will not be able to resist betraying them if asked inappropriate questions."

Sister Agika inclined her head. "A reasonable request."

Glass opened her mouth, then closed it. "I'm told the taste of this mixture is incredibly bitter. If I choke or spit it isn't because I am being poisoned." A smile towards Sherzal. She opened her mouth again.

The taste when Melkir placed the pill upon her tongue was far worse than anything Glass had imagined. She clamped her jaw tight, sucked her cheeks in hard, and screwed her eyes shut, willing herself not to vomit or cry out.

It was shouts and exclamations of shock that forced Glass to open her eyes. When the commotion reached through her distress she wondered if the pill had perhaps done something ghastly to her appearance. Then, on focusing her vision, she wondered if Apple's concoction really had poisoned her and the scene before her was hallucination.

Sera had fallen to her knees, hands at her throat, crimson with the blood pulsing between her fingers. Safira stood behind her, knife held steady, its edge scarlet. Sherzal had shaken off her chain and moved from the rail. Several of her house guards flanked her as she approached her throne.

Glass spat out a bitter, black mess from her mouth, pressing her puckered lips into a grim line. Such an attack had always been a possibility but she had felt that the weight of probability lay with Sherzal throwing herself upon her brother's mercy. If Crucical had any murderous instincts towards his siblings then they had certainly given him enough past excuses to act upon. Likely this time he would have banished Sherzal to the ice. The ice being the symbolic punishment, the banishment real. From the ice, no doubt burdened with funds, Sherzal would have been able to return to some other country along the Corridor and live a comfortable life in exile. That was how Glass had anticipated events unfolding. However, she had always known that the chance Sherzal would throw caution to the wind and take to violence was a real one.

Sherzal reached her throne and turned in an imperious swirl of white. "My friends, lords of the Sis, I brought you here not just for the pleasure of your company but to make an announcement."

Sera pitched forward with a clatter and lay still in the spreading pool of her blood. Melkir, ashen-faced, bared his steel and went to stand with the judges, placing himself between them and Safira.

"The moon is falling." Sherzal stood before her throne, hands moving to underscore her words. "The ice is pressing, closing its jaws upon the empire, squeezing all of us from the lowest peasant on the margins to each of you, my brothers and sisters of the Sis. The same ice advances on the Durns and on the Scithrowl, and on their most distant borders it presses equally on the witch-cults of Barron and the Kingdom of Ald."

Lord Jotsis stood up from his chair. "Your servant just murdered an Inquisition enforcer! I demand an explanation, not a lesson in geography!"

"My brother cannot save this empire!" Sherzal carried on

as if Lord Jotsis were still silent and seated. "His armies can barely contain the Durns. Our coast is washed by the Marn but three miles out it might as well be called the Durnsea." She gestured east, waving an arm towards the banqueting hall. "When the Scithrowl come they will not be stopped. These mountains have been all of the empire's strength in the east but they are no longer tall enough to hold back this tide."

The scattered protests at Sherzal's assertion rose above a background of worried silence. Word of the Scithrowl numbers had been spreading westward like a plague.

"The moon is falling!" Sherzal raised her arms. "Listen to the words. We say 'When the moon falls' and by that saying we mean *never* . . . but I'll repeat myself. The moon *is* falling." She scanned the room, her stare challenging any dissent. "The moon is falling but it has not fallen yet. It will fly a lifetime more, and another perhaps, but in that time the northern ice will hasten its advance towards the southern."

"What do the Scithrowl want with us, my lords? Why brave the harsh slopes of the Grampains? Why spend their blood here instead of racing across the hills of the Ald?" Sherzal allowed no time for answers. "The Ark can control the moon. She who controls the moon owns the Corridor. Adoma, battle-queen, knows this. She also knows that my brother would break the Ark asunder before he let it fall to those who had destroyed our empire, and rightly so."

Lord Jotsis, still on his feet, found his voice again. "If the Ark controls the moon why is Crucical not exploiting such a power?"

"How could the moon be used to save us?" Lord Tacsis asked from his seat. If Glass was any judge it was a question posed to allow Sherzal to answer. Lord Tacsis had been alone in his lack of surprise at the unfolding of recent events.

"The Ark can aim the moon," Sherzal said. "It can make the moon's focus spend more time in one part of the Corridor, less in another. With such control we could push back the ice from the empire—"

"And the price?" Lord Jotsis demanded.

"Somewhere else the ice would advance more swiftly," Sherzal replied.

From the muttering behind Lord Jotsis it seemed that many of the Sis didn't consider this too high a cost.

"Why then does Crucical not use this power?" Lord Tacsis presented Carvon Jotsis's first point as if it were his own. "The emperors have dwelled in the Ark for centuries."

Sherzal acknowledged the question with a nod. "The Ark needs to send energy to the moon so that it may flex and turn. To provide sufficient energy four shiphearts are required, and because of an ancient covenant set to ensure unity of purpose between the tribes, they must be the hearts of ships from each of the four tribes. Without these shiphearts the Ark cannot even be opened."

A ripple of understanding ran through the crowd, followed by confusion.

"There are only three shiphearts in all of the empire." Lord Glosis, her voice rusty with age and querulous. "And even if you *have* stolen from the Church you do not own the other two!"

"Strength is built from alliances, Lord Glosis." Sherzal exposed her shark's smile. "The strength of the great bow comes from the alliance of different woods, each with their own contribution to make." She turned to the judges. "I said I would not plead guilty or claim dispensation. But I did not plead innocent. The truth is that I ordered the shipheart taken from Sweet Mercy convent. I state it now, with no shame. Guilty of taking from a handful of nuns, isolated on a lonely rock, something of incalculable benefit to all of the empire. Guilty of putting all our futures before the elitism of the Grey and the Red, and before the selfish abstractions of Holy Witches." Sherzal walked behind her throne, facing the room over its high back. "The Noi-Guin have a marjal shipheart."

A muttered discontent rose immediately. Many families among the Sis had lost members to the Noi-Guin. The deaths were often commissioned by other families, most of the remaining casualties were ordered "in-house" as a means of advancing personal prospects within a family.

"If you would see an end to the Noi-Guin," Sherzal said, "I know of a way that will succeed where hundreds of years and thousands of troops have failed. Bring them into the fold. Let them take their place at the high table as the Noisis and there will be no more Noi-Guin. Let them add their shipheart to our cause."

"That's two." Old Lord Glosis, hunched within her robes despite the heat.

Glass found herself sweating with the crackle and roar from the hearth behind her. She began to unwind her chain though she had no hope of escape.

"Two." Sherzal held up a pair of fingers. "And Adoma has the last two required." She raised the remaining fingers on her hand.

"You plan to invade Scithrowl?" A lord at the back barked a laugh.

"I plan an alliance." Sherzal lowered her hand.

"With the battle-queen!" Carvon Jotsis's outrage had nowhere left to take him, so he sat down. Others rose to their feet—many of them—cries of "Treachery!" on their lips.

"You would sell us into Scithrowl chains?" Lord Mensis cried.

Shouts of "Heresy!" from the judges' bench.

"Adoma will provide two shiphearts and her war clans will clear our path to Verity," Sherzal said, her voice rising above the swell of complaint. "My brother will be faced with two choices, where before he had only one, though he will not admit it.

"The first choice is to have the Scithrowl take the empire under their control, have their heresy in every church of the Ancestor, have our people enslaved, our nobility overthrown. Surely Crucical would ruin the Ark to deny them such a prize, but it would be a hollow victory, one battle in a lost war. This is currently his only choice. The Scithrowl cannot be held.

"The second choice is to accept me as the new emperor, maintaining the Lansis dynasty. To take the offer of Adoma's shiphearts and by adding them to our own to gain dominion over the moon itself.

"Adoma will, through the sigil-work of her mages, retain the ability to destroy her two shiphearts from her own throne and in doing so destroy the Ark. This is her assurance of our good faith. But *we* will control the moon, and in exchange for its use in preserving Scithrowl and in furthering Adoma's interests to the east, she will withdraw her forces.

"Our borders will be secured, our future ensured for generations to come, our honour restored. We will let the ice crush Durn and the moon will burn their ports to ash. And you, my friends, by joining your forces to my advance, will ensure that the flower of the empire survives this crisis and that your position as prime among the Sis is assured, favoured by my throne."

The shouts of protest continued but began to ebb, many lords falling to intense discussion with their neighbours. Glass knew enough of folk to see that the tide had turned and all that remained was for Sherzal's guests to realize it themselves.

"The only casualties that are unavoidable stand before us." Sherzal recaptured the lords' attention. "The Inquisition will never accept a Scithrowl alliance. I will need to make an end of the abbess and her organization." She waved a hand at the judges. "Can any among you claim that the Inquisition is a thing of worth, an asset that should not be sacrificed in the cause of greater good?"

And Abbess Glass, her tongue possessed by a poison that compelled the truth, had to answer. "No."

GLASS FOUND HER voice again as Sherzal's guards advanced on the judges' bench.

"The Inquisition may be a price worth paying, Sherzal, but your assassin killed an innocent child when stealing from the Church of the Ancestor. A child's life was too high a cost. As are all the lives that will be spent when the Scithrowl hordes sweep along the roads to Verity. The battle-queen may withdraw, she may not, but even if the hordes do return to the east it will be like a storm-tide retreating, leaving devastation." Glass spoke nothing but the truth and she spoke it with the confidence of her office, exerting a magic all of her own, one that stilled the chatter of the lords and even made Sherzal's soldiers pause in their advance on Melkir. "All this blood spilled for your ambition, Sherzal! If this myth of shiphearts and wielding the moon were true then Crucical himself could strike such a bargain with Adoma. If you shared your knowledge with him no Scithrowl would have reason to cross the Grampains. *If* it were true."

"Well, *take* her!" Sherzal urged her guards on.

Melkir levelled his sword but Safira moved faster than the eye, stepping around the blade and locking her right leg behind his left to send him clattering to the floor.

Glass spoke on, even as the guards closed around her. "And all the peoples of the Corridor are children of the Ancestor, whether they know it or not, whatever borders enclose them. Crucical would not use the moon as a weapon of aggression. It is our gift from those far deeper in the Ancestor's great tree than we. The emperor could seek ways to better employ the moon's blessing, and to deter others from attack. The empire could become the jewel on Abeth's belt, not a dark and murderous master, condemning whole nations to icy ruin."

Two guards took Glass's arms, seeming unsure what to do next while she kept on addressing their mistress.

"Your plan has much in it that is good, Sherzal. What it does not require is *you*. No part of the greater good requires you to sit as emperor!"

"Silence the woman!" Sherzal shouted. "Or must I do it my—"

The sound that overwhelmed all others was an enormous and physical thing, as if a giant's hammer had struck the palace—not against the outer walls but here within the chamber. Chairs and their occupants flew in all directions, centred on the area where the Sis families had been seated. Cracks, wide enough to receive fingers, even whole hands, ran out across the marbled floor, a cloud of powdered stone rising from the impact site.

Motion behind and above the scene caught Glass's eye, a large figure driving smaller ones from behind a screen in the musicians' gallery. Darla! Her opponents were archers, crossbows useless at such range. Their weapons must have been trained on the one guest that Sherzal knew had the potential to be her greatest physical threat. Slipping away during the trial to deal with Ara's watchers would have been an impressive feat for someone closer to seven foot tall than to six, but Darla had managed to get herself escorted out, saving the need for subterfuge.

The dust began to settle. In its midst a figure on one knee, one hand to the floor. A woman in the tatters of a dress. The fabric, indeed the whole of her form, shuddering, shifting . . . warping . . . as she struggled to contain her power.

Arabella Jotsis! The archers must have been instructed to shoot her at any sign that she had begun to walk the Path. The last of their number fell, wailing, from the gallery.

And Ara stood, the glow around her limbs and torso almost too bright to look upon.

42

⸺ ✦ ⸺

THE DETONATION UP in the main levels of the palace drew all the guards from their subterranean barracks, leaving just three of the four who had been on duty in the corridor.

"If they get to the sigil-work on the walls we're done for," Clera said. "I don't know what it does, but Sherzal puts enough faith in it not to have a gate between her and the Noi-Guin."

"And we can be pretty sure there are sigils there that will strip away shadow-work," Nona said.

"So, you go up there and incapacitate them, Clera." Kettle waved her on. "They'll let you get close, then . . ."

"I'm not sure I could stop them all in time." Clera frowned.

"Jab a pin varnished with lock-up into them," Nona said, remembering a certain cave and unable to keep a trace of bitterness from her voice.

"They're dosed with standard venoms every month to keep their tolerance high. Sherzal knows the Noi-Guin's tricks. Besides, I don't want them to know it was me."

Nona unwrapped the chain around her waist. She'd fixed it there as a belt for the remains of her prison smock, and to provide a place to thrust the spare blades picked up after the battle at the cell-block. She set down her weapons and gave the chain to Kettle. Next she crossed her arms, back to back, the knuckles of one hand resting against the inside of the elbow of the other. "Bind me."

Kettle started to wrap both limbs together, turn after turn of the chain. "I used this ploy with Zole at the entrance to the

Tetragode. I don't think it will work here though . . . I look like a Lightless."

"That's why I'm going alone," Nona said.

Kettle finished binding Nona's arms and tucked the end of the chain away. "If Clera doesn't think she can disable the three of them quickly enough what makes you think you can?"

"That's right." Clera scowled. "I'm as fast as you are! These men aren't pushovers. It just takes a moment for them to touch the right sigil and then—"

"Because I *want* to kill them." Nona let Keot take her tongue, her voice becoming a snarl, something alien. "I hunger for their deaths. I want their blood to spill. I've been trapped, boxed, poisoned, abused, and now it's my turn. I don't fear destruction. It's the desire to survive that slows you, girl. I—" Nona wrested control back from Keot, coughed and added in her normal voice, "If that's all right with you?"

Clera, pale now, backed against the tunnel wall, her eyebrows raised, and offered her palms in the "be my guest" gesture.

Nona walked on alone, the ribbons of her smock loose around her, body filthy with grime and gore, her chained arms held up before her. Days of starvation had taken flesh from her bones and she hadn't any to spare before she was captured. She put a limp into her step and hung her head as she came into the circle of the first lantern's light.

"Ice!" An oath from the trio in the corridor ahead of her.

"Help me." Croaked out, too soft for them to hear perhaps.

"It's a girl." The sound of swords clearing scabbards.

"One of their prisoners?" A deep voice.

"A child." The one with a hint of sympathy. "Chained."

"Get away!" Barked at her, harsh.

Nona kept up her advance all the while, slow, steady. "Help me."

"We can't help you, girl."

"Get yourself back. There's ways out. You might find one before they catch you." This one took a certain pleasure in her predicament. The Noi-Guin would not be kind to any escaped prisoner.

"Help me."

"I'm warning you! Come any closer . . ."

Nona set her fingertips to the chain and rippled her flaw-blades into being.

"Help." She lifted her head. "Me."

In the moment while the three men registered the alien blackness of her eyes Nona tore one arm across the other, shredding iron links beneath her blades. She scattered chain segments at the guards and sprinted the remaining five yards, hurling herself sideways into the air. Deep in the moment, Nona twisted to ride both above and below the sword blades reaching towards her. She hit all three men with her back to them, one arm extended to drive blades into the neck of the leftmost man, the other arm crooked to skewer the groin of the middle man, her legs tangling with the legs of the man on the right.

All of them fell. Before they hit the ground Nona had ripped her blades from the leftmost man's neck and doubled up to stab the rightmost in the head. She cut short the cries of the groin-stabbed man with a slash across his throat.

Kettle and Clera ran from the shadows where corridor gave way to natural tunnel, and found Nona sitting across the three bodies, panting, blood arcs spattering the sigil-scribed walls.

"I thought we were going to . . . knock them out," Clera said in a small voice.

Nona levered herself up, her exhaustion returning with a vengeance. "Let's go."

NONA WATCHED THE corridor while Clera and Kettle searched the dead for keys or anything else of use. The symbols etched into the walls pulled at the corners of her vision. Which of the sigils would collapse the tunnel Nona had no idea, but had there been even a single additional guard it would have been hard to stop them activating one and bringing the roof down. Had there been a whole barracks full of them, it would have been impossible.

Kettle distributed the throwing stars she had recovered from the bodies of her earlier targets. Nona found a length of rope in the barracks room to replace her chain belt. She thrust her Noi-Guin sword through it and accepted two stars from the nun.

Clera led them on, nerves showing. "I've no idea how you talked me into this, Nona." She flattened herself against the wall and peered around the corner before moving on towards a flight of stone stairs. "I mean, I missed you . . . but I had a good thing going here. Sherzal and Lord Tacsis are—"

"Vicious maniacs who would fill the Corridor with blood just to float themselves a little higher than their already lofty stations," Kettle finished for her.

"Well." Clera advanced soft-footed up the stairs. "Yes." She paused and advanced again. "But very rich."

Nona brought up the rear, a throwing star in each hand.

I like your friend. Keot seemed louder in her skull than he had for some time.

An understanding struck Nona as moments of clarity sometimes do when all the parts of a problem come momentarily into some chance alignment. *When I kill and rage . . . your grip on me grows stronger.*

Only a silence where Keot should be.

And when I show mercy or kindness you're driven to the surface.

"Nona!" Kettle beckoned her to the corner ahead. "Servants." The nun reached a hand around Nona's shoulder, the other arm around Clera, sharing her weight on the pair of them rather than her injured leg. "I'll hide us." Shadows rose to wrap them and although Nona still felt visible, albeit darkly shadowed, she knew that Kettle had worked the trick of hers that would deceive any casual and untrained eye into seeing nothing but perhaps a thickening and a flicker of the shade. She concealed them from the worry-faced servants who came and went. Of Sherzal's guards there were few signs.

Stealth is best achieved in the patience trance. Nona had conquered the clarity trance first, and finally serenity, but she had never truly mastered patience. She tried though, focusing on her mantra, an image of a green shoot just broken through the soil and waiting to grow. She found that being exhausted helped. With Kettle's weight on her shoulder and the shadows flowing cold around her, she found a kind of patience and schooled both her breathing and her footfalls to match the palace ambience, fitting them into the spaces provided by the moan of the wind, the distant clatter of feet or shutting of doors, the sounds that underwrote each day beneath that roof, unmarked and unheard.

They paused at a second flight of stairs.

"We've been incredibly lucky so far," Kettle whispered. "So lucky it almost feels like a trap. We can't count on things staying this way. Whatever problem is drawing the guards off is unlikely to keep them away for long."

"Once I've got my hands on the shipheart it won't matter," Nona said. "Let them come." She could feel its power even now, and Hessa's memory promised so much more as they got closer.

The arm with which Kettle held Nona to her stiffened a little and, after a pause, the nun spoke. "A shipheart is a dangerous thing. As dangerous to the person who holds it as to anyone they aim that power at. If we're going to do this I think I should be the one to carry it . . ."

"You can hardly walk!" Nona said.

"I don't know what it would do to you, Nona." Kettle's voice was tight with conflicting concerns. "There are books at Sweet Mercy that say the shipheart is too strong for mortals to get close to. It twists them." She was talking about Keot. Nona felt sure Kettle knew she carried a devil beneath her skin, and the nun didn't believe her pure enough to touch a shipheart. It hurt to hear Kettle's doubt in her. But it was probably well founded.

"Well we're not going to find out standing here." Clera bumped them both back into motion.

With Clera's direction and Kettle's shadows the three of them wound their way deeper into the palace, through galleries and halls so numerous that Nona wondered who used them, and whether Sherzal saw any of these grand spaces more than once a year. They crossed a small internal courtyard, like a deep sky-roofed pit in the palace, at the heart of it a lonely fountain, and came at last to a corridor where an iron gate blocked their progress.

"Locked." Clera ran her hands up the scroll-worked bars. "Solid."

Kettle sat, leg held stiffly to the side, fresh blood glistening amid the dried. Taking three heavy picks from her sleeve, she addressed the lock. Within seconds the mechanism yielded, clunking as she rotated the picks together. "Done."

They helped Kettle up and went on, advancing down a long lamp-lit corridor, passing many closed doors.

"We're getting close," Nona said. The shipheart's presence pushed on her, filled her, set her nerves tingling, the feeling both exciting and a little terrifying.

"We are." Clera shot her a look. "There's a barracks room ahead and to the left. They say Yisht's quarters are around here too, but I've not seen her since that day with the barrel." Clera bit her lip, frowning. "And you know what? I really don't want to see her again. Especially not when all I've got for protection is you two walking wounded." She shrugged off Kettle's arm. "We really should go back."

"We're going to get our shipheart!" Nona helped Kettle on alone.

"Sherzal's guards are scared of Yisht." Clera's voice came from behind them now. She wasn't moving. "They say she came back changed."

"There's a reason the shipheart was kept walled up in the caves," Kettle said.

Nona's mind was full of the shipheart now, close, powerful, the beat of it running through her, not kind, not comforting, just vast and endless.

I feel it too. Keot's voice held a certain hunger.

You do?

Like a memory. I know this thing. It's old, as old as I am. He sounded stronger by the moment.

But . . . the shiphearts are older than the empire! Nona wasn't sure how old they were but certainly thousands of years. Enough time for nations to rise and fall, for knowledge to fail and be rebuilt. *The shiphearts brought the tribes to Abeth.*

Do you think so?

You don't? Nona didn't like the smugness in the devil's voice. *Everyone knows they did.*

Maybe they drew your people here. They didn't carry them.

What do you know about it? You never know the answer to anything interesting. All of a sudden you know things?

The heart is waking up my memories.

And why would it do that? Nona kept her eyes on the doorways ahead, trying not to let Keot distract her.

Because it's where I was born.

Nona made no reply, returning her attention to the corridor. Keot's certainty unsettled her. There *was* a draw to the shipheart's presence. Perhaps the fascination that the flame holds for the moth. She felt its pull in the marrow of her bones.

They advanced around another corner. From her time with Hessa Nona knew that the shipheart had to be within fifty feet or so now. Keot blazed across her chest and down over her abdomen. He seemed to be feeding on the shipheart's power in ways that Nona couldn't understand. His natural anger and lust to kill began to bleed out into her. Earlier she had felt his grip on her weakening and thought that one day she might be able to drive him out. Kettle must know of the devil now, having worn Nona's flesh and bones back in the Tetragode. What she might do about it was a problem for later. If there was a later.

A cold shiver ran through Nona, toes to head, pulling her away from thoughts of Keot. Something had changed. Suddenly the halls of Sherzal's palace seemed echoingly empty, not conveniently empty but as if Nona had turned around in a crowded market square to find in that instant the place stood deserted with just the wind to stir the space where people should have been.

"She's watching us," Nona said, knowing it to be true though not knowing how. She tried to reach for her own anger rather than Keot's and found only fear. Over her shoulder she saw that Clera was backing away.

The cracking of stone was their only warning. Shards of masonry broke from the wall at the margins of the area from which Yisht stepped. She emerged behind them, the stonework releasing her with reluctance, as if she were pulling free of thick mud.

Clera spun around with a squeal of fear. Nona and Kettle disentangled, turning as they did, the nun hopping back on her good leg.

Yisht broke clear about the same time that Clera recovered enough of her wits to hurl the throwing stars she'd been given. Kettle and Nona threw theirs a fraction later, six in the first volley, more following.

Clera had never been particularly accurate with throwing stars. Her right-hand throw at least centred on Yisht's body mass, the left angled wide of target. Lacking hunska speed, though, the warrior should have been hit at least five times. She stepped through the hail of sharp metal unharmed. Her ability to read the immediate future allowed her to begin plotting a path that would evade the stars even before her opponents had decided to throw them.

Yisht *had* changed. She wore the same black garb, knives across her chest in a black leather harness, her tular—the flat-bladed sword favoured by the ice-tribes—at her hip. She seemed to wear the same body too, though it moved in unnatural ways as if occupied by some larger presence. The flat bones of her face cut the same angles, but her black eyes sat in a crimson sea rather than the whites she once had, and her skin had become a moving patchwork of scarlet, deep purple, black, grey, and bone-white.

Nona knew exactly what she was looking at. "She's full of devils."

Where Nona had one, and Raymel had returned from death's border with four, Yisht had so many that they competed for space, surging across any exposed skin. Nona could almost hear them screaming for her blood.

Clera, who had been closest to the point where Yisht emerged, now passed Kettle and Nona, moving fast. "I know another way out!"

"We want the vault, not a way out!" Kettle called after her. To Nona's ear the nun didn't sound as convinced as she had before.

Nona gathered her courage, reaching for another weapon. Kettle set her back against the wall, calling on the shadows. The sword Nona drew from her rope belt felt unfamiliar in her hand, a Noi-Guin blade, a little shorter, straighter, and heavier than the swords Sister Tallow trained the novices with.

Yisht had never been one for smiling, but she smiled now, her teeth bloody. She pulled her tular from the grip of its scabbard, along the side slit as tulars are nearly twice as broad at the end as at the hilt. By rights she should be the one afraid, facing a sword-trained novice whose speed could leave her swinging at air.

Nona held her ground, making test cuts to learn the feel of her weapon. Behind her the darkness began to thicken and clot as Kettle focused her strength to give the night claws.

Yisht came in at a steady pace, sword before her, arm extended.

"Clera!" Nona called after her departing friend. Yisht had defeated them both once before, along with a classful of other novices, but they had been children then.

"Friends are a weakness," Yisht said. "I taught Zole this lesson."

She attacked as she spoke and at the first parry Nona's sword was all but taken from her hands. The ice-triber's strength was incredible. Nona struck back, launching a blinding sequence of blows, moving as fast as she ever had. Yisht met each one with a perfectly placed parry. Nona tried to carry her slices over the interposed edge but Yisht somehow twisted her blade to stop such moves, almost disarming her.

A vicious swing at stomach level had Nona leaping backward, pulling in her hips and belly as the end of Yisht's tular sliced within a finger's breadth.

How can you be losing? Keot howled.

She knows everything I'm going to do! Nona turned a thrust from her chest. *She can see the future.*

She can't see the future, just what you and your friends are going to do next, because you're such primitive things. She can't predict a dice roll or see what I will do.

Well, do something then! Nona deflected another attack, feeling the wind ripple behind Yisht's tular as it passed her face. *Don't just talk!* But she knew that talk was all Keot had.

It's easy, Keot said. *Do something she can't stop even if she knows it's coming!*

Nona fell back another step then leapt into the moment. She swung at Yisht's head from the woman's right and their two blades met in a jarring crash. Nona pulled her sword away, starting to rotate on a heel. She accelerated into the motion, turning her back on Yisht, relying only on the lack of time to keep the woman from cutting her down. Yisht's sword was high up on her right side, still shaking with the echoes of that last parry. If Nona could spin around and cut in low from the left there was no way Yisht could physically move her blade fast enough to interpose it.

Yisht's boot heel smacked into Nona's backside as her spin turned her through the half-circle. She must have started the kick before Nona started turning, and it sent her sprawling away onto her front. Nona barely managed to avoid being skewered by the follow-up, pinned to the floor. She rolled away beneath Yisht's descending blade with an inch to spare.

Kettle's shadows launched themselves at Yisht over Nona's prone body. Nona saw the ice-triber fall back before the mass of rending darkness, just as she had once fallen back before Nona's own avenging shadow.

A moment later the nightmare of claws and teeth fell apart, collapsing into a wash of darkness. Nona rolled just in time to see the chunk of stone and plaster that had struck Kettle fall to one side as the nun dropped bonelessly to the other. Yisht must have used her rock-work to break the lump free. Nona could see the spot where the piece had fallen from, high above Kettle where the wall joined the ceiling. But the blow was a glancing one. Kettle had sensed it at the last, and managed to pull back far enough to save her skull from being smashed.

Yisht came on at speed, neatly sidestepping a knife that came winging down the corridor. Nona only just got to her feet in time to meet the attack. She held her place between Kettle and the ice-triber, trading blows. Although her speed kept Yisht on the defensive each clash of swords threatened to tear Nona's from her fingers. Her arm ached and she was tiring swiftly. Of Clera there was no sign other than the knife.

Kill her! Keot sounded desperate. The devil drove himself into Nona's right hand, strengthening her grip on the sword hilt.

Kill her!

Too crowded for you inside Yisht, is it? Don't fancy sharing?

Nona fought on. To her side she caught a glimpse of Kettle starting to move. An arm lifting to her head. A groan followed.

Yisht stumbled, her footing wrong after a difficult parry, one boot skidding on scattered ceiling plaster. Seeing her chance, Nona pressed the advantage but suddenly found her sword stolen from her hand by some wrist-rolling action that went unrevealed until the result had become inevitable. Yisht surged up, her stumble a ruse, and Nona, now letting time escape only in the smallest fractions, suddenly became aware of several square feet of ceiling plaster descending upon her. The falling mass had already covered more than half the distance to the floor.

Nona dived back, twisting from the thrust of Yisht's blade, turning her shoulder to the plaster as it hammered into her. She hit the ground hard in a white cloud of dust and fragments, rolled and kept rolling, knowing that a razored tular would come scything out of the dust any moment.

But none did.

The air cleared to reveal Yisht, her blacks now whitened, the slow colour-tides across her skin pale beneath powdered plaster. She stood with one foot pressing Kettle's head to the floorboards, the blade of her sword against the nun's pale throat. Whatever looked at Nona from her eyes did not appear to be human.

"Friends are a weakness," Yisht repeated. "You should run away now . . . but you won't." She moved the sword a fraction and Nona cried out. Yisht smiled, the devils fighting over her tongue. "You should have let me kill you back in the convent. I was different then. Not kind, but not cruel. That has changed. Now I am cruel."

Run away, Keot said. *The nun's doomed. In any case, she's just a burden.*

"I will cut her throat on the count of three. One . . ."

No! Run! Keot shrieked. *Run, you idiot . . .* His voice growing faint and thin.

Nona threw herself forward empty-handed. Yisht timed her move perfectly, lifting her sword with a spray of blood just as Nona's feet left the ground, committing her to her trajectory.

The tular came level with Nona as she reached it, ready to impale her. She lashed out with her flaw-blades, her fingers scarlet where Keot had invaded them. Her blades met steel, slicing the weapon into bright, tumbling sections, but Yisht had seen what would happen, and had seen the last foot of her sword, deflected from Nona's chest, piercing her upper thigh instead and grating over bone.

Yisht sidestepped Nona's tackle and the girl fell to the ground beside Kettle with a scream, her leg a hot, wet agony. The remains of Yisht's tular fell beside her, torn from the woman's grasp.

"I could leave you both to bleed to death. I doubt you'd last until Sherzal's guards found you." Yisht stepped back, beyond range if Nona had the strength to swing at her.

The blood pumped from the wound in Nona's leg at an alarming rate. If she hadn't had to slaughter pigs on Sister Tallow's instructions she would not have believed how much blood was in her or how fast it could leave. Of course she had inflicted worse wounds on others, but in the heat of battle there was no time or desire to observe the aftermath.

Direct pressure on the wound. That was the most important thing. Unless something else was about to kill you more quickly, of course.

Yisht had a small package in her hand. "Grey mustard. I had hoped to spend more time helping you make a slow exit from this world." The creature didn't sound like Yisht any more. "I hear that Lord Tacsis wanted the same pleasure. But grey mustard isn't exactly a kindness . . ."

"No!" Nona didn't want to beg, but she knew what the stuff could do. "Please." She raised her hand as if she could somehow ward off the coming cloud of spores.

And as she did so, something red left her fingers, a crimson cloud, its tendrils seeking purchase on her skin but losing their grip one by one as though some force were sucking it from her. *No!*

A moment later Keot lost his last connection with her and shot away as though drawn by a bowstring, to hit Yisht square in the forehead.

The ice-triber drew in a huge breath like the gasp made when you fall into freezing water. She dropped the grey mustard package and staggered back, still gasping, wheezing for air. All across her skin the devil taints swirled, flowing over her, converging on her head. Somehow Keot had been sucked from or driven from Nona, or both at once, and his initiation into Yisht's crowded flesh did not appear to be a gentle one.

The pain in Nona's leg demanded her attention. She pressed her fingers hard into the wound where the blood spurted with each beat of her slowing heart, and rolled, awkwardly, to see Kettle, with both hands pressed to a crimson throat, eyeing her frantically. Nona reached out to pull Kettle's robe open, exposing the tight-bound bandolier of poisons and cures. In amongst them would be stanching powder, which when applied to wounds would, along with causing excruciating pain, dramatically reduce the blood flow. Nona could see only two containers that looked as if they might hold powder, and snatched one at random. Kettle gave a slight nod. Behind them Yisht bellowed and roared, underlining the need for haste.

Nona readied the stanching agent, raised herself from the ground, and pulled one of Kettle's hands from her throat, trying not to grimace. The cut wasn't as deep as she had feared given all the blood. Kettle must have managed to jerk her head back and lessen the damage. The nun held the middle of the slice together, pinched between finger and thumb, while Nona applied the powder. Kettle immediately went rigid, showing her teeth in agony's grimace. The wash of blood slowed, clotting darkly around the powder.

Nona rolled to her side and applied the remains of it to her leg wound. It hurt less than the Harm, despite her fears. She had Thuran Tacsis to thank for showing her that whatever hurts she suffered in life, worse were possible.

"Come." A pained rasp from Kettle.

Nona reached out for her sword, thrust it through her belt, and together they began to crawl away down the corridor. Behind them, Yisht was throwing herself around, impacting the walls, roaring, shattering masonry.

With every yard they put between Yisht and themselves Nona's fear grew that the ice-triber's raging would summon Sherzal's guards. It seemed, though, that whatever the emergency was that had drawn away those charged with the defence of the emperor's sister, it was proving to be a big one.

After twenty yards Nona got to her feet using the wall for support and helped Kettle up. Apart from the pain and weariness she felt a kind of emptiness, a hole where Keot had been. She had tried so hard to be rid of the devil, especially in the early days, turning the whole of her will against him, but to no avail. And then, at her weakest, he'd been ejected without conscious effort, like a sickness coughed out . . .

The reason came to Nona as a small epiphany, only half-believed. Every time she forgave, every time she showed love or loyalty, the devil's hold on her had been weakened . . . Was that really all it had taken? For her to throw herself between a friend and certain death?

Kettle and Nona hobbled on, leaning on each other, and as they approached the junction where another passageway intersected their own Nona saw Clera peeking from the corner.

"Ancestor's balls! What did you do to her?" Clera stared past them.

Kettle made no reply, hurrying around the corner and out of sight of Yisht. Nona let the nun go and took a last look at Yisht before joining her. The woman was hunched on the floor, curled around whatever battle was raging through her. Her howling had subsided to terrifying groans.

Nona longed to go back and kill the ice-triber, to give her the end her crimes demanded, but the shipheart lay close at hand and time was short. She pulled back out of sight, turning to see that Kettle had crouched down against the wall, a small ceramic tub of black ointment in her hand. The nun removed some of it on the end of a thin wooden applicator and offered it to Nona, pointing the blackened end towards her throat where she still pinched the sides of the cut together.

The stuff had an acrid smell and Nona knew it for flesh-bind, a costly adhesive that stuck flesh to flesh with frightening swiftness, forming a bond that was hard to break. The price of the ingredients, along with common sense, forbade its use by any but the oldest novices in Holy Class. Too many girls had been glued together in compromising positions in past years to allow its use by the younger and more mischievous novices. An unfortunate side-effect was that if left too long it would permanently dye the skin black too.

Nona applied the stuff to the edges of Kettle's wound and, steeling her stomach against the grisly business, pressed the skin together, taking care not to get glued in place. The end result proved messy but effective.

Kettle repaid the favour on Nona's leg, more quickly and with far neater results. Clera hovered anxiously, taking quick glances around the corner to check on Yisht.

Nona stretched her injured leg. It hurt like hell. "Where's the vault?" she asked.

"Back there." Clera waved absently towards double doors that stood ajar at the end of the corridor. "It's a steel box big enough to fit a horse in. Stuffed full of Sherzal's treasures. You can't carry it and you'll never get it open." She sounded wistful, as if the proximity and inaccessibility of such wealth were a source of great sorrow to her.

Nona could feel the shipheart. The hidden fire that had drawn her forward had now grown into something awful, too fierce to dare. Like the fire in the hearth it was something you wanted to come close to until suddenly you were close enough and another step would see you burned. She lifted her hand, fighting weariness, and forced her flaw-blades into being. They flickered unevenly. "I'll get in."

"It's sigil-worked. I don't think you'll cut it." Clera flinched as a particularly loud howl from Yisht shook the air. "We have to go! I checked ahead. There's some kind of battle going on in the great halls downstairs. It's the ideal distraction."

Nona shook her head. "We came for the shipheart."

"No." Kettle gripped Nona's arm with surprising strength.

"No?" Nona blinked. "But we—"

"The shipheart . . . does things . . . if you get too close. What happened to Yisht . . . It's too powerful. It takes anything bad in you and gives it voice. It makes—"

"Devils!" Nona said.

Kettle nodded. "I think you just lost something that you don't want back. How would you fare if the shipheart makes six replacements of your very own from the darkest parts of your mind? Speaking with your own voice?"

"But—"

"It would take someone of extraordinary purity to carry a shipheart unscathed. We're none of us that." She looked down. "I hadn't understood how quickly the effects could occur or how bad they could be," Kettle said. "We have to go."

"Now!" Clera shouted. "We have to go *now*!" Her loudness suddenly made Nona realize how quiet it had become. Yisht had fallen silent, and Nona doubted it was a good thing.

Even so Nona hesitated. "We came for the shipheart . . ." Amidst the consuming aura of the thing she felt something more, there was a bond. Something of her lay in there too . . . her shadow! She understood it in that moment. The shipheart had drawn her shadow in, whether in Yisht's defence or by its own nature. "We can't come this close and just leave."

Clera screwed up her face, locked in some inner battle. At last the words blurted from her. "Ara's here. That's what the fighting downstairs must be. They're trying to rescue the abbess."

Nona stared at her in disbelief that she would have kept such a thing quiet.

The shipheart was just a thing: but downstairs her friends could be dying.

"Let's go."

43

---◆---

ABBESS GLASS

ARABELLA JOTSIS SHONE brighter than Abeth's sun had burned during the lives of men. A white light broke from her, like the Hope that stood as a lone diamond in the ruby heavens. Abbess Glass turned away from the girl, shielding her eyes. Someone blundered into her, a perfumed woman, tripping over her long gown. Glass caught her shoulders, steadying her. "Cover your eyes, dear. It will be all right."

It took Glass a few more moments to realize she held Joeli Namsis. Her grip tightened. "Joeli?" Even now she wasn't sure, her vision full of afterimages. "Joeli! You can try to end this! With your skills you might make peace here. Try to change Sherzal's mind towards moderation—"

The girl ripped free, stumbling away. It had been a vain hope. Sherzal would likely be too well warded even for Joeli.

For a long minute screams, shouts, and the thud of falling bodies filled the hall. Glass saw Thuran Tacsis and his son Lano escape into the main corridor, the boy shoving older and less hale lords aside in order to reach the doors.

The blinding white intensity lessened as Ara spent the power she had taken from the Path. Glass watched the girl through her fingers, a white shape, as if stolen from the heat of the smith's forge, moving swiftly. She wove a path among the silhouettes of palace guards that stumbled towards her, leaving them in her wake, blind, insensible, or smoking, depending on the length of contact made between them. Each step brought her closer to Glass and the judges.

Above the sounds of combat Glass could hear Sherzal shouting orders from the corridor outside the main doorway, commands that the Jotsis girl be taken down and that nobody escape.

As Ara's light dimmed Glass began to see the rest of the room. Guests wandered, dazzled, or crouched in fear, or lay groaning where they'd been trampled in the exodus. Guards continued to close on Ara, in greater numbers now they could look her way, with more arriving from the adjoining chambers.

Darla had descended from the gallery, possibly by hanging and dropping from the railing. Glass watched her use some kind of heavy wind instrument to flatten a guard then steal the woman's sword just as two more guards closed on her.

Across the room Regol and Safira were locked in unarmed combat, their battle blisteringly fast. Having witnessed many contests between hunskas Glass could tell that both were full-bloods and extremely skilled. Perhaps Safira had the better technique but Regol's greater strength restored the balance. Glass suspected Safira too proud to use her Noi-Guin blades or poisons. She had been proud as a novice. Too proud to let Kettle go. She would want to beat this cage-fighter bloody with her own hands.

Ara came through a wall of five guardsmen. A flight of arrows hissed in from the doorway. Ara avoided them with motions too quick to see, one arrow spinning away, another finding the leg of a guardsman hurrying to intercept her.

"Abbess!" Suddenly Ara stood before her, surrounded in light that seemed to emanate from the air around her. "Your instructions?" She snatched another arrow from the air before Glass could speak.

"We had better leave. Don't you think, dear?" Glass looked back at the doors to the main corridor. Four archers stood abreast there, with many palace guards behind and Sherzal somewhere in their midst. An arrow caught Brother Dimeon in the neck and he fell, twisting, gurgling in what sounded like outrage.

"We can't go that way." Ara batted an arrow to the floor, glancing around the room. Darla and a few of the Sis who had found weapons were now fighting a retreat towards the banqueting hall. The big novice felled the guardsman before her with a blow that opened his chest, then beckoned them to follow. "Servants' entrance!"

"Let's go." Glass hurried towards the melee on the far side of the chamber. She kept her head bowed, terrified that any moment an arrow would transfix her. In all her long years this was her first time in a battle and it appalled her. The swiftness and the violence, the sheer noise of all that shouting, clashing metal, the injured howling, the stink of blood and death. All of it numbed the mind and reduced a person to a collection of animal fears and the basest of instincts.

Ara kept pace, shielding the abbess, knocking aside any that intervened. Seldom and Agika followed, flanked by Melkir holding up a chair as an improvised shield. Glass picked her way through the detritus of the hastily abandoned room, toppled chairs and benches, here a necklace scattering pearls from a broken string, there a silk shawl edged with gold rings, smeared crimson. A handful of guests still wandered in shock, an old lady toppling gracefully as an arrow meant for Glass or Ara took her between the shoulders.

The blurred whirlwind of fists and feet that was Regol and Safira spun nearer. Ara eyed the conflict, clearly torn between intervening and protecting Glass. If the pair came any closer the two choices would be the same thing. Melkir took the decision from Ara, perhaps driven by thoughts of Sera lying by the judges' bench with a slit throat, and hurled himself at Safira's back. Somehow her foot struck him in the stomach, but his armoured bulk still drove her back and Regol took advantage, felling the woman with a punch to the face. Glass heard Safira's cheekbone shatter and winced.

Moments later Ara had downed two of the guards that were harrying those of the Sis retreating with Darla, and made a path for retreat through the banquet doors. Glass, Regol, Seldom, Agika, and Melkir followed. An arrow caromed off Melkir's shoulder-plate, another hammering into the door to Glass's left.

"I'll hold them, Holy Mother." Darla towered over the escaping clergy, a wild grin on her face, scarlet splashes across the blue taffeta gown she'd been squeezed into.

Regol sidestepped a guardsman's thrust and pulled a sword from the hand of a dying lordling. He swept the guard's blade up and ran him through, then took his place beside Darla, holding the doorway. Ara had hurried ahead, down the passage they proposed to escape along, to check for defenders.

Four long tables ran the length of the banquet hall, leading towards a dais where the high lords must have dined with Sherzal at the circular table. The remains of the feasting were still scattered across the tables. Candles lit the room, scores upon scores in brackets on the walls, and dozens of silver lamps were set in lines down the centre of each table. Across the hall Lord Carvon Jotsis was leading the Sis into the servants' corridor. The shuddering light gave the scene an unreal quality.

"Hurry, abbess!" Melkir took her arm, trying to lead her on.

Glass held back for a moment. Through the doorway to the reception hall, narrowed by the partly closed doors that framed Darla and Regol, she could see the musicians' gallery. A figure in cream and saffron skirts approached the broken rail. Joeli!

"Abbess!" Melkir at her shoulder. "They can't hold for long!"

The crowd of guards before the entrance was growing rather than shrinking. Some had hold of the doors, heaving them back against the makeshift wedges that had been set, so that more could attack the pair denying them passage.

"Joeli . . . you can end this." A whisper as Melkir pulled her away. The girl would have a clear vision of Sherzal and space in which to work. Even if she could get nothing past Sherzal's sigil wards but a little doubt it might buy them time.

Up on the gallery Joeli reached out a hand as if to steer someone's will. But her gaze turned towards the wrong doorway, her unfocused eyes seeming to find Glass. The girl's fist closed, not in the delicate manipulation of thread-work but a violent snatch. Between the widening doors Regol suddenly leapt back, turning. A moment later he was sprinting past Glass, bewildered terror on his face.

"Dung on it!" A cry from Darla as an arrow sprung from her shoulder. She roared, sweeping her sword out and driving back four palace guards.

"Don't . . ." Glass's heels dragged the floor as Melkir hauled her towards the servants' corridor.

Joeli repeated her action and this time Darla froze in mid-parry, as if suddenly distracted by some vital thought. A heartbeat later the guard to her left drove his sword into her side. Darla had nothing but a tattered gown to armour her. She folded around the steel, cursing, now lost among her attackers.

They closed in, swords rising and falling.

44

———— ✦ ————

CLERA LED KETTLE and Nona back through the palace, aiming to reach the tunnel by which they had entered not long before. They had approached the chambers where Sherzal's guards crowded but whatever battle had raged seemed to be over, the other participants fled or corpses. Wrapped in Kettle's shadows, they saw no sign of Abbess Glass.

Nona limped along behind Clera, trying not to wonder whether her friends still lived. She could still sense the shipheart at her back. "We could have . . ." She tried to think what exactly they could have done. Dragged the vault? Hacked their way in with axes. None of it would have worked.

"We're lucky that the shipheart wasn't just resting on a table," Kettle said. "I didn't know quite how dangerous its effects on people were close up, or how fast they took hold."

"It would have been a price worth paying to take it from Sherzal." Nona had meant to say to take it back for the Church, but the truth was that denying Sherzal would give her the most pleasure.

Kettle shook her head. "If it had turned you into a thing like Yisht who knows what you would have done with it or where you would have gone?"

"Yisht brought it all the way here!" Nona protested. "I could have held it for an hour."

"I doubt that she did. Sherzal would have had transport and containment waiting and ready close to the Rock. The shipheart likely warped her within an hour."

"Shhhh!" Ahead of them Clera raised her hand.

They both limped up to join her. Voices could be heard on

the stairs: ". . . back to help the guards chase them down." A young man's voice. One of the Sis.

"You'll accompany me to my rooms and stand guard like a son should!" An older man, familiar.

"Istead will look after you," the younger man replied. "What's Sherzal going to think of us if we just scuttle off and hide? I'll make for the gates. They don't know the palace—that's where they'll go. They're not getting out. I'll bring Sherzal the old woman's head!"

"Lano—"

"You know I'm right. We outnumber them fifty to one." The sound of running feet followed, fading into the distance.

"Damn boy!" Thuran Tacsis's voice. "We'll get to the rooms and wait this out, Istead."

"Yes, my lord."

Clera had already turned from the corner and hurried back along the hall, waving frantically at Nona and Kettle to follow. Kettle turned but Nona remained, gripped both by a debilitating fear and by a rising anger. Just the sound of the man's voice brought back the full horror of those endless hours waiting for his return, it made her remember the unbelievable agonies from just a brief touch of the Harm and her gut-churning disgust at the tortures he planned. But the fear brought rage with it, a fire roaring out its defiance, refusing to be made small by an old man's threats—threats issued when all the advantage was his.

Nona put her weight on her injured leg, gritting her teeth against the hurt. She didn't know who this Istead was. He could be a deadly warrior employed as Lord Tacsis's personal bodyguard. In her current state it wouldn't take much of a fighter to take her down, and then she'd be in Thuran Tacsis's clutches again, the whole nightmare that she'd escaped reinstated simply because she was too proud to run. The silence where Keot should be felt like a hole. The devil would have had advice, and she probably would have opted to do the opposite.

You can only hesitate so long before choice is lost. The two men's shadows preceded them. Nona pressed herself into the corner. The unknown quantity, Istead, came first. A tall man,

well-built, his blond hair and square jaw reminiscent of Raymel Tacsis. Nona wasted no more time. She surged up as fast
as she could on her good leg and punched him at the junction
of chin and neck, driving flaw-blades deep into his brain. Ripping free in a crimson spray, Nona made to throw herself at
Lord Tacsis.

Abused flesh can only tolerate so much. Nona's leg collapsed beneath her and she fell sprawling before her enemy.
Thuran immediately began to turn to flee, drawing breath to
shout for aid. Nona managed to swing her non-traitor leg to
kick his trailing foot and he toppled facefirst onto the rug that
ran the length of the corridor.

Nona scrambled onto Thuran's back, grabbed two handfuls
of greying hair and banged his face repeatedly into the floor
with measured violence. It was an expensive rug but not so
thick that it would stop Lord Tacsis feeling the floorboards
below.

"Unlock that door." Nona gestured to the nearest door with
her head.

Kettle, who Nona knew would have returned for her,
limped past and set to work with her picks. The lock surrendered in moments.

"Help me drag him." This to Clera who had just that second popped her scarf-wrapped face around the corner. "Wait."
Nona sliced and lifted Thuran's thick jacket, winding it around
his head so there would be no trail of blood.

"You're mad," Clera hissed, but she took a leg and between
the three of them they got the man into the room, closing the
door behind them.

The chamber was a spacious drawing room, perhaps for
one of the many guest suites in the wing. The furniture was
draped with sheets and the place had a musty smell as if it
were not often used.

"Under here." Nona lifted the sheet covering a table set
against the wall that must be the palace's outer wall.

Clera rolled Thuran into place, keeping her head averted in
case even in his dazed state he might recognize her over her
scarf. She left him face down.

"Flesh-bind." Nona held her hand out to Kettle, and the nun

dug into her robe. She retrieved and handed over the small tub without comment, passing across a wooden applicator a moment later.

Nona knelt, put the tub to one side, and further sliced apart Thuran's jacket, a thing of gold thread and silk embroidery that must have cost more than a labourer could earn in a lifetime. She found the leather pouch containing the Harm and extracted the sigil-worked disc of iron with considerable care. Her fingers didn't want to go anywhere near it. She forced them to their task, requiring the same effort as if she had wanted to hold them to hot coals. Next she applied the last of the flesh-bind to the sigiled surface. Her mouth twisted as she contemplated the pallid skin covering the small of Lord Thuran Tacsis's back. He had started to moan, returning to his senses.

"A better person wouldn't do this . . ." Part of her wanted Keot to be there in her mind, screaming at her to act. She glanced at Kettle, finding the woman's face free of expression.

"Any fair court would give the death sentence for his crimes," Kettle said at last. "It's for you to decide how."

Nona remembered the Tacsis, father and son, leaning over her in that Noi-Guin cell, and pressed the Harm firmly into the small of Thuran Tacsis's back, holding it there as he went rigid with an agony whose measure she could not forget. She held the disc in place long enough for the flesh-bind to form its bond.

"Why isn't he screaming?" Clera whispered.

"You can't," Nona said. "It hurts too much."

She moved back, lowered the sheet, and got up. "Lock the door behind us." There was no knowing how long it would take before he was discovered. If they took too long perhaps the pain would kill him or maybe he would survive until he died of thirst. Twinges of regret and shame ran through Nona while Kettle set to work on the lock again, but each time she thought of returning to put an end to the man some image from the cells would rise to stop her.

"Done." Kettle stood from the lock.

"Can we leave now?" Clera asked.

Nona glanced back at the door, heart heavy, not feeling the release she had anticipated. "No."

"No?" Clera seemed on the point of mutiny.

"Lano Tacsis said the abbess was escaping with others. They're going to be caught at the gates. We need to go there and help them get out."

45

---◆---

ABBESS GLASS

ARABELLA JOTSIS LEAPT higher than Glass had seen anyone leap, or had imagined that they might. She had sheared away the bottom half of her skirts but still what remained trailed behind her like fluttering plumage. Her leading foot broke the neck of a palace guardsman, her sword scythed through another's throat, and she was attacking a third before either of the first two could start to fall.

While Melkir dragged Darla between the doors and clear of the melee Ara spun amid the crowd of her foes, creating an ever-wider circle of injured opponents. Her speed couldn't last, but while it did the results were breathtaking.

Glass worked as quickly as she could, snuffing the flame from one silver table-lamp, flinging it towards the doors, picking up the next, its oil sloshing within, and repeating the process.

Darla, bleeding fiercely from several wounds, shook free of Melkir and hauled herself up him, trying to return to the fray. Melkir caught hold of her again, offering sharp words. Glass couldn't hear what they were but they worked and Darla accepted his support as they hurried towards the servants' door. Glass flung a seventh lamp before abandoning her task and setting off after Melkir.

The seventh lamp was still lit. There had been no plan, no words exchanged. Ara had simply exploded from the passage and hurled herself across the room to rescue Darla. Now, planting a foot in a guard's groin and driving off, she threw herself back across the flames blossoming between the doors. She arrived at the entrance to the servants' passage simultaneously with Glass, moments behind Melkir and Darla. Glass patted her on the back, taking the opportunity to put out a burning patch of Ara's dress.

They wedged the door and moved on, Darla stumbling white-faced, the floor behind her painted by the rapid pattering of blood.

LORD CARVON JOTSIS seemed to have the best knowledge of Sherzal's palace among the group who had escaped the banqueting hall. He led their party through the palace's underbelly, through roaringly hot kitchens, steaming laundry rooms, and past endless servants' chambers.

Their group numbered a score or so: four Sis lords—Jotsis, Mensis, Halsis, and old Glosis, who appeared not yet ready to die despite having enjoyed at least eighty years in her seat. With them were various family members and additional guests, including a merchant or two, and the cage-fighter, Regol. Now, shamefaced over his flight from the battle at the banquet doors, he was helping Terra Mensis along. The girl had broken a wrist during the escape though otherwise appeared astonishingly pristine. Had there been time Glass would have explained to Regol the reason for his lost courage. But time had run out on them and they were chasing it. Glass walked alongside Darla, trying to bind the cuts on her arms and side with strips of cloth torn from her habit. All were too deep for dressings to be much help. The injury in Darla's side was a puncture wound and the sword that made it must have penetrated her vitals. Glass talked all the while, hardly aware of what she said, just comforting noise. Words of praise for Darla's courage and skill, words of comfort and of hope that she didn't feel, the words of the Ancestor, mother and father to them all who would surely gather each of them into the eternal embrace soon enough.

Carvon Jotsis led them with a certainty common to those of his station whether or not they knew where they were heading. In the distance shouts rang out, the sounds of running feet came and went, and the darkened corridor behind them promised attack at each moment. But it never came. Eventually they emerged from a long service tunnel into a cellar and up into the main stables. Ara felled the trio of stablehands who showed some inclination towards barring their way, using her fists and feet rather than her sword, but it still looked a brutal business. Ara's uncle left her to it and went to the main entrance, Glass following. Some yards back from doors as wide as those of any barn a huge carriage stood beneath protective sheets. Sherzal's, no doubt. The wheels were nearly as tall as Glass.

"Twelve hells." Carvon turned from the narrow gap between the stable doors. "The main gates are shut. There's a line of soldiers in front of them, two dozen archers on the walls above those." He walked back towards Glass and the inquisitors.

"There must be another way." Ara left Darla in Melkir's care, resting against a hay bale, and came to join Lord Jotsis in front of Glass. "It won't take long before they're coming up behind us."

"There's no other way, not for us." Carvon shook his head. "They say there're ways into the mountain from the basements but I don't know how to get there, or how to get through the caves if we found them."

"So we go out there." Ara drew herself straight, trying to look fierce, but her exhaustion showed. "Regol and I could make it onto the walls. Attack along both sides. Clear the archers."

Glass didn't bother to point out that it would be suicide. Reinforcements would arrive before they got to the gates. And even if they got above the gates opening them would be no simple thing. And merely leaving the palace wouldn't save them . . . The weight of this knowledge pressed down upon her shoulders. Her arrival had killed these people. Whole families condemned to die.

"I'm game." Regol flashed Ara a wolf's smile. "I came for a free meal. I get enough of fighting to the death back in Verity. But I'm damned if I'm supporting that woman against the emperor or inviting the Scithrowl over the mountains."

Seldom spoke up behind Glass. "We're done for."

"We are." Agika joined them. "We should pray."

Glass smiled. She turned back towards the inquisitors and nodded. She had never been a zealot in the mould of Sister

Wheel but she believed that at the end of things the Ancestor would gather them to the whole and all division would be set aside. It was an end worth praying for. She reached out for Agika's hand, then Seldom's. "Sister, brother, it has been an honour to serve with you."

Lord Glosis, last to arrive, clambered up the stairs from the cellar, helped by a young nephew. "They're on our trail." She paused to catch her breath. "I could hear them in the corridor right behind us." Another wheezing chestful of air hauled in under her ribs. "They're coming!"

Ara and Regol moved quickly to flank the stairs, both with bloodstained swords in hand. The sounds of a fight would draw guards and soldiers from other directions; it would be over quickly. The sounds of footsteps on stone stairs grew louder, closer. A dark head popped up. Regol swung. Ara swung. Swords clashed, Ara's blade turning Regol's aside as the head jerked back.

"Clera?" Ara shouted. "What in hell are you—"

"Don't kill me!" Clera came up again, hands raised.

Regol stepped back, frowning. Ara gave a cry and pushed past Clera, heading down the steps. She emerged a moment later in a staggering, limping, moving embrace with Nona Grey and Sister Kettle, all three of them clutching swords.

"I've seldom had a prayer answered so swiftly . . ." Glass released the inquisitors' hands and hurried across to Nona and Kettle.

Glass wrapped her arms around Kettle's altogether too-skinny frame, then Nona's, similarly lacking in softness, all hard angles.

"Sister Kettle! So good to see you, Mistress Shade asked me to bring you back to the convent in one piece and I would hate to disappoint that woman." Glass found her smile so wide it hurt. She took Nona's hands. "And, novice, I've reconsidered your punishment. I've decided death was too harsh. Banishment seems extreme too. So . . . no visits to town for a month and you're to attend the optional Spirit classes on seven-days instead."

Glass stepped back and found both of them teary-eyed. To her dismay she discovered her own eyes misting. "Enough of this! The gate is heavily guarded. How are you going to get us out?" She noticed that Nona was limping. Kettle too; and the young nun also sported a livid black-and-scarlet wound across her throat.

Nona's gaze wandered over the various stalls with horses in, the rope and tack hung across the walls, the hay heaped beside sacks of grain. Her eyes came to rest on Sherzal's huge carriage. One of the Sis had pulled back the sheeting from the door. It gleamed darkly, lacquered in black, emblazoned with Sherzal's coat of arms: a storm cloud above a mountain, both lit by the jagged golden lightning that joined them.

"Is it a clear path to the outer gates?" Nona asked.

"Apart from all the archers," Regol said. "And the soldiers."

Nona looked across at the cage-fighter, registering him for the first time. She stood frozen for a heartbeat then looked away, almost shy. "Everyone needs to get into the carriage."

"How will that help?" Lord Jotsis pushed through the survivors starting to gather around the newcomers.

"I will move it." Nona turned her wholly black eyes on the man. "There are palace guards entering the cellar below as we speak. Get in the carriage and you might survive."

"Uncle." Ara was already pulling the lord towards the carriage.

Glass watched without comment. Nona's unassuming air of command was remarkable. The girl had Sis lords hurrying to do her bidding.

Kettle turned around and scattered caltrops down the stairs. "Better hurry, abbess, they're coming."

Glass nodded and followed Carvon Jotsis. A sense of urgency took hold and the guests in their soiled finery started to hurry towards the carriage. It looked large enough to hold them all though there would be no room for modesty. It would take eight horses to pull and horses wouldn't see them through locked gates. What one girl could do Glass couldn't imagine, but she had prayed and Nona had come. Now she would have faith.

Nona reached out, took a lantern from one of the passing guests and smashed it at the base of the piled hay. She pointed to a pitchfork. "Block the stairs." Regol moved to begin the task while the others stood horrified.

"You'll burn us alive!"

"She's mad. Look at her!"

The air was already hot on Glass's face and her eyes stung. The memory of her burned hand returned to her, not the unreal agony of the burning but the long dark misery of pain in the weeks that followed. She hoped Nona's plan reached beyond torching the palace.

Nona ignored the cries of protest. "Make sure the horses can get out, Terra."

"But . . ." Terra held up her broken wrist.

"Just do it."

Nona limped towards Sherzal's carriage. Kettle limped after her. Clera chased both of them. "Burn to death in the carriage. Is that the plan?" She stopped in her tracks. "I liked Sherzal's better!" Behind her the panicked whinnying of horses had begun.

"I am rather wondering what the plan is myself," Kettle said. Behind her the flames were leaping up across the hay, smoke billowing from the stairs to the cellar. Regol stumbled out of it, coughing, wiping his eyes.

"I'm going to walk the Path," Nona said. "Unlock the doors!" She waved towards the stables' main entrance. The two inquisitors ran over, hauling the locking bar clear.

"You won't be able to!" Kettle said. "Not so soon. You walked an hour ago!"

Glass had no practical experience but she had heard Sister Pan's stories. On rare occasions the old woman, her tongue loosened perhaps by convent wine, spoke of past days, and of the deeds of the greatest Holy Witches. Walking the Path was always dangerous, a step too far. Take too much power to yourself and it would rip you apart. It took time to recover from. When extremity drove a Holy Witch to return to the Path too soon it always ended in disaster, often for everyone around. The old saying was "seven moons to be sure." Some of the greatest had walked again after a single moon, a single night to recover their focus, and for some of those it had been their last moon too. The curtain wall of Heod's Fist, a great castle close to Ferraton where Glass had grown up, held a scar yards across and feet deep, and in its midst the shape of a person etched into the blackened rock. Sister Pan's teacher, Sister Nail, had died there in defence of the castle against the army of the rebel king. A second walk attempted at the sunset of a day when she had walked the Path at sunrise.

Ara hurried back from the carriage to help Melkir lift Darla from her resting place among the hay bales.

"You can't walk again, Nona." Ara struggled with Darla's weight. "You know you can't."

Nona opened her mouth to reply, then froze. Glass realized that until this moment Nona hadn't seen the gerant novice, lying down among the hay bales.

"Darla . . ." Nona dropped her sword. "What have they done to you?" She was beside the girl in a moment, kneeling over her, oblivious to the crackle of the fire, rising towards a roar. "What have they done to you?" Her hands moved across Darla's wounds, inches above them, trembling.

Darla lay, white-faced, lips blue-tinged. "What kept you . . . runt?" Darla managed a smile, then grimaced and coughed. Dark blood ran over her lip, dribbled down her chin.

Nona swung around to stare up at the people standing around her: Glass, Melkir, Ara, Kettle. She fixed on the nun. "You can help her."

"Nona . . ." Kettle looked down, head shaking.

"You *can*! You've got supplies. You've got—" Nona bit off whatever she had been going to say, suddenly stricken by some realization.

". . . s'too late . . ." With immense effort Darla closed a big hand around Nona's. ". . . tired . . ." Her brown eyes clouded with confusion, a kind of wonder, staring at some distant place above Nona's head.

A moment passed. Another. Darla's gaze remained fixed.

"She's gone, Nona." Kettle put her hand on the girl's shoulder. Nona flinched it off as if it burned.

Sister Agika bowed her head. "The Ancestor has taken her to—"

"Damn the Ancestor!" Nona gripped Darla's fingers. "Get up. Darla, get up. I'm taking us out of here. We're going back to the convent. We're going . . ."

Ara took Nona under both arms, drawing her up, choking back tears. "She's gone, Nona." Smoke rolled over them both.

Glass retreated from the heat and smoke, coughing, making for the carriage. A panicked horse ran past her, nearly sending her to the floor. She reached the steps and helped Lord Glosis into the carriage ahead of her, Agika coming up behind. The survivors were packed along two broad bench seats, crowding the stuffed leather, and crammed upright in the space between.

Nona, Ara, and Kettle came from the fire. It swirled around the three of them like a cloak of shadows and flame. Nona, pale in her rags, her black eyes unreadable, looked as though the blaze had birthed her. She looked like something not of the world.

"You can't. It's madness." Ara lacked conviction now.

But what choices were there?

46

"THE SHIPHEART IS here. I've stood before it. I am restored." Nona took Ara's hands from hers. She needed
Ara safe. "Get into the carriage."

"There's no room."

"Then get onto it and watch for arrows."

Nona closed her eyes, closed her ears to the roar of the fire,
and opened her heart to the banked fury that had trembled in
every limb since she left Darla, still warm, among the hay.

The Path had seldom seemed so distant. Just a thread. Little more than the crack that had run through her dreams back
in the day when Giljohn first put her into his wooden cage. She
saw it as a wisp, there and not-there. Her feet remembered the
blade-path, its narrow treachery, the fall yawning beneath.
Darla had hated that thing. She never managed more than four
steps. But she returned to it time and again, no fear in her.
Nona had asked her why once. Darla had given that fierce grin
of hers. "My father told me, your weaknesses have more to
teach you than your strengths."

General Rathon wouldn't know his daughter was dead. Not
yet. He wouldn't know that Nona had used the last of the flesh-
bind that might have saved her. He wouldn't know that it had
been spent on hollow revenge against a man not fit even to
look at his daughter.

Seven moons to be safe. Nona hadn't any interest in being
safe. If the Path tore her apart she would welcome it and hope
only that no stone of Sherzal's palace was left atop another.
She would turn her helpless rage to a fire that would purge the

mountain, a fire that would consume the pallid flames behind her, scouring the tunnels of the Tetragode.

She looked again for the Path and found it blazing, a river, twisting through more dimensions than a mind should know, running at right-angles to imagination. The shipheart's pulse beat in her ears. Without hesitation Nona threw herself forward.

This time it was different. The Path wasn't something narrow, veering through sudden angles, trying to throw her at every step. The Path had become a plane, a flowing expanse of molten silver so wide that falling from it seemed an impossibility. Even if she weren't running, the Path would draw her on. She could race forever, untiring, each step bringing new energy. The world lay behind her. Time had no hold. The Path enfolded, filled, led, gave direction.

The hard part wasn't staying the course, it was turning from it. Too many steps taken, and leaving would cease to be an option—at least leaving and remaining whole. That was true of many paths perhaps. Nona saw Clera's dilemma now, how hard it must have been for her to do what had seemed so simple from Nona's side, how easy it would be to return to her course.

Nona ran the Path and all her hurts were left behind her in the very first step. Her wounds, her exhaustion, even the ache of Darla's death, something small behind her, growing pale and faint. Each step flooded her with an energy so fierce, so exhilarating, that it overwrote her, became her, replaced her centre.

In the end only Darla brought her back. Nona would have run the Path forever. Something so right couldn't be denied. But for the fact of her friend's death diminishing behind her. Something like that couldn't simply be thrown away, discarded, abandoned as if it held no worth or meaning. And with a howl Nona turned in a place where there could be no turning, and fell back into the world.

She hit the ground and only with effort managed to stop falling. The world held too many possibilities and her body wanted to explore them, wanted to flow like the smoke, dance like the flames licking around her, follow gravity's pull deep into the ground; wanted to run as she had run on the Path, not in one direction but in all of them at once. Aspects of Nona began to separate, some to answer the horses' distress, some to explore the smoke, others to play with fire.

A faint noise penetrated the vastness of Nona's wonder and she turned towards it, towards the black carriage, wrapped in smoke. A figure clung to its side. Ara!

Nona drew a breath as if breaking the surface of some bottomless lake. It hurt, as if her lungs were wrapped in broken glass, but she had been schooled in pain of late. Nona drew the breath and drew back into herself the possibilities, the myriad choices, until at last she was focused, one, whole, shuddering with power.

She approached the carriage, suddenly aware of the fragility of everything around her, even the flagstones beneath her feet. In the past she had thrust the Path's power from her rather than keep it. She had thrown it as heat when she brought fire to the forest outside Verity, and as lightning against the Noi-Guin. Now, though, she turned it inward, running it through muscle and bone, owning it as strength, not just the kind that moves mountains but the kind that preserves the flesh doing the moving. Sister Pan had explained that one at length. The strength to punch through walls is of little use if the arm you punch with shatters before the rock does.

Nona moved behind the carriage. She inched her hands forward with caution. Too much pressure too swiftly and her palms would break through the timber before her and she would be elbow-deep in splintered wood. Hands met lacquered panelling, pressure mounted. And Nona's bare feet began to slide across the flagstones.

"No!"

Armoured in the Path's energies, Nona kicked at the stones beneath her feet, pulverizing the rock, excavating small craters to push against. The boards beneath her palms creaked and the huge carriage stole into motion. Nona kept up the pressure, feet scraping the flagstones, shattering several more.

The front of the carriage hit the stable doors at a brisk walking pace and they shuddered aside, billowing smoke out into the courtyard. Sherzal's carriage emerged, wheels clattering, thick white smoke all around, terrified horses streaming past on both sides.

The archers lining the walls hesitated, uncertain what they were dealing with. Sherzal's carriage carried on past those of the Sis, lining the walls to either side. With every yard Nona imparted more speed to it. The palace gates, more accurately described as fortress gates, would of course bring its progress to an abrupt and devastating halt.

The first arrows began to hammer into the carriage. Those inside had already made efforts to reinforce the shutters with seating. On the outside Ara was a popular target, but even with only one hand free she managed to deflect those arrows that would otherwise have hit her.

With the carriage moving at a good speed, Nona let it run and sprinted to get ahead of it. Every archer on her side of the courtyard took the opportunity to let fly at a clear target and their arrows hissed around her, breaking on the flagstones, hammering into the carriage's sides, or finding her flesh. The same energies that allowed Nona's body to contain and use the Path's strength also resisted arrowheads. The arrows ricocheted from her as if she were a statue, leaving just pinpricks.

Feeling the Path-energies begin to ebb and fade, and with Sherzal's carriage rumbling along behind her, Nona threw herself at the palace gates. Her final leap took her six feet off the ground and her shoulder hit the heavy timbers with a bone-jarring impact. The doors stopped her dead and she slid into a heap at their base. Arrows hammered into the timber on both sides, several hitting her in the back.

"Too light," Nona muttered. It didn't matter how strong you were, nobody could knock a man down by throwing a feather at him.

She stood, the carriage only twenty yards behind her now. The gates' huge locking bar had not been lowered but they were still held by a series of bolts driven into the stonework above and below by some system of cables anchored across the inner surface. Nona lacked both the time and the reach to rip it all clear.

How to open the gates when her own strength would just throw her aside? Even if she had the time to dig footholds

Nona thought that they would probably give way before the bolts surrendered.

Academia lessons came to Nona's aid where her Blade and Path education kept silent. Inertia keeps even the lightest of things stationary in the face of great forces—you just have to act fast enough. Nona punched the left gate a foot from the edge where it met the right one. The speed of the action allowed no time for her to be pushed back. Instead her fist burst through the timbers and she stood with her arm elbow-deep in a splintered hole, her fist just emerging into the wind that scoured the outer surface. Nona slammed herself forward until her shoulder met the timbers and her elbow cleared the far side of the door. She bent her arm and clung on. More arrows studded the woodwork around her. More hit her back and fell away leaving just shallow wounds.

Now, anchored by the thickness of the gates themselves, Nona set her other hand, palm out, to the other gate. And pushed. When she punched the door had no time to move and so she punched through. Now she pushed with slow, inexorable force. Anchored to the left-hand gate, she couldn't move back. Instead the gate had to take all the pressure. She curled around, setting her shoulder and hip to the other gate, using all the core strength of her body, magnified a thousand times by the fading energies taken from the Path. Behind her the rumbling clatter of the carriage grew ever closer.

With squeals of protest the bolts above and below began to fail, pieces of stone shooting away, shards of wood as long as an arm breaking free as the housings gave way. A shadow loomed. Time had run out. Sherzal's carriage smashed into the gates, Nona caught between its hammer blow and the gates' anvil.

A moment of darkness, of light, of whirling motion, screams and broken wood. Nona found herself on the ground with something huge rushing above her.

47

---◆---

THE ROAD DOWN from the side valley that housed Sherzal's palace was a long curving sweep of modest gradient. It ended at the highway that threaded the Grand
Pass.

Despite the arrow transfixing her left calf Ara had managed to scramble on top of the carriage, climb to the heavily
damaged front, and find the braking levers. The slope was too
steep for the brakes to fully arrest the carriage's motion but
they helped to tame it.

Steering proved to be a different matter. The carriage
steered itself by scraping along the rocky wall where engi-
neers had cut into the valley's side to make the road. It was a
process that removed a new section of the carriage's side every
twenty yards or so and threatened, at every collision with a
larger outcropping, to send them all veering across the narrowness of the road to pitch over the drop into whatever heart-
stopping fall the darkness hid.

Eventually, with about two-thirds of the mile-long journey
to the pass road complete, the ruins of Sherzal's grand carriage lurched sideways and came to a halt with the front right
wheel hanging over an unknown drop. Ara stood panting,
braced against the brake lever.

A minute's work saw most of the carriage's passengers dis-
embarked, or carried off. Two older men had been killed by
arrows that found their way past shutters and seat bases. A
matronly woman in a voluminous dress had been shot through
the shoulder, the arrow still in place, its steel head emerging

from her back. Regol, Kettle, and Ara kept close around the abbess.

NONA CRAWLED FROM beneath the wreckage of the carriage, her arms aching, legs scraped and torn. She had lunged for the axle and let it drag her, with only the fading power of the Path to shield her from harm.

"Nona!" Ara hobbled across to help her up. Behind Ara Nona could see the distant flames licking up above Sherzal's walls. She hoped the conflagration would spread and gut the place from lowest cellar to tallest tower.

"Where's Clera?" Nona asked looking over the survivors.

"She never got in," Ara said.

"I called to her." Kettle pressed her mouth into a speculative pucker. "She backed away into the smoke."

"But—" It made no sense. The abbess would have taken her back. Nona knew it.

"She made a choice, Nona." Abbess Glass spoke in a low voice. "She helped you when you needed help, but she fancied her chances better with the emperor's sister."

Nona looked around her. Starlight washed the roadway through a wind-torn hole in the clouds. It lit the ruined carriage, one side torn away, the roof sagging, and shone red across a score of Sis in ballgowns and formalwear, ill-suited for walking the mountains. Many bore injuries, including Kettle, Ara, and herself. Her gaze settled on Regol, the only fighter among them fit for combat, save for Melkir.

"My lady." He executed a half-bow, showing her that same old smile, even now.

She found herself suddenly aware of how tattered and inadequate her smock was, the wind playing it around her, and how filthy everything beneath it lay. "Regol." She had meant to tell him she was a novice rather than a lady, but she wasn't sure she was either right at that moment. And with his gaze upon her she was no longer sure which she would rather be.

"Every time I dine somewhere that you are also a guest, Nona, I find myself attacked." He rubbed his jaw as if remembering a punch. "By the same woman!"

"Safira?" Kettle stepped forward. "Is she . . ."

"I punched her pretty hard," Regol said. "But she'll get up again. I can't claim it as a fair fight, though."

"Are we safe?" Terra Mensis broke into their circle, cradling her injured wrist. She seemed to have picked up new injuries in the carriage and sported a livid bruise across most of the left side of her face.

"I rather doubt it," Abbess Glass replied. "Sherzal will send her soldiers after us. How soon depends on how bad a fire we left her with, but I can't see us outrunning them."

As if to answer her the sky cleared further and beneath the starlight the whole curve of the road could be seen, leading back to the broken gates of the palace. A troop of perhaps fifty soldiers was advancing along it at speed. They'd covered half the distance already.

NONA SET HER back to the rocks beside the road, as spent as she had ever been. Yisht had called friends a weakness. The pain that Hessa's death, and now Darla's, had caused her was very different from that of the Harm, but it was deeper and longer-lasting. A weakness, though? It had been friendship that had Kettle follow her half the length of the empire, friendship that had Clera spirit her out of the dungeons of the Noi-Guin, and if she had to die she would rather do it here under the scarlet heavens with her sisters of the Red and the Grey, free and fighting, than any alternative she could imagine.

Kettle stood, throwing aside the halves of the arrow she'd taken from Ara's calf, and came to stand beside Nona. Ara followed, testing her weight on her tightly bound leg with a grimace. "Ouch." She leaned back beside Nona, the wind spreading golden hair across the rocks.

"Nice dress," Nona said.

"Thanks. Terra helped me choose it. It was stupidly expensive."

Regol came to stand before them. His dark hair swept by the Corridor wind, he glanced across at the approaching troops. All around them the rocks lay red with starlight. He turned his gaze upon Nona and suddenly it felt as if the focus moon were blazing, making her sweat. "Will you hold the road with me, sister?" he asked. "I've wanted to see you fight again."

"I'm not a sister, just a novice." The moment the words left her she felt stupid. Was that the best she could think of to say? And why did it even matter with fifty swords approaching?

Regol grinned. He always grinned. "You're my sister of the cage."

A chill ran the length of Nona's spine despite the heat of his regard. How did he know she would be Sister Cage, a secret shared only with Ara and Mistress Path?

"We were both born from Giljohn's cage after all!" He laughed, breaking any tension, and turned towards the palace, swinging his sword in a figure of eight.

Abbess Glass stood revealed as Regol moved aside. She too was smiling, albeit a smile tinged with sadness. "You three have done astonishing things to bring us so close to an impossible success. Astonishing." She reached out her hands and Nona took them, Kettle and Ara laying theirs over hers. "But the world is not changed by individual acts of violence, no matter how good the cause. Neither can it truly be changed by the power of the Path. The greatest of the Mystic Sisters all knew this. However much strength is concentrated in a single Martial Sister, however far the reach of a Sister of Discretion, it is overreached by the strength and reach of the masses. You may be rocks but humanity is the tide and you only have to stand upon the sand to see how that contest concludes.

"In the end it is not whether we live or die here, but how the message echoes through the empire and beyond. We are not leaders, merely servants. Even the emperor's power is illusion. Ultimately the will of the people drives us, as inevitably as the advance of the ice. And the people are, each and every one of them, the children of the Ancestor, holy, chosen. We have shown them Sherzal's true heart and they will judge her actions. Those who cannot slow the pursuit must flee. They must scatter across the slopes and we must trust that some will find their way to safety and speak of what happened here."

Abbess Glass stepped closer, staring into each of their faces in turn, her eyes kind. "I've always prided myself on being able to look ahead, on being able to see the consequences of actions. It's a meagre skill perhaps, compared to the talents that the Ancestor has placed in you girls, but it has served me well until this night. But you should know, the greatest joy to those who see the future is that life remains full of surprises. And you have all surprised me."

"Holy Mother . . ." Kettle's voice grew too thick with emotion to continue.

"I had a son once." The abbess smiled, remembering. "I couldn't have loved him more. But I never had a daughter. I would have been proud to call any of you my own." She lifted her hands, forestalling any embrace. "You are my children, children of the Ancestor, daughters of the Rock of Faith, daughters of Sweet Mercy. I expect you to meet your enemy with ferocity and make a good account of yourselves."

Nona turned towards the road where Regol stood ready, behind him a thin line of the Sis with Lord Carvon Jotsis at the centre. Sherzal's soldiers were close, close enough for her to hear the tramp of their boots as they jogged forward, eight abreast. Each man was chain-armoured, each bearing shield and spear. The stars still watched, their light gleaming on steel.

Beside the carriage Agika and Seldom led the elderly and infirm in prayer. Terra Mensis stood, having cut away the singed length of her skirts. Clutching the knife awkwardly in her left hand, she went to stand beside her father, tears in her eyes, ready to follow the others who were already making for the main road. Soon the story of Sherzal's treason would be spreading along the Grand Pass in both directions.

"Something's coming . . ." Nona said as Kettle led the way to stand by Regol.

"Well . . . yes," Ara said, hefting her sword.

"No. Something else." Nona glanced out into the night, down across the slopes, dark and beyond her seeing, edged with the faint crimson starlight. On high the wind tore the clouds still further and the Hope blazed forth, adding its light to the world. Nona strained her senses. She heard . . . footsteps? A beat at least. Something that had been growing for a while but that hadn't registered above all the loud emotion. Suddenly it came to her.

"It's a sh—"

The cracking of rock drowned her out. With no warning a great wedge of the mountainside slid down across the road ahead. In just seconds it was over save for a few dozen loose boulders that continued to roll away down the slopes, crashing and bouncing into the distance. Nona watched in confusion as cascades of loose stones died to trickles. An untold weight of bedrock had slumped a score of yards, obliterating the road and the soldiers upon it.

Everyone from the carriage just stood and stared, unsure of what they had seen. Even as they watched the failing starlight stole away the details. Only Nona turned from the scene. Only Nona looked behind them to see a grime-covered hand clasp the edge of the road. A moment later the rest of the person followed, hauling itself up one-handed to stand and return Nona's stare. The figure clasped something glowing to its chest. Something spherical, the size of a human head, lit from within by a deep violet light. The glow from it was so deep that it seemed as if it might be the edge of some blaze to challenge the focus moon if only the eye could follow it off the far end of the rainbow's spectrum.

"Zole."

It was the ice-triber, her habit as stained and tattered as Nona's smock, her face as impassive and unreadable as ever.

Beside Nona, Ara turned, then Kettle and the abbess.

"You did that," Nona said.

"How?" The abbess seemed too stunned for more than one word.

"She has the shipheart," Nona said.

Kettle shook her head. "It can't be. Sherzal's vault was too—"

Zole held the sphere up, its light somehow both fierce to look upon yet too faint to illuminate the road past glimmers here and there. "It is the Noi-Guin's shipheart."

"How could . . ." Abbess Glass started.

Zole bowed her head and raised the sphere higher. In the action Nona saw it, just a glimpse, a stain, dark and purple, flowing from the hand that held the heart, down across the wrist, quickly lost beneath the sleeve of Zole's habit.

Abbess Glass gathered herself. "How is this possible?"

Zole raised her face to them, her eyes burning with the shipheart's light. "I am the Chosen One."

EPILOGUE

———— ✦ ————

Lano Tacsis had brought two armies to the Convent of Sweet Mercy. A Pelarthi army that had now been spent, and an army of his own house that had yet to test its strength against the sisters who barred the way. He had hundreds of warriors at his command. But he knew that the eight who stood around him were more dangerous than all the Pelarthi purchased with Tacsis wealth and all the soldiers sworn to his name. And of those eight Noi-Guin one was rumoured to be more deadly than the other seven together.

The Singular of the Noi-Guin was said only to leave the Tetragode when the Tetragode itself was torn down and reconstructed in some new stronghold, hidden from the world. The Singular would move from the old Tetragode to the new, and resume his place as the dark heart of the organization. The Singular was keeper of the Book of Shadows, linked by shadow-bond to every Lightless and every Noi-Guin, the spider at the centre of the web. And yet here he was, at Lano's right hand, in the light of day and yet so deep in darkness that he seemed a silhouette.

Lano signalled to his captain. "Lead the troops in. Take her down. Crippled would be best but dead if you must. Kill everyone else. The nuns first, then the children." He wanted vengeance on Sister Cage, of course he did, but dead was dead. Reaching for more than that had been the downfall of his older brother and his father. Nona Grey had given him his lordship and he was prepared to miss out on watching her gruesome death if a quick death was safer and more certain.

Lano allowed himself a smile of satisfaction as his warriors began to ready their advance. Today he would watch Sweet Mercy fall.

Clera Ghomal stepped amongst the Noi-Guin as if she were some noble, an equal rather than the turncoat daughter of a failed merchant. Lano resisted the urge to backhand her. Today was a day of victory, not to be tarnished by squabbling with underlings.

"She'll run," Clera said. "Now she has her friend she'll run. She's terrified of falling into Tacsis hands again." She glanced around her. "Or Noi-Guin hands. She'll make for the caves and you'll never find her. Not unless you know them like I do."

"My troops will find any that try to run." Lano had no intention of being goaded into giving chase himself. He regretted not shutting Clera's mouth with his fist the moment she had opened it uninvited.

"No." The Singular started towards the distant pillars. The Noi-Guin began to follow in his wake, the girl with them. "Come."

Lano made no move to go but a Noi-Guin to either side took his elbow and started him forward. Lano glanced helplessly at his soldiers. He had never intended to lead this charge.

The Singular accelerated across the plateau. "Let her die on a Noi-Guin blade. Let this be certain. Let there be no escape for her."

"Escape?" Lano intended to bark his laugh but it came out nervous. "She won't run. Not from here. It's her home. Her family. Besides"—he gestured to the smoking horizon—"where would she run? The whole world is on fire."

Read on for a special preview of

HOLY SISTER

Coming April 2019 from Ace

IN THE DARK of the moon by the side of the Grand Pass two dozen citizens of the empire huddled away from the wind. Dawn would show them an unparalleled view of that empire, spread out before them to the west, marching between the ice towards the Sea of Marn.

Nona stood close to the rock wall, pressed between Ara and Kettle. Her leg ached where the stump of Yisht's sword had driven in, pain shooting up and down as she shifted her weight, the whole limb stiffening.

Abbess Glass had gathered the survivors in a bend where the folds of the cliff offered some shelter. There were among their number men and women who owned substantial swathes of the Corridor, who had been born to privilege and to command. But here in their bloodstained finery, with flames from the palace of the emperor's sister licking up into the night behind them, it was to Abbess Glass they turned for direction.

"It will take Sherzal's soldiers a while to navigate around Zole's landslide but they'll come. It won't take long then to alert the garrisons and send riders down the road to Verity. There's no chance of making the capital that way."

"We don't need to reach Verity." Lord Jotsis spoke up. "My estates are closer."

"Castle Jotsis is formidable," Ara said, looking between her uncle and the abbess.

Abbess Glass shook her head. "Sherzal will bottle us up anywhere but the capital. She might not be insane enough to lay siege to your castle, my lord, but she would likely encircle your holdings to prevent word reaching the emperor. And besides, I fear that closer is not close enough."

"So we've escaped only to be hunted down on the road?" One side of old Lord Glosis's face had swollen into a single bruise but she still had enough energy to be temperamental. "Unacceptable."

"It's the shipheart that Sherzal wants above anything else." The abbess nodded to where Zole waited, some thirty yards closer to the landslide, her hands dark around the glowing purple sphere she had recovered from the Tetragode. "If we give her good reason to think that it has gone in another direction she won't spare many soldiers for chasing us. Maybe none."

"And how," Lord Jotsis asked, "can we make her think we haven't taken the shipheart with us?"

Abbess Glass turned to stare at the darkness of the slopes rising above them. "By making them think it has gone south, towards the ice."

"How can we make them think it's been sent south?" Lord Glosis asked, leaning on the arm of a young relative.

"By actually sending it south, to the ice," the abbess said. "Zole will take it and let them see the glow upon the slopes."

"But that's madness." Lord Jotsis drew himself to his full height. "You can't entrust a treasure like that to a lone novice!"

"I can when it's the lone novice who somehow stole that treasure from the heart of the Noi-Guin's stronghold in the first place," Abbess Glass replied.

"She won't be alone." Nona limped forward.

Ara hobbled to stand beside Nona. Kettle put her hands on their shoulders. "In our state we're going to be slowing the abbess down on the road. None of us will be any use to Zole trying to outdistance soldiers across the mountains."

Kettle was right. Nona gritted her teeth against the pain in her thigh and refused to let the admission out.

The abbess advanced on them, wind-swept, grey hair straggled across her face. "The Noi-Guin's shipheart is a marjal one. It's said that in the hands of a marjal healer it can mend any wound but that it can also bring harm."

"Well, I don't want to go near it." Nona shuddered. She knew what harm the shipheart could bring. It had even squeezed a devil out of Zole, the most tightly bound person she had ever met. "And we don't have a marjal healer."

"We have Zole," the abbess said, and raising her voice she called to the ice-triber. "Zole, time to show us what Sister Rose has been teaching you."

ZOLE BECKONED THEM rather than approach and bring with her the awful pressure of the shipheart's presence. Nona took a few uncertain steps towards the girl, Ara behind her, then Kettle, all of them limping, the novice because of the arrow wound in her calf, the nun because of a knife wound in her thigh.

"We shouldn't be doing this, abbess." Nona looked back. "The Sweet Mercy shipheart did terrible things to Yisht."

"And yet Zole is untouched." The abbess and the others were black shapes now, with just edges picked out here and there by the deep purple light of the shipheart.

But Zole was not untouched . . .

"Find your serenity." Zole's voice resonated through the night. "Serenity will preserve you."

Nona didn't feel serene. She felt scared and in pain, but she reached for her trance, running the lines of the old song through her head, imagining the slow descent of the moon and the children of her village chanting in a circle around the fire. And with the moon's fall a blanket of serenity settled upon her, setting the world apart, her pain not gone but no longer personal, more a curio, an object for study.

Zole held the shipheart out towards them, a sphere the size of a child's head, resting on both palms, dark purple, almost black, but somehow glowing with a violet light that seemed to shade beyond vision. Nona advanced. She felt the pressure of the thing, as if she had fallen into deep water. She had plunged into the black depths of the Glasswater sinkhole before, and this was no less terrifying. The need to breathe built in her and threatened her serenity, before, with a gasp, she remembered that there was no reason not to draw breath.

With just a yard between them Nona's skin began to prickle and then burn, as if the devils were there already just waiting for their true colours to be made known. Nona had shared her skin with a devil before, Keot, not one of her own making but one that had infected her when she killed Raymel Tacsis. The rocks around the man's corpse had been stained black beneath the crimson.

"Hold to yourself." Zole closed the remaining distance that Nona's feet proved unwilling to cross. Zole had seen Nona's old devil and kept the secret. Zole said they called them *klaulathu* on the ice. Things of the Missing.

Without preamble, Zole pressed the heart's orb to the wound above Nona's knee. Nona had expected her flesh to sizzle, the blood in her veins to boil like the water in Sweet Mercy's pipes, but instead icy fingers wrapped around her bones and a black-violet light stole her vision. For a moment she saw strange spires silhouetted against an indigo sky, swept away in the next beat of her heart as if by a great wind. The Path opened before her, not the narrow and treacherous line that had to be hunted, but broad, blazing, so wide that its direction became uncertain, a place one might wander, drunk on power until the end of days. Voices began to sound within Nona's head, all of them hers but speaking from different places, some raging, some jealous, some whispering secret fears or wants, a babble at first but each taking on a separate identity, becoming clearer, more distinct.

"Done." Zole pushed Nona back, the base of her palm against Nona's sternum.

Nona staggered and Ara kept her from falling with help from Kettle. The heart-light caught their faces, making something alien of them both.

"Are you all right?" Kettle asked.

"I . . ." Nona stood straight, stamped her leg. It still ached but the flesh had been made whole, a white line of scar tissue marking the passage of Yisht's blade. "Yes." The voices that had filled her mind became jumbled together once more, fading back into the shadows.

"Go on." Kettle sent Nona back towards the abbess and the rest of the group, giving her shoulder a small shove to get her going.

By the time Nona reached the ruins of the wagon that they had escaped the palace in she was calm again, her serenity intact.

"How do you feel?" The abbess watched Nona's eyes with an uncomfortable intensity.

"I don't know," Nona said. "Tired. But full of energy. If that makes sense." She looked back down at her leg, the scar visible through the tattered smock. The cold no longer touched her. "I don't know how Zole can stand it." Part of her wanted to tell the abbess about the devil she had seen at Zole's wrist when she first arrived with the shipheart. She bit down on the impulse. She had lived with Keot for years and Zole hadn't informed on her. Zole would have to deal with her own demons. The abbess probably couldn't help in any case. And the inquisitors with her would want to burn the devil out of Zole.

Abbess Glass took Nona's hand and led her back to the main group. "You're mended? You can walk the distance now?"

"I could run it!" Ara caught them up, her hair rising around her head as if backcombed, a blond confusion defying the wind. She had a wild look in her eye. Nona met her gaze and a grin broke across both their faces, a shared understanding, and something more complex that perhaps neither understood. Nona wanted to run with her, to chase her. Wanted her friend.

The three of them turned to see Kettle silhouetted against the shipheart's glow, Zole on one knee, applying the heart to the nun's inner thigh. Kettle broke away with a cry after just a moment's contact. She came hurrying down the road, not glancing back. She moved quickly, though still with a slight limp.

"Sister Kettle?" The abbess stepped forward to meet her.

"Mother . . ." Kettle's wide eyes sought the abbess as though she were night-blind.

"Here." Abbess Glass took the nun's hands. "You're safe."

Nona raised her brows at the enormity of that lie but said nothing.

"I can't go near it again. I can't." Kettle shot a glance over her shoulder as if Zole might be approaching with the shipheart even now.

"It's all right, sister." The abbess led them farther away. "I need you to protect us as we journey west. Even if all Sherzal's forces follow the shipheart towards the ice, the empire roads are no longer a safe place for the vulnerable. And unguarded Sis lords are likely to be a tempting prize to any bandits we might pass."